Talking Of Michelangelo

A Novel

S. Frederic Liss

First Edition, April 2025
Library of Congress Control Number: *pending*
ISBN 978-1-965784-18-1 Hardback
ISBN 978-1-965784-19-8 Paperback

Cover Graphic Design & Book Typography by Kurt Lovelace.
Cover artwork by Pierian Springs Press
Cover type *Bauhaus Dessau* **Alfarn** by Céline Hurka,
Elia Preuss, Flavia Zimbardi,
Hidetaka Yamasaki, and Luca Pellegrini.
Chapter titles in **Jenson** by Robert Slimbach.
Chapter titles in **Baskerville**; Body text set in **Nimbus**.
Chapter dropcaps set in **Mrs Eaves XL**
by Emigre Foundry designer Zuzana Licko.
Flourishes set in Emigre Foundry **Dalliance** by Frank Heine.
Emigre Foundry **ZeitGuys** by Bob Aufuldish, Eric Donelan.
Typefaces licensed Adobe, Linotype, Emigre, & URW GmbH.

PSPress.Pub
Pierian Springs Press, Inc
30 N Gould St, Ste 25398
Sheridan, Wyoming 82801-6317

For J, a pillar of creation.

Contents

Part 1

April 30, 1968–June 6, 1968

PART 2

June 25, 1967–April 24, 1968

PART 3

June, 1962–November, 1964

PART 4

September, 1949–1957

PART 5

June 6, 1968–June 16, 1968

ABOUT THE AUTHOR   449

ALSO BY S. FREDERIC LISS   451

In the room the women come and go
Talking of Michelangelo.

T.S. Eliot
THE LOVE SONG OF J. ALFRED PRUFROCK

"Life can only be understood backwards; but it must
be lived forwards."

Søren Kierkegaard
JOURNALEN JJ:167 (1843),
SØREN KIERKEGAARDS SKRIFTER

"…the illusion that since the past exists only in one's
memories and the words which strive vainly to encapsulate them, it is possible to create past events
simply by saying they occurred."

Salman Rushdie
MIDNIGHT'S CHILDREN

"…a lot of people flatter themselves that their memories are much more accurate than they are and they
forget that the perspective of a kid is so limited and
unsophisticated."

Nell Zink
The New Yorker
May 18, 2015, p. 41

Talking Of Michelangelo

Part I

April 30, 1968–June 6, 1968

April 30, 1968

4:30 PM

If you are the type of person who looks away from Nicolas Poussin's *Rape of the Sabines*, whose stomach becomes queasy at the blood in Caravaggio's *David with the Head of Goliath*, who is offended by Courbet's *Woman with a Parrot*, or who does not understand why the beheading of St. John the Baptist is such a recurring subject in Western art, (like all law students, I must cite, cite, cite: see e.g. Di Paolo's *The Beheading of Saint John the Baptist*), then you probably are not reading this, having tossed aside my memoir in disgust. As he painted, did Poussin imagine himself as one of the Roman soldiers or one of the Sabine women? Did Caravaggio see himself as David or Goliath? I search the paintings for clues, hints of some childhood trauma that might explain the artists' frame of mind as he applied paint to canvas.

I have placed such a clue in my paintings, the same in each one, there to be deciphered by those astute enough to do so. For those who cannot, I offer my life story told backwards to weed out readers who shun anything more than a simple narrative. Life is not a simple narrative. I do not want readers who dismiss life because it may only be understood, past or future, through the present. Told forward chronologically, my life, my art, would have no meaning. Paperback psychologists masquerading as art critics would trumpet truths that are as false as intelligent design, astrology, or the alchemy of turning lead into gold. And told backward the meaning is the same, just more nuanced.

Another reason. Memory works that way, the past unrolling backwards, the brain vomiting up bits and pieces of the past that oft times bear as close a resemblance to actual events as the vomit does to the meal just eaten. I don't know if I am a reliable or an unreliable narrator. I just narrate as best I can. Memory, fallible or not.

On the other hand, if you care little about how I came of age, how to interpret the clue I hide in my paintings, or whether the bits and pieces of my past I've shared with you compare with actual events, if you only wish to know whether my vision clears, whether I replace my discarded brushes and return to my oils and watercolors or hide from life in a three piece suit with a pocket square and a Phi Beta Kappa key adorning my vest, or whether I have a future after June 6, 1968, a real future, not just marking time as time passes, you could skip ahead to the end. I don't know what you will find there. No, I don't know. Maybe nothing. For now, best you stick to the path I have placed you on lest you get lost in the dark wood of April 30, 1968.

❧ ❧ ❧

I stand at a window in the library of the Columbia University School of Law (to give the school its formal name) and sketch the riot unfolding on Amsterdam

Avenue. Sounds of the rioting penetrate the sealed glass as waves of students and community activists roll up the avenue. Mobs surge through the Columbia University campus in random motion and I search for something to focus on, perhaps the woman in the red beret or the man wearing the American flag as a diaper. I see the ebbs and flows of the motion, see if those ebbs and flows create wave patterns that I may be able to use in a future painting; but the mob dissolves into chaos the way water dissolves watercolors and I discern no patterns. The fading light shades the colors of the jackets and vests the rioters wear, the banners and posters they carry, their faces, some white, some black, some bearded, some clean shaven, and their hair, every color under the rainbow, colors Clairol has yet to invent, will never invent, yet, all combining in a living Jackson Pollock drip painting. I imagine a giant Jackson Pollock dripping and dropping and flinging rioters to the earth from on high the way the real Jackson Pollock dripped and dropped and flung paint as he walked round and round his floor bound canvases, a Wyoming rancher walking the fences of his range. Random motion and not Pollock's planned abstractions now controls Columbia University in the spring semester of my first year at Columbia Law School. Part of me wants the University to close down, the part that wants to paint for the rest of the semester. Like Paris in 1965. The rest of me does not want to have to repeat the term.

Bodies pack College Walk which bisects the campus between Amsterdam Avenue and Broadway. It's Times Square on New Year's Eve. College Walk usually presents nothing more hazardous than freshmen playing Frisbee; but on this night, Students for a Democratic Society, a liberal protest group at birth, but now, in its adolescence, militant leftist radicals for whom a single act of destruction is worth a million words, march in formation up the center of Amsterdam Avenue and turn left on to College Walk with the precision of a platoon of Marine recruits trying to impress their drill sergeant. Their front ranks carry posters depicting a bleeding Vietnam. The mob parts, cleaved by the chants of the marchers:

"L.B.J.! L.B.J.! How many babies did you kill today?

"CIA! CIA! Why'd you kill M.L.K.?"

I press my ear against the glass of the library window. Somewhere in the mob a bass drum reverberates with a steady beat, a cadence. I search the mob, trying to trace the sound to its source, but the drum remains invisible in the descending darkness. I see instead how the mob marches to the beat of this invisible drum and I hear how they chant to the beat of this invisible drum and I relive when I, too, marched through a chanting mob behind a bass drum: my junior year at Durfee High School when a very visible bass drum, its skin red and black, the colors of the Durfee High School Hilltoppers, led the basketball team on to the parquet floor of Boston Garden for the finals of the Tech Tourney, the state high school basketball tournament, Durfee High School vs. Somerville High School for the Class A Massachusetts championship. Stationed under one of the baskets during the game, the drum's rhythmic beat as I brought the ball up court increased when I crossed the mid-court line. I dribbled in rhythm to that beat as I waited for the pick and roll to develop, or the back door to open, or a path to the basket to appear. The cheerleaders screamed and the Durfee fans in the stands behind the basket chanted. The pick and roll did not develop. The back door did not open. A path to the basket did not appear. The clock ticked down. Inside ten seconds. Inside five seconds. Four seconds. Three seconds. Two seconds. Once again, I am suspended in the air behind the foul circle, a defender's hand in my face. One second. The ball arcs toward the basket, perfect back spin, zero seconds, the buzzer sounding, the ball hitting the front of the rim, bouncing straight up, higher and higher until it seems to brush against the Boston Celtics championship banners that hang in the rafters, then straight down, swish, the winning shot because the ball is in the air before the buzzer buzzed. Every ball player's dream, making the winning shot in a championship game. One lucky shot, another trophy for Durfee High School, a letter jacket for me, and a citation for being named to the third team all Bristol County team as a guard. The rest of the starters made first or second team. Life would be much simpler, if I had missed that shot.

In the stands behind the Durfee bench Father Giuseppe Ozoni, my former parish priest, cheers and claps and shouts my name. His cassock undulates with the fat that rolls up and down his body as he jumps as excitedly as my coaches and teammates, as excitedly as the cheerleaders, as excitedly as the members of the marching band. He reeks with the same enthusiasm as when he first bought watercolors and brushes and special paper for me and Merisi "Minnie" Minifie, when he first arranged for us to be tutored by an artist on the faculty of the Rhode Island School of Design in Providence, paying our fees, chauffeuring us back and forth to my art lessons. Without him I doubt I would I have painted *Talking of Michelangelo*, my other paintings, that Minnie would have painted *Life with Coffee Spoons*. I doubt I would be a painter who refuses to sell, to exhibit, his work. Minnie would still be alive. The single hair growing out of the giant freckle on Father Ozoni's cheek beneath the corner of his eye points at me like a rifle tracking a deer, as unaware of its fate as I once was.

The inside of my mouth goes dry. My tongue feels like sandpaper against my lips. I blink, rub my eyes, blink again. Father Ozoni mocks my reaction. He looks exactly as he did when he was alive, except he now sports an eye patch over one eye like the Hathaway shirt man. Christ resurrected, I wonder, then banish the thought from my mind. I count on my fingers the number of years he has been dead, both hands required. I attended his funeral mass, his burial, the first Mass of his replacement, Father Octavio Crizal. I shout at one teammate then another, point at Father Ozoni, but it is evident from their expressions they see nothing but the celebration of victory. Later, on the bus returning to Fall River from Boston, I tell Coach what I saw. Coach laughs and blames it on the adrenalin high of making the winning shot. At the time I agreed, but countless sightings of Father Ozoni over the years convince me adrenalin had nothing to do with it.

Now, back in the law library, I fill page after page of my legal pad with quick pencil strokes, studies and sketches to take back to my apartment as raw material for future paintings. I stack the studies and sketches with my lecture notes on the Parol Evidence Rule, still confounding me after hundreds of hours of study. Only men who count angels on the head of a pin can contrive something as arcane and meaningless as the Parole Evidence Rule. Yet, compared to the Rule against Perpetuities, it is as understandable as a theorem of Euclidian geometry. Parallel lines extended to infinity will never intersect. I shift to another window, leaning against the library stacks arrayed behind me, shelves of law books that create a fortress sufficient to repel the rioters. The law inside the books offers little protection, but the books themselves, pages and pages of court opinions and statutes and learned essays on the law, form a barrier no bullet can penetrate. Maybe this is the law's real function.

Down Amsterdam Avenue, squadrons of mounted

police from New York's Tactical Police Force, the dreaded TPF who take special delight in breaking up student demonstrations and who are sued at least weekly by the National Lawyers Guild, mill about in front of the Cathedral of St. John the Divine. In spite of their training, the horses are skittish and neither the reassuring pats of their riders nor the cubes of sugar in the riders' hands calm them. For once I will have something to write about in my letters to Minnie that will bear witness the way his letters from Vietnam do. At last, I will have raw material to warehouse for future paintings that measures up to what he's harvesting in the jungles of Southeast Asia.

I finish another sketch and prop my legal pad on the shelf of a study carrel. I analyze it from various angles. I need close-ups, things I can only see if I walk the campus, become one with the mob. Artistic distance comes when you stand in front of the blank canvas, not when you observe the world, something that must be done from within. At least that's what Minnie maintains.

Minnie's taunt, 'law school's for cowards,' haunts me the way the truth haunts a person afraid to face up to it. We are both cowards, each in our own way. Minnie flees the past by putting his life on the line for his art, now in Vietnam, before in Alabama, other times, other places, dodging cars in traffic as a child, drag racing and playing chicken as a teen ager, challenging bullets in Vietnam as an adult, daring God to call his number. My flight barricades me in the library of a law school that feeds the insatiable appetite of the Wall Street law firms, Fortune 500 corporations, the Federal government, all of which feed on us then excrete us as bodily waste.

Once upon a time, Minnie and I were going to conquer the art world together, but when I opted for the safety of law school instead of the risk of finding a loft, converting it into a studio, scrambling from temporary job to temporary job to pay the rent while hoping that the draft board back home filled its quota with boys who went from high school into the mills, Minnie's first taunt was 'law school's for cowards'; then, when Minnie saw the building housing Columbia Law School, a second taunt: 'here's to life in the pop-up toaster'. I submit a sketch of the building with 'Sunbeam' carved into its facade to the law school newspaper, but lawyers in training at a school like Columbia that drips with prestige like a donut left in the cooking oil too long, a school where three hundred students compete for a handful of openings on the Law Review like passengers on a sinking luxury liner fighting for seats in the lifeboats, law students at a school like this lack a sense of humor. Minnie closes every letter from Vietnam with one taunt or the other. Both hurt. But, not enough for me to drop out.

"Napalm Dow Chemical!" someone shouts over an amplified megaphone and the mob cheers. Maybe it's the great Mark Rudd. Or Ted Kaptchuk, President of SDS. Neither controls the mob the way Pollock controls the flow of his paint. I quickly sketch what I imagine this person to look like. A student, of course. Sunglasses even though it's dusk. An army jacket over a tie-dyed tee shirt. An SDS armband. A headband spotted in the green, black, and brown of camouflage. Imagination is my eye on the world.

"Waste Westmoreland!" The mob cheers. "Bomb the Pentagon back to the stone age!" The mob is now in a frenzy, but the law books surrounding me on three sides, the Atlantic Reporter, the Northeast Reporter, the Southern Reporter, the Southwest Reporter, the Pacific Reporter, deflect the frenzy and I feel safe. Another function of the law. To make me feel safe. A noise startles me and I see the reflection of a private security guard in the library window, one of the many the Law

School hired to supplement the University Police. The guard points a container of mace at me, his finger on its button.

"I'm a first year," I say before the guard speaks. "I have I.D."

He returns the mace to its holder in his utility belt, babying it as if it's a live grenade; then shoves his hand into his pocket to adjust his underpants. "Building is being shut down to keep out the riot." The guard shakes his pelvis to untangle his scrotum from a seam in his underwear and waits while I gather my books and papers.

April 30, 1968

5:00 PM

Dinitia Marbury Madison, wife of less than one year, turns off the lamp, the bedroom now as dim as the New York City dusk and stretches the telephone cord to the window. She leans out and looks up Broadway toward the Columbia University campus and down Broadway toward 110th Street while she talks to me. The lamp, the bedroom furniture, all the furniture except for Dinitia's Eames chair, looks like salvage from discards put out on the streets of New York for pickup by the sanitation workers. Her parents offer to pay the rent for an East Side apartment and to buy new furniture, but I refuse. As long as we're students, we'll live like students. Her father castigates me because it forces Dinitia to get a job rather than go to the Museum School for a graduate degree. I don't mind, Dinitia tells her dad. I'll go later. Two more lies. Since the wedding, only lies enable Dinitia to be civil toward her father. Or, to me. "Liar! Liar! Pants on Fire!" I imagine her thinking every time she looks at me.

Dinitia wears frayed blue jeans torn at the knees and my old blue dress shirt. The colors from *Talking of Michelangelo*, my latest creation, transform the shirt into a work of art. The eternal optimist, Dinitia will save my shirt for the day when relics of the artist become collectibles for which people who do not know better will pay big money that she will spend on college tuition for the grandchildren. Unlike her mother, she won't take 'no' for an answer.

Dinitia shivers with envy, shivers with awe, shivers because she's cold since we turn the heat down to save money, shivers whenever she looks at *Talking* leaning against the wall beside the dresser away from the heat of the radiator and the draft of the window while its coat of damar varnish dries. She tells me I have twice Minnie's vision, twice her vision, twice the vision of any young painter currently being exhibited in the galleries on Madison Avenue, opinions she shares with her mom but not her dad. Twice his vision, but none of his courage; but I don't count it as courage the way weds himself to risk and takes danger as a lover. More lies. Like the way Picasso's women talked to him while he fucked them. I believe her genius equals mine not to validate her praise, but because it does. I should have liberated her to paint rather than consigning her to supporting a Sunday painter, a weekday lawyer. Maybe not. Time will tell, the cliché goes. Time tells nothing, I say. Dinitia says if Michelangelo's *Creation of Adam* is about the creation of man, then *Talking of Michelangelo* is about the creation of an artist. Or, an artist's destruction. I fear what will time tell.

On the opposite wall leans *Life with Coffee Spoons*, Minnie's masterpiece that we are baby-sitting while he is in country, an oil on canvas, hundreds of coffee spoons spiraling into infinity, disappearing into the painting's first vanishing point. And more that regress into infinity at the second. Original, yes; but Minnie's greatest masterpiece, says Dinitia, says the great god Pratt, will be an underdeveloped photograph in comparison to my least, to Dinitia's least. Minnie understands this, but he does not concede it. Instead, he exposes his life to the needs of his art – the lie he tells himself, tells us, tells the world, to suppress the truth of why he really exposes his life – while engaging Dinitia and me in philosophical discussions about the chromophobic nature of Western Art. Color is subordinate to line, Minnie rants. Color is superficial, cosmetic. Color is infantile and vulgar. Line communicates the ideas of a work of art. M.C. Escher without the math. The rant is eternal, from Plato and Aristotle to Wittgenstein and Berenson. *Life* is line, *Talking* is color, Minnie raves. It is a reprise of the argument between Michelangelo and Titian as told by Vasari some four centuries later. *Colorito* v. *disegno*. Venice v. Florence. Composing with color v. composing with line. Monet v. Renoir. Delacroix duels Ingres who duels Delacroix. No one will duel Minnie when he rhapsodizes about the greens he tastes in Vietnam. He fancies himself another Matisse. Another Van Gogh. Another Frank Stella. It's how he justifies his perseverance. Art offers no choice, Minnie likes to taunt me. I live by the sword and die by the sword, his third taunt. As if creating art is an obsessive/compulsive disorder. Yet, art is nothing but making choices.

Dinitia kicks the dresser inches from *Talking*, a close call, the same feeling she gets when she almost runs down a pedestrian in her car. The handles on the dresser drawers rattle, but the dresser, venerable and made of real wood, absorbs her kick the way paper absorbs watercolors. She's pleads with me to drop out of law school. Begs me. Attempts bribery, first with sex, later by abstinence. Praise. Guilt. You belong in front of an easel, she says, not in front of a classroom being fucked over by a professor who believes the only way to teach law is to embarrass his students to the point of tears. I wouldn't feel scummy about sacrificing the Museum School, she tells me, if you drop out of law school. Scummy. That word lodges in my mind like a piece of shrapnel from a cluster bomb. I know what it is to feel scummy. For too, too many years I have felt scummy. It is why I barricade myself in law school like a young child hiding from the monster in a Hollywood horror flick. It pains me that I make my wife feel scummy. I doubt she would feel this scummy married to Minnie. Being made to feel scummy is not ground for divorce in New York. Though it should be.

Dinitia's tricks do not work because I have miles to go before I sleep and promises to keep. Maybe if Minnie returns from Vietnam, he can persuade me by romancing her away. Easy pickings, she'd be. Nothing will change my mind. Minnie hasn't in the past and we know each other from our finger-painting days in nursery school. A sense of loss enters through the open window in our apartment with the late April breeze and brushes against her cheek, the sense of loss that comes with death, not the death of an old person, four score and seven years of age; but the death of someone whose bloom time will tell. The death of two someones if she counts herself. Dinitia lowers the window, leaving a gap of several inches. No grimy pane of glass will shield her from April's cruelty.

The window overlooks the intersection of Broadway and West 112th Street. Police muster on all four corners like soldiers awaiting the order to charge. The storefronts are dark except for the Chinese restaurant and the place that sells Sicilian pizza by the square. The waiters at Tom's Restaurant cover the plate glass windows with sheets of plywood. Most of the storefronts lining both sides of Broadway are already boarded up.

At the Korean green grocer's, the owner and his wife bring the sidewalk displays of fresh fruits and vegetables inside as does the owner of the news stand his newspaper racks. Sanitation workers remove the trash barrels from the corners. Subtract the cops and the scene reminds Dinitia of the hurricane watches of her childhood. This hurricane shows no sign of veering out to sea. Most do but enough do not. Only fools ignore hurricane watches. Her father lost a factory in a hurricane. 1954 or 1955. Insurance rebuilt it, he always said. Dinitia doubts insurance will rebuild the damage from this hurricane. Down Broadway toward West 110th Street a phalanx of police vans waits. Their engines rumble like distant thunder. The exhaust smells like ozone after a lightning bolt strikes the earth, something one smells if one degree removed from ground zero.

"I hear the screams from here," Dinitia now says into the telephone.

"They told us to take our books," I reply. "They don't know when the building will reopen."

"Monsieur Badin called again. Twice actually. He's up to $10,000.00 for *Talking*. He'll go higher. Your Ma needs the money. You promised your Da you'd take care of your Ma after he died."

"*Talking*'s not for sale."

"I'll work two jobs if you paint. I resent working one to keep you in law school."

"Not for sale."

"Why should I give up the Museum School if my dad's willing to pay?"

"I'm not taking handouts."

"There'd be no Renaissance art if it weren't for patronage."

"Pimps and Popes. That's what the Medicis are." Florence at the time of the Medicis produced some of the world's great art. Fall River at the time of Father

Giuseppe Ozoni would produce only the still born. In my mind's eye I see the original Salvador Dali Dinitia gave me as a combined college graduation and wedding gift, Dali's *Inferno: Canto XXV* also known as *The Punishment of Vanni Fucci*. She insisted we hang it on the wall above the bed. At first, I argued we should store it with her parents as it was too valuable to hang in a student apartment in New York; then I realized a break-in, a burglary, the theft of the Dali would be a perfect solution. But not perfect enough. "I love you, Din Din."

Silence.

"If I walk home real slow, will you have time for a bath with lots of oil?"

Silence.

"Talk to me."

"I'm tired of your selling a painting is like selling a child bullshit,"

"It is."

"Or that selling a painting dispossesses you of your art."

"It does."

"Liar! Liar! Pants on fire.!"

At times like this, can't overcome the feeling Dinitia wishes she didn't love me. Wishes she married Minnie. When I'm most depressed, I, too, wish she married Minnie. With Julia, my high school flame, we would not argue about whether I should sell my paintings. With Julia there would be no paintings. Just pants. By the dozens of dozens.

April 30, 1968

7:00 PM

Sergeant Benjamin Greenbaum of the New York City Tactical Police Force sponges the flank of his horse, Blue Note, and coos to her as if he is humming a lullaby to a baby. The noise from the campus several blocks north makes Blue Note skittish and Greenbaum keeps a firm grip on her bridle, gently pulling down, afraid she'll rear up. Blue Note doesn't panic in crowds. Loud noises don't scare her. She is not afraid of the dark. But she anticipates and during the moments before she feels Greenbaum's weight on her back, his knees on her flanks, his hands pulling back on the reins, during those moments she acts like a filly being paraded to the starting gate at Belmont for the first race of her career. Greenbaum knows his horse like a jockey knows his mount. He feels her feelings, not because he shares them, but because he feels them himself. On the football field. In high school. Waiting for the opening kickoff. Waiting for the first hard hit. In the TPF waiting for the order to move out. He strokes Blue Note as he continues cooing and she whinnies softly.

Like the pillars of creation, the great spires of the Cathedral of St. John the Divine hover over Greenbaum and the TPF and their mounts. Greenbaum doesn't believe in omens, but he prefers bivouacking on the grassy knolls of Riverside Park or among the trees of Morningside Park rather than beneath God's spires. Unlike the other cops in the Tactical Police Force, he does not see himself as doing God's work. Jews make lousy missionaries.

Greenbaum and the rest of the TPF wear riot gear, helmet with face guard, leather boots to just below the knee, gloves to the elbow. They carry oversized batons almost the size of Frank Howard's baseball bat and mace as well as side arms. Greenbaum keeps his face guard raised while he ministers to Blue Note. He wants her to see his eyes. She likes his eyes and he likes hers.

"This OT's killing me, Ben." Sergeant Gil DeNisco, Greenbaum's partner, joins him. Greenbaum and DeNisco ride together, have for years, first in blue and whites, then on the horses, two cops who entrust their lives to each other but whose families never break bread together. "If I don't get back to my beat, I'll lose my pad."

"That'll make history." Greenbaum smiles and DeNisco laughs. Tip a waitress. Tip a doorman. Tip the cop on the beat. New York runs on tips the way some cities run on electricity. There are other ways, better ways, to distinguish the honest cops from the corrupt. DeNisco cuffs Thompson between the ears and Thompson, a gelding who is a half-brother of Blue Note, whinnies. Bobby Thompson, DeNisco says when people ask who the horse is named after. Greenbaum figures it's a cover for the truth, that Thompson is really named after the submachine gun carried by gangsters and federal agents during Prohibition. DeNisco obsesses over the prohibition era, reading every book, seeing every movie.

He names his twin sons Eliot and Al. Greenbaum never knows for certain which side DeNisco would be on if he could travel back in time, Ness's or Capone's. Greenbaum wouldn't be on either side because neither side rode horses. For Greenbaum, the 1930's are fifty years too late. Isaac wants to go here, Greenbaum tells DeNisco who jokes, today it's Columbia, tomorrow it's Staten Island Community College.

If Jews in the New York Police Department are no longer an anomaly, there are fewer Jews in the Tactical Police Force than on the regular force and still fewer in the Seventh Cavalry, the elite group of mounted police that fancies itself as a reincarnation of the legendary Seventh Cavalry of the old West. Most Jews of Greenbaum's generation growing up in New York City rarely got closer to horses than summer camp if they were rich or a child's pony ride at a country fair or the merry-go-round in Central Park or a movie matinee, Sunday if the parents are Orthodox, Saturday if not.

Horses and Jews don't mix, Greenbaum's father said when Greenbaum returned from a matinee, John Wayne or Hopalong Cassidy, and told his parents he wanted to be a cowboy when he grew up. Horses and Jews don't mix, his father repeated when Greenbaum told him he was assigned to the Tactical Police Force where he would ride horses rather than drive a blue and white. Blue and white, his father reminded him, are the colors of Israel.

Years later when Greenbaum sat Shiva for his father his Uncle Melvin explained that in the old country, the country his father and his uncles escaped as youths, the country of pogroms and forced conscription and blood libels, the Czar's cavalry rode down Jews the way American cowboys rode down cattle. They trampled our parents to death, his uncle says. Our oldest sister.

Now, the noise from the campus stills and the horses

whinny and neigh and try to break free from their riders as if they smell a silent predator of the night hiding behind the great brass doors of the Cathedral, locked to protect God's sanctuary.

"Easy, Blue Note. Easy," Greenbaum coos.

April 30, 1968

9:00 PM

I balance my casebooks and notebooks on my hip as I wait in a line that backs up from the main entrance of the Columbia University School of Law through the lobby, around the escalators, and up the stairs to the reference desk in the library. The mob on the plaza over Amsterdam Avenue connecting the Law School to the main campus surges toward the doors like teenage girls trying to storm the stage at a Beatles concert. The University Police, armored with the same riot shields the Alabama state police use during civil rights marches, repels wave after wave while a gauntlet of private security guards force open a path for students who exit the building. Mobs don't respect law students. No one does.

Sounds like a riot going on out there, I say to the guard when I make it to the door. He sneers and bitches about the way the Strike Coordinating Committee organized a food march to feed the hippie dippie fag fucks occupying the buildings. The guard brightens when he tells me the Mau-mau are providing security for the SCC. He has a dull flat voice, this guard, the voice of a newscaster who reads the same story dozens of times each hour and cares as much. No reason for him to care. A black in the employ of honkies protecting a building teaching honkies' law from a mob of honkies. No stake in it beyond a pay check. There are safer ways to earn a living. Like standing watch over the paintings at the Metropolitan Museum of Art, shooing away patrons who stand too close. Maybe he still wouldn't care, but maybe he would. Art does that to people. To some people.

"Mau-mau?" I ask.

"The Harlem street gang."

"What're they doing down here?"

"Wilding." He makes no effort to mask his enthusiasm.

On the main campus, New York City police guard Low Memorial Library and Butler Library while the faculty rings Havemeyer, Schermerhorn, Avery, Fayerweather, Mathematics, and the other academic buildings, druids standing vigil, arms locked against the world. If only they had the stones of Stonehenge. Inside, protesters stack chairs and desks to the ceilings to barricade the doors and ground floor windows. Classrooms where students discuss the Renaissance, the Enlightenment, classical Greek civilization, become bunkers, munitions dumps, command centers. Under siege, Columbia University cowers before each new slogan the mob hurls its way. Its image of itself as a guardian of the values of Western civilization paralyzes it. Some believe values are relative, but relative to what? No one asks; no one answers. Instead, the faculty and students shatter into schisms, each trumpeting its own version of revealed truth, each accusing the others of heresy. It's like the medieval church or the early decades of Communism. But, then, any painter will tell you the sixties were only Cubism fifty years late. Picasso truly was ahead of his time.

A long column of marchers snakes through the campus probing for weak spots in the faculty blockades to break through and deliver food and supplies to the occupiers of the buildings. In the courtyard between Earl, Lewisohn, and Dodge, chanting begets taunting and taunting begets violence, amateur violence, sophomoric violence, punching and kicking and pulling of hair, the violence of drunken fans at a football game mixing it up whenever the other team scores a touchdown. It's as ugly as professional wrestling, but it keeps the food out. I concentrate on faces with my painter's eye, cataloging lips and mouths and cheeks, all twisted in fear, exploding with anger. Up ahead, I see a student with curly hair squatting atop his head like a stocking cap. The student's hands clench into claws. One finger tugs at the side of his mouth and pulls his lips taut enough for me to see both his teeth and gums. I stand with Carpeaux as he sculpts his *Ugolina*. Reality is much more inspirational than imagination.

At the far end of the overpass by the staircase leading around the north end of Philosophy, two SDS foot soldiers identifiable by their armbands pin someone against the rail. They wear faux military uniforms, one with sergeant stripes, the other without, and I dub them Sgt. Bilko and Private Doberman. Both have camouflage stripes on their faces. As I get closer, I recognize their victim, Joel Davidow, another first year law student who is in my Torts section. An Orthodox Jew, Davidow never attends Saturday classes and during the winter he leaves early on Friday afternoons to arrive home before sunset. His professors cut him no slack. Nor do his classmates. One less person in the hunt for Law Review. I envy him for his devotion to a higher calling.

Bilko and Doberman struggle to lift Davidow on to the railing and I realize they intend to dump him on to

Amsterdam Avenue as if he is a water balloon being dropped on a passing car. I beg help from the University Police who ignore me, preferring to protect the Law School building. The old debate, human rights vs. property rights, but I don't recall discussing it in this context in my Real Property class. It should be. Count the number of people who die defending, or attacking, a section. An acre. A quarter acre. A square foot. A square inch. No monuments memorializing them.

Bilko bends Davidow over the railing as Doberman struggles to lift his legs. Two of them; one of me. Fighting dirty evens the odds. The ends justify the means. Doberman lifts Davidow's feet off the ground. His body seesaws on the railing as Bilko and Doberman toy with him, tilting him over, bringing him back, over and back, over and back. I fight my way through the mob.

"Need a hand, guys?"

I punch Doberman in the ear, splitting it open. Blood flows down Doberman's neck. "You deserve a Purple Heart," I shout as I catapult Doberman over the railing. He bounces off the roof of a passing bus and lands on Amsterdam Avenue where a cab slams on its brakes, skidding to a stop, one of its front wheels between Doberman's legs.

Bilko drops Davidow on the plaza's concrete floor, then squares to confront me. I circle around, positioning myself a few feet in front of the railing, enough room for me to drop down and ride Bilko over the railing on my feet, a maneuver any first-year judo student masters. Anticipating Bilko's charge, I lean forward, light on my feet, beckoning with my hands, exhilarated the way painting exhilarates me when my vision, my conception, takes physical form.

"You be watching your back, you hear." Bilko dissolves into the mob.

I pick up Davidow's skull cap. "You all right?"

Davidow brushes the dirt from his skull cap and kisses it before replacing it on his head. "Animals. They're animals." He straightens his shirt and tucks it back into his pants and I notice the fringes around his waist. I knew Jews from high school, from college, from law school. Before Dinitia, before Julia, I dated Barbara and Brenda, nice Jewish girls. And played basketball with Marc and Herbie and Jeff and Bob, but never Ric who wasn't into driveway basketball. Nice Jewish boys. None of the Jews I knew dressed or acted like Davidow.

"Where're you heading?" I retrieve my books.

"The train."

"I'll walk you 'cross campus."

Davidow and I avoid College Walk, the most direct route from the Law School to the subway station at Broadway and West 116th Street, walking instead in the shadows between the back of Low Memorial Library and Uris Hall. Night controls this part of the campus. Several students race by us, fleeing the war zone surrounding Mathematics. Fear replaces frivolity. The moment is no longer a lark, no longer a spree, no longer a panty raid. Davidow and I step deeper into the shadows. SDS foot soldiers dressed like urban peasants rather than faux military, black coveralls with red headbands, as if their costumes add virtue to their cause, charge the faculty brigade ringing Mathematics. They are reinforced by Mau-mau. The two groups collide, meld like a rugby scrum, alternate pushing each other forward, then back. In the shadows of Earl, two Mau-mau empty a gunny sack of bricks, bisected, light enough to throw accurately and heavy enough to inflict real hurt. The faculty and the SDS foot soldiers scatter under the barrage of half-bricks, then regroup to provide first aid to their fallen comrades. For a moment, they are no longer enemies. No longer teacher and student either. Not allies, but no longer enemies.

I binge on the moment. Feelings of exhilaration whip through me, more intense than what I felt on the plaza after dumping Doberman on Amsterdam Avenue, more intense than what I feel when I sign my initials to a finished canvas, than when I add the small crucifix in a pool of blood, the clue I hide in every painting. I feel ready to take on the universe. I could become addicted to this feeling. Easily. Too easily. "Get the University Police" I tell Davidow.

Using my Torts casebook to shield my face and head, I dodge bricks as I draw the fire of the Mau-mau. Three University Police trailed by Davidow bear down on the Mau-mau who separate, one racing toward the statue of Alma Mater in front of Low, the other toward Avery. I chase the one heading toward Alma Mater, dodging knots of people like a broken-field runner. On the plaza, I tackle him. The brickwork rips the skin from his cheek. I let him bleed, a souvenir, something to shave around, something to remind him of this night every time he looks in the mirror. I scream at the night sky and by the time the University Police relieve me of my burden, I bring my high under control. The righteousness of my cause justifies, excuses, what I feel, the lessons of the rioting.

"Reminds me of Daumier's *Uprising*," I say to Davidow.

"Who is this Daumier?"

"He painted French peasants rioting. Any of them had more purpose than all these people combined."

"This Daumier, would he paint this?"

"This madness. Who knows? Goya would. The later Goya. The Goya of the etchings. The Goya of the firing squads."

"Who is this Goya?"

"Picasso? Rembrandt? Michelangelo? Do these names mean anything to you?"

"I never studied them. Talmud and Torah. I studied

Talmud and Torah."

"So why are you going to law school?"

"To become a lawyer."

The simplicity of his answer startles me, causes me to wonder if that is why I am going to law school. Unless, I'm a slave to a hidden agenda. Someone else's agenda imposed on me by my past.

On the vast expanse of grass in the courtyard formed by Hamilton, Hartley, Livingston and John Jay, extending across the campus between Butler Library and the Sundial to Furnald and Ferris Booth, Mau-mau break into small groups that roam like soldiers on search and destroy missions, picking off individual students, all white, beating them and leaving them on the ground, debris to be swept up in the morning. SDS no longer orchestrates the demonstrations and building occupations, no longer sets the political agenda, no longer controls the flow of the pain. Mau-mau care little for stopping the construction of the new gym in Morningside Park or severing Columbia's ties with the Institute for Defense Analysis, or amnesty for students who participated in previous demonstrations, the issues precipitating this evening's frolic. Mau-mau care only for the hunt and the kill and hunting/killing season is open. The plains of Columbia University throb with game, white game, wounded, sickly, unable to defend itself, the kind of game hyena packs easily cull from the herd, run down, devour.

Davidow and I work our way along the side of Hamilton Hall toward the wrought iron gate at the Amsterdam Avenue entrance to College Walk. The night sky, clear, cloudless, full of stars, is invisible over the city's lightscape. It smothers the crowd, trapping the crowd's energy, the way thick cloud cover traps the heat from the earth's atmosphere. A crescent moon hangs over the Law School like a pervert's grin. The mob evolves into an organism, a life form, perhaps a paramecium, or an amoeba or some other single cell creature. It extends a pseudopod and suddenly we are surrounded, ingested as if we are a speck of food.

"Hey! Law School Boy!" Someone steps out of the shadows. Doberman. An ace bandage wraps his left hand. Adhesive tape and gauze pads cover his right ear and the right side of his face. "Ever ride the roof of a bus before?"

"Fare jumping's illegal."

Bilko joins Doberman. "Remember me?"

"Bilko's gonna break your head," Doberman says.

"Him and what army?"

Four Mau-mau step out of the shadows and surround me and Davidow. "Him and this army."

I await the surge of another high as I maneuver to stand back to back with Davidow, but the high never arrives. Instead, I feel as dead inside as when Minnie taunted me that law school was for cowards, mocking me by saluting life browned to perfection in the pop-up toaster. Don't show fear. I drop my law books to free my hands and look each of the Mau-mau in the eye, ignoring Doberman and Bilko the way a person about to be attacked by a pack of wolves ignores a cocker spaniel. I spit on the ground, then spit a second time, an imaginary line that I dare the Mau-mau to cross. My heartbeat pounds inside my head like a bass drum and I wish for a real bass drum, red and black, a cadence I can fight to. Maybe I'll hit another lucky shot. Davidow breaks the back to back formation. "Stay put," I whisper.

"Think you can handle the Jew?" one of the Mau-mau asks Bilko.

"I doubt they could handle your mama," I say.

The Mau-mau smiles at me.

"Why do you want to get busted up for honky trash like them?" I ask.

"Who says we're doing it for them," the Mau-mau replies. "Can honky trash handle the Jew?"

"Blindfolded and with our hands tied behind our backs," Doberman says.

"And Law School Boy?" the Mau-mau asks.

"He's all yours, brother," Bilko replies.

"Don't fucking brother me," the Mau-mau snaps.

Bilko and Doberman struggle to wrestle Davidow to the ground. He thrashes around like a person trapped inside a giant paper bag trying to free himself.

"Regular Killer Kowalskis," I say.

Doberman finally trips Davidow and Bilko begins kicking him when he hits the ground.

"Let me bust up those two motherfucks," I say to the Mau-mau, "and then I'll dance at your party as long as you want."

One of the Mau-mau answers by cracking the side of my head with a police nightstick, but the leader restrains him. "I could use me some entertainment." The Mau-mau step back. "You whip their asses we let the Jew go."

"And me?"

"You owe us a dance."

I pull Doberman off Davidow by the hair, rip the bandages from his face, then head butt him, reopening the split in his ear, the laceration along his cheek. Blood drenches his shirt and he staggers toward College Walk. I kick Doberman in the small of his back and he sprawls on the bricks. I lock my arm around Bilko's neck and jerk him away from Davidow, then shove his head into the wrought iron fence, wedging it between two spokes. "You a wrestling fan?" I ask Doberman before I execute an Atomic Knee Drop between his shoulder blades. I squeeze the side of his neck with a Jivaro Finger Pinch and he passes out.

"Not bad for a honky," the Mau-mau leader says.

I fill my voice with bravado. "Get out of here, Joel."

The leader snaps his fingers and one of the other Mau-mau shoves Davidow to the ground and stands with his foot on Davidow's neck like a hunter on safari posing with the carcass of a trophy kill. "I guess it's time for our dance," the leader says to me.

"We had a deal."

"It's been re-negotiated."

I circle until the wall of Hamilton Hall is behind me. What cuts off my retreat also cuts off their attack from my backside. One of the Mau-mau charges from the side. I spin and sidekick him in the chest, knocking the wind out of him. Before he recovers, I slip behind him and immobilize him in a strangle hold. Drool flows from his mouth as I slowly close his windpipe. "You let me and the Jew go and I let him go."

"He ain't worth dried shit."

"The Jew then."

"I ain't had my dance yet."

"Fuck you!" I shield myself with the Mau-mau. One jerk to crush his windpipe, to suffocate him. Not homicide. Self-defense. A great question for the Criminal Law final, but I don't want to become a law school final. I don't want to become a defendant either. Better a live defendant than a dead law student. Columbia is not Alabama; this Mau-mau is not M'Boto. I am not Sheriff Cyrus's whistling deputy. Davidow is not Minnie. The leader nods and two Mau-mau flank me, closing in from each side, moving slowly, deliberately, preventing me from leveraging my speed into an escape. The leader approaches from the front, closing off the angle of escape, trapping me inside a triangle. I jerk my forearm tight, then shove my hostage into the arms of the leader and dodge to the right, trying to burst out of the triangle with a juke to the right, a feint to the left, but the Mau-mau brings me down with a perfect open field tackle, arms wrapped around my knees, pinning my legs together, twisting to the right to drive me into the brick of Hamilton Hall. I break my fall with my forehead and feel my skin flay like the skin of an orange peeled with a chain saw.

I struggle to get up. The leader splits my ear open with a police nightstick, knocks me back against the wall. My skull, my cheeks, my nose, my jaw, my forehead, the nightstick pulverizes my bones. I try to curl my arms around my head, but that exposes my rib cage. The other two Mau-mau, armed with brass knuckles, pound my ribs as if they are Sonny Liston and I am a punching bag. My ribs crack and my rib cage contracts around my lungs. I try to crawl between the Mau-mau, but they push me back against the wall of Hamilton and continue beating me, two with brass knuckles, the leader with the nightstick. I am a lump on the ground, barely alive. Lights flash on and off in my eyes as if my brain, my retinal nerve, is a loose wire randomly allowing electrons to flow from wall socket to light bulb. The beating continues as the Mau-mau chant, 'CIA! CIA! Why'd you kill MLK?' in rhythm to each blow, to each kick. Again, I try to cover my head with my arms and curl myself into a fetal position, but the other two Mau-mau grab my arms and legs and straighten me out, exposing me like a prisoner bound to a medieval torture rack. I will not give them the satisfaction of begging for death. The beating continues and the chants of the Mau-mau, uniform beats, no longs, no shorts, fade in and out of my consciousness like a tape with dead spots. "CIA!... Why'd... MLK?" The Mau-mau land their blows on my head and chest and groin like drummers laying down a backbeat. Only my rage at the joy in their voices keeps me alive.

"Ain't no more shit left to beat out of him," one of the Mau-mau says.

"Ain't shit we're beating out of him." The leader punctuates each word with a kick to the groin.

I sense myself tumbling over and over. I'm a child again rolling down the dunes of Horseneck Beach into the surf; but what wets me now is my blood pooling in the gutter of Amsterdam Avenue. If I still have a head, I no longer feel it. If I still have fingers, hands, arms, I no longer feel them. Nor my feet, legs or thighs. The dead zone expands from my chest to my stomach, from my stomach to my testicles, from my testicles to the very core of my being. My consciousness seems disembodied, my intellect disconnected. The pounding continues, always in rhythm to the chanting, 'CIA! CIA! Why'd you kill MLK?' At last, I black out and the chanting, at least for me, ceases.

9:45 PM

Sergeant Benjamin Greenbaum jumps off Blue Note and positions his horse to create a breakwater forcing the mob to divert around me. "I got him," he shouts to DeNisco. "You get that one." Greenbaum's fingers search for my pulse. He activates his walkie-talkie. "Two civilians down. One with a crushed skull. No pulse. Losing blood. The other unconscious. Need an ambulance." Greenbaum covers me. "It's worse than Esther after the accident, Gil."

Blue Note flinches as the red emergency light of the ambulance sweeps along her flank. Greenbaum grabs for her reins. This happens at Columbia, he thinks. Ivy League. The school of Hamilton and Jay. Older than the United States itself. The ivoriest of ivory towers. It doesn't matter whether it's Mau-mau or Martians. If it happens at Columbia, no school is immune. Not Fordham. Not Yeshiva. Maybe we should move to Israel, Isaac and me, Greenbaum thinks. At least the Israelis know what they're fighting for, who they're fighting against.

Greenbaum leads Blue Note to the side of the ambulance, making room for the EMTs to load me. Blue Note whinnies at the sound of the ambulance door being slammed shut. The driver cranks up the siren and Blue Note rears back and slams the side of the ambulance with his front hooves, two more dents to add to those made by tire irons or cinder blocks or baseball bats or brass knuckles, souvenirs of neighborhoods where anyone in uniform is the enemy, even the blues worn by the ambulance crews. The ambulance races down Amsterdam Avenue past the Viennese pastry shop where I eat breakfast after my 8 o'clock classes, past the post office annex where I buy overseas air mail letters for writing to Minnie, past the newspaper store where I buy *Thor* and *Spiderman* and *Fantastic Four* and *Dr. Strange*, past the tenements that are permanent homes to the people who live in them, to St. Luke's Hospital. The horses of the Seventh Cavalry panic. Some throw their riders; others break formation and flee the noise and lights. Horses, unlike people, respect the sound of the siren. The ambulance arrives at the emergency room and the mounted police regroup and march down Amsterdam Avenue toward the Columbia campus. Somebody cracks a joke about taming the Wild Upper West Side. No one laughs.

At St. Luke's, Willard Cushman Hayes, a hospital orderly, yet one who fancies himself the smartest mind on the floor, wheels me across a loading dock into a corridor leading to the emergency room while the ambulance driver struggles with Joel Davidow because his gurney freezes up, its wheels twisted inwards. The right front wheel of my gurney clicks each time it revolves because of a wad of dry gum, flat from time, black from age. No one can hear the clicks over the cries of the patients, bloody, bruised, and battered as a result of the Mau-mau search and destroy missions. The patients crowd the corridor and lay siege to the doors of the emergency room, fighting for position like rabid football fans waiting for the box office to open hoping to purchase standing room tickets to a playoff game. The police lock arms and form a human chain to clear a path for the gurneys, a human chain to block the mob from crashing the emergency room. Only the near dead are granted access.

"Severe head trauma," Hayes tells the triage team converging on me. "There could be raised intracranial pressure. Better check for herniation of the brain through the foramen magnum."

"Outta the way, probation prick." Dr. Jamaal Kofu, Chief Resident in the St. Luke's Emergency Room, pushes Hayes aside. "You leave the medicine to us and we'll leave the bed pans to you."

"Watch who you're shoving," Hayes says.

"Hey, Tony!" Kofu shouts to one of the hospital's security guards. "Call Dr. Kildare's probation officer. I want his ass out of here."

"He'll violate me," Hayes says.

"Not the way he should," Kofu replies.

To a person, the emergency room staff hates Hayes, a Cornell pre-med student who acts as if he's already Board certified in emergency medicine. After killing his fiancée in a DWI, Hayes received a year of community service as an orderly at St. Luke's in lieu of jail, a year's probation, a sealed record, a plea bargain that will enable him to have sufficient good character to be licensed as a physician in New York. Hayes griped about the year's delay, but then he didn't know how much his father contributed to the judge's re-election campaign to pay for the plea bargain. If New York were a state where judges were appointed rather than elected, Hayes would be breaking rocks at Sing Sing or Attica and subsisting on bread and water.

Kofu who lives in a railroad flat on the other side of Morningside Park while he pays off his college and medical school loans especially hates Hayes because Kofu knows that if he were driving drunk, he'd be doing ten years hard time at Attica rather than getting in everyone's way in the St. Luke's emergency room. In New York, integrity, like the pastrami, is well cured.

"Skull's depressed," the nurse says.

"Any bleeding from the nose or ears?" Kofu asks. "There's bruising around the eyes, Doctor." "This one's for Hendu."

"Hendu's been in O.R. the last sixteen hours."

"He's on for another twenty, isn't he? Page him. STAT."

Hayes wheels my gurney into the Intensive Care Unit. In the quiet of the ICU, the gum on the gurney's wheel echoes like a metronome. With each click, my eye lids flicker. Above me, the ceiling tiles and fluorescent lights pass in a stroboscopic blur, but the light does not register on my pupils which are fixed and frozen. A nurse drapes a cloth over my eyes and I sense my soul settling back into my body. As the gurney picks up speed, the clicking gets louder, more persistent, now the sound of the lever on the Lincoln Park grocery wheel hitting the pins as it goes round and round, white lights flashing, red lights flashing, slowing down until it picks another winner of a can of peas or creamed corn or a box of stale crackers or a mill dolly for the shill.

The grocery wheel stops on the line between two and three. I flip the number board. Dimes cascade on to the conveyer belt, then into a funnel that deposits them in a locked box, dented from banging against the shaft in which it rests.

The hospital gurney stops on the line between life and death. Whether my number is up depends on the flip of the board.

April 30, 1968

10:30 PM

Dinitia ties the belt of her bathrobe and steps from the steam filled bathroom to answer the telephone. The heat of her bath seeps beneath her skin, relaxing her muscles and heightening her anticipation of my return, but the frigid bedroom shivers away her desire. Goose bumps are never sexy.

"Madame Malone." The speakerphone distorts Monsieur Badin's French accent, making it sound like he acquired it at Berlitz. Dinitia doubts any of his clients speak French. If they did, they wouldn't be his clients.

"Mais, non. Madame Madison."

Dinitia closes the blinds and sprawls in the Eames chair beside the window. Her retaining her maiden name feeds my anxieties, my fear Malone is not a good enough name for her. As good as Minifie would be. She counters with questions of her own. Marriage, children, gender, is that why there are few women artists. Few Georgia O'Keefes. Mary Cassats. Frida Kahlos. Judith Leysters. Sofonisba Anguissolas. Lavinia Fontanas. Artemisia Gentileschis. Dinitia memorized their names, studied their biographies, counted the number of their paintings reproduced, the number of references to them, in Janson's *History of Art*. That Dinitia Marbury Madison has ceased to exist. Marriage. Working a shit job to support a broke law student. Not a starving artist. Not Minnie.

She grew up in a home replete with original works of art whose owners selected artists whose names were the equivalent of the labels of the Paris fashion houses. Now, she lives in an apartment whose only original works of art are *Talking of Michelangelo* and *Life with Coffee Spoons* by artists whose names would not grace the labels on the rack of a 14th Street jobber house selling off brand clothing through street vendors and flea markets. Dinitia adjusts to living at my economic level more easily than I adjust to living at hers. Maybe, in the future, I say, if I succeed in my own right. As a lawyer, she asks. I hate it when she sounds like Julia.

"Has Madame spoken with Monsieur?" Badin's voice echoes through the speakerphone as does a woman's cough. Dinitia tries to massage the goose bumps into her arms, but they're as stubborn as I am about not selling my paintings.

"Do you know the time?"

"Great art is timeless."

In her mind, she laughs at the cliché. "My husband appreciates how generous $10,000.00 is. He wants me to thank you." Dinitia chooses her words more for the unknown buyer than for Badin. "I don't know if my husband would reconsider." Other voices filter through the telephone, clearly audible above Badin's efforts to silence them. 'I've got to have it,' a woman says. '$25,000.00,' a man says.

"Madame?" Badin says.

"Did I hear $25,000.00?"

"Your husband is acquiring a reputation, Madame," Badin says. "This is not bad. Temperamental artists sell better. Scarcity breeds demand; demand begets inflation. I can make Monsieur Malone wealthy. Famous. The future of art."

And me, Dinitia thinks. If it were my name on that painting, Dinitia wants to ask, would you make me wealthy? Famous? The future of art? She bites her tongue.

Since I was told I may kiss the bride, I worry she regrets she forfeited her place at the Museum School to support a law student who fears the blank canvas, who paints only on Sundays, a law student who refuses to sell his painting to fulfill his pledge to his Da to support his Ma. If she catalogued all the regrets, the marriage may not survive its first anniversary. Love does not conquer all.

I worry her attitude toward me changed as her father's did when I refused his offer to finance a studio, arrange portrait commissions, introduce me to art dealers, that she realized her marital mistake. Amherst College will no longer be good enough for me to gain entry to her world. If not a mic, now a wop. Still, Italy gave Western civilization the Renaissance. And Ireland. Joyce and Yeats and St. Patrick and the potato famine and hundreds of years of bloodshed. Two writers and a saint who might not have existed against a horde of painters and sculptors. With da Vinci designing the weaponry, Italy in a cakewalk.

Amherst now admits Jews, her father whimpered in her ear. And Negroes and Irish and Poles and Chinese and Japanese. Nor will Columbia University School of Law which also admits Jews and Negroes and Irish and Poles and Chinese and Japanese be good enough to get me past the gatekeepers of her world. I am Irish. The son of mill workers. God knows who my ancestors are. Where they come from. What they did to survive. No United States presidents in my lineage. Not the Madison's kind; nor the Pratt's. Maybe good enough to tend the grounds at their Newport cottages, but certainly not worthy of entering the main house as guests, much less as a member of the family. Her father whimpered these things in her ear like a judge pronouncing a death sentence, but Dinitia married me anyway because she loved me, she said, and believed in me, she said, and will spend her life, if necessary, to get me in front of an easel, she said. I do, she said. A slip of the tongue when she meant to say I don't. As I do when I refuse to sell *Talking of Michelangelo* for $25,000.00 when Ma desperately needs the money. For this Ma persuaded Da to let me go to Amherst.

At one time, I offered to sell the Dali, but Ma said no. "A gift from your wife, it would be a sacrilege," she said.

It is pigheaded stubbornness, mulish like Da's da, that causes me to refuse $25,000.00 for *Talking of Michelangelo*. Genetic, stubbornness. A dominant gene, recessive. Advanced Placement biology sophomore year. Mendel's peas. My genes determine, control, my future. If I have two dominants for stubbornness, it means one must have been lurking in Ma's DNA; or that one is enough to make me pigheaded, mulish. Mendel's peas do not answer all my questions. Nurture rather than nature must play a part, the same nurture that causes me to hide a tiny crucifix in a pool of blood in each of my paintings.

Dinitia says to Badin, "My husband says selling a painting is the same as selling a child."

I do say that and she does not believe me, never did, never will. I see it in her eyes, the way they dim whenever I offer up this excuse she knows I don't believe myself. The truth, she demanded the first several times. Now she no longer bothers. Liar! Liar! Pants on fire! Love, love's opposite.

"And does he make love only to procreate?" Badin

asks. "If a tree fell in the forest, Madame, and there was no one to hear it, would it make a sound?"

"Cogito ergo sum," Dinitia replies. "Au revoir, Monsieur Badin."

Dinitia's goose bumps collapse back into her skin. She wants me home. She needs my touch to kill the regrets and silence the whimpering of her father. She needs my touch to distract her from the fact that someone wants to pay $25,000.00 for the painting leaning against the dresser that I will not sell. She needs my touch to remind her she did the right thing when she said 'I do'. So easy to mistake her love for lust.

Dinitia eases herself back into the bath, thankful the water is still hot. She adds another measure of oil to make her skin glisten. She likes the way my hands glide along her body when her skin is well oiled and we both like the oil's fragrance and taste. She sinks into the water until it laps against her chin the way the ocean laps against the chin of a young girl lying on the beach at the family's summer cottage in Newport trying to count the stars in the heavens, a little girl dreaming about becoming an artist and selling her work to museums to inspire other little girls the way Georgia O'Keefe and Frida Kahlo whose art her father refuses to purchase inspire her.

Tonight, she decides, when we snuggle after making love, she will tell me she will not be another Mrs. Jackson Pollock. She will enroll in the Museum School, she vows to say, the day after I graduate law school. She will sell her paintings. But what if we can't afford it, she anticipates me responding. What kind of lawyer cannot support his wife, she will say. What kind of painter can, she hears my voice in her head. You are not a painter, she will say. A chill courses through her as if someone dumps several buckets of shaved ice into the bath. All the money in all the Madison and Pratt checkbooks will not put Humpty Dumpty back together again.

Dinitia squeezes a drop of scented oil on her fingertips and massages it into her inner thighs. Her fingers linger at the place where she likes to be kissed. If I won't yield up my secrets to my wife, she thinks, maybe I will to a French whore. The fragrance excites her and she closes her eyes and imagines the fragrance mixing with her own aroma after a good fuck. She should bottle that aroma, market it at Saks and Bonwits and Bloomingdales. Call it Intercourse. Bottle it in long, tall phials, very phallic, very penile. She wouldn't sell it to women over thirty. Such women would not use it properly. They would wear it to benefits or dinner parties or Metropolitan Opera openings. Thank God menopause is several life times away. Maybe when I am deep inside her, she thinks, I'll confess why I will not sell his paintings for $25,000.00 or $250,000.00 or $2,500,000.00. Truthfully confess. I painted it for you and you alone, she imagines me saying. She knows I lie. She knows there is no logical or rational reason. But there is, one Minnie and I vowed to each other to take to our graves. Mendel's peas, I will tell her. Mendel's peas. From doubt to disbelief to regret is a hop, skip, and jump. My voice, squalling from the ecstasy of sex, fills her head, muffling the incessant ringing of the telephone.

"Mrs. Malone?" A stranger's voice, as cold and precise as an incision made by a scalpel. "Your husband's at St. Luke's Emergency. You better get over here right away."

"Is he?" Her voice quavers, then steadies, hardens. "Is he... ?"

"Do you have a priest? If not, the hospital will provide one."

Dinitia hurries into her clothes, too upset to notice she wears the bath oil like a shroud.

April 30, 1968–May 1, 1968

Not all memories are pleasant. Remembering some events causes greater pain and anguish than experiencing them as it is with this particular night in April, the cruelest night of the cruelest month. My mind pictures these events as if they are Egyptian funerary art on the walls of a Pharaoh's tomb. Ti watches his slaves hunt hippopotami in 2400 B.C. and 1968 A.D. Nebamun hunts birds in 1400 B.C. and 1968 A.D. Sen-nedjem lives his life during the Nineteenth Dynasty and he lives it again in 1968 A.D. What I share with you in 1968, some trespasser will experience in 2968 and 3968, a register of scenes proceeding from one to the next to the next in a Pharaonic burial chamber. My Pharaonic burial chamber.

✲ ✲ ✲

Before Father Urbano telephones, Ma knows nothing about the troubles at Columbia University. The local television stations, Channels 10 and 12 in Providence, do not consider it newsworthy and Ma does not watch the Boston stations because the reception is too fuzzy. Nor does she read the sketchy wire service reports that the *Fall River Herald* publishes because she cancelled the paper to save money. Television and radio, more radio with its five minutes of news and weather on the hour, keep her informed. Before Father Urbano's call, Ma is as oblivious to the Columbia riots as I am to her deteriorating financial condition. Ignorance makes me a bad son unlike Da who was not ignorant. Da was a good son. I am blessed to be descended from two strong women. Genes keep me alive.

At the train station in Providence, Ma hides behind a luggage cart while she waits for the train to New York that originates in Boston. Most of the other passengers are my contemporaries, Brown students going to New Haven to visit friends at Yale or New London in the hope of getting laid at Connecticut College. They celebrate out of brown paper bags. Although the train departs Boston on time, it is twenty minutes overdue because a gate malfunctions at a grade crossing in Attleboro and the engineer has to lower and raise it by hand. Ma last rode the train during World War II when gas was rationed, pregnant with me, a trip to New York for a last farewell before Da shipped out for the European Theater. I was not kicking yet and the only external evidence of my existence was a slight rounding of Ma's abdomen and tenderness of her breasts and nipples. From the womb, I sensed Da's presence, his touch. And I heard his voice, a voice I next heard sixteen months later. I'll be back for the first birthday, Da promised. Ma cried. Da cried. I cried.

Meanwhile, in New York, the fiercely mournful melodies of Miles Davis's *Sketches of Spain* reverberate off the walls of the doctor's lounge at St. Luke's Hospital where Dr. Archibald "Hendu" Henderson sprawls on a couch sleeping off sixteen hours of emergency brain surgery on a postal worker who was run over by a mail truck. Unlike the prestigious private hospitals on Fifth Avenue that provide luxurious lounges, St. Luke's carved an area out of the back of a supply closet and furnished it with used furniture, a radio old enough to have tubes, and a coffee pot, not the brand hawked by Joe DiMaggio, but one of its discounted imitators. Hendu sleeps through the noise of people coming and going to retrieve sheets, pillowcases, towels, bed pans, plastic glasses, but Dr. Karen Robey, a surgical resident who sprawls on the other couch, cannot. Her metabolism, imprisoned by caffeine and adrenaline, still races because of the life she and Hendu saved in surgery. Yes, the postal worker almost died, but Hendu told her what to do and how to do it as he continued working inside the patient's brain and, somehow, she was able to follow his instructions. Don't get too high when you save them, Hendu told her as he sutured the skin along the side of the skull. Don't get too low when you lose them. Unlike Hendu, she's a rookie at playing God.

Once, Robey asked Hendu how he went from hours of surgery to dispensing bad news to the husbands or wives, mothers or fathers, of his patients and he told her that jazz is his oasis. Now it is hers as well. On her rare nights off she haunts the Village Gate or the Village Vanguard or the Blue Note or one of New York's other jazz clubs. Whenever Sam Goody has a sale, she spends her month's entertainment budget on records. She falls asleep, when she is able to sleep, to Brubeck or Coltrane or Davis or Ellington. With jazz, she feels inside the music while, simultaneously, the music is inside her. Rock is surface music that never penetrates the skin. Still, on this particular night, Robey curses Scott Muni, one of her favorite radio disc jockeys, for playing Miles

Davis because he brings back memories she does not want to have.

Rennie Coolidge also loved jazz, but Karen Robey was too young then to appreciate why. It will be one of those differences, she thought at the time, that will make their marriage work. Rennie has never been part of her nightmares and she does not want him to be, but extreme exhaustion liberates memories that burn into her vision like the desert sun at mid-day. Robey's memories linger after the music stops, after Scott Muni does a time check, 11:30 PM, after he reminds his listeners to stay tuned for Alison Steele, the Night Bird, who comes on at midnight. Midnight. Memories are always worst at midnight. Smith College. Senior year. Eisenhower's second term. Rally Day. Smith's winter festival.

Rennie, a senior at Amherst, presented her with an engagement ring, the diamond a family heirloom that his grandmother last wore. For Robey, like many in her class, a diamond by graduation was no longer the prime objective it was when her mother, Class of 1932, attended Smith. Graduate school, jobs with career paths, many wanted more than an apron with a toddler or two tugging at its hem; but she loved Rennie and she said yes and with his encouragement and the urging of her Organic Chemistry professor she applied to medical school. She hesitated to tell her parents. She was an only child and their grandparents' clocks ticked loudly, louder when they announced her engagement in *The New York Times*.

Memories. The weekend before the Amherst prom. She and Rennie planned ahead. She will sign out to visit a friend at Radcliffe who will cover for her if the housemother makes one of her random telephone checks. Rennie reserved a room at the Parker House and made dinner reservations at Locke-Ober. After dinner, back at the hotel, where they calmed their nerves with champagne and made love to a Stan Getz album, *Moonlight in Vermont*, and, because Rennie was gentle, it was not, as her roommate warned, like an obstetrics exam. In the morning Karen woke first and brushed her teeth and, because she was eager to make love again, blew in his ear. When he didn't respond she shook him. He was cold to her touch. Slowly, the realization crept over her that Rennie had died in his sleep. An autopsy resulted in a long medical explanation that she first began to doubt as soon as she became Dr. Robey. The week before graduation, Smith convened a disciplinary hearing, convicting her of signing out to a false address, but waiving the penalty, mandatory expulsion, out of compassion. She skipped graduation. Smith mailed her her degree and Phi Beta Kappa key.

Now, back in the lounge at St. Luke's, the coffee, stale and bitter and burnt, dissolves her memories the way acid dissolves flesh. The inside of her mouth feels like the morning after a bad drunk and she spits the coffee into the waste basket. She reaches to silence Scott Muni, but the intercom squawks, rasping like the feedback from a Jimmy Hendrix guitar riff after it doubles back through the sound system.

"Dr. Henderson. Emergency Room. STAT. Dr. Henderson. Emergency Room. STAT."

Robey calls the switchboard. "Hendu's in the lounge. Drop dead exhausted. Get someone else."

"Negative. Severe head trauma. Loss of consciousness. Probable brain damage. Possibly irreversible. Worse than the postal worker."

"Vitals?"

"Erratic."

"Oh fuck!" Robey shakes Henderson. "White knight time, Hendu."

"Again?" Henderson groans as he puts on his hospital scrubs. "Just think, Karen. Someday this will all be yours." Hendu is fully awake by the time he reaches the emergency room and steps inside the curtains surrounding the bed where I lie. "Films?"

Hayes mounts several X-rays on the light box. His face brightens as the lights come up. "God damn! We got edema. We got clots. What a big motherfucker."

"Blow it out your ass!" Robey pushes Hayes aside.

"Here," Hendu says.

"Maybe here." Robey points.

"O.R. 1. STAT."

"Ice packs," Robey says.

"To lower his body temperature," Hayes says. Right?"

"Prep him and shave his skull," Hendu orders.

As Hayes wheels me away, humming to the rhythm of the clicking wheels of my gurney, Hendu reaches for Robey's hand and gently squeezes it. "Ready for a little carpentry, Doctor?"

In the operating theater, Robey's nose itches and she wishes she could scratch it, but she doesn't because it would violate surgical protocol. Her nose always itches before surgery. Fear, she thinks, but Hendu explains it's adrenaline, tells her that when the itching stops, she should hang up her scalpel. Robey glances at the clock. Fifteen minutes to Alison Steele. She wishes she were the Night Bird.

❧ ❧ ❧

In Providence, the Brown students serenade the world with the hits of Frankie Valli and the Four Seasons and Ma cowers behind the baggage cart like an illegal immigrant afraid of being deported. A few miles away in Attleboro, the engineer struggles with the gate while the train sits by the grade crossing.

Hendu and Robey concentrate on my skull while the rest of the surgical team monitors my heartbeat, my respiration, my body temperature. Hendu knows this team, likes them, calls them his foxhole team. Guy Stevens, the only anesthesiologist at St. Luke's who never loses patients, puts them asleep, keeps them asleep, wakes them when it's over.

Raz Fernandez babysits the equipment that monitors the patient's readouts, heartbeat, respiration, body temperature. If a patient flatlines, Raz sounds the alarm. A doctor in his native Bolivia, Raz is not eligible to be licensed in New York because he is not a graduate of a medical school accredited by the American Medical Association.

Bobbye Briscoe, chief surgical nurse, twelve years emptying bed pans and changing the sheets in Alabama hospitals because it was illegal in Alabama for Negroes to provide medical treatment to whites. At St. Luke's, Briscoe makes sure the right tool or implement is in the surgeon's hand before he requests it. Every surgeon at St. Luke's wants Briscoe, but she works only with Henderson because many of the patients assigned to Henderson, patients like me, need more than surgery. We also need miracles.

Lizzie Wrick, the daughter and granddaughter of nurses, handles the soft goods, bandages and gauze and sponges and dressings. She's royalty, the Countess, because she counts everything twice to make certain nothing is left inside the patient that should not be there.

Ella Valery, content to be on the periphery, operates the sterilizer. Gaye Sillers does everything else.

And, Dr. Karen Robey assists. Smith College, Harvard Medical School, internship and surgical residency at Massachusetts General Hospital, a second surgical residency at St. Luke's because she want4ed to work with Dr. Archibald Henderson who, when he's not teaching at Cornell Downstate, haunts the operating theaters at St. Luke's because St. Luke's needs him more than the fancy Fifth Avenue hospitals.

Hendu wishes he had this team with him in Korea. His MASH unit would have saved many more lives. Robey wouldn't have liked it, he figures. The war part wouldn't bother her, but being forced to be a nurse, not being allowed to be a doctor because of her gender, that would have been a problem the army probably would have solved with a court martial. Hendu smiles at her beneath his surgical mask and nods his head. Robey winks, then begins to strip the skin from my skull.

"Don't yank it, Karen. Peel it back easy."

"Like peeling a tomato."

"Tell me, Karen. If you had to choose between saving an artist and saving a lawyer, you can only save one, who would you save?"

"What kind of question is that?" Robey asks.

"One that'll keep me awake for the next six hours. Humor me."

"Triage. The one most likely to live."

Briscoe slaps a rongeur into Hendu's hands and he carefully begins to bite out sections of my skull. "Is that what passes for medical ethics these days?"

"You'd try to save the artist, I suppose," Robey says.

"Artists don't sue doctors," Fernandez says.

"Maybe not in Bolivia, Raz," Hendu replies.

"Everyone sues in America," Wrick adds. "Doctors and nurses both. My mom's a defendant in two cases where she did nothing more than sit in the gallery and observe. Lawyer says she should have intervened when she saw the doctor fuck up."

"Kill the attorneys," Steven says. "Isn't that Shakespeare?"

"No," Hendu says. "That's common sense. Gaye. What do we have for music?"

"Mozart okay?" Sillers asks.

"We'll have to drill burr holes, Karen," Hendu says.

Briscoe has the drill in Robey's hand before Hendu finishes speaking.

"Mozart. Anything livelier?"

"Beach Boys," Sillers suggests as she covers Robey's eyes with surgical goggles.

"*Surfer Girl*," Hendu says.

"*Little Deuce Coupe*," Robey suggests. "You're way too old for a surfer girl."

"I'll never be too old for a surfer girl." *Surfer Girl* fills the operating room, mixing with the whine of the drill, the buzz of the bit as it burrows into my skull, the wheezing of the respirator, the sounds of the other equipment, and the nasal doo wop of Dr. Archibald 'Hendu' Henderson.

⁂

Meanwhile, from her studio many blocks downtown, Alison Steele urges lovers all over the metropolitan area to snuggle close together while a few blocks north on the Columbia University campus the riots continue unabated. In Providence, the train arrives and the Brown students haul their celebration into the nearest passenger car. Ma selects the one furthest away and avoids eye contact as she walks down the aisle toward the last empty pair of seats. In her mind it is 1916 and I am a casualty of the rebellion.

⁂

In O.R. 1 at St. Luke's Hospital, *Surfer Girl* becomes *Surfin' USA* which becomes *Surfin' Safari*. After *Catch a Wave*, Dr. Karen Robey asserts herself and the lake pipes of *Little Deuce Coupe* roar, followed by *409*. Everyone joins in singing *Be True to Your School*. Dr. Archibald "Hendu" Henderson's foxhole team cruises the operating room like high school kids cruising some downtown strip while on the radio Alison Steele breaks for the 1:00 AM news.

Robey drills her final burr hole and Hendu removes another section of my skull and exposes my brain, then adjusts his magnifying lens and leans over me. "Judging by
how fast these clots developed, there must be a rupture somewhere."

"Why'd you become a brain surgeon, Hendu?"

"Getting familiar, are we, Karen?" Hendu nudges one of the nurses with his foot and she wipes his forehead with a damp cloth. "Suction off some of this blood. We need to find the bleeders." Hendu shakes his head, hard enough that his surgical mask almost twists off.

"You, okay?" Robey asks.

"I feel like Mr. Sandman's filled my eyes. Why'd I become a brain surgeon? Hollywood's fault, actually."

"Bone fragment," Robey says. "I've got it. Hollywood?"

"God. Half his skull's inside his head." Hendu pauses to assess the situation. My brain tells him nothing about me. No matter how unique I may be, my brain looks pretty much the same as every other brain except for the trauma. Brains don't have black skin or thick lips or wiry hair. Brains don't have big noses or big ears. Brains don't have blue eyes or brown eyes or green eyes or blonde hair or brown hair or black hair or red hair. Henderson concentrates only on the brains, ignores the skin or hair color or eye color or physical features that surround them, ignores whether the person is a teacher or an auto mechanic, a cop or a felon, a priest or a minister or a rabbi. Once when he still believed in Camelot, he drafted a letter to Senator Jacob Javits volunteering to testify before the Senate in support of President Kennedy's civil rights legislation. I can educate the Senators, he wrote, on the similitude of brains, perhaps persuade them to adopt President Kennedy's legislation. Hendu knew Senator Eastland of Mississippi wouldn't listen to him. Nor Senator Thurmond of South Carolina. Nor the other southern Democrats. They'll laugh, make jokes about monkey brains, blind to his brain because of the color of his skin. Yet, if he testified from behind a screen, he knew that by the time he finished every one of those southern Democrats would want him and no one else to operate on them or their wives or their children. Him. Not the surgeons from Walter Reed. Him. Not the surgeons from Massachusetts General Hospital. Him. A Negro. At home in a hospital a few blocks south of Harlem's southern border. Him. Hendu never mailed that letter to Senator Javits. Never sat in at lunch counters. Never registered voters in the deep South. Never did anything but show up at St. Luke's Hospital and operate on patients in need of miracles. And to this day when people ask him why he became a brain surgeon, Hendu blames it on Hollywood. Someday, he thinks, maybe in his lifetime, he won't have to. *Fun, Fun, Fun* sing the Beach Boys. Somewhere it's always summer, all summer long.

"You saw some movie about a brain surgeon?" Robey now asks.

"Not quite. I saw *Donovan's Brain*. Lew Ayres."

"The brain in the fish tank?" Ella Valery asks and Hendu nods. "My boys saw it on Creature Double Feature on Channel 11."

"Drill another burr hole, Karen. There."

Briscoe slaps the drill in Robey's hand.

"Bobbye, we got a backup for that brace and bit?"

"Sterilized and ready to go." Valery places a sterilized brace and bit on Briscoe's equipment tray.

"This guy dies," Hendu says. "Shot in a robbery or something."

"A car crash," Valery corrects him.

"Where does it say nurses upstage doctors, Ella? Car crash. Gun shot. No matter. What does matter is that Lew Ayres removes his brain from the body. Keeps it alive in a fish tank. Before long the brain takes control of everyone. ESP or something. I don't remember how it ends."

"That inspired you to go to medical school?" Robey asks.

Hendu laughs. "I vant to be Doctor Diabolical." He speaks with what he imagines a German accent would sound like if married to the South Bronx.

"Et tu, Herr Frankenstein?" Robey replies with a worse one.

Hendu lifts up another section of my skull. "See, Karen. There. Three of them."

"Another of nature's perfect symmetries."

"What about you, Karen? How'd you end up here?"

"To train with you."

"No. I mean why medicine. Why surgery? Why brain surgery?"

Robey suddenly feels very self-conscious inside her operating gown. She looks at Hendu without anger. He's only trying to make small talk as they try to save another life. He knows nothing of Rennie. No one in her current universe does. "Why?" she says in her most non-confrontational voice. "Because I want to succeed in a man's world."

On the train at last, Ma stares out the window, avoiding eye contact with her own reflection, while in the surgical waiting room at St. Luke's Hospital Dinitia fidgets and thumbs through copies of *Time*, or *Life*, or *Sports Illustrated* that are six months out of date. She does not share my enthusiasm for the 1967 Impossible Dream team or my heartbreak when Bob Gibson of the St. Louis Cardinals outpitched Jim Lonborg of the Boston Red Sox in the seventh game of the World Series. Reading about it now, weeks after the 1968 baseball season began, only saddens her because if I were not wait-listed at Harvard Law School, I would be in Boston, not New York, drinking pints of Watney's bitter at the Wursthaus in Harvard Square rather than undergoing brain surgery in St. Luke's Hospital.

"Any word yet?" Dinitia asks at the nurse's station, but the nurse just shakes her head, a response by rote that reminds Dinitia of the original telephone call from the hospital, cold and business like, the warmth of a prerecorded message. Fragments of her mind scatter on the floor like a handful of jacks and she only hopes when she bounces the little red ball, she can sweep up enough of them to make her mind whole again.

Downtown, Alison Steele dedicates *White Rabbit* to the brave revolutionaries who occupy Philosophy Hall at Columbia University, Ray, Jay, Mark, and the two Teds. When Gracie Slick finishes singing, the Night Bird reads the 2:00 AM news, stories datelined Saigon, Hanoi, Washington, and Moscow, but none datelined Columbia University; stories about body counts and troop levels; stories about Senator Robert Kennedy's campaign and Vice President Hubert Humphrey's albatross; stories about General William Westmoreland's prediction that the war will end by Christmas and his request for another 50,000 troops to guarantee his prediction will come true. In protest, she doesn't report the scores of the Yankees or the Mets or the Knicks or the Rangers. Upset by the news, she pops one of Gracie Slick's magic potions and reprises *White Rabbit*. In New London, a sailor in dress whites takes a seat in the same car as the Brown students those who prefer the men of Yale to the women of Connecticut College, pause in their celebrations and mutter under their breaths. No one offers the sailor a beer.

❧ ❧ ❧

In O.R. 1 Hendu tells Karen it's time to seal the trap doors.

"Wire or will you let them re-grow?"

"This many? Wire wouldn't you think. God, I'm fucking tired."

"Gaye. Find someone else to do the honors." Robey nudges Hendu away from the table, then leads him to the bench that lines the back wall.

"You taking me out of the game, Karen?"

"Who, moi? You're taking yourself out."

"In Korea... "

The Countess presses a damp sponge against Hendu's forehead. "You're in New York. Not Korea."

Hendu sighs. "I have to finish... "

"Even God rested during the creation," Raz says.

"Patients like this make me wonder," Robey says, "about the statistics that say the mortality rate for brain surgery is the same 5 or 10 percent as other surgeries."

"Statistics lie," Bobbye says.

"Except baseball statistics," Guy Stevens adds. "They never lie."

"Who holds the record for most home runs in a season?" Hendu asks. "Ruth or Maris?"

Gaye Sillers returns with a doctor in tow before Stevens can reply. "I'll close for you, Hendu," the doctor says.

"That you, Joe? I thought you went off duty at midnight."

"It's been a busy night, Hendu."

"Monitor him for edema, Joe. Round the clock. Any swelling... "

"I know the drill, Hendu. Go home and go to bed."

Robey helps Hendu to his feet and leads him into the wash room like a mother leading a tired child too heavy to carry. Hendu rests his chest on the edge of the sink. After a few minutes, he twists his head under the faucet and turns on the cold water.

"What're you going to tell his wife?" Robey asks him.

Hendu rotates his neck. Water washes over one cheek, then the other. "The truth."

"Which is?"

Hendu opens his mouth and lets the water collect inside his cheek, swallowing when it is full, refilling, swallowing, refilling, swallowing, until, his thirst abated, he stares into the black hole of the drain. "That any swelling the next 24, 48 hours likely will kill him."

"How do you do it, Hendu?" Robey's voice mixes with the water and slaps Hendu in the face, but he's too exhausted to feel it.

"With difficulty, Karen. Great difficulty."

❧ ❧ ❧

Meanwhile, somewhere in Connecticut, the Brown students stare at the sailor, trying to intimidate him into leaping from the train. Greater dangers await him than a bunch of drunks who celebrate their privilege out of brown paper bags and he ignores them.

🙢 🙢 🙢

After rescuing Joel Davidow from the hooligans marauding through the Columbia University campus, Sergeant Gil DeNisco joins his partner Sergeant Ben Greenbaum in the nave of the Cathedral of St. John the Divine. Greenbaum admires the vastness of the cathedral's inner space, in awe of the majestic God it takes to fill this space. B'nai Israel, the synagogue of his youth, the synagogue of his middle age, is small and cramped in comparison to St. John. Fifty B'nai Israels would fit inside the cathedral's main sanctuary. Maybe a hundred. Maybe more. The God of his youth, his middle age, was also small and cramped. The God of the First Temple wasn't. Nor the God of the Second Temple. But the God of Congregation B'nai Israel was. Rabbi Ziskind would box his ears for such thoughts; his father would paddle him. Not his son Isaac. His God died on the Cross Bronx Expressway.

DeNisco has their copies of the memo Deputy Commissioner Harcourt Dodds distributed earlier that evening at the briefing in the Cathedral's main social hall. Over a thousand cops crowd the hall, but at the podium the Office of the Mayor outnumbers the Office of the Police Commissioner 3 to 1. Sid Davidoff, Barry Gottehrer, and Jay Kriegel, three of Mayor John Lindsay's top assistants, flank Dodds to emphasize the political imperative. We negotiated an agreement, Dodds announces, between Dr. Grayson Kirk, President of Columbia University, the Office of the Mayor, and the Police Department regarding the evacuation of the university buildings. Police cadets distribute copies of Dodds' memorandum summarizing the agreement as Dodds speaks.

Some of the points make sense. A University representative will order the students to vacate each building because it is not criminal trespass unless the University asks them to leave and they refuse. Emptying the buildings in the early morning when fewer people are on campus and the neighborhood still sleeps also makes sense. Most of the points, however, dictate that the Mayor's office, not the Police Commissioner's, acts on behalf of the City. The campus will not be cleared before the bust. There will be no unnecessary arrests; no unnecessary violence. The number of plain clothes officers will be minimal. The police will provide first aid to all injured civilians. There will be no police vehicles on campus. Cries of Shit! Fuck! No way! bubble up from the mass of blue. Dodds signals Mayor Lindsay's assistants to remain silent. Let the anger dissipate on its own, he whispers.

"The PBA won't be able to save their butts if they violate this," one of Lindsay's assistants says. He talks as if he dares the cops to breach the contract.

"They hate these kids," Dodds says, speaking just loud enough for the microphone to pick up his words. "They hate 'em because they can't afford to send their kids to school here. Because they burn the flag. Because they're against the war. Because they don't cut their hair or shave or bathe." The longer Dodds speaks, the quieter the men become. "And they hate this bullshit because people like you have no conception of what it's like to be in the middle of a riot. The PBA will take 'em out on strike before it lets one cop be disciplined." Dodds ignores the cheering as he rushes off the podium leaving Lindsay's men to face the mass of police. They scamper after Dodds as the cheers turn to boos, the boos to catcalls, threats, obscenities. Two cops jump behind the podium and lead a cheer like cheerleaders at a football game:

Bust 'em high;
Bust 'em low;
Bust 'em in the balls;
Go! Go! Go!

༄ ༄ ༄

Now, the Seventh Cavalry, the elite mounted division of the Tactical Police Force, spreads across Amsterdam Avenue from curb to curb, a dozen horses across, a dozen rows deep. The night air is redolent of the fresh horse manure that steams on the cool pavement. The men, as superstitious as witch hunters in colonial Salem, welcome the smell because it's considered good luck if your horse shits before battle; the bigger the shit, the better the luck. Greenbaum and DeNisco wait for the signal to lead the men north on Amsterdam Avenue toward Columbia University. Blue Note and Thompson, calmed by the odor of their own shit, no longer react to the noise of the riots. The other horses share their serenity. They will march uptown on Amsterdam Avenue in close formation. At 114th Street they will form a column, four horses across, the maximum width to fit between the Amsterdam Avenue gates. Once on campus, they will herd the protesters evacuated from the buildings toward Broadway where police vans wait to transport them to booking stations set up in precincts throughout Manhattan. Greenbaum reminds the men, we're not Cossacks.

Greenbaum and DeNisco halt the procession at 114th Street. The men reform into a narrower column. As they wait, police enter Hamilton Hall through the underground tunnels linking the campus buildings. Another squad pushes its way through a faculty picket line and smashes open the front door. The Mayor's office accepts the demands of the black students who occupy Hamilton Hall for its evacuation. The black students will not resist. After their arrests, they will be escorted from the building to busses on Amsterdam Avenue through the underground tunnels. Civil rights lawyers will be present to observe. Eighty-six students will be arrested without incident.

As easy as Hamilton Hall is, the other buildings are not. At Low Library, the faculty cordon is stronger and the police need more force to break through. The number of students is much larger than estimated. They do not submit to arrest but go limp, the classic act of passive resistance, and are dragged from the building. Some are clubbed. Kicked. Punched. Rumors of police brutality race through the campus. Avery Hall and Fayerweather Hall are similar to Low Library; but in Mathematics Hall the barricades are higher and take time to dismantle. The students soap the stairs and the police charge plays like a scene out of *Abbott and Costello and the Keystone Kops*. Alison Steele fills New York's airwaves with head music and folk-rock and sounds that AM radio refuses to program. All of these things happen during the late-night hours of April 30, 1968, the early morning hours of May 1, 1968, while I lay on an operating table, my brain open to the night air of the operating theater.

And more happens because the campus is not empty that early Tuesday morning. Word that the police bust will occur Monday night/Tuesday morning spreads as if Alison Steele herself broadcasts it and the campus fills up with students, agitators, people from the neighborhood, people looking for a good time, people looking for trouble, all of whom have one thing in common, a profound hatred for the New York Tactical Police Force and a fierce determination to off a pig.

"We've been ordered," Greenbaum tells his men, "to clear South Field, drive them toward the Broadway gates of College Walk." Greenbaum does not know these gates are locked and the students have no place to go when the mounted police charge through the Amsterdam Avenue gates. Once on the campus, the police switch to spread formation, three deep, and sweep the campus. Protesters have a choice between being trampled or fleeing toward Broadway where the locked gates trap them in the path of the Seventh Cavalry who use their batons and nightsticks. A convoy of police vans, lights flashing, sirens blaring, follows the mounted police on to campus. Squads of police in riot gear surge from the vans. The air fills with the fumes of the vans' idling engines. Students run in every direction but there is no place to flee because the police control the buildings and the campus. One by one, the buildings empty and the vans fill, their open doors beckoning to the protesters like a genial host welcoming guests. The crack of a billy club restrains anyone who tries to escape. Soon only the rhetoric remains and that, too, is locked inside the police vans.

Over 100 people require hospital treatment, 87 at St. Luke's; yet inside O.R. 1 neither Dr. Archibald "Hendu" Henderson nor Dr. Karen Robey nor anyone else on his foxhole team will learn about the Columbia bust until late Tuesday afternoon. While Alison Steele rehearses her 5 AM newscast in the safety of her studio, a newscast that will include a story about the bust at Columbia University, Hendu and Robey, still deep inside my skull, listen, at last, to Mozart.

❧ ❧ ❧

Meanwhile, Ma dozes on the train, oblivious to the slums of Harlem that appear like a vision in the dim light gathering outside her window. The train stops at the 125th Street station, then enters the tunnel to Grand Central Station. It is night again. Less than a mile away, Greenbaum and DeNisco rest on the plaza beside College Walk at the feet of Alma Mater, Blue Note and Thompson tethered to a nearby railing. The top floor of the buildings on the east side of campus glows as the sun edges over the Brooklyn skyline and crosses the East River. Mounted police in pairs patrol a deserted campus, guiding their horses around the bricks left over from the previous night's battle. Books and notebooks and papers litter the campus. Pens and pencils. Brief cases and purses. Slide rules. Hand calculators. Jackets. Sweaters. Shoes and sneakers. Wrist watches. Ear rings and necklaces and jewelry incorporating the peace symbol. And eye glasses. Dozens and dozens of pairs of eye glasses. Hundreds of thousands of dollars when new, but now trash. As worthless as the university surrounding them. For the time being, the battle for Columbia is over. For now, the University wins this battle. The invaders are vanquished. The University is liberated. But, one battle a war does not make. The light hardens as it brightens, illuminating the names carved into the frieze of Butler Library: Ask those names if winning one battle a victorious war does make. Ask Homer, Herodotus, Sophocles, Plato. Ask Aristotle, Demosthenes, Cicero, Vergil. Honored by a University ignorant of their teachings. Taught by a faculty who do not appreciate them. Read by students who do not understand them. If stones could cry, this frieze would weep.

May 1, 1968

Artists play God. As do writers. They create their own heavens and their own earths. Their own hells. Rarely in six days. They populate their universes with creatures of their own creation. One-eyed Cyclops's. Men who metamorphose into bugs. Desert planets with sand worms big enough to swallow armies of men in a single gulp. They enact their own laws of physics, their own laws of chemistry and biology. They write imaginary histories, paint imaginary scenes. Realism is in the eye of the beholder.

❧ ❧ ❧

Doctors do not play God. Dr. Karen Robey whispers these words because she and Dinitia stand beside my bed in the Intensive Care Unit at St. Luke's Hospital where I lie in a coma after my first surgery. Dr. Robey tries to smile, but her muscles freeze. Medical school doesn't offer a class in communicating bad news to the families of patients. When Robey petitioned the dean to start one, her classmates, the men and the handful of other women, shunned her as being too feminine to be a good doctor. Doctors have balls, regardless of gender. Nurses don't. One of med school's oldest clichés. This cliché attached itself to Robey like a smell that cannot be washed away, accompanying her through her internship into her surgical residency. Dr. Henderson at least treats her as a colleague. He thinks she has balls. He's ahead of his time. Maybe that's why he's good at breaking bad news to the families of his patients. That and because he does it much too often. He's home, asleep and she's in the ICU wondering whether my wife will accept bad news from a woman. I don't know if I would.

"All those tubes," Dinitia says. "What do they do? Each one."

Dr. Robey knows this reaction. In the beginning, the patient's family survives on adrenaline. Before the adrenaline runs out, before they crash, they can deal with things. Dr. Robey leads Dinitia by the arm to the consult room behind the nurse's station. "We don't know how much awareness a person in a coma has," she says. "We never talk about the patient in his presence because he may be able to hear. We assume the patient hears and understands everything. Some people remember everything that goes on around them. Other people remember nothing."

Dinitia takes a small notebook from her purse. Robey has also seen this before. I won't forget something this way, most people say; but to Robey it's a way of not listening. Robey knows her words will pass through Dinitia's brain on their way to her notebook without stopping to be understood as if Dinitia is a college student in a boring lecture class taking notes by rote. Like the professor, Robey feels obliged to give the lecture.

"Those things on his feet. They're called space boots.

They lock your husband's feet and ankles into position to prevent deformities that will limit his future movement. His legs are wrapped in TEDS. They go half way up his thigh. They support the muscles and prevent the blood pooling in his legs."

"So he won't have an embolism?"

"Your father a doctor?"

"One of my uncles."

"The Foley Catheter," Dr. Robey continues, "drains his urine to prevent kidney failure. The GI tube allows us to introduce liquids, food or medication, directly into his stomach since he can't swallow. We could use an NG tube, but, well, it's kind of crowded around his head."

"What's the vest for?"

"The Houdini jacket. Keeps him stationery. We don't want him to rip out the tubes."

"He's unconscious."

"Comas are not deep sleep. Coma patients exhibit reflex activities. Some sleepwalk. In a manner of speaking. We restrain them for their own protection."

"He was an artist, a painter."

When the family begins to talk about the patient in the past tense, Dr. Robey knows the adrenaline is beginning to wear off.

"Will he still be able to paint?"

Dr. Robey wishes she understood this instantaneous leap from past tense to future tense. It's more common than the notebooks. She knows it's the subconscious at work. Experiments prove this. Most people don't remember changing tenses. Maintain they had not even when they hear their own voices on tape. It's the subconscious debating with itself. Denial. Hope. Both.

"The occipital lobe," Dr. Robey explains, "processes visual information. It's where the mind recognizes shapes and colors. It's near the back of the brain. Near the cerebellum which coordinates balance and movement. Damage to the cerebellum causes ataxia which means the muscle movements are uncoordinated, spastic, hard to control." She pauses and Dinitia can catch up with her note taking. "He took a pretty bad pounding on the back of his head."

"Bad enough?" Dinitia asks.

"The brain's not like other organs. It's hard to predict."

"I feel helpless."

"You're... "

"Don't tell me to pray," Dinitia says. "If he's dying, tell me straight out."

"You're as important to him as I am. Maybe more. Sit and hold his hand. Tell him how much you love him. Read his get-well cards. Talk about your honeymoon, your plans for the future, what you had for breakfast. Tell him he's getting better. Tell him what great doctors he has. If he can hear you, it'll make a difference. We don't know why, but it does."

Robey wants to hug her because women hug at a time like this, but she's a surgeon now, not a woman, and it's unprofessional for a surgeon to hug the spouse of a patient. She recognizes the symptoms of battle fatigue, the subconscious storming the rational, forcing connections she trains her conscious mind to suppress. Only cowards get battle fatigue.

"I've got to finish my rounds. I'll ask Father Urbano, the hospital chaplain, to visit. It's up to you, Ms. Madison, to finish what Dr. Henderson and I started. We may not be God's agents, but you are."

Straight out, Dinitia wants to know if I'm dying. I do not hear the reply. Dead I already am, having died years ago when I destroyed Minnie's sculptures, having died because I thought I was too good for life in the tannery. Or, maybe I had died before then, in my childhood, but had not realized it. No matter now.

Minnie's lust for Dinitia, revenge for my destroying his sculptures. Often, the simplest explanation is the truest, the truest the simplest. The other side of the equation doesn't compute. She married me, not him. Yet, love him she does. It's an equation without an equal sign, an arcane area of math I do not understand. I was never good at math. I was good at destroying sculptures. And keeping secrets.

❧ ❧ ❧

Death, my death, my last gift to Dinitia. Freedom to marry Minnie. If he survives Vietnam. They will make art together. And children. And, maybe, as a thank you to me, they will name either a child or a work of art after me, maybe a son, maybe an Elmwood
sculpture in the style of Henry Moore.

May 2, 1968

3:00 AM

Father Urbano Miranda, the St. Luke's Hospital chaplain, reminds Dinitia of Cardinal Don Fernando Nino de Guevara. Both have long, thin faces, pointed beards going white at the tip, and wear black rimmed eye glasses that emphasize the vertical plane of their foreheads. Both sit as if they have tie rods for spines. When Father Urbano recites the rosary, he clutches his beads with the same fervor with which Cardinal Don Fernando grips the arm of his Cardinal's throne; but Father Urbano's eyes lack the ecclesiastical authority that radiates from El Greco's portrait. If you are in the Cardinal's presence, you believe he lives. A thousand El Grecos could not work a similar transformation on Father Urbano.

Father Urbano reminds me of my old parish priest, Father Giuseppe Ozoni; not by appearance. Unlike beauty, ugliness is more than skin deep. If Urbano had been my parish priest, I would hide a crucifix in a pool of blood in each of my paintings.

Father Urbano makes the sign of the cross over me. I

lie in bed anesthetized from my first surgery. A respirator fills my lungs with oxygen and empties them. A catheter drains the urine processed by my kidneys. The fluids that sustain me do not produce solid waste. Unconscious, but conscious, I do not understand my hybrid mental state. Nothingness, I can sense the void. I try to fill the void. With memories. With imaginings. With whatever a normal mind conjures up. Nothing. Until I hear voices.

"You're bad luck," Ma says to Father Urbano. "James won't get better until you go."

She's got that right, I think.

"Shhh!" Dinitia says. "He may hear you."

"He's the angel of death," Ma hisses in Dinitia's ear.

Aren't all priests, I ask myself.

"He can't wait to administer the last rites. Look at him. It's blasphemous the way he hovers there like an evil spirit."

Dinitia clamps her hand over Ma's mouth. "The doctor," she whispers, "told me he might be able to hear everything we say. If you tell him he's going to die, he'll believe you and die. Either be still or go back to the apartment." Ma struggles and Dinitia squeezes her cheeks. "You will sit here and you will comfort him. Do you understand?"

Since Da's death, Ma considers all hospital priests to be angels of death. In another incarnation, Father Octavio Crizal waited outside Da's room in Charlton Memorial Hospital in Fall River while Julia and I played at being grown-ups in the dunes of Horseneck Beach. Ma welcomed him then, took comfort in his homilies, prayed when he said pray, believed when he said believe, confessed her sins when he said confess, donated when he said donate. All for naught. After Da died, Father Crizal talked of paradise and resurrection, of a better place where Jesus clasps Da's soul to His heart and God grants Da eternal peace. The angel of death won that time. Ma let him. But not now. Not this time. No. This time she will chase the angel of death from my bedside. Offer herself in my place. Wrestle him like Joseph in the Bible if he refuses her. For all eternity if she has to. For all eternity. Ma fidgets with her rosary, praying it will protect me from the Prince of Darkness who haunts the corridor outside the door to my room. Satan is a shape-shifter. As are the demons who serve him. The power of the rosary will defeat Father Urbano. I wish I knew then what I know now, but time only moves forward even if my story unfolds backwards.

Ma's jaw hurts, but she forgives Dinitia. It has been three days, but she is still exhausted from riding the mail train that departs Boston and stops at every city or town between Boston and New York that has a post office or a train station. Father Urbano called during the 11:00 news. Something about a riot. Emergency surgery. She didn't understand everything he said because of his accent, but she understood enough to telephone a neighbor who drove her to Providence where she boarded the mail train at about the same time the Tactical Police Force finalized its plans for clearing the protesters from the buildings on the Columbia University campus that was also the same time Dr. Karen Robey drilled the final burr hole in my skull to complete the preliminaries of my first surgery. My skull has more finger holes than a bowling ball. Westward rolled the train, slowly because of the condition of the track bed and the curves in the right of way. While the train unloaded mail in New London, the Tactical Police Force cleared Hamilton Hall and as the train entered the outskirts of New Haven the TPF moved on Fayerweather. By the time the yard crews in New Haven changed engines and disconnected the cars bound for Hartford and Springfield, the TPF entered Mathematics. Somewhere west of Bridgeport the bust ended as did my first surgery. By the time Ma arrived at Grand Central Station I was in intensive care, unconscious. A police officer directed her to the stop for the 104 bus from 42nd Street to Broadway and 112th street, one cross-town block and one uptown block from St. Luke's Hospital, four uptown blocks from College Walk on the Columbia campus. Da died while Ma was in a cab and she vowed not to repeat her mistake.

"The cafeteria's open," Dinitia says. "You should eat something. Coffee? A muffin?"

"No. Nothing."

"I'm going anyway."

"Take the devil with you." Ma moves around the bed to block the door if Father Urbano attempts to enter.

Bandages wrap my head in a cocoon of white. Inside them is not the me of the school photographs Ma carries in her purse, thirteen wallet size photos, one from each school year, kindergarten through senior year in high school. Inside them is not the me of my college yearbook photo, handsome in my suit, my one suit, my suit for all seasons. And inside them is not the me of my wedding photo, glamorous in formal wear, a wedding gift from Minnie, my best man, my best friend then, relegated to best man when he should have been the groom. Inside the bandages is a new me, one Ma has never seen, one she cannot imagine. But I can and I imagine Theodore Gericault standing at my bedside sketching me in his quest to express the truth of death and dying. Maybe Gericault will take me home with him after I die to study me at his leisure. I will have plenty of company.

Ma cups my hand in hers and rests her head on the edge of the bed. Her breathing synchronizes with the breathing of my respirator. In spite of her fears of Father Urbano, she falls asleep, a black, dreamless sleep, silent except for the sudden sound of a factory whistle like the one that once controlled her day, telling her when to start work, when to stop, when to start again, when to stop again, when to go to lunch, when to return from lunch, when to smoke a cigarette, when to go to the ladies' room, when to go home, a lifetime under the control of a whistle. Da, too, lived by a whistle working in the mills. As did I during school vacations. There are no factory whistles at Columbia Law School,

but a premonition bubbles up from the depths of my coma that soon a factory whistle will control my schedule, one that signals whether I live or die.

A whistle, screeching, high pitched, thin, reedy, drives my dream down into the depths of my coma. Ma awakes. Screams. I thrash about, babbling nonsense syllables. The hospital bed shakes like a young child possessed by the devil. It rams against the nightstand knocking over the water pitcher and the intravenous pole. It beats against the wall trying to break into the next room. Father Urbano and two nurses converge on my bed.

Pin his legs, one shouts to Father Urbano who yells, Caramba! He kicks like a mule. Ma pulls at his cassock, but he brushes her aside. Dr. Henderson sprints into the room. Two orderlies follow with a gurney. One throws his body across my abdomen while the other immobilizes my shoulders. A nurse exposes my buttocks and Henderson spikes me with a needle. The shrieking resumes and I am a factory whistle once again except my legs now move like they are underwater. Someone straps me to the gurney. O.R. 1. STAT! Dr. Henderson orders. Ma attempts to follow, but a nurse traps her in a chair and sedates her. After a few minutes, it's Christmas Eve and she is cheery from the eggnog. Caroling. Midnight Mass. The Latin Mass. Sitting between Da and me. Never more happy. Never more proud.

"Where's Malone?" Dinitia's shadow falls across the pile of linens torn from my bed.

"Caroling with Minnie," Ma says.

"Another seizure," the nurse says.

"Fluid builds up." Dinitia knows the words. Dr. Robey taught her them. Explained them. Repeated them while Dinitia entered them in her notebook. Dinitia recites by rote. "Intracranial pressure. Swelling. No place to go inside the skull. Pressure. Seizures. The spiral effect. Every event. Every event... he'll... he'll... " The words stick in Dinitia's throat like a broken chicken bone she can't cough up.

In the corner, his back to Ma and Dinitia, Father Urbano straightens his cassock. Reciting the rosary, he sounds like he's speaking in tongues.

May 2, 1968

3:30 AM

Classic Greek vase painting, whether red period or black, whether Archaic, Classical, or Hellenistic, whether this, that, or the other, I detest, as I will declaim with the eloquence of Demosthenes if you care to listen. Not sculpture, especially friezes, whether from the Parthenon or the Treasury of the Siphnians or the Temple of Zeus or the Temple of Hera. Countless amphitheaters or agora do the Michelangelos and Berninis of ancient Greece fill. My hands lack the genius to sculpt today's Panathenaic Procession, but not my imagination. I conjure up in my mind a St. Luke's Hospital Procession that, when today becomes antiquity, will be as enlightening, no, more enlightening, than anything surviving from those six or seven centuries prior to the life and death and resurrection of our Lord and Savior, Jesus Christ. There will be no chariots in my St. Luke's Hospital Procession. No ranks or files of soldiers, mounted on horse or marching on foot. No spears. No bows. No arrows. No shields. No helmets. No lyres. No gods. No goddesses. But there will be gurneys.

Hospital gurneys. As many as it takes to frieze the facade of St. Luke's Hospital.

⁂ ⁂ ⁂

Hospital gurney races, like alligators living in the sewers or vampires nesting in abandoned subway stations or playground ballers who would make Bill Russell look like an amateur, are one of New York's enduring urban legends. Every hospital has them. Teams of residents, interns, and orderlies compete. Student nurses lead the cheers. A referee enforces rules that he steals from professional ice hockey, assessing penalties for boarding, slashing, tripping, unnecessary roughness, and certifies the winner of each race. Intramural and inter-hospital. Six weight classes in fifty-pound increments from empty gurneys to gurneys with three hundred pounds of cadavers from the hospital morgue. Everyone claims to know someone who races gurneys with live patients, but no one admits to doing so. Sprints, obstacle courses, and endurance events for each weight class. As many leagues as college basketball has conferences. League standings. Borough by borough. Championship trophies. One for each borough. One city-wide. One for the state. A banquet after the post-season tournament. Top teams only. A single elimination tournament. Last team standing. Like high school basketball back home except none of the teams wear red and black. No outsiders ever witness these gurney races. Other than me. I am in one. I play the role of the cadaver. I'm a natural.

"We're racing the grave, Hendu," says one of the orderlies who navigates my gurney from my room to O.R. 1 for my second surgery.

The corridor is an obstacle course and the gurney zigzags like a tailback breaking through the defense for a long run, veering around Toby Swift who holds hands with his IV pole as if it were his high school sweetheart as he strolls from his room to the patients' visiting lounge; swerving around a laundry cart whose hamper overflows with the linens stripped from Harriet Richter's bed, the same Harriet Richter, seven years of age, whose body is now being autopsied in the hospital morgue to determine why she died the night before her tonsillectomy; cutting back to avoid a dietitian's cart with glasses of clear liquids for the patients able to have a morning beverage; juking around a cart with doses of sleeping pills in paper receptacles that hospital regulations require nurses to administer to patients who already sleep; dodging an empty gurney that delivered Harriet Richter to the hospital morgue, carried Dorothea Douglas from the recovery room to the ward and which, like an empty cab in queue at the airport, waits in readiness for its next fare. Henderson holds a morphine drip over my head in his right hand and pushes aside obstacles with his left.

I roll around, kicking and thrashing and screeching like I'm being electrocuted. Henderson hands the drip to a nurse and attempts to lash my feet to the gurney; but I continue kicking, babbling, the pitch of my voice rising and falling with my kicks, nonsense syllables, pre-verbal, pre-language. Instinct rather than thought controls my brain. Random electrical impulses rather than conscious thought manipulate my muscles. I sound like a prehistoric man screaming as he flees a pack of carnivores who have not eaten in days. The nurse opens the flow valve on the drip a half turn and a drop of violence drains from me with each drop of morphine that enters my bloodstream.

"Bet you wish you was in pathology," the orderly says.

"I wish I was in bed is where I wish I was," Henderson replies.

The intercom continues paging Dr. Robey to O.R. 1, a code blue to inform Robey, but not the civilians in the hospital, not the patients, not their families, that another life hangs in the balance, one of dozens every twenty-four hours, the fifth or sixth since Robey came on duty. Dinitia knows the code. She knows whose life hangs in the balance. She attempts to distract herself by watching television, the syndicated version of *American Bandstand* broadcast years later in New York's early morning hours. Ma dozes in the corner. Dick Clark. One of Philadelphia's urban legends. The same boyish face as junior high school when Dinitia was a dreamy adolescent who believed life would be one never ending love song. Seventh grade when she and her girlfriends giggled at Darlene's and Marlene's and Maureen's and Noreen's and Doreen's oversized boobs and wondered if their boobs would ever grow big enough for witless boys to tease them about wearing-over-the-shoulder-boulder-holders. Dinitia is grateful hers did not, but the boys still teased and she teased back and told them the joke about the boys who choked to death on hairy lampposts until George or Greg or Gary or Geoffrey or Gordon dared her to look at his. Seen one, seen 'em all, Dinitia sneered, silencing them for once and forever. She wishes she could silence Dr. Robey's page. Her father's voice makes her wish come true.

"I'm surprised everyone doesn't die of infection in this filthy place."

Reginald Madison's voice precedes him down the hospital corridor, tuneless, off key, a voice that becomes thinner as he becomes angrier, a voice that sounds masculine only when he has a severe head cold. Madison is a monument builder who builds monuments only to himself by donating as much of the Pratt fortune as his wife suffers to allow to colleges and universities, museums and symphony orchestras, hospitals and medical research centers, provided they name an endowed chair, a building, a gallery, a laboratory, anything of significance, after him. Not his wife. Not his father-in-law. Him. Elizabeth draws the lines at politicians depriving her husband of what he really lusts after, the power of a king maker of governors and senators and, in his dream of dreams, presidents.

"You!" Madison shouts at a nurse whose name tag identifies her as Bette. "Where is Mr. Malone?"

"She's not one of the servants, Reginald," his wife, Elizabeth, whispers. Taller than her husband, Elizabeth stays thin by playing tennis, singles and doubles, against opponents her daughter's age and by eschewing the martinis and canapés at the benefits they attend several nights each week. On their backyard tennis court, she lets Reginald win often enough for him to believe he's her equal, but at the club she beats him consistently enough that he now claims a stiff ankle or a sore knee or some other hypochondriac ailment whenever she offers a game.

Dinitia rushes past her father, bawling, a little girl with a scraped knee. "He's back in surgery." She wraps herself around her mother as if she were clinging by her fingers to the edge of a cliff. "Another edema. He may not... Oh, mom. He won't die, will he?"

"I'll call Chase van Dorn," Reginald says. "Arrange a transfer. Cornell Downstate. A real hospital with real doctors."

"Reginald! This is not what Dinnie needs right now."

"Dinitia needs what all young women need," Reginald says. "The firm loving hand of her father."

"Keep it down," Bette says. You're upsetting the patients. If you don't quiet down, I'll call hospital security." She picks up the phone.

"That won't be necessary," Elizabeth says softly. "My husband's just distraught. He'll behave."

"Elizabeth!"

"Reginald! If you don't cease acting boorish, Bette will complete her call with my blessing."

"I built Madison Industries by acting boorish."

"Yes, dear."

Elizabeth rolls her eyes. Reginald's grandfather, the grandson of President James Madison, founded Madison Industries. Reginald's father took it public during the boom years after World War II. Reginald, at best, a caretaker for a coterie of Harvard Business School graduates who run the company and report to the Board of Directors, thinks he gives the orders; he does, but not the ones that are obeyed. Reginald suffers from coupon clipping envy, unable to accept that Madison money will always be minuscule compared to his wife's share of the Pratt family fortune.

"Thank you for coming, Mr. Madison," Brigid Malone says.

"Ignore his harrumphs," Elizabeth says. "He'll leave soon enough for some important meeting."

"Do you think James would be better off at another hospital?" Brigid asks.

"I'm sure his condition's too critical for him to be moved," Elizabeth says.

"Then I'll bring the doctors here," Reginald says.

"Daddy." Dinitia puts her hand on her father's shoulder. "The doctors are here. Dr. Henderson teaches at Cornell Downstate."

May 2, 1968

4:00 AM

The black faces of the monitors on the wall above the bed in my hospital room stare down at Brigid Malone, Elizabeth Madison, and Dinitia Marbury Madison, my mother, mother-in-law, and wife. The green lines that squiggle across the screens from left to right like fluorescent snakes in a primitive children's cartoon now hide in their lairs waiting for the heartbeats, the brain waves, the respiration, that will chase them into the open and start them squiggling once again. Brigid, Elizabeth, and Dinitia also wait. They talk to no one, not even to each other. They feel as dead as the air in the room. In the corridor Father Urbano, the hospital chaplain, and the nurses guard the door as if the three women must be imprisoned as plague carriers and my room quarantined. I am the plague. And the carrier. Not them. Brigid opens and closes a silver-plated brooch that hangs around her neck. When Ma was younger, it held a photograph of her Da; now one of my Da and me on the day of my First Communion.

In the operating theater, Dr. Henderson and an orderly struggle to transfer me from the gurney to the operating table for my second surgery. I flop around like a freshly caught fish on the floorboards of a young boy's rowboat. One summer Da rented a row boat and we fished for yellow perch, Da and me and one of his army buddies and the buddy's son, on a small lake in Brewster on Cape Cod. We caught a few and Da used one of the oars to stun them, then boned them, fried them over a campfire. I wish I were a yellow perch and Hendu an oarsman who would row me across the River Lethe into the arms of forgetfulness.

"Somebody, sit on him," Guy Stevens, the anesthesiologist, shouts. "Raz. Lizzie. Grab that arm."

Dr. Robey sprawls across my midsection and I smell her fear. "Another edema?" she asks.

"Another edema," Henderson replies.

Stevens isolates a vein and inserts the IV. "One hundred, ninety-nine, ninety-eight." He sneezes into his shoulder and rotates his jaw beneath his surgical mask. Bobbye Briscoe scratches his nose with a clamp, then returns it to the autoclave to be sterilized. "Just a few more seconds. Ninety-one, ninety, eighty-nine, eighty-eight, eighty-seven, eighty-six. He's all yours, Hendu."

Henderson tests the drills, selecting one by the sound it makes. The steadiness of the buzz tells him whether there's any meaningful variation in the number of revolutions per minute. He likens it to a speedometer. If it's not accurate, you get a ticket for speeding. If the drill speeds up or slows down, he loses control and the drill bit may puncture the brain, scrambling it like an egg beater scrambles raw eggs. That's my brain. Raw eggs.

"Where's the goddam music?" Hendu demands.

"Early Beatles?" Briscoe asks.

"*A Hard Day's Night*" Hendu says, "because that's all

we've gotten from this patient."

Henderson's team operates as music fills the silent spaces surrounding them.

"Bone fragments," Henderson says.

"How could we have missed them?"

"Suction out that dead brain tissue, Karen."

"Devitalized," Robey says.

"Never run from the language, Karen. A doctor, especially a surgeon, should never run from the language."

"We all have our own coping mechanisms."

Robey curses under her breath as the instrumental version of *And I Love Her* begins. At another time, this was her special song. Someone, not Rennie, told her he loved her while this song played and she said yes, I love you, too, and he wanted to make love and she wanted to make love, but as he slowly and gently unbuttoned her blouse she saw Rennie, inert on the bed, and before her blouse slipped off her shoulders she grasped his hands and said I'm sorry, I can't, please forgive me, and he apologized and asked what's wrong and she assured him it wasn't him and he said are you sure, are you sure, because I love you, and she said yes, I'm sure, and kissed him good night and the next seven times he called she was too sick to go out and finally he stopped calling and she rationalized it by convincing herself that no man will love her the way Rennie did or need her the way her patients need her, the way this patient, me, lying anesthetized upon the operating table, needs her. Love is too debilitating. Too debilitating. A good medical term. Diseases debilitate; love shouldn't. Robey bites her lip to prevent her hands from shaking and a spot of red stains her surgical mask.

"Gently, Karen," Henderson says. "We don't want to damage the good stuff."

"Oh God! I didn't suction out his vision, did I? I did, didn't I?"

Henderson reaches across the table and steadies Robey's hand. "You suctioned out dead brain tissue, Karen. Dead. Devitalized. Brain tissue that will never re-generate. If he's lost his vision, he lost it long before you got out of bed this morning. Stay with me, Karen. I need you to help me save this guy's life."

After the Beatles, they switch to do-wop, the Five Satins, the Fascinations, the Ink Spots, groups Robey doesn't know, records from Henderson's private collection. Henderson sings along with *In the Still of the Night*, keeping time with his foot. "Street corner music," he says. "Uptown Saturday night. The Apollo. Amy and I'll take you there, Karen. All of you. We'll do some Q first, then the Apollo, then an afterhours club where Monk and Mingus and Coltrane and Davis hang out when they're not playing downtown. Finish up with a sunrise breakfast. How about this Friday? If we're out of this guy's skull by then."

"I'm on duty," Karen says.

"I may have some pull with the guy who fills out the schedules." Henderson winks. "Bring a friend. Bring a lover. Bring a spouse. All of you. The surgical team that parties together saves lives together."

Robey allows the blood to accumulate in her mouth as the operation continues.

Meanwhile, in my hospital room there is no Beatles, no do-wop, no street corner music. "This silence terrifies me." Ma's words hang dead in the air like grief at a wake.

Dinitia bursts from my room and zeroes in on the nurse's station, shrugging off Father Urbano like an old coat resting lightly on her shoulders. "Bette. Again. Please."

"It's only been ten minutes." Bette dials a number, listens for a moment, then hangs up. "He's still in surgery, dear. It'll be a while."

Dinitia shudders and swoons, but Bette catches her and helps her to a chair, then administers smelling salts. "I'll be widowed like that bride on the news last night," Dinitia says. Bette gathers Dinitia into her arms and rocks her gently and rubs her cheek against the crown of Dinitia's head. "My son's in country. I pray for him every night. Pray for your husband, dear. Prayer keeps my boy alive. It'll do the same for your husband." Bette recites the Lord's Prayer. Father Urbano joins her, then the other nurses. Dinitia stares at the floor. In my room, Elizabeth whispers the words and Ma faces the photo of Da and me toward the door. We hear the voices and share in the words. Only Dinitia and the blank faces of the monitors remain silent.

When Bette finishes, she returns to her nursing station and Dinitia returns to my hospital room where Ma sits beside my bed comforting someone who isn't there and Elizabeth stares at the words on the page of her book. Dinitia sits, then paces; paces, then sits. She silently recites the Twenty-Third Psalm, the one psalm she memorized when she was a little girl afraid of the dark. She tries to bargain with God, but has nothing to promise Him. Her talent? Her life? The Pratt fortunes? She has nothing to say to a God who ordered Abraham to sacrifice Isaac. To a God who murdered His own Son. He is not her shepherd. She does want. She will not lie down. She invokes the Devil. Maybe he'll offer better terms. Her soul, a vaporous appendix, a bargaining chip of little value.

"Your husband's in recovery." Dr. Henderson's voice startles Dinitia. "He's not out of the woods yet. Not by a country mile. But he should live."

"I want to see him," Dinitia says.

"I think we got in before there was too much permanent brain damage," Dr. Henderson explains, "but we won't know for certain until he awakens." Dr. Henderson pauses and Dinitia tenses. False hope is the stepchild of ignorance, a false idol not to be worshipped, and the sooner she knows the truth, the sooner she can begin to cope. Ma, she senses, fears the truth and Dinitia wonders if that's a difference in their personalities or the difference between a mother and a wife. Elizabeth doesn't seem afraid, but then I am not her son. "I'm less optimistic about his vision," Henderson continues. "We found some dead brain tissue we had to suction out. He might be blind."

"You blinded him?" Dinitia asks.

"We suctioned out dead tissue. If he's blind, he already was blind." Henderson's voice is conversational, concerned, not the voice of a doctor trying to explain away an embarrassment. He escorts them to the door of the recovery room and introduces Dr. Robey.

"Resting comfortably," Robey whispers. "Vital signs stable."

Dinitia covers her eyes. Bandages wrap my head as if I am a mummy. Tubes connect my nose to an oxygen tank. An IV runs from my arm to a bag of fluid suspended on an IV stand. The sheet covers my torso to my chin. There is no visible skin. No visible hair. No visible facial features. There is nothing about me anyone can recognize. "Malone?" Dinitia can't bring herself to accept the doctor's word that this gauze mannequin is me. She wants to peek under the covers, to satisfy herself that there is a freckle on my left thigh opposite the scrotum, a scar from an emergency appendectomy on my abdomen, a configuration of veins just above my right foot forming the letter H; but the medical equipment and the oxygen and the IV and the doctors and my fragile condition intimidate her.

Explain about his eyes again, Ma says and Henderson does, "We had to suction dead tissue from the area of the brain that controls vision. He may be blind. If he is, it's because the tissue died, not because we suctioned it. We won't know until we remove the bandages." Dr. Henderson's voice soothes, the voice of a doctor who knows how to give bad news to the families of his patients. A man with a voice this soothing would not palm off a stranger on his patient's wife. "If he is blind," Henderson says, "that doesn't mean he can't practice law. The firm I use has a blind partner. He even goes into court."

"Does he go to art museums, this blind lawyer of yours?" Dinitia asks. "Does he create art?"

May 2, 1968

10:00 AM

Exhausted from my second surgery, depressed because of her clumsiness with the suction tube, Dr. Karen Robey nurses a cup of tea in the hospital cafeteria, more out of habit than thirst. If she drinks the tea, the caffeine will roil her system and keep her awake when her body craves sleep. If she doesn't, she still won't be able to sleep because she sinned. She took an oath to do no harm and she did harm. A colleague suggested hot water with a wedge of lemon for moments like this. Another pushed chicken soup. A third Scotch, the more rotgut the better. One or two smoked dope. The senior resident slept it off with a prostitute, two for those really horrific moments. Hendu went home to his wife. Robey opts for hot tea. Maybe because she associates tea with the British and what she needs is to be encased inside some of that famous British reserve to suffocate her feelings. She wishes she were a teacher. First or second grade. Children. Laughing and smiling and playing. It is not a sin to wish to be surrounded by happy children. Once she and Rennie, both without siblings, talked about that. A farm size family. An old fashioned 19th century family. Once. Now, she makes crumbs out of her corn muffin and her mother's voice fills her head and yells at her for playing with her food. There is no exit.

"Dr. Robey?"

A cop. In uniform. Tactical Police Force. With the unmistakable appearance and smell of someone who spends long nights at hard labor. Someone she thinks she recognizes. She knows everyone in the local precinct, but he's a stranger, one of the imports brought in to clear demonstrators from the Columbia classroom buildings. Not a patient because St. Luke's is a neighborhood hospital and few cops live in Morningside Heights. New York is full of familiar faces who look like someone else, people on cross-town busses or on line outside movie theaters or squeezing the produce at the local Korean green grocer. Every New Yorker has a mistaken identity story. Robey's occurred one Sunday morning waiting on line for Nova at Mama Joy's Deli. She was convinced the man buying white fish was the janitor from her high school until he walked by and she saw his manicured fingernails. She does not want to play the 'do I know you from somewhere' game with this Mr. TPF. She sticks the tea stirrer in her mouth and it dangles like a cigarette.

The cop sits without being invited and as he does his sidearm catches on the table and points at her. Robey jerks back, shielding her heart with her arms. "Safety's on," he says. "I always keep it on when my weapon's holstered." He adjusts his weapon then folds his hands and rests them on the table, trying to make her feel at ease by keeping his hands in view. "I'm Ben Greenbaum. Your patient, Malone I think his name is, I brought him in. How's he doing?"

Robey chews on the stirrer, shifting it from one side

of her mouth to the other. She imagines holding out her hands to be cuffed and saying she won't cause any trouble. I'm not here to arrest you she imagines his reply and she asks him whether it's a crime in New York to blind someone and he says it is and she says I plead guilty and when he still doesn't arrest her, she lays the stirrer on the table beside the crumbs from her muffin and sips her tea. It's cold and bitter and beyond saving by sugar or lemon.

Greenbaum rubs his forehead with his fingertips. "I didn't think he'd last the ambulance ride."

Robey realizes he's going through the same decompression she is. But not really. Only if he shoots somebody, shoots an innocent bystander. A page over the loudspeaker. Not for her. She gouges out a chunk of muffin.

"What was it like on campus?" she asks.

"A war zones. What about Malone? How's he doing?"

"We've treated almost a hundred people from your war zone. Faculty. Staff. Graduates. Undergraduates. Cops. For what? A gym?"

"I'm not the enemy. All I want to know, is he going to make it?"

"How many scalps did you collect?"

Greenbaum pushes away from the table. "You wouldn't believe the truth if you saw it firsthand."

"Surgery wasn't easy." Robey grinds her lower lip wishing she could shoot down her words before they reach Greenbaum's ears. She draws comfort from the familiar taste of blood. No one warned her about the nightmares. Not at Smith College. Nor Harvard Medical School. Nor Massachusetts General Hospital. Nor at St. Luke's. Because of one patient, Malone, whose name she hesitates to say in front of this cop, sleep for Robey is a recurring bad dream in which she is trapped in a tenebrous, windowless room full of broken lamps. The room has one door that opens into an identical room with identical lamps except without light bulbs. The single door to this room leads to a third with lamps whose plugs are severed from their cords with the neat, clean slice of a scalpel. The rooms have no electrical outlets.

Hendu told her on her first day at St. Luke's that exhaustion was a surgeon's worst enemy, not because of what may happen in the operating room, but because of what the mind dredges up hours later when it relives the surgery. She doubted him then because only cowards got battle fatigue, but I teach her otherwise.

"Will he make it?" Greenbaum says softly.

She asked Hendu the same question as he stitched a flap of skin on the side of my head, the final procedure of my second surgery; but she already knew the answer. The next edema will likely kill me. Edemas are a risk of any surgery, especially brain surgery, and are fatal more often than not.

Suppose I live. Her clumsiness probably blinded me, something that will be confirmed when my bandages are removed. The blind make music, some of jazz's greatest are blind, but I'm not Ray Charles or George Shearing. And write books. Helen Keller. Beethoven composed with encroaching deafness, but he could see the notes and hear them in his head. But, I paint. Monet painted with failing eyesight. Some say Degas did also. Neither were blind, Minnie would hoot. Dinitia would echo him.

"Edemas," Robey says. "Probably blind. My fault." She slips off her left shoe and massages the sole of her foot with her toes. She runs her fingers through her hair, oily with the sweat of surgery, and wipes them on her scrubs. "If he were famous, I'd be a headline in the *Daily News*."

"Be back," Greenbaum says.

A cup of hot tea with a fresh stirrer appears before

her, the bag already in the water.

"Jazz is my oasis," Greenbaum says. "Yours, too?"

Robey wishes the intercom would squawk her name. She thinks about calling hospital security, you can't call security on a cop, a TPF cop.

"I saw you at the Blue Note a few weeks back. Coltrane. You were at a side table. Alone."

Robey does not want to have this conversation, any conversation. She makes one of those polite noises that substitutes for conversation in awkward situations.

"I named my horse Blue Note," Greenbaum says. "After the record label and jazz club. They keep me sane, jazz and Blue Note." He rips a page from his note pad and scribbles a telephone number. "Let me know how he's doing." He stands and adjusts the way his sidearm sits on his hip.

Robey chews on the plastic stirrer. Her desert has no oasis.

May 3, 1968

Dinitia paces back and forth in my hospital room where I lie in a coma. She wants to scream, but doesn't because Robey explained to her that patients in comas frequently have some level of sensory perception and can hear and understand in a subconscious way. Some also remember. You can't remember, Dinitia challenged Robey, something you don't experience or perceive. When Robey launched into a technical dissertation replete with the jargon of the science of the mind and the chemistry and biology and neurology of the brain, Dinitia waved away the answer and decided it was easier to accept the science on faith than to understand it. For this reason, she and Ma take turns talking to me and holding my hand, soft words, words of love, future words of hope and encouragement, past words about happy memories, familiar words about familiar subjects, words I would recognize and understand if I heard them. Dinitia reads me letters from Minnie in Vietnam, leaving out the teases about my choosing law school over life, not telling me those letters are addressed to her, not me. Her voice fills with love as she reads, love for Minnie, always love for Minnie. If I never awaken, she will be his.

"The light glows," Minnie writes in one of his letters, "with humidity, making the colors intense enough for me to taste. Try to imagine what green tastes like. Spinach? Creme de menthe? Mint? Absinthe? No. Green tastes like Beethoven's *Eroica*, Stravinsky's *Rite of Spring*, the opening verses of *Genesis*. Green tastes like van Gogh's *Cypresses*, Rousseau's *The Repast of the Lion*, Monet's *Nympheas (Water Lilies)*."

"I'm gathering a lifetime of material," Minnie writes in another letter. "Two lifetimes. War always produces great literature. This war will produce great art, art to make Caravaggio look like a Sunday painter, El Greco a realist, and Goya, damnable Goya, as sane as you or me."

Dinitia reads me poetry, especially T.S. Eliot's *The Love Song of J. Alfred Prufrock*, asking me whether I think this phrase or that phrase would make a good subject for a painting, restaurant floors covered with saw dust and oyster shells or ragged claws scuttling in pairs across the ocean floors or the eternal footman always snickering or women coming and going, talking of Michelangelo. I have seen it all already, I have seen it all. She does a daily sports report, making up news about the early season Boston Red Sox, the late season Boston Celtics. On Dinitia's sports report, the Sox and Celtics always win, Yaz always hits another home run, Russell always blocks another shot or grabs another rebound. And she prays for the day when I will confront her about the truthfulness of her reporting.

Ma speaks of Da and my childhood in Fall River. She speaks of my first box of crayons, my first set of watercolors, the time I finger-painted on the bathroom wall and cried when the shower dissolved the paints and washed them away. She speaks of Minnie and the afternoon we tried to dig a hole to China. She speaks of the trip to Howe Cavern and the boat ride on an underground river, the trip to Niagara Falls and the boat ride under the falls; but mostly she speaks of Da, how important it was to him that I escape the mills, how he was as proud of my painting as he was of my going to college, how frightened he was that his beloved Briggie will suffer the same old age as his beloved Ma, no heating oil in the tank, no electricity. But I won't, Brigid says. And you don't have to become a lawyer on my account she reminds me.

❧ ❧ ❧

Ma's voice triggers other memories that play against the black wall of my coma like a movie. I am trapped inside the projector, trapped inside each frame of film as it races past the projector's bulb. If one hole on the edge of the film slips its sprocket, if the projector jams, the bulb's heat will set fire to the film, cremate it like a gas oven cremates a dead body. I cannot escape the projector.

❧ ❧ ❧

For days, more days than Ma or Dinitia care to remember, they talk while I lie on the hospital bed fit for nothing more than being Rembrandt's model in the *Anatomy Lesson of Dr. Tulp.* If not for the wavy lines on the electronic monitoring equipment, the periodic beeps, the orderlies who change my drip bags and empty my catheter, the nurses who check my chart hourly, the daily visits of Dr. Henderson and Dr. Robey, no one would know my body still lives.

I will never know if Julia would have been as loyal, as steadfast. If we had married, Julia and I, I would be at business school learning how to transform a pants factory into an international conglomerate. Unlikely Columbia Business School. The Ivy League wouldn't be at home in a Fall River textile mill.

As for Dinitia, in love with Minnie out of guilt, sympathy, shame. If Malone the lawyer, the Sunday painter, repels her, Malone the sightless, Malone the invalid, would be much more repulsive. My body still alive is my curse.

May 4, 1968

12:00 noon

Dr. Robert Fludd, a/k/a Dr. Robertus a Fluctibus. A subject of the first Elizabeth, she of the pale white complexion and red hair. A contemporary of Shakespeare, whoever he or she might be. A magetizer. A zealous proselytizer of the "weapon-salve." If Dr. Fludd Fluctibus lived today, he would be on the staff of St. Luke's, the faculty of Columbia Physicians & Surgeons. Or, Dr. Robey's. Perhaps Dr. Henderson's. Three chambers divide the brain, Dr. Fludd Fluctibus lectured his eager students. The first chamber, behind the forehead, hosted the imagination which transforms the elemental quinternity of the five senses into shadowy duplicates (others aver into glowing, visual images) that imprint themselves upon the brain like a stamp imprints initials on the molten wax Elizabeth I used to seal her royal decrees. In the warm, moist central chamber immediately behind the first, reason ordered these shadowy duplicates (or glowing, visual images) into things recognizable warehoused by the brain in the third chamber (just inside the back of the head beneath the skull's crown) until the central chamber recalled them. The third chamber stored the memory, Dr. Fludd Fluctibus lectured, a record of all things that ever happen, enabling the second chamber to make sense of the ever changing quinternity the first chamber imagines.

Thus, science explains infallible memory. If my surgeries restore the flow between the chambers of my brain, my memory will become infallible. I'll remember the secret Minnie and I vowed to take to our graves. If there is any silver lining to my injuries, it is the possibility that secret was forever beaten from my brain, kicked to the gutter like an empty beer can being used by the neighborhood kids for a game of street soccer. I'd think twice, thrice, before saying no to that trade.

As for Dr. Fludd Fluctibus's scientific explanation for my multiple edemas, blockages in the pipeline between the brain's chambers that trap the flow inside one chamber or another. If these surgeons, skilled plumbers that they are, dissolve and remove these blockages, my memory will flow out the seams of my skull, pool on my pillow the way my blood pooled on Amsterdam Avenue. I want a second opinion from Dr. Fludd Fluctibus. I want his "weapon-salve." Multiple surgeries, multiple edemas, and I am still at risk. Why, I ask Dr. Fludd Fluctibus who has no answer.

⁕ ⁕ ⁕

Deep in the bowels of St. Luke's Hospital in a room adjacent to the radiology lab, Dr. Karen Robey straps a magnifier to her forehead and mounts my x-rays in order chronological on all the available light boxes, usurping the entire room; the x-rays done before my first surgery, after my first surgery; before my second surgery, after my second surgery; bench mark x-rays, current x-rays as recent as that morning. But no x-rays prior to the trauma. No x-rays when my brain and eyes functioned normally. If chest x-rays are part of a routine physical, x-rays of the rest of the body should be as well. Especially the brain. Especially if the object of the exercise is to discover, then recreate, once upon a time. "Dr. Henderson's orders," she says when the interns complain. There are no such orders, but she doubts anyone will call her bluff. She outranks them and she's not looking at pornographic slides which are what the interns often mount on the light boxes.

Robey doesn't know what she's looking for; but she knows she'll recognize it when she sees it. For now, nothing, nada, the big rien as the French would say. She doesn't speak French but she once went out a few times with a Dartmouth College student who tried to seduce her in French. Raspberries and strawberries and the good wines they brew and here's to the girls in the country side and all that rot. Rien is all he deserved. Rien is all he got. Rien is all that remains of that relationship. Rien is all she sees in my x-rays.

"Why?" Henderson asks her when the head of radiology tells him what she is doing.

"He's not a lawyer you sacrifice in triage," she replies. "He's a painter. His wife showed me one of his paintings. He's got talent."

"It's not healthy to get close to the patients. Sometimes they die."

"Or worse," Robey says.

Henderson lets the subject drop, but later he buys Robey coffee and a muffin in the hospital cafeteria and leads her the way a professor leads a first-year medical student through her first human dissection to a corner table that is always empty between meals.

"Stop blaming yourself," Henderson says.

"Easy for you to say."

"Each one tears me up as bad."

"How do you handle it?"

Henderson stares. "I get my Colt down from the closet, put one bullet into the chamber, spin it twice, put the gun in my mouth, and pull the trigger."

Robey throws her coffee in his face and Henderson throws his coffee in hers. She unscrews the salt and empties the shaker on his wet shirt. He dumps the pepper on her blouse. She squeezes mustard on him like he's a hot dog and he replies with the ketchup. She bounces the remains of her muffin off his forehead and he picks it off the floor and wings her in the shoulder, then pins her wrists, lightly but firmly, to the table.

"Medicine is one would've, could've, should've after another. Sometimes it's a malpractice case. Sometimes it's peer review. But the worse are the ones you inflict on yourself. Learning to live with it is as basic as learning how to drill a burr hole or peel the skin off the cranium. If you don't, one day you will put that gun in your mouth and you will pull that trigger."

Alone in radiology, Robey thinks about what Hendu told her in the hospital cafeteria and also that night at supper over stuffed cabbage, stuffed peppers, and retsina at the Green Tree, a goulash joint on Amsterdam between 110th and 111th. His advice, she accepts, will get her through every future would've, could've, should've; but only she herself can get herself through the would've, could've, should've, that is me.

Robey stares at the tenth pair of films, one from the recovery room after the first surgery, the other hours old. What's that? And that? The same place on both films. She examines two more films on another light box, one taken before the second surgery, one taken after it. Same dark squiggle, same place, two more times. A third pair of films, pre-first surgery and after second surgery, same dark squiggle, same place, two more times. She pages Henderson and compares more films. Everywhere the same dark squiggle in the same place. Fuck me, she thinks. If I'd done the suctioning right.

"I'm in radiology," she says when she answers the phone as if no one in the world would call radiology except Dr. Archibald "Hendu" Henderson. "It's not dead brain tissue. It's lesions from the bone fragments that caused the edema. It's right here on the films."

"I'm on my way."

An hour later, Henderson and Robey escort Dinitia Marbury Madison and Brigid Malone to the same cafeteria table where they had their food fight. Splotches of mustard and ketchup still stain the wall.

"Now it's lesions," Dinitia says after Henderson finishes. "What next? A missing scalpel?"

"The visual pathway may have some scar tissue," Henderson says, "but we won't know without operating again."

"If we do nothing," Brigid says, "will my son be able to see?"

"Maybe," Robey says. "Maybe tomorrow. Maybe next month. Maybe never. Nobody knows. If we do nothing, Mrs. Malone, the odds are your son will wake up blind."

"This visual pathway, what's that again?"

"It's like the cord connecting your TV to the wall socket." Henderson speaks with a low, steady voice, a respectful voice, the voice a teacher would use to explain a difficult concept to a bright student. "Pull the plug and the screen goes black."

"Don't patronize me," Dinitia says. "I don't have bubble gum for brains. I graduated Smith College. Phi Beta Kappa." She bites her tongue before she says anything else, angry that the stress of the situation makes her boast like a six-year-old. Malone needs the grownup, not the child.

"Me too," Robey says, "while you were still agonizing over whether you'd be invited to the junior prom." She uncrosses her legs and squares her chair to the table. "The part of the brain that controls sight is the visual cortex. How do we see? A visual stimulus enters the eye through the retina, proceeds along the optic nerve, through the chiasma, into the optic tract and the lateral geniculate body to the optic radiation and from there into the visual area of the cortex."

"Is that like one street with a bunch of different names?" Brigid asks. "Or a bunch of different streets?"

"For our purposes, it doesn't matter," Robey says. "There are two eyes, two optic nerves. Somewhere along the way, you'd figure they'd merge two streets into one, but they don't. They cross over each other in the chiasma. The stimulus that enters the right eye goes to the left part of the visual cortex and the stimulus that enters the left eye goes to the right part of the visual cortex."

"Do I need to know this?" Dinitia asks.

"Yes," Robey says, "because it's possible that only one of your husband's eyes is at risk, not both. We won't know until we get in there."

Brigid looks at Henderson. "You said he might wake up blind."

"If both visual pathways have lesions, he might," Henderson says.

"He can paint with one eye, can't he?" Brigid asks Dinitia.

"It's not that simple," Robey says. "The visual cortex is divided into a primary zone and a secondary zone. Both the left and right are divided into these zones. The primary zone receives the visual stimulus from the eye. The secondary zone synthesizes it, codes it, organizes it. Because of the secondary zone when you look at my face you see my face and you know what it is and who I am. If the lesion is in the primary zone, your husband may be blind in the right eye, if it's on the left side or in the left eye if it's on the right. And in both eyes if there's one on each side. Depending on the location and size of the lesion, he may only be partially blind. Sometimes it's a blind spot in the middle of the field of vision. Sometimes it's like a donut around the peripheral vision."

"I get the picture," Dinitia says.

"Not the complete picture," Robey says. "Blindness isn't the only risk. There's visual agnosia. If the lesion is in the secondary zone, your husband will be able to see, but he may not comprehend what he sees. That's visual agnosia."

"May I have your glasses?" Henderson asks Brigid. He folds them and places them on the table. "We all see eye glasses. In geometric terms, we have two circles connected by a horizontal bar. Someone with visual agnosia would see the geometry but would not be able to recognize the circles and connecting rod as eyeglasses. He would try to use logic to figure out what it is. He might decide it's a bicycle, also two circles connected by a horizontal bar. Or a typewriter ribbon. He could look at a dial telephone and think it's a clock or look at a peacock with its tail feathers spread and conceptualize flames. If the lesions are bad enough, things might be too fuzzy to see."

"The interesting thing," Robey says, "is a person with visual agnosia does not lose his intellectual function. He can't read because he can't decode the letters, but if you read to him, he would understand. The same with mathematical calculations. He wouldn't recognize the numbers, but he could do the calculations in his head."

"And his other four senses would work normally," Henderson adds.

"He couldn't paint with agnosia," Brigid says, "could he?"

"Just the physical act of putting the paint on the canvas, Mrs. Malone," Robey says.

"This operation... "

Henderson leans forward. "First we have to find the lesion or lesions. We think it's in the visual cortex. Then we have to figure out how to deal with it. If it's scar tissue, we'll try to remove it; but you have to understand, Mrs. Malone, that it's very hard to remove scar tissue from anywhere along the visual pathway. The risk of doing greater damage is very high. But if the operation works, your son will be able to see normally."

"And if it fails, he's blind for life," Brigid replies.

"Yes. Or has visual agnosia."

"Is the surgery difficult?" Brigid asks.

"All brain surgery is difficult," Henderson says.

"What approach gives him the best odds for recovery?" Dinitia asks.

"We can't handicap it like a horse race," Henderson says.

"So how are we supposed to decide?" Dinitia asks.

"We don't have the luxury of time," Robey says. "The more the lesion hardens, the riskier the surgery."

"Why?" Dinitia says. "If it's already hardened and won't get any harder, why can't we wait and see if his sight's normal. If it isn't, he can decide for himself."

"I don't want to crack open his skull after the bone sets," Henderson says. "It adds a whole new layer of risk." Henderson removes a surgery consent form from his file and places it on the table in front of Dinitia with a pen. "Under New York law, a spouse has precedence over the parent of an adult child."

"I say wait." Dinitia pushes her chair back and lowers her forehead to the edge of the table. She makes panting sounds as if she is in labor. Henderson nudges Robey's foot and glances down at his coffee cup.

"I'll get refills," Robey says.

"We won't be here long enough," Brigid says. "If Da were here, he'd sign the consent, dear."

Dinitia sits up. "It's his right." Her voice quavers. "He's the father."

"And now it's your right."

Dinitia rubs the palms of her hands against her arms, the rapid strokes of a person trying to rub away a chill. "You want me to?"

"You have my blessing, dear. Whatever you decide." Dinitia wants to take a coin from her purse and flip it, but she knows whether she calls heads or tails that she'll flip it again whichever comes up, then a third time and a fourth, flipping it over and over until the surfaces of the coin wear smooth and she can no longer differentiate between heads and tails. Or, until it lands on its edge. Heads or tails. Scissors, paper, stone. One, two, three, shoot. He loves me, he loves me not. Childhood ways of making decisions. Spin the wheel. Roll the dice. Take another card. Games people play. Bet on a horse. Bet on a stock. Bet on the hands of two doctors. Gamble the odds. Light a candle. Make a sacrifice. Say a prayer. Hedge the bet. Pick a card at random. Play dice with the universe. Isn't that, she thinks, what I'm really doing.

She thinks of *Talking of Michelangelo* and her conversations with the gallery owner, Monsieur Francois Badin, and her husband's stubborn refusal to sell his paintings. She thinks of the time Malone knocked the Zippo from Delaney Pratt's hand. And the stories she overheard Brigid tell him as he lay in a coma. And she thinks of the shame and pain of a man who can't keep his mother warm, who can't give his mother light. But, Dinitia thinks, I can give my husband light. And I can keep him warm. And I will sacrifice my art if I have to. Painter or lawyer, it does not matter. If I don't sign the form, she thinks, I'll be the electric company shutting off the power. Dinitia knows Da would sign the consent for his son and his son for Da. And if the operation fails, Da would thank his son for taking the chance as his son would thank Da. But never, never, Dinitia understands, would Malone thank me for shutting off the power. Nor forgive me. Regardless of how long we stay married, how much I sacrifice for him. Nor will he ever thank me. Never. Never. Love leaves no choice. Dinitia knows this as much as she knows anything. Closing her eyes, she picks up the pen and signs the consent.

May 4, 1968

3:00 PM

In 1931, Salvador Felipe Jacinto Dali Y Domenech painted *The Persistence of Memory* whose limp and flaccid timepieces horrify, astonish, fascinate. It depicts, the cognoscenti aver, the destruction of the concept of time. (Is that the same as the destruction of time? Dali v. Einstein. The fight of the century. No, of the millennium.) Other cognoscenti interpret the symbolism as a commentary on time and decay and the quest of the artist to defeat time and achieve immortality through creativity. The watches, they pontificate, symbolize both finite time and infinite or eternal time. They bend because the artist bends time to his will. Dali laughed at all this and said don't be high falutin' low pollutin'. Time is nothing more than a piece of Camembert cheese wilting in the midday sun. And, in 1951, he painted *The Disintegration of the Persistence of Memory* in which the clocks blurred, became disjointed, lost their form, fell apart. The joke was on us.

❧ ❧ ❧

The logic of these paintings escapes me. I doubt memory persists while time is destroyed. Or, outside of time. Independent of time. The physicists don't understand. Time is a construct of memory having no independent existence. Yet, memory disintegrates over time and time ends when memory fully disintegrates. My brain with its surgically installed memory is Dali's Camembert cheese, not the rock in Dali's landscape. Still, my existence repudiates the symbolism of Dali's paintings as surely as Spain's hot sun melts a wedge of Camembert. Time out of mind.

❧ ❧ ❧

Dr. Karen Robey, less than two hours before my third (and what will be my final) surgery, roots through her purse searching for her BankAmericard, praying it is not stolen because she doesn't have the money to pay the bills a thief would rack up, nor the money to hire an attorney the way one of her medical school classmates did when his Master Card disappeared. She would have to file for bankruptcy. She would not limit it to financial bankruptcy. She would include a schedule of bad memories in the schedule of bad debts. Wipe out those memories and start fresh.

Rennie? She wonders who she would be if Rennie never happened. She tries to imagine a Karen Robey who never met Rennie. It's like imagining the children she'll never have. Baseball players or bankers, sinners or scientists, no matter. There are no bankruptcy therapies like bankruptcy laws and there are no bankruptcy therapists like bankruptcy judges who can unhinge you from your past with the bang of a gavel. Dali's Camembert cheese is eternal.

Robey dumps her purse on the table in the doctor's lounge at St. Luke's Hospital and paws through its contents. She flips through the pages of her address book, thanking God when she finds her credit card cemented to the Z page by a forgotten partially decomposing lollipop. Maybe she should let Hendu root around inside her brain until he finds the synapse labeled Rennie and excises it. If the operation succeeded, it would make her a new woman, a woman who, once more, has the capacity to love. If it failed, he would have to excise another synapse, and another, and another, until he lobotomizes her.

Robey pries her credit card from the lollipop. Stuck to the other side of the Z page is the paper with Sergeant Benjamin Greenbaum's phone number. She does not understand Greenbaum's interest in her patient, in Malone, though she recalls having similar feelings about her patients during her first year as an intern. Any involvement with a patient, no matter how cursory, makes the patient hers and spawns a proprietary interest. As she progressed from internship to residency, she suppressed those feelings, now rationing her interest to those patients who have been under her knife. Callous, but an effective survival strategy. She couldn't fathom why Greenbaum, a veteran on the force, a member of the Tactical Police Force, the toughest of the tough, now acts like a police cadet, a rookie, a first-timer. Unless he was responsible for Malone's injuries, but she cannot comprehend a cop for whom jazz is an oasis beating someone up because he has long hair. Robey glances at the clock. Enough time to make a phone call. She ponders what to tell Greenbaum. That she has a theory. That Dr. Henderson buys it. That they're giving it the old college try. That they won't know if it works until they remove the bandages. She decides not to call.

Robey returns each item to her purse with a surgeon's precision. Everything, her mother nags, has its own place, the one place where it belongs, and you must find it or else your purse will be out of balance and won't hang properly on your shoulder. Robey's sense of fashion does not extend to how her purse hangs on her shoulder, but she still follows her mother's advice for no reason other than it's her mother's. Of course, her mother also nags her to give up medicine and work for a book or magazine publisher, a respectable career for a woman with a college education, a career where she will meet a plethora of eligible bachelors. Rennie, she imagines telling her mother, is, was, the only eligible bachelor. Only cowards, she imagines her father responding, succumb to battle fatigue. She crumples the paper with Greenbaum's phone number into a tiny sphere, then creates a catapult with her thumb and ring finger, a trick she learned in the second grade to defend herself in spitball fights, and balances the sphere on her fingernail. Deadeye, they called her in the second grade, although some of the boys always added 'for a girl', because she could flip a spitball into a wastebasket from twenty feet. Once on a dare from Frankie Dobbs, the class bully, she did it blindfolded and became the proud owner of his Ted Williams rookie baseball card. She may still have it. Maybe in the box of things from home she never unpacked. This memory she does not want discharged in bankruptcy. Or the memory of Frankie going straight from twelfth grade to the House of Correction three weeks prior to graduation. A nurse intrudes to fetch some urine cups and penile catheters. The draft blows the spitball off her finger. If she doesn't call, she'll be distracted by spitballs in O.R.

"Speak!" a young boy orders.

"Sergeant Greenbaum, please. Dr. Karen Robey."

"Hey, Dad!" A door slams in the background.

"My son's at a very loud age," Greenbaum says. "How's your patient?"

"We're going back in." Robey explains what they intend to do, her voice as cold and clinical as if she is describing a surgical procedure to a new group of residents. "The visual pathway may have some lesions, but we won't know without cracking his skull. We think they're in the visual cortex. We'll try removing them, but it's delicate everywhere along the visual pathway and the risk of damage is astronomical. If it works, he may be able to see."

"If anyone can do it, Karen, you can."

"Hendu's the miracle worker. I just try to stay out of his way. I gotta run. Time to change into my scrubs."

"Quickly, Karen. Getz. Stan Getz. He starts a week's run at the Village Gate tomorrow night. He's probably going to play some of the Brazilian music he's experimenting with. Like to go?"

"I told you about my schedule."

"You tell whoever does the scheduling I'll arrest him if he doesn't give you a night off."

"Overworking residents, is that a felony, Ben?"

"In my book. Which night? I'm on days this week."

"I don't know how many hours of surgery I have ahead of me."

Greenbaum clears his throat. "I guess you're right. A cop with a teenage son. A brain surgeon. Jazz isn't enough."

"It's not that, Ben."

"I'll get a reference from my Rabbi."

Robey laughs. "Wednesday night if Malone behaves and there are no emergencies."

"What about Thursday morning?"

"Officer Greenbaum!"

"I mean if you're on duty Thursday morning we'll go to the early show. If not, the midnight show."

"Jazz plays better at midnight."

"You like Chinese? I know a place on Mott street."

"Street level?" Robey asks. "I refuse to eat at street level. Up a flight, down a flight; but never street level. And never at a place that serves Jell-o."

"This one's in the basement. One flight down. And they don't serve green, red, yellow, orange, purple or any other color Jell-o."

Oh, shit, Robey thinks. After all these years, she still sees Rennie when she sits across the table from a date. Maybe the jazz will rescue her. Maybe Getz will be her savior. And maybe surgery will numb her mind until the music begins.

May 4, 1968

11:00 PM

Some 350 years ago, more or less, Galileo Galilei, an accomplished watercolorist and favorite son of the Inquisition, painted a series of watercolors of the moon's surface based upon observations he made through a telescope. The moon was not a common subject of Western art, especially high art, in Galileo Galilei's time. Nor in the centuries before or after. Not until deep into the current century when artists like Jackson Pollock sought inspiration in the myths of indigenous peoples like the Indians of North America for whom the moon was an integral part of the life cycle. It took longer than long to go from Galileo Galilei's scientific reproductions of the face of the moon to Pollock's *The Moon-Woman*. Maybe, it was the moon's association with alchemy and astrology. Or, the menstrual cycle of women. Or, the night. Or, because the moon, as many people still believe, is made of blue cheese.

❧ ❧ ❧

A crescent moon hangs over St. Luke's Hospital, but Dr. Archibald 'Hendu' Henderson and Dr. Karen Robey do not see it. Inside O.R. 1 they listen to Guy Stevens, the anesthesiologist, count backward from 100. Because of my prior surgeries, my skull looks like a baseball stitched by a drunk. Unlike archeologists who dig to uncover the past, Henderson and Robey dig to uncover the future as the secret of my future awaits them inside my skull. Yet, after they finish digging, they will not know my future until it happens. It's the paradox of what they do, the perversity of playing God.

"Any Getz in the juke box?" Henderson asks.

"I'm seeing him at the Gate Wednesday night," Robey says.

"With the Gilbertos?" Henderson asks.

"He's under," Stevens announces.

"Vitals?" Henderson asks.

"Stable," Raz Fernandez replies.

"Any blips, Raz, even small ones... "

"Every flicker."

Henderson begins the laborious task of reopening my skull. "Get that bleeder, Karen. Better cauterize it. Bobbye! Angle that light!"

Bobbye Briscoe, the chief surgical nurse, adjusts the light to eliminate the shadows cast on my occipital lobe by the edge of my skull. Henderson traces the optic nerve bundles through the optic chiasma to the visual cortex, the eye's highway to the brain.

"If we don't have Getz, how about *Highway 61 Revisited*?" Henderson asks.

First, Al Kooper's organ backed up by Paul Griffin's piano, then after a few seconds, Bob Dylan's vocal: "Once upon a time you feel so fine... "

"Looks like lesions on both nerves," Henderson says.

Lesion. The first medical term Robey learned. While still in college. Spring of her senior year. A coroner defined it for her, a morbid change in an organ or body part, when he told her that Rennie, her fiancée, died because of a brain lesion. Now that she is a doctor, she understands that the mystery of curing the common cold will be solved before the mystery of Rennie's death.

Henderson studies the lesions while Dylan asks 'how does it feel to be on your own, with no direction home, a complete unknown, like a rolling stone?', then flexes his fingers and begins. He works in close. His surgical cap darkens as it absorbs the sweat caused by the hot lights and Gaye replaces it with a fresh one. The magnifying lens strapped to his forehead strains his neck muscles and he taps his toes inside his surgical boots in beat to the music to distract him from thinking about the ache in his neck when he should be concentrating on me. Robey watches, more a student than a doctor because there is room for only one pair of hands inside my skull. Dylan moves through *Tombstone Blues*, *It Takes a Lot to Laugh, It Takes a Train to Cry*, the other songs on the album. "They're selling postcards of the hanging," Dylan now sings, the opening lyric to *Desolation Row*, the last cut on the album.

"Vitals?" Henderson asks.

"Stable," Fernandez says. "I like this Dylan. In my country the generals would execute him."

"American generals don't like him any better," Robey says.

"Why don't they kill him?" Fernandez asks.

"You think his motorcycle accident was an accident?" Henderson asks.

"How many brains have you operated on?" Robey asks as Dylan begins a second set, a perfect reprise of the first.

"Stopped counting at a thousand," Henderson says.

"Doesn't it get to you?"

"The tension drains me. Makes me feel like an invalid sometimes." Henderson continues operating as he talks.

"Do you think I can handle it?" Robey asks.

"Do you want to handle it?" Henderson looks up from my brain. His eyes are enlarged and distorted by the magnifying lens, their blood vessels thick and red, engorged as if they are about to hemorrhage. "You can make a lot of money doing safe surgeries."

"You don't."

"Negroes don't have the opportunities for safe surgeries whites have."

"If I wanted to do safe surgeries, I'd be downtown," Robey says.

"You have to teach yourself to face the spouses or parents who beg for the million to one chance you represent then curse you when you fail. One mother called me every night between 2 and 4 for weeks. I can't sleep she would say and I'm gonna make damn sure you can't either."

"You should've called the police," Robey says.

"She lost her son." Henderson glances at Fernandez.

"Still stable."

"You'll take the patients home," Henderson continues. "My wife knows when I need a hug and when I need to be left alone and she carries me through the rough times."

And the unmarrieds become alcoholics or dope heads, Robey thinks. She studies Henderson's hands, his fingers, the deft way he maneuvers the probes, the shunt, the delivery of liquid nitrogen through a thin plastic cannula. His hands are as calm and steady as if he is cutting into a serving of stuffed cabbage at The Green Tree or a piece of chocolate cake at the Viennese

Pastry Shop. Robey knows what it is to work inside the brain, her hands as steady as Henderson's. And she knows what it is to face a patient's loved ones. My loved ones. My wife. My ma. But she does not know what it is to tell them that their son or husband died or that the surgery failed and he will be blind for life. Surgeons do not let coroners do their dirty work.

"One more speck," Henderson says. "There."

Dylan reprises *Desolation Row*, the beginning of the end of the second set. Henderson's shoulders slump. Exhaustion ripples through his body like a convulsion.

"I'll close," Robey says. "I have to do something to earn my keep. How's the inventory, Lizzie?"

"All accounted for."

"...[T]he fortune telling lady has taken all her things inside..."

"Let's hope for another miracle," Robey says as she undertakes the initial suture.

"Sorcery, my dear," Henderson says. "We're nothing but sorcerers."

Robey listens to the fatigue in Henderson's voice. She has doubts she'll survive to her hundredth operation, much less her thousandth. She fears she'll succumb to battle fatigue long before then. When it came up in a lecture at medical school, she asked her dad, a World War II veteran who saw action in the Pacific, about battle fatigue and he told her only cowards got battle fatigue. If I were a coward, she replied, I would have gone to nursing school. Only cowards got battle fatigue, her dad insisted. If he were a doctor, he'd still be prescribing leeches.

Henderson steps back from the table and Gaye trades him a wet towel for his surgical cap and face mask, tossing both into the laundry hamper. He drapes the towel over his face and head. Vigorously, he rubs his cheeks, forehead, and scalp, then his hands and fingers.

In the bright light of the operating theater, the moisture makes his skin shine and he glows.

"... he was famous long ago for playing the electric violin on Desolation Row."

May 8, 1968

I dream I hear music. I dream I hear voices talking about Stan Getz at The Village Gate. I dream I am playing Bach in the stern of the Staten Island Ferry. I dream the great God Delaney Pratt, Dinitia's uncle on her mother's side, challenges me to paint musicians making music. Picasso did, Pratt says. And Lorenzo Costa. I dream I am dreaming.

In my dream, Lorenzo Costa's three musicians meld into Picasso's. The lute morphs into a guitar, the recorder into a flute. Costa's musicians make music. Look at the shapes of their mouths. Their eyes. Their hands. Their fingers marking the beat on the table. Nothing can be said of Picasso's trio with their tiny hands and misshapen heads, their unplayable notes hanging from a music stand, nothing that speaks to making music. If I play Bach in the stern of the Staten Island ferry, I must decide whom would I commission to paint me. It's a choice between the greatest painter of the 20th century or an obscure Italian painter from the 15th. The ultimate irony, to be famous as the subject of a painting, not as the artist who painted it.

How I envy musicians, composers. If deafness deprived Beethoven of the beauty of his art, would that only blindness deprives the painter of the beauty of his. $25,000.00 for *Talking of Michelangelo*. A years' income for a newly minted Wall Street lawyer, if not more. A years' freedom to paint, if not more. For me. For Dinitia, stubborn Dinitia. But, I am not ready to consign my art to memory. Memory is too fallible.

I lie to myself. To my wife. To the world. Selling a painting is not the same as selling a child. Selling a painting does not dispossess the artist of his art forever. I will take the answer to those questions to my grave along with the secret Minnie and I swore to keep.

Still, I dream I hear music and voices talking about Stan Getz at The Village Gate.

✻ ✻ ✻

At The Village Gate, Sergeant Benjamin Greenbaum fingers the body of the wine bottle, replicating the way Stan Getz fingers his tenor saxophone, while Dr. Karen Robey taps the base of her wine glass with her fingertips. Her nails are trimmed close to the skin, unfashionable, but necessary because long nails interfere with the delicacy of surgery. Such dainty hands to be arbiters of life or death. She wears nail polish, bright red, and Greenbaum wonders if she wears it in the operating room, if it shows through her surgical gloves. He busies his hands by peeling the label from the wine bottle with his fingernails, tiny bits and pieces as the glue is too strong, too evenly spread, for the label to come off in long strips. It's a Wednesday night and The Village Gate is sold out, the tables packed together. The room is silent except for the music as Getz solos *Moonlight in Vermont*. His sax softens and Gary Burton's vibes enter in the background, carrying the melody and creating a framework around which Getz weaves his solo like a breeze wafting through a pine grove on a Vermont mountain slope. Behind Getz and Burton, Gene Cherico leans on his base, nodding his head in rhythm to the music, and Joe Hunt taps his drum sticks against his open palm. A shroud of cigarette smoke, like a theater scrim, separates the stage from the audience. Getz arches his back to reach a high note and a flash of light reflects off his gleaming golden sax and catches Greenbaum in the eye.

Greenbaum stares into his wine, wishing that the deep burgundy would absorb the melancholy triggered by the music. He assumed Getz would play Brazilian music, the bossa nova, that Astrid Gilberto would sing. It did not occur to him that *Moonlight in Vermont* would be on Getz's play list even though Getz recorded it on *reflections*, an album he, Greenbaum, stashed in a box in the attic after Esther's accident. *Moonlight in Vermont*. The Christmas before the accident. Skiing in Vermont, a few days at the Middlebury Inn. A few at the Woodstock Inn. Isaac bivouacking with his grandparents in Delray Beach. A Hannukah present from Esther's parents. The moon was bright and there was night skiing on the lower slopes. They talked about making another baby, a brother or sister for Isaac. Everywhere they talked. In front of the fire. In bed. On the ski lift. In the craft shops. And, finally, their stomachs warm with Indian pudding, in the parking lot of The Dog Sled beside a brook now iced over, where they decided they would, that summer, because, as Esther said, one hot weather pregnancy was enough for a lifetime. And now Getz at the Gate, sharing *Moonlight in Vermont* with a woman who is right in every way but one. Greenbaum coughs and wonders if she can see the No Vacancy sign hanging above his heart.

Cherico's bass enters behind Getz and Burton; Hunt follows, first with the cymbals, then the drums, a light beat, lighter than a heartbeat at rest, the rhythm of flames dancing in a fireplace in a country inn in Vermont. Greenbaum likes the way Robey presents herself, posture erect, face not caked with make-up, red fingernail polish her only adornment. He likes the way she smiles when she spots him in the restaurant, the way she waves hello as she snakes her way through the tables to his booth. He likes the timbre of her voice and wonders if singing lessons might have led to a different career, concerts at Town Hall singing old English folk ballads or cabaret at the Rainbow Room singing Gershwin and Porter. He likes the way she acts, like a lady, not a surgeon, and the way she treats him, like a gentleman, not a cop. And he likes the way she tries hard and he wonders if this is how she naturally is or whether she also is trying to escape something from her own past. He likes everything about Robey and he wishes they were somewhere else, anywhere else, Carnegie Hall listening to Bach or the Village Vanguard with Judy Collins or the Battery waiting for the Staten Island Ferry or Times Square laughing at the tourists being suckered by three card monte, anywhere but Getz at the Gate, anywhere but *Moonlight in Vermont*. Cherico solos now and Greenbaum rages at the label on the wine bottle until the quartet finishes its first set and exits through the smoky scrim to an ovation.

"Why do you use your trigger finger?" Robey asks when the applause dies down.

"It's a cop thing, I guess."

The man at the table to Greenbaum's right jerks his head in Greenbaum's direction and edges his chair away. He wears several pounds of Mardi Gras beads and Greenbaum recognizes some of the krewe emblems, Comus, Rex, Poseidon, Zeus. Breakfast at Brennan's.

Dinner at Antoine's. Jazz at Preservation Hall where the saints always go marching in. Parades. Conceiving Isaac in a bed and breakfast in the French quarter, third floor, corner room, balcony brocaded in wrought iron scroll work. Greenbaum smiles at the man in the Mardi Gras beads, then steadies himself with another sip of wine and resumes his attack on the label.

"Would you rather go for a walk?" Robey now asks. "Skip the second set?"

Greenbaum freezes. "I'm sorry, Karen. I'm not ready for this. I thought I was."

Robey's eyes flicker and she pinches the bridge of her nose. "Will you call me?"

Greenbaum sweeps the label scraps into the ashtray. "I'll always love Esther."

Greenbaum imagines them standing on opposite subway platforms shouting at each other through moving trains. At the end of each platform, stairs lead to a crosswalk, one platform to the other. They pace the platforms, unwilling to risk the crossover, afraid they'll miss their trains. There's always another train. There always is. That's how the subways operate in New York, but true New Yorkers never want to wait for the next train. They live in the here and now, lugging their past with them in a hobo's bindle. And, Greenbaum now appreciates that that's what they have in common, this cop and this surgeon, hobo's bindles. Except she knows what's in his.

A crescendo of applause explodes and The Stan Getz Quartet remounts the stage through the smoky scrim. Getz signals the downbeat and the audience quiets on cue as the music starts, a Duke Ellington standard, *Tonight I Shall Sleep with a Smile on my Face*. Someday the music will stop, if it hasn't already. He's a cop with a teenage son and she's a surgeon and they have nothing in common but jazz and their hobo's bindles. He places his hand in the center of the table a few inches from Robey's and curls his trigger finger under his palm. The Quartet reprises Ellington, this time Burton leading the solo and Getz, aided and abetted by Cherico and Hunt, providing the framework. Greenbaum knows that if he wants the song to come true, if he wants to sleep this night or any night with a smile on his face, he must close the gap. He must touch her fingers. And, if he does, he must hope that when the music stops, she does not break contact to applaud.

May 12, 1968

Mother's Day

Black. Black black. Blacker than the blackest pigments. I occupy my mind with thoughts of black pigments to root myself in a reality other than the restraints, thick and padded, encircling my wrists. And the darkness. Either I'm I blindfolded or blind.

Ivory black. Primary black pigment. Used for all techniques. Made by carbonizing bones. I don't know how you carbonize bones or what carbonized bones are. What remains after the flesh is cremated, maybe. A much better black than ordinary bone black. Made from better bones. Made with greater care. My favorite black. Minnie's too.

Lampblack. The smell of burning oil. Greasy and fluffy at the same time. Too difficult to work with.

Carbon black. The most intense of all. Always used alone because it mixes poorly with other colors. One-part carbon black, five parts ultramarine blue, and five parts ochre, Payne's gray. A simple recipe, but impossible to mix. Like red. A primary color. Impossible to mix. Crucifixion paintings. A field. Summer. Hot. A knife.

Blood. Seeping through a handkerchief. Thread by thread. Black. Concentrate on black.

Vine black. The favorite of artists who don't eat their vegetables when they are growing up. Pales in comparison to ivory black.

Mars black. Heavy and dense. Named after the planet because of its slight reddish cast. Easier to use than carbon black, especially in a water medium.

I hear voices. Too indistinct to understand. Maybe a man. Maybe a woman. I lie still, sensing the weight of my body. My back aches like it does after a shift at the tannery lifting bales of cowhide. I fear soon becoming a cripple like Da. I will my eyes into my fingertips. My fingers press downward. A slight give. Familiar. Might be a bed. A mattress. With a sheet. I test the restraints. Either they're too strong or I'm too weak. I relax. I want the advantage of surprise. I don't want them to know I'm awake.

Inside the black, I open and close my eyes. Black is black is black.

In the background a beep. Monotonous. Steady. I try to count the seconds between beeps, but I can't. I recite the alphabet to myself. Stop at F. Q. Q comes after F. I hold my breath, listen to my heart beat. It synchronizes with the F Q beep. It's like I'm connected to an alarm. Or, a bomb.

I roll my eyes. Needle-like pain, a headache throbbing to the beeps. Swimming in black. Dizzy. Symptoms of a concussion. The voices are closer now. Something about sorcery. They're saying something about sorcery. Sorcerers talking of sorcery. Something about the next twenty-four hours. Must be a deadline. Hostage situations always have deadlines. I'm a hostage of sorcerers debating what to do with me if the ransom isn't paid.

I struggle to remember. A robbery at the amusement park. A botched getaway. The first aid room. Of course, the bed, the sheet, the woman's voice. She must be the nurse. Another hostage. I concentrate on counting voices, listening for children's voices. The amusement park is always full of kids. All summer. Full of kids. God! I hope they didn't grab any kids.

I hear voices, but I don't know how many. I swallow a yawn. I don't want the voices to know I'm awake. I fight the urge to sleep. I'm falling through the darkness. I must be on drugs. As harmless, as helpless, as a newborn. No wonder my restraints are loose. Too loose. Big mistake, Mr. Voice. A big F Q mistake. The male voice says time should tell how good we are at sorcery, the last thing I hear before the void.

Awake. Again. I wiggle my toes. Booties. Like a young child bundled up to play in the snow. I tighten my calf muscles. Something wraps my legs half way up my thigh. Tight, but pliable. I contract the muscle controlling my penis. Something's inside it. The whole length. My heart skips a beat. I'm being held by fucking weirdoes who mean to kill me. I inhale, but something restrains my chest. I try to relax my stomach, extend it to its fattest. The same restraint. I inch my right elbow toward my ribcage. A straitjacket. But not my arms. Makes no sense. I try to visualize the men holding me, their motives, objectives. Nothing makes sense. The easy way, tie my hands behind my back, my feet together at the ankles. They didn't. This ain't Hollywood.

I listen for breathing. For voices. Silence. I must be alone. I say my name, surprised my voice still works. If I call for help, no one would hear me except the sorcerers. Surprise is my only ally. I must play dead until I can figure things out. I feel my mind shutting down. I struggle to fight it, then stop. Sleeping is the easiest way to play dead.

Awake, again, everything still, blacker than the blackest pigment. New voices. Strangers. A woman saying he's still unconscious. A man replying optimism is key. The man believes what he says. The woman sounds edgy, afraid, uncertain.

Another voice. Familiar. Asking how is he today.

Ma? Ma! A hostage. Oh, God!

Yet, another voice, this one calling for Dr. Robey. Dinitia! I can't restrain myself. "Dinitia? Ma?"

A new voice. "I'm Dr. Henderson. You're in St. Luke's Hospital recovering from surgery."

"Am I dying?"

Dr. Henderson, "No!"

"Ma?"

"You're not dying, son."

"Do you feel any dizziness?" A woman. Is Dr. Robey a woman?

My head spins and I feel like I'm whipping around inside one of the wire cages on the Death Wheel at the amusement park. I worked the Death Wheel that summer. Just once. Handing out the pamphlet the park's insurance company required patrons to read before they rode the Wheel. Collecting the releases management insisted the patrons sign. Fear sold. It still does. It's how Hollywood advertised the horror movies I gobbled popcorn through at Saturday afternoon matinees. Double features. Monsters. Creatures from other worlds. How I hated the mushy, kissy parts. Monster killer, that's what I wanted to be when I grew up.

Fear. It's how the amusement park shilled the Death Wheel. Suckers all, I thought as I distributed the pamphlets, collected the releases, until Kurt, the regular operator, dared me to ride the Wheel, offered me a free pass, tested the restraints strapping me to the back wall of the cage, and smiled. Oh, how Kurt smiled like a death head on a Halloween mask as he pushed the lever that started the ride. The Death Wheel tilted from horizontal to vertical and whipped around, faster, faster, rotating clockwise, while the cages spun counterclockwise, faster, faster. Everything, the amusement park, the highway, the parking lot, the buildings, the sky, whipped by in a blur until, after a minute, maybe two, maybe three, maybe an infinity of minutes, I screamed and blacked out. At the completion of the ride, Kurt carried me off the Death Wheel and revived me with smelling salts. I awakened to Kurt's shit eating grin and the reassurance that it happened several times a week.

"Fading in and out of consciousness is normal," Dr. Henderson explains, but, still riding the Death Wheel, I do not hear him.

I open and close my eyes. My eyelids scrape against something. A blindfold. Hostages always wear blindfolds. Makes them easier to control. A new sound. A squeak. Like the wheels of a shopping cart. Not a shopping cart. A hand truck. Moving cases of soda and crackers and wax beans, ugly yellow wax beans, into the storage area behind the grocery wheel at the amusement park. Mill dollies and wax beans and whatever happened to Julia. Now the sound of breathing and a different squeak. Like sneakers on a gym floor. Early in the school year before the summer's polish wears off.

"Good morning, Mr. Malone. Dr. Robey again."

The last how many hours have disappeared.

"Hi, honey." Dinitia. Hold a gun to a person's head and she'll say anything.

"I'm here too, son."

Ma sounds coerced, threatened, not normal. There's little they can threaten her with. Not her life. That wouldn't work. *Johnson's Motor Car.* Except my life. She'd be a puppet on a string.

"I'm going to remove your bandages," Dr. Robey says.

"Blindfold."

Robey takes my hand and places it on my face. "It's Johnson & Johnson medical tape."

"You're in a hospital, son."

"St. Luke's, honey. A block from our apartment."

"I want you to close your eyes," Dr. Robey says.

"How long?"

"Until I say open them."

"How long have I been here?"

"I'm going to leave the gauze pads in place. I have some special sun glasses I'm going to put on you. They're very dark and wrap around. Keep your eyes closed while I pull the gauze pads out from behind the glasses. When you feel up to it, open your eyes a tiny slit. The light will hurt through the sun glasses. You have to open your eyes very, very slowly."

I feel the motion of the scissors against my temple. "Hold still," Robey orders as she snips the bandages. More squeaks and now her scent is stronger on my right.

"Am I blind?"

Robey stops, resting the scissors against my temple. "I don't know." She recounts my last surgery and the circumstances leading up to it. "Your wife made a very brave decision. Whether you can see or not, she made the right choice."

Dinitia: "Could I have a few minutes alone with my husband?"

"Not too long." Robey retracts the scissors. "Don't remove the bandages."

More squeaks, then the click of the door. One person breathing. Warm against my neck. A faint odor of tea. I remember kissing someone who tasted of tea. Julia only drinks coffee. I pucker up, but the bandages, the God damn bandages, surround my mouth like sandbags piled high around a foxhole against an enemy assault and our lips cannot touch and our tongues cannot reach and I must satisfy myself with the memory of the taste of her tea laced kiss.

Two hands now enfold mine in familiar softness. The sweet aroma of hand lotion replaces the faint odor of tea. I caress the crowns of her knuckles at the base of her fingers, dainty, barely rising above the plane of her hand like the stems of expensive watches. Talented fingers able to paint circles around me and Minnie. Stubborn fingers. I rest my fingertips on the sleekness of her fingernails, as hard as shields but pearly pink and shiny because she only uses clear translucent polish. I gently press my fingers into the puffy flesh of her palms, firm like pillows stuffed with the finest down, smooth like pillows covered with the finest silk. I trace her life line, her love line, both straight, deep, true. Palm reading, crystal balls, astrology, fortune tellers. One good sideshow deserves another.

"We're alone now," Dinitia's voice says. Her voice is liquid, landing on my ears like a gentle mist, seeping into my consciousness.

"Am I'm really in a hospital?"

"St. Luke's."

"I'm not a hostage?"

"Only to your injuries."

"I don't want to be a burden."

"I love you," she says.

I sense a skip in her voice, the Sunday painter skip, the lawyer/artist skip. The 'I married the wrong Musketeer skip.' I entwine my fingers in hers. She places my palm on her cheek and I feel the wetness of her skin beneath her eyes. I curl my fingers behind her ear and gently pull her toward me and she burrows within the sandbag of bandages surrounding my mouth and with her breath and with her kiss she deposits the taste of tea upon my lips and upon my tongue and I know that as long as I can taste her and smell her and touch her and hear her voice I will be able to see her.

Robey returns and finishes cutting away the bandages. "Remember. Eyes closed."

The tape comes off and my head feels lighter. I'm in the third grade again with a broken leg. How weightless my leg was after the doctor sawed off the cast. It levitated toward the ceiling. Da made noises like a ghost and waved his arms like a magician. Ma laughed and didn't stop until we were back in the car. Now I only hear the soft pant of Ma's breathing, quicker and shallower than Dinitia's or Robey's or the nurse's. I remind Ma about my leg, Da's ghost, ask her to laugh again, but she says it was my arm, not my leg, and that she took me to the doctor because Da was at work. Now I laugh for both of us and with the laughter I feel my head rise to the ceiling and bounce along like a helium balloon.

Robey fits the sun glasses over my eyes, then removes the gauze patches. "You look like a jazz musician. Just a slit. Open slowly to let your eyes can adjust to the light."

I cup my hands over the sunglasses. "It's like the sun's a foot from my face."

"Rest your eyes," Robey says.

It is thirty minutes before I can open my eyes completely. "Tomorrow," Robey says when I ask if I can remove the sunglasses.

"Everything's blurry."

"How long?" Dinitia asks.

"Days. Weeks." Robey motions for Dinitia to follow her into the hall. "Maybe never."

Week of May 19, 1968

Vietnam.

The humidity that makes the colors glow in the mind's eye of the artist mildews everything it touches: the cloth of the uniforms, the leather of the boots, the metal of the guns and grenades, the skin of grunts like Merisi 'Minnie' Minifie. The dirt on the sides of the foxholes weeps with humidity. The pressure bandages the medics squeeze into wounds gurgle with humidity. The rotors of the choppers give off a misty spray like garden sprinklers bringing life to suburban lawns. The humidity saturates the skin of the grunts, turning it green until it's the texture of moss growing on a rock. Minnie licks moisture from his lips and vows that green will never grace his palette again.

The problem of humidity pales beside the problem of the stench. Not the stench of soldiers who haven't bathed in weeks. Not the stench of uniforms that have not been laundered in months. Not the stench of garbage from the field kitchens. Not the stench of shit from the field toilets. It's a unique stench. A new experience for the grunts. A new experience for Minnie who worked summers in his dad's funeral home bathing bodies, embalming them, applying cosmetics, laying them out for wakes. A new experience for Hobo who grew up in Alabama with the smell of crosses burning in his yard. A new experience for Spiker whose bedroom window opened on an alley that served as the neighborhood garbage dumpster. A new experience for Miguel who almost disappeared into the barrio before the draft board located him. A new experience for all the grunts in Vietnam.

The stench, unseen like Victor Charlie, originates in the jungle and flows over the landing zone on every breeze, attaching itself, like the humidity, to the cloth of the uniforms, the leather of the boots, the metal of the guns and grenades, the skin of the grunts. It's the stench of decomposing plants, the stench of rotting flesh, some animal, some human, battlefield dead that neither side allows the other to recover. There are two points of honor on this battlefield both sides live by: recover your dead and prevent the enemy from recovering theirs. Kill or be killed. Life is simple on the battlefield. Death is simpler. War is neither good nor evil. War is. Peace isn't.

Everyone breathes the stench of rotting flesh from unseen corpses who, once upon a time in another life, shot hoops on the playgrounds of Harlem, or hit baseballs on the sandlots of St. Louis, or tossed tight spirals on the streets of Pittsburgh, or skated on the frozen lakes of Minnesota, or hung out on street corners in Los Angeles watching the high riders and low riders and no riders cruise by.

To perfume the stench, to calm nerves, to mark the passage of time, everyone smokes. Just as in prison, cigarettes are a medium of exchange except for the wounded who get a free pass. The worse the wounds, the freer the pass. Cigarettes and sympathy from a first looie who doesn't understand that getting A's at the Point doesn't guarantee survival for himself and his men in country. The better first looies discard 'the book' before the choppers touch down. The survival statistics of their platoons confirm their wisdom. The ones who care about becoming generals don't. The army no longer travels on its stomach. It travels on procedures and procedures kill as every grunt knows. Grunts know little or nothing. If they were smart, they'd be stateside in college smoking dope, fucking cheerleaders, and throwing water balloons filled with piss at pigs, hippies, and fags.

Heavy clouds obscure the moon and stars. In his foxhole, Minnie withdraws into the smoke of his cigarette and pats down his breast pocket to reaffirm he still has his sacred scalpel, the scalpel he stole from his dad's funeral home when he was a young child; the scalpel that saved his life many, many years ago; the scalpel that did not save M'Boto because the Alabama night supped on his bravado like a vampire bat supping on blood, a death for which he now and will forever blame himself regardless of the bullshit shrinks have tried to foist on him over the years. From New York, to basic training, to Saigon, into the shit, he obsessively checked to make sure his sacred scalpel still accompanied him. It is a talisman. Minnie knows as long as he has his sacred scalpel, he will survive Vietnam and return home a whole man, his chest weighed down with the medals the Army bestows on fools like him.

Feeling safe, feeling secure, he lets his imagination bathe himself in imaginary pussy, wet and sweet and quivering with anticipation, anonymous pussy, a Playboy pinup, a movie star. Not Laurie Williams. Not Dinitia Marbury Madison. For Minnie, pussy with a name, pussy he knows, pussy he went to school with, pussy he dated, pussy he fucked, will never be as good in real life as imaginary pussy in his foxhole. In the middle of this fantasy, Hobo plops down and begs a light off his cigarette.

"Sketch me a sketch," Hobo says. "A pack of Pall Malls in it for you."

"Miss Edna ever tell you about Alabama?" Minnie asks.

"Something I be sending my daughter back home."

"I killed M'Boto," Minnie says.

"A second pack if you do one for Miss Edna," Hobo says.

"Same as if I tossed the rope over the branch myself."

Hobo lights a second cigarette off his first and douses his butt in a puddle of humidity. "A couple of sketches. That's all."

A crescent moon whose boundaries blur from the moisture in the air breaks free from the clouds. The landing zone glistens. The grunts extinguish their cigarettes. No plumes of smoke to give away their location to an enemy who launches mortars or grenades or other ordnance at anything that looks out of place. A third point of honor both sides live by: never let the enemy enjoy a smoke. Minnie retrieves a pen and pad from his pack, souvenirs from an R & R in Saigon.

"A letter to Malone?" Hobo asks.

"To Dinitia. Malone wouldn't understand."

"He won't be jealous, you writing his wife?"

"Not my problem."

Minnie riffs through his pad until he finds a sheet of paper dry enough to write on. "I'm gathering a lifetime of material," Minnie writes. "Two lifetimes. Every war produces great literature. Some wars produce great music. This war will produce great art, art to make Caravaggio look like a Sunday painter, El Greco like a realist, and Goya, damnable Goya, as sane as you or me." Minnie scratches his nose with the pen. "If I were a writer, I would write the narrative of your husband's life. I would write of chino pants and law books and painting water colors in Florida while awaiting his next Social Security check. I would write of quitting basketball and quitting painting and quitting life. I would write of a man who is as at home in his time as a man running from a wounded bison was when he first appeared on the walls of Lascaux. And I would write the narrative of the woman who in a moment of madness married that man, a narrative without an ending, as incomplete as an unfinished symphony, as a chalk never realized as a painting, as one of Michelangelo's unrealized sculptures lining the corridor of the Galleria dell'Accademia leading to his David. But I'm a painter, not a writer nor a composer nor a sculptor. We live in meaningless times, Dinitia, a time of *Life with Coffee Spoons*, and I shall be the painter of record. Love, Minnie."

With the dawn, the early morning dew mixes with the humidity to create a thin, watery soup that turns the field rations soggy and dilutes the coffee. The stench rises with the sun, intensifying as the light brightens. Photosensitive, it feeds off daylight. It surrounds the landing zone the way the photosphere surrounds the sun, radiating stench instead of heat and light. The water molecules in the air carry the stench into the darkest shadows and deposit it on things, living, dead, inanimate. The men joke about joining the French Foreign Legion and being stationed in the Sahara, but laughing only makes them sweat more. As the men prepare for another day of drills, another day of sorties into the jungle, another day of hitting Victor Charlie, of Victor Charlie hitting back, a chopper lands. Mail call and for Minnie a letter from Dinitia postmarked April 27, 1968, almost four weeks travel time from New York City into the shit.

Hobo and Minnie squat at the edge of the jungle beneath leaves that remind Minnie of elephant ears. Minnie doesn't know the fancy Latin name for these leaves because he's an artist, not some fucking Audubon making an accurate record of the flora and fauna of an exotic world. Yesterday, he photographed these leaves. Someday he may paint them though it will be difficult without green on his palette. No matter. Leaves don't have to be green. Color is a form of artistic expression. He'll paint them red. Blood red.

When Hobo asks what Malone be saying, Minnie reads the letter aloud. "Dear Minnie: Malone's brain's all twisted up trying to master the difference between a counteroffer varying material terms and a counteroffer that doesn't while you're making the world your model. Back here, everyone's rioting, occupying buildings. It'd be a big giggle if the bastards weren't armed. Mau-mau down from Harlem. Black power from black powder. And schisms. You'd think it was the *Battle of Algiers*. Whole God damn university's shut down, cowering before each new slogan, paralyzed by its fucking self-image as a fucking guardian of fucking western civilization. There's probably more fucking civilization where you are.

"He was jumped by a bunch of rioters 'cause he was taking pictures. They thought he was a spy or something. They didn't believe he was warehousing material for future painting. I don't either. Lawyers don't paint. He talks the talk, saying he's cataloging lips and mouths and cheeks twisted in fear, exploding in anger, distorted by emotion. You should hear him. I know the faces Rubens knew in *Fall of the Damned*, he says. I stand with Carpeaux as he sculpts his *Ugolino*. Bullshit! Have I earned the right to paint what I see, he asks. Sorry for the unladylike language. Miss you. D."

"Shit, no," Minnie tells Hobo, confident Dinitia

echoes him.

Dinitia's letter marks the end of Minnie's fourth month in country, most of it in the shit. Minnie trades the first looie a portrait for five day passes for himself and Hobo, five days R & R in Saigon. Hot showers. A bed with sheets and pillows. Real food. Real Scotch if you buy it in on base. Mail only a week old. And pussy. For every taste. For every budget. Fantasy land.

Hobo props photos of his wife and daughter on the night table, then stretches out on a hotel bed a foot shorter than he. With his sacred scalpel, Minnie shaves in the bathroom bending over a sink that only reaches his knees. Another superstition, for the scalpel to bathe him in good luck, he must incorporate it into his daily life, not merely carry it with him. In the center of the room, a ceiling fan, one of its blades missing, struggles to move the thick air, the difference between a luxury hotel and the hovels where the locals stay. Minnie's socks hang from one blade, Hobo's socks from the other, a strip of fresh flypaper from the third. The afternoon sun forces its way through the shutters and heats the interior air. The slants of sunlight, Hobo says, remind him of summer afternoons inside Miss Edna's railroad shack. Hobo usually shuns reminders of home. In the field, being homesick can be fatal. Grunts, especially cherries on their first tour of duty, daydream about home and walk into sniper fire, trip wires, ambushes. Hobo doesn't want to die because of someone else's homesickness.

"You coming with me?" Minnie says. "Soo Phat's Noodle House supposed to have the fuckingest whores in Nam."

"I ain't bringing home no souvenirs."

"So they'll blow your horn."

Minnie and Hobo detour to check the mail, a letter from Miss Edna for Hobo, another letter from Dinitia for Minnie, that they read on the jinrikisha ride to Soo Phat's. The coolie who pulls the jinrikisha has a wispy white beard and wears a conical hat tied loosely beneath his chin. His skin, the color of brown mustard, looks like it has already been made into a lampshade. His sandals are cut from tires and bound to his feet by rope. The way his head bobs up and down reminds Minnie of the horses that pull the carriages in Central Park. One or two die each summer. Minnie wonders about the death rate of jinrikisha drivers in Saigon. Dogs nip at the coolie's heels and the jinrikisha's wheels. Children in rags compete with the dogs for running room. Some sell broken shells or chipped beads or their sisters or mothers; others just beg. The coolie turns down a narrow alley lined with hootches selling meats barbecued over open drums. Locals clamor to buy cups of steamed rice or noodles ladled with fresh barbecue. Paper lanterns hang from wires strung between windows on opposite sides of the alley. Whores stand in these windows, the mothers and sisters of the children who crowd the dogs and the jinrikisha, advertising themselves with waves and flashes of tit or pussy. They are as appetizing as the garbage piled around the barbecue drums. A pungent aroma fills the alley and some of the dogs stop to sniff the drums and beg for handouts. One of Saigon's truths, Hobo tells Minnie, is that the dog chasing you today is tomorrow's barbecue. Vegetarian is the only way to go unless you eat on base where the odds favor (nothing's a sure bet in Nam) the chicken being chicken, not pigeon; the beef being beef, not dog; the pork being pork, not rat or cat; and the special of the day being something other than snake.

Minnie closes his mind to Hobo and the jinrikisha and the coolie with the conical hat and the children and the dogs and the alley and the lanterns and the whores and the pungent aroma of roasting dog meat as he reads

Dinitia's letter for the fourth time, hoping her words, now old and out of date, yesterday's news, will change: "Malone's in the hospital, a casualty of the campus riots, beaten within an inch of his life because he tried to rescue a classmate being attacked by Mau-mau. He may be brain damaged. He may never regain his cognitive functions. He may be blind. He may die. I don't know how long it will take this to reach you. I may be a widow by the time you read it. Minnie, I need you. Please come home."

Minnie folds the letter in half, then in half again, and again, until it is a tiny square that he slips into the secret pocket sewn into the inside of his shirt over his heart. Rescuing a classmate, he thinks, not taking photos. A lie, but why? And, who did he lie to? Me or Dinitia? Minnie's arm dangles over the side of the jinrikisha and the dogs nip at his fingers. But if he were beaten unconscious, he wouldn't be able to lie. Someone else must have told the lie. The rescued classmate, an eyewitness, the cops, all possibilities. Malone would not have let M'Boto be lynched. Minnie knows this now. For all his bravado, for all his living in the line of fire, he, Minnie, is the coward and Dinitia would never have married a coward. Days and days from New York to Saigon. Somewhere between there and here is another letter. Maybe San Francisco. Maybe Honolulu. Maybe Tokyo. Maybe waiting to be sorted in Saigon. The dogs nip his fingers and the children laugh and chatter and clap their hands like they're watching a circus act, the lion tamer being eaten by the lion. Now, the dogs gnaw at his fingers and the children no longer laugh or chatter or clap their hands.

Minnie knows how much burying kids upsets his dad. He tries to imagine how upset his dad would be burying one of his friends. Malone. A friend rather than a once upon a time blood brother. And, I won't be there when Malone's buried, Minnie realizes. I'll be in Vietnam where life is cheap, but not as cheap as life on the Columbia University campus.

Pain ravages Minnie from his fingers to his shoulder. He feels as helpless as he did in Alabama listening to M'Boto scream, plead, beg. He doesn't feel responsible for Malone's death the way he does M'Boto's. Malone made his choice and he'll have to live with it, maybe die because of it, a choice he, Minnie, heroism pulling him by the short hairs, was too chickenshit to make. He wants to telephone Dinitia, but even in emergencies it takes days to arrange a line and the army won't consider this an emergency since Malone's not his brother. Once upon a time blood brothers don't count. There are no musketeers in this man's army, just guilty grunts, him being Exhibit A.

"Shit, man!" Hobo grabs Minnie's arm and yanks it inside the jinrikisha. The dogs yelp their disappointment and drop away in search of something else to eat. The children seek other American joes to beg from. Minnie's fingertips are red with blood and pulpy with open flesh. "I gotta get you to the medics. You need shots and shit."

`Minnie digs a pint of whiskey out of his pants. "I'm not letting you go back into the shit without me." He drinks a swig, and pours the rest over his fingertips, then serenades the coolie and the whores and the locals huddled around the barbecue drums with *White Rabbit* while Hobo wraps his fingers in a bandage. Blood seeps through the cloth and Minnie relives the summer day he wrapped Malone's finger in a handkerchief and they joked about the color of blood in crucifixion paintings.

"How much longer to Soo Phat's?" Minnie shouts at the jinrikisha driver.

"No long. No long."

"Five minutes or no tippee!" Minnie leans forward

and snatches the coolie's hat and sails it into the nearest barbecue hootch where it lands on a drum and bursts into flames, a glorious geyser of yellow and orange. The driver runs faster and a half hour later, Minnie and Hobo sip beers at Soo Phat's and watch Vietnamese strippers with tiny tits and pussies shaved like inverted arrowheads dance on an elevated stage to loud acid rock, Jimi Hendrix, the Jefferson Airplane, the Doors, Canned Heat, Big Brother and the Holding Company, Moby Grape. Minnie doesn't give a rat's ass. Tit is tit and pussy is pussy and I'm dead, he believes, and M'Boto is dead, he knows, and humping disease on a cot is nothing compared to facing death in the shit whether that shit be in Alabama or Vietnam or the Columbia University campus.

Soo Phat's is one large room bisected down the center by a runway allowing every patron to see every side of every stripper. The room is segregated by military service. Marines sit with Marines, Navy fliers with Navy fliers, grunts only with grunts. Minnie and Hobo sit by themselves. Square tables, capacity of four, cram the floor, spaced for the talent to hawk their wares table to table. Rattan window screens that roll up and down at the tug of a draw string let the outside in, the inside out. Cigarette smoke, too thick to be disturbed by the ceiling fans, perfumes the body odor of the patrons, the strippers. The beer is warm and watered, the hard liquor soft. Behind the runway a door covered with cheap strings of beads leads to a warren of small rooms where American joes can pay to touch or be touched. Officers do not patronize Soo Phat's. They have their own fantasy lands where the skin is whiter, the tits bigger, the pussies blonder. Servicemen wave American dollars at the strippers, shouting out what they want to buy, what they're willing to pay.

"Too much like a slave auction," Hobo tells Minnie.

"Let's go."

Minnie rotates his bottle until the label faces Hobo. "Been a hundred refills since this had Bud in it. I paid for the fucking king of beers. I want the fucking king of beers."

"Beer's beer. What's eating you?"

"Her." Minnie waves his bandage at one of the strippers who bumps and grinds to their table.

"American joe want fucky fucky?" She opens her legs and rotates her hips, exaggerating the motions of intercourse. Her cunt, as red and raw and pulpy as Minnie's fingers, looks like it needs a month's leave.

"How 'bout sucky sucky?" Minnie asks.

"Two joes, two suckys, twenty-dollar American." She flicks her tongue in and out of her mouth like the jungle snakes that invade the landing zone at night and slither into sleeping bags and ponchos.

"Two joes, two suckys, two dollars."

"Count me out," Hobo says.

"One joe, one sucky, one dollar," Minnie says.

"Too cheap. Too cheap. Me not cheap."

"I ain't paying American prices for gook cunt." Minnie grabs her wrist and throws her down on the table, standing over her as he tries to undo his pants, but he can only use one hand and his shirttail gets caught in his zipper and before he can get his pants down Hobo grabs him by the collar and slams him back in his chair.

"Go," Hobo tells the stripper, but she remains on the table, her legs open for business, her office inches from Minnie's face.

"Fifty-dollar fucky right here." She pats her pussy. "Fifty-dollar fucky."

"One joe, one sucky, one dollar."

The stripper swivels off the table. "Me no cheap."

"Let's go!" Hobo says.

"Lemme finish my king of beers." As Minnie

swallows, a Navy airman brushes his arm, knocking the bottle into his lap where the beer spills, white and foamy.

"Lookee, lookee." The stripper points. "Joe do it in pants." She waves to the other strippers who gather, jousting with each other for position as if they are competing for a thousand-dollar fucky sucky. "Joe do it in pants."

Minnie whips the bottle at the Navy airman who jumps Minnie and starts pummeling him. The brawl quickly spreads throughout Soo Phat's. Grunts beat up fly boys. Fly boys beat up grunts. Marines beat up everybody. The strippers kick whoever they can reach. Five grunts, ignoring the sirens of the Military Police, gang rape Minnie's stripper, revenge for the casualties their platoon suffered. Hobo wrestles the Navy airman off Minnie and leads Minnie toward the beaded doorway. When Minnie trips over his own feet, Hobo tosses him across his shoulders in a fireman carry.

"You looking to get yourself killed," Hobo says.

"Heroes die in combat."

"Bar brawl ain't combat."

"All life's combat."

Minnie's bandaged hand bounces against the small of Hobo's back, bloodying Hobo's shirt and the top of his pants. Hobo kicks open the back door into the alley behind Soo Phat's kitchen, scattering a pack of dogs who scavenge the garbage. Today they scavenge, tomorrow they are scavenged, a dog's life in Saigon. Hobo hauls Minnie from alley to street to alley to street to alley, checking to make certain he's not being followed by MPs or Navy fly boys or Marines or strippers or dogs ravenous from the scent of blood. He turns into the alley with the barbecue hootches and props Minnie against a wall behind one of the oil drums.

Minnie gives Hobo Dinitia's letter.

"Why didn't you say something?" Hobo folds the letter and returns it to Minnie's inside pocket, then makes his way to the mouth of the alley where he hails a jinrikisha whose coolie does not have a conical hat or a wispy white beard or skin that looks like a lampshade to take them back to their hotel.

*　*　*

Landing Zone Yellow Jacket. A secret location. Everyone but the pilots wears blindfolds on the flights in and out.

While Hobo tends to Minnie's fingers in Saigon (thank God I don't paint with my left hand, Minnie tells him), two platoons of Army engineers led by a Rambling Wreck from Georgia Tech, an ex-linebacker who volunteers for Nam to toughen himself up for the National Football League, begin construction of LZ Yellow Jacket in a clearing in the middle of the jungle. The men call him R.W. which he interprets as a sign of respect because he doesn't realize the R stands for 'Ratfucker', not Rambling. He's the Ratfucker Wreck from Georgia Tech and that's how his men sing his college fight song behind his back when they're not speculating about the invasion that will be launched from the LZ. Cambodia. Laos. North Vietnam. China. Ratfucker who speculates about nothing and who believes that the only truth in life is the final score of a football game won by his beloved Yellow Jackets (a losing score being solely the fault of incompetent or dishonest game officials) wears his college football jersey under his uniform for luck and prays to Bobby Dodd because Jesus Christ never beat the Bulldogs of the University of Georgia.

With napalm, the engineers burn away the trees and vines and other jungle undergrowth, baking the snakes and vermin too slow to escape. With bulldozers, they flatten the earth and grade it. With backhoes, they dig trenches along the jungle's perimeter, eight feet deep, two feet wide, walls plumb and true. With forklifts, they rim the outer edge of the trenches with three feet of sandbags. With hammers and nails and lumber they build wooden sidewalks to line the bottom of the trenches. With cement they construct landing pads and with yellow and black paint they decorate them with yellow jackets inside circles, targets for the Huey pilots and dustoffs. With iron piping they erect two sets of cross bars and with wiring and light bulbs and buttons and switches they jerry-build a clock and scoreboard for the men to play football in the evening or on Saturday afternoons when Georgia Tech would play if it were October and there weren't a twelve-hour time difference.

One afternoon, a combat soldier relaxing in the shadow of the wall of sandbags places his empty soda can atop the wall. A Victor Charlie sniper opens fire, hitting the can with his fifth shot. A game is invented, a distraction, something to bet on other than the poker games that fill idle time. Empty soda cans are lined up along the sandbags, ten at a time. Book is made in two categories: how many cans will Victor Charlie hit and how many shots will it take him to do so. Even odds. A dollar per entry, the pool divided equally between the winners in each category. Cash is minimal at the LZ. Tallies are kept, agreements made to pay all debts in the future, the men joking the debtors will volunteer for the point on patrol to avoid paying up. To flaunt their manhood, some do. When three of the first six winners die on patrol, superstition reigns. Talk of curses, demons, other worldly beings, bedevils the men who attempt an exorcism by burning the tally sheets. They seek other distractions. Ratfucker Wreck who equates religious ceremonies with voodoo practices and worships only football provides one.

Atop an observation tower shielded from Victor Charlie snipers by bomb blast suppression blankets, in the shadow of a beach umbrella above the construction equipment, above the dust, above the stench of the jungle and the sweat and stink of the men, above the muted hum of his bastardized college fight song, above the world of Landing Zone Yellow Jacket, Ratfucker Wreck sits, observing his men through binoculars like a football coach monitoring his players. Every day in the heat of the midday sun when the men break for lunch Ratfucker entertains them from atop his tower (it'll help you relate to them, Saigon command assures him) through an official army issue field sound amplification system by strumming a guitar and singing Paul Simon tunes in an accent half rural Georgia and half Flatbush and too thick to be deciphered by men from either place. Or from anywhere else. It's enough to scare away Victor Charlie, and maybe it has, because neither the Viet Cong nor the North Vietnamese nor the Chinese make any effort to stop the construction of LZ Yellow Jacket. Or, maybe they patiently await the completion of construction when they'll seize the landing zone for themselves. As for Ratfucker, someone must have told the snipers that killing him would aid the American war effort. They leave him to his midday entertainments. Ratfucker opens and closes every lunch time set with his favorite Paul Simon tune, *America*, although he always botches the chorus, singing 'we have found America' rather than 'All come to look for America'. Maybe Ratfucker has found his America at LZ Yellow Jacket, but not his men. Their America is somewhere else and they hope someday to return to it. To them, the rest stops along the New Jersey Turnpike would be paradise compared to LZ Yellow Jacket.

As for Hobo and Minnie, they, too, reside at LZ

Yellow Jacket. Minnie hides the remnants of the fingers of his left hand inside bandages he explains away as an accident, someone slamming a door on his hand. Are you sure you weren't run over by a jinrikisha while you were drunk in the gutter, the first looie asks. Saigon streets don't have gutters, Minnie replies. But they do, at least some of them. Like the rest of their squad, the rest of their company, the rest of the combat troops slowly accumulating like the mildew induced moss, their mission is twofold: keep LZ Yellow Jacket secure and beat the shit out of Ratfucker's engineers in football, something they regularly do because on the playing fields of LZ Yellow Jacket where there are no ringers the combat troops have the edge.

About 2:00 in the afternoon local time on Minnie's and Hobo's first Friday back from R and R in Saigon, the twenty-fourth day after Dinitia mailed her letter to Minnie, the referee in violation of a direct order from Ratfucker Wreck suspends the day's football game, Combat Troops 28, Engineers 6, because the daily mail chopper hovers above the landing pad nearest the north end zone excreting long green duffel bags of mail that fall to earth like shit from a very large dog and plop on and around the yellow jacket painted in the center of the pad with a dull thud that, if it were night, would be mistaken for the sound of shells exploding in the distance. The men gather around the pad, close but not too close because being bopped by a stray mail bag merits neither sympathy nor treatment from the medics, much less a Purple Heart or a trip home. To everyone but Ratfucker, mail call takes precedence over touchdowns and he would court martial the referee for stopping play if he weren't afraid of being fragged. When someone frags his guitar, Ratfucker gets the hint and plays Stones and Doors and Kinks and Beach Boys and Motown and Elvis and Jefferson Airplane during lunch. The men, combat troops and engineers alike, clump together by squads for mail call. Minnie's squad gathers in the shadow of Ratfucker's observation tower where Hobo makes a game of calling out the names by mispronouncing them or using nicknames he invents on the spot. As the stack of letters shrinks, Minnie becomes more despondent and by the time Hobo hands out the last letter, Minnie stands alone, the only man in his squad without mail, nothing from Fall River, nothing from New York, nothing but the last letter from Dinitia, already weeks out of date when he received it. Like all grunts in a war zone, Minnie knows there is nothing lonelier than watching your buddies read their mail.

Minnie retrieves his sketch pad and a set of color pencils and a bottle of Scotch from Saigon he saves for special occasions and tiptoes around and through the combat troops, around and through the engineers, around and through hundreds and hundreds of men, as if he is tiptoeing around and through a mine field. Their letters, whether on white ruled paper or perfumed pink stationery or office letterhead or the back side of supermarket shopping bags, are land mines and sooner or later Minnie knows he will receive one postmarked New York that will explode in his hands as he reads it. Tripping inside their letters as if they are on LSD, the men do not notice Minnie as he slides a wooden plank across the perimeter trench, as he walks the plank and climbs a fire ladder, as he sits himself cross legged in the lotus position on the rim of the sandbags facing into the sun, facing the jungle. He feels as empty as a can of soda gulped down on a hot, sweaty day. He unsheathes his sacred scalpel from the leather carrier he made in Arts & Crafts in a previous life, a summer camp life, and places it on the sand bag beside himself. Minnie opens the sketch pad and spreads it across his lap. He guzzles the Scotch that, according to its label, is slightly older than he is. Humpty Dumpty perched on his wall.

A dragonfly, the national insect of Vietnam, buzzes around the sandbags like a bomber about to begin its run, then lands on the scalpel beside Minnie, staring at him. He stares back and once again he is a young boy drawing a stick figure on a horizontal black line in a nursery school finger-painting, another on a green blob of grass below the black line; once again he is a school boy staring at dragonflies at Camp Aquidneck, the summer camp where he made the leather carrier for his sacred scalpel, where he learned how to swim and sail and water ski and fish and braid bracelets out of gimp or rope and tell dirty jokes even if he didn't understand them. Like LZ Yellow Jacket, a marsh bounded Camp Aquidneck, a marsh as murky and mucky as any in Vietnam, a marsh overrun by fiddler crabs and periwinkles and dragonflies like the one now sharing his scalpel with him, a marsh which had a different smell for each stage of the tides, a marsh with swamp grass long and thin and sharp enough to cut the tender feet of boys fool enough to walk on it barefoot. On those long-ago summer days of his childhood when the Scotch he now drinks still aged in some barrel in a warehouse somewhere in Scotland, Minnie believed every dragonfly in the whole wide world lived in the marsh at Camp Aquidneck. Now, wise with age, he knows better.

Minnie begins to sketch the dragonfly atop the scalpel, its long cylindrical trunk, the double sets of wings on each side, the triple sets of arms, the camouflage spots on its wings, the bulbous eyes jutting out from its head like door knobs. He wonders how many of him the dragonfly sees. Dozens if it sees the way other flies do. Dozens. Minnie drinks another swig of Scotch and holds it in his mouth. The alcohol enters his system through the membranes of his cheeks and tongue. And he draws. And each line he draws makes him think of

Fall River. And with each line he wishes Malone had been at Camp Aquidneck with him, staring at dragonflies and learning how to swim and sail and water ski and fish and braid bracelets out of gimp or rope and tell dirty jokes even if Malone didn't understand them. How different their universe would be. Malone would not go to law school. M'Boto would not be dead. Malone would not marry Dinitia who would be Mrs. Merisi Minifie, married to a man who wore the scars of bravery on his face, the scars of cowardice on his soul. Minnie completes a second sketch looking down from above at the dragonfly. A third from the back. A fourth and a fifth, the dragonflies of Camp Aquidneck. A sixth with the Three Musketeers, Malone, Dinitia, himself, flying astride dragonflies into the sunset. One for all and all for one.

Inside the landing zone, the men finish reading their mail and the football game resumes. Minnie can tell by the cheers when touchdowns are scored. He can tell by Ratfucker's obscenities broadcast over the official army issue field sound amplification system which side scores. The combat troops. Always the combat troops. Cheers but no cheerleaders, the one thing missing from Ratfucker's football games. Minnie misses their short black skirts and red undies and heavy white sweaters with a capital D over the breasts. He misses their red and black pompoms and their megaphones. He misses their pyramids and cartwheels. He misses Laurie Williams and the sense she gives him of being rooted in a particular place at a particular time. Nursing school. An R. P. N. Working at Charlton Memorial Hospital. She understands. In a way Dinitia doesn't. Poor Minnie never realizes it.

The cheers quiet down and Minnie hears a gun shot and he looks at the scoreboard to check the final score, but the clock says there are still three minutes to play and the men are still on the field lined up waiting for the center to hike the ball to the quarterback and Minnie realizes that the fire spreading through his gut is not from the Scotch but from whatever now causes his uniform to darken and liquefy. Minnie topples backward off the wall, the scalpel falling with him. The dragonfly rises up and alights on his chest and now they look at each other like two neighbors gossiping across a backyard fence and Minnie can see himself and himself and himself many times over reflected in its bulbous eyes. And he can feel the fire spread down his legs and the wetness with it and he wonders why the wet doesn't douse the fire and he tries to lift his head but the dragonfly buzzes and Minnie obediently lowers his head and rests it on a leftover sandbag.

Hobo also hears the gun shot and sees Minnie sprawled at the base of the sandbags and races through LZ Yellow Jacket to the trench and across the plank where he tries to brush the dragonfly aside, but Minnie, weakly, grabs his arm and whispers something about the king's horses and the king's men.

"Medics are coming," Hobo says. "Stay with me."

Minnie smiles at Hobo and winks at the dragonfly and sees his wink reflected back a dozen times and the dragonfly lifts off Minnie's chest with the slightest and lightest of buzzing and flies into the jungle bearing away Minnie's soul on its vibrating wings, bearing away the secret Minnie vowed to take to his grave. And Hobo checks Minnie for vitals and closes Minnie's eyes when he feels none and retrieves Minnie's sketch book and is about to close it when a breeze lifts the page of dragonflies and on the next two pages Hobo sees sketches of himself, one for his daughter, the other for Miss Edna, pencil sketches that make him look braver and stronger than he's ever been and handsomer and nobler than he ever will be, and he tears them from the sketch book and folds them neatly into a square and places them inside his shirt above his heart, clipping them to the chain that holds his dog tags, and he knows the way combat soldiers in a war zone know things ordinary people don't, things about life and death, that as long as he carries these sketches over his heart he will survive the war and return home from Vietnam to his wife and daughter and to Miss Edna a whole man.

Men gather now. Some help carry Minnie's body to the LZ morgue to be tagged and bagged and stored until the dustoff picks it up for the first step of its long journey from LZ Yellow Jacket to Fall River, to Vincenzo and Therese, to the Minifie Funeral Home. In the confusion, Minnie's sacred scalpel slips from the sandbag and falls into the loose dirt where it will rust in the rain and humidity and be buried in the mud until the jungle swallows it up as it will, someday, LZ Yellow Jacket. Other men comfort Hobo, each of them sad, but each of them also grateful, grateful that this particular bullet in this particular place at this particular time had Minnie's name on it, not theirs. It is the peculiar nature of sadness in a war zone that Hobo, the saddest of these sad men, is also grateful.

Vietnam.

May 31, 1968

I regret not having made peace with Minnie before his induction, his shipping out to Vietnam. If not for his sake or mine, for Dinitia's. Absolve her, them, for her loving him. I couldn't if Minnie told her the secret that we vowed never to tell anyone. Telling her to seduce her. To favor him over me. I understand now why Dinitia gave me the Dali. To remind me every day of our marriage she preferred Minnie over me. The dead have no regrets.

Come nightfall, in Boston's Fenway Park the Red Sox will shut out the Baltimore Orioles, a five hit complete game by Gary Bell, solo home runs by Yaz and Hawk Harrelson, their 22nd win against 23 losses. 29,301 fans will attend. If Harvard Law had accepted me rather than wait listing me, there would have been 29,302. Or, 29,303 if I had married Julia who shared my devotion to the Red Sox. Dinitia would not have gone. She sails alone; I go to Sox games alone. We'd clash over which our children would embrace, if we had children. Either? Both? Neither? But I will not be at Fenway Park this evening. I will be in a hospital room three blocks downtown from the popup toaster of Columbia Law School. Maybe I should have gone to Boston College Law or BU or one of those accounting colleges Da favored. My head would be in one piece.

The next morning, Dinitia will read the box score to me and I will know the truth of the Red Sox victory. When she reads Frank Robinson pinch hit, I ask why didn't he start, but she doesn't know. Julia would have.

I will ask Dinitia to close the door to my room. I will ask her to close the curtain until it surrounds my bed. I will ask her to peel back the blankets, lift my hospital johnnie, expose me, I will ask her to use her hands and mouth to relieve the tension that I cannot relieve for myself because neither of my shoulders are fully functional. She will say no, as she always does. Julia, more egalitarian would say, as she often did, I will if you will. At least Dinitia reads me the box scores.

Day by day in May, the weather warms and the trees along Broadway, Dinitia tells me, are in bloom. The month drags along. My vision begins to clear and St. Luke's transfers me out of the Intensive Care Unit to a regular bed. My broken ribs and other non-cranial injuries heal enough to enable me to begin physical therapy and I now spend several hours a day slowly relearning how to do things like walking or using the bathroom. My muscles and nerves and brain must be retrained, reprogrammed, muscle memory restored, my physical therapist tells me as if I were an Isaac Asimov robot whose memory circuits shorted out. Robots dream of electric sheep. No, it's androids. I undergo a battery of tests to determine the extent of my brain function. Match the shapes. Match the colors. Match the patterns. List the differences between these two pictures. Connect the dots. Draw a circle. Draw a stick figure. Toss the ball from one hand to another. Toss the bean bag through the hole. Paint by number. Recite the alphabet. Count backwards from one hundred. I see Dick run. Jane run. Spot run. I see Dick and Jane run. I see them play ball and chase the ball and do whatever else first graders do. At times their faces are clear. At times blurred. At times double-imaged. Patience, Dr. Robey counsels. Will he be able to paint again, Ma wants to know, Dinitia wants to know. As for me, que sera sera.

Can I skip second grade, I ask Dr. Robey. She approves a television for my room when I promise not to watch it when my eyes tire. Ironside solves another crime. The Defenders win another case. The Cartwrights capture another rustler. Tarzan thwarts another ivory poacher. *Million Dollar Movie* reprises classic Westerns like *High Noon, Shane, Stagecoach,* classic monster movies like *Them, Creature from the Black Lagoon, Invasion of the Body Snatchers, The Thing.* On *Star Trek*, Bones McCoy reconnects Spock's brain, stolen from his head by aliens, to his nervous system. Kirk watches. It's delicate surgery, Bones says. Very risky. A million things could go wrong. The operation succeeds. Spock recovers. Instantaneously. Without therapy. Without tests. In time to joke with Kirk and Bones on the bridge of the Enterprise before the final fade out. As good as new, Spock is. Better than new. I'm not. The next time I see Dr. Robey I ask if she earned her medical degree at Star Fleet Academy. She doesn't know what I'm talking about. Robots or androids, no difference.

On the Tuesday before Memorial Day, I hobble for the first time without the assistance of a cane or walker to the patients' lounge. When I return to my room, Dinitia huddles in a chair, hugging herself, weeping into her shoulder like a bird burying its beak beneath its wing. When she sees me, she wraps her arms around me and nestles her cheek against my neck.

My body shakes violently with the force of her sobbing my legs and sides ache. My bones, still brittle from the beating, feel on the verge of shattering into thousands of shards. I stroke her hair and whisper in her ear and, as I do, the room fills with blank canvases, easel after easel each with a blank canvas waiting for an artist to make it complete and I suddenly realize I see places I haven't been and things I haven't experienced, visions as clear and detailed as if I am the man on the cave wall being attacked for all eternity by a wounded bison.

"Dead," she whispers. "Sniper while doing pencil drawings in his sketchbook."

"Suicide by sniper."

"At least he died doing what made him happy."

"He stopped being happy years ago."

I feel complicit with the sniper, his co-conspirator. I gave up too easily trying to persuade Minnie to abandon his death wish. We were just kids. Sinners in God's eyes; sinners in our own. Absolution not from reciting Hail Marys but from the sharp blade of Minnie's sacred scalpel. For me, but not for him. Jesus in heaven would have had no more success than I did. It was His finger on the trigger. Not mine. Minnie's dead and I killed him.

This, the last time, the time when Minnie succeeds, makes me think of the first time. We were young kids then, our brains pre-adolescent, our intellects too immature to calculate risk. It had happened, the it we vowed never to speak of to others, a few weeks before Minnie made what I later recognized was his first suicide attempt.

We had exited North Park on to the sidewalk beside President Avenue opposite High Street, waiting with our bikes for an opening in traffic to zip across. President Avenue was (and still is) a long steep hill from

Highland Avenue down to North Main Street. Several streets intersected it, creating flats, some like Belmont and Rock continuing into North Park, others like Underwood, High and June dead-ending at President Avenue. It was a perfect hill for sledding, but the city never closed it to traffic because it was also Route 6, the main route through Fall River from Watuppa Pond to the Taunton River before the Interstate now bisecting downtown was built. Cars, especially those driven by teenagers, raced up and down President Avenue, bottoming out on the flats, sparks flying as tailpipes and mufflers, sometimes bumpers, scraped the pavement. Drag racing in the dead of night claimed one or two lives every summer. Long haul trucks, whether going up or down, labored, straining their gear boxes, the stink of their burning brake pads fouling the air.

The more we waited, the more Minnie fidgeted. I teased him about having ants in his pants. Not in my pants, he said. Minnie wheeled his bike back into North Park, a fifty-yard dash from President Avenue. He had a Schwinn three speed, an English racer, with caliper hand brakes mounted on the handlebars below the hand grips, pencil thin black fenders, pencil thin tires. Red and black streamers, the colors of BMC Durfee High School, flared out from the hand grips when he pedaled at full speed. My bike, bought used at a church rummage sale, had one speed, fat wheels, fat fenders, and old-fashioned pedal brakes that only engaged when I stood up and shifted my weight back.

"Watch this," Minnie shouted as he mounted his bike. With a loud 'Hi, Ho, Silver, Away!' he pedaled hard toward President Avenue, not slowing at the sidewalk, accelerating into the downhill traffic, missing the rear of a panel truck by a hair. The car behind the panel truck slammed on its breaks, fishtailing, straddling President Avenue, its front end pointing up High Street. A pickup truck broadsided the car.

Minnie pumped his bike as if he had superhuman strength, not veering left or right, sneaking between traffic in the uphill lane, slapping the hood of one car with the flat of his hand. "Hi, ho, Silver! Away!" he shouted again as he pedaled up High Street.

The driver of the pickup noticed me, waved, yelled, started toward me. I retreated into North Park as fast as my bike would let me, exiting on Hood Street. My legs ached as I squeezed as much from the bike's one speed as I could. I knew the neighborhood from winters throwing snowballs at traffic on President Avenue then running to escape drivers who stopped. I knew what yards connected to other yards, what streets had houses with tall hedges or thick bushes to hide behind, what garages had side doors left unlocked. The pickup driver cursed as he crossed back and forth in front of the house in whose bushes I hid. In the distance I heard police sirens. To keep quiet, to avoid crying, I bit my tongue.

The next day at school Minnie laughed and called me a sissy when I told him he was crazy, that he could have been killed. Better than the roller coaster at Lincoln Park, he said. I didn't know; I had never ridden it.

A few weeks later Minnie tried again at the Belmont Street intersection, then a third time opposite Underwood, a fourth at Rock Street. After Rock Street, Minnie said, it was like kissing his Aunt Honora, that he had to find something more exciting to replace it. And, he did. Maybe I should have tried harder to stop him. Maybe I should have told his folks. Maybe I should have given his name to the police or one of the drivers involved in the accidents he caused. But, I didn't. We were just kids. Now, we're adults and Minnie's dead and I killed him.

Dinitia soaks me with her tears, my cheek and hair,

my neck and shoulder, the cloth of my hospital gown. The wetness drips down my back and my arm and in spite of the heat of her tears and the way they burn my skin, they chill me like a soaking November rain when the temperature hovers above freezing and the sky is leaden gray. Would she cry like this for me? Did she while I lay in my coma? Would she answer truthfully if I ask her? Questions whose answers I pray I never learn.

Pain fills my emptiness and I know that I will live with this pain for the rest of my life. When I walk too much or stand too long or the weather changes. When I sleep in the wrong position. When I get in and out of a car. When I make love. When I steady my hand to add a brush stroke to a painting. If ever I add a brush stroke to a painting. Pain will be the only answer God will ever give me as I spend my life trying to understand why the law student survives and the artist dies.

Pencil in hand, Minnie died. His boots on. Mine will be off, at my desk, encased in a three-piece suit, surrounded by memos and contracts and wills and trusts, my eyes glazed over by whereases and heretofores, stacks of pink telephone message slips overflowing inboxes and outboxes. Lawyers don't die pencil in hand. They die when they're sworn in as members of the bar, when they're given their first Montblanc pen as a law school graduation gift, if they haven't died when they first enroll in law school. I squeeze Dinitia and she hugs me. The force of her hug detonates explosions of pain throughout my body and I beg her to hug me harder and she does. Minnie's dead. He died pencil in hand. I hope Dinitia didn't die with him.

Our secret. I ask myself if Minnie's death relieves me of my vow to take it to my grave.

Before the time of television, before the time of Movietone News, before the time of photographs, art, paintings and drawings and to a limited extent sculpture, were the media for the visual depiction of history. The earliest art, the art that came before writing, before language, the cave paintings of Lascaux, France, Addaura, Sicily, El Cerro Felio or Altimira, Spain, told stories with the same certainty as Herodotus or Thucydides or Gibbons or H. G. Wells or Bruce Catton writing about the Civil War. We stand before a cave painting in Lascaux. 15,000 years ago, a wounded bison attacked a man. 15,000 years from now, if the cave painting survives, if there are sentient beings to stand before it, a wounded bison will attack a man. The philosopher argues that only the past and future exist, that the present has no existence. For the artist, the past and future do not exist, but conflate in the present. For the artist, only the present exists. On June 4, 1968, a wounded bison attacks a man.

❧ ❧ ❧

On Tuesday night, June 4, 1968, the three networks broadcast the results of the California presidential primary. Kennedy. McCarthy. Humphrey. Because of the progress of my recovery, Dr. Karen Robey, after consulting with Dr. Archibald 'Hendu' Henderson, schedules me to be discharged in a day or two or three barring a relapse. Thursday or Friday. Medical progress. The only progress. Everything else is regress.

Home. An apartment a block from the hospital, a one bedroom in graduate student housing owned and operated by Columbia University, the friends we've made who live in the building, the gourmet group, the bridge group, the children who give us all a chance to play mommy and daddy without having to change diapers, Tim and Tom from the business school, Jack from the physics department, Al from... I cannot remember from where. I remember Columbia. British Columbia? District of Columbia? Columbia, Missouri? Columbia University, Roll on, Columbia. Columbia, Roll On? My memory is as scrambled as eggs on a hash house grill.

Home. The middle floor of a three decker in Fall River, Ma and Da, no brothers no sisters, a bus driver and stitcher on the top floor, a furniture salesman, the landlord, on the first floor. A steep hill. Stairs. Thousands of stairs. More stairs than the Washington Monument or the Empire State Building. Enough stairs to climb from the pit of Hell to the crown of Heaven. All of Fall River visible from the living room window. All of New Bedford from the back bedroom. All of Providence from the kitchen. All of Lincoln Park. The Ferris wheel. The roller coaster. The Death Wheel. The grocery booth. The cigarette booth.

Dinitia brings me photos of our apartment. Familiar things, the doctors advise. Stimulate his memory, they urge. Forge new neural connections. Maybe I don't want new neural connections forged. Maybe I don't want my memory stimulated. Maybe I want it erased. Or, at least certain parts of it. The part I vowed to take to my grave. I deserve a say in what to pick, what to choose. To reject a memory, I need to remember it. Photos, I urge. More photos. The tiny galley kitchen where I cooked coq au vin when it was the husbands' turn to prepare dinner for the gourmet group. The living room with the desk where I studied law. The bedroom with my oil painting, *Talking of Michelangelo*, that someone wanted to buy for $25,000.00. $50,000.00. $100,000.00. I don't remember. Not that how much matters. I refused to sell even though Ma needed the money. Dinitia does not forgive me for abandoning Ma. Little, if anything, does she know about needing money, heir to two fortunes, one eight figures, the other nine. It makes no sense that she, rich enough to light her joints with c-notes if she chooses, gives up her career as an artist to work a shit job and support an impoverished law student. If all happy families are happy in the same way, all stubborn people are stubborn in their own way. Why blame me. I am not a musician, I tell her, who can play the music again, an author who can buy another copy of his book or borrow it from the library. A print, a poster, is no substitute for the real thing. Nor is visiting it in a museum which is like visiting me in the hospital when I was still in a coma. She does not understand. But she does for she knows I am lying when I explain why I won't sell my paintings. I see it in her eyes. I see it in the twitch of her fingers. The slight tightening in the muscles in her neck.

Her pushing me away when I try to initiate sex. Neither did Julia understand; but in Julia's ignorance there was a seed of tolerance that one day, maybe, would bloom. If Dinitia harbored such a seed, it had hibernated long ago.

On television, Senator Robert F. Kennedy stands at the podium in the ballroom of the Ambassador Hotel in Los Angeles to deliver a victory speech to his cheering campaign workers. The Senator tells them and a national television audience, "Rosey Grier said he'd take care of anybody who didn't vote for me." When the laughter and applause and cheering quiets, Kennedy reminds us that "we are a great country, an unselfish country, and a compassionate country."

Anne Harley, my favorite nurse, pauses in the door. Her neck, long and thin and perfectly cylindrical, and her eyebrows, symmetrical arches of black on white, remind me of Gainsborough's Lady Rodney. If I had the talent, I would be her Rembrandt. She deserves it.

"We want to deal with our own problems," Kennedy says, "in our country and we want peace in Vietnam."

Anne playfully wags her finger at me. "Do I have to be putting you to bed like my five-year old?"

"So my thanks to all of you," Kennedy says, "and it's on to Chicago and let's win there."

❧ ❧ ❧

In our apartment, Dinitia exercises, Royal Canadian calisthenics, while she watches the California primary results, supercharged by the prospect of having me at home again, eating at the same table again, sleeping beside her again, eventually making love to her again. She cannot sleep. It's like the night before our wedding. She knows she'll be up all this night and the next night and every night until I return home and she hopes I won't look like the skull in a Frans Hals oil painting when she picks me up. She does pushups as the announcer informs the nation that "Senator Kennedy is exiting the ballroom through the back door. He will travel down a kitchen corridor to a nearby dining room that serves as a temporary press room."

Gunshots and Dinitia freezes at the top of a pushup.

"Somebody has set off some firecrackers," the announcer says. "Oh, my God! Gun shots. There have been several gunshots." The announcer and reporters rush in the direction of the gunshots, but security personnel block their way. "Several people have been wounded," the announcer says. "One of them is lying on the floor. It's... it's the Senator. Senator Kennedy has been shot."

Dinitia collapses from the top of her pushup.

❧ ❧ ❧

In Fall River, Massachusetts, Brigid Malone, my Ma, home from her vigil at St. Luke's Hospital, warms some milk. Since Da's death she no longer sleeps when it's dark. As the milk warms, she sits at the kitchen table and turns the pages of an album of family photographs, the same photos she looked at while warming milk the night before and the night before that, stretching back more nights to the night she'll never forget. She pauses as she has every other night at a photo of me as a young child playing with Da in the crawl space under the porch. She pours the warm milk into a cup, turns on the television, now her loyal companion, and returns to her memory book.

"I don't know how bad," the announcer says.

Brigid sips her milk and touches the images of Da

and me in the photo.

"He's on the floor," the announcer continues. "Surrounded by people."

The urgency of the television voice makes her look up. People run around, screaming, shouting. "They're calling for doctors," the announcer says. "Oh, no. A priest. A priest is kneeling beside the Senator. Please. Not again. Don't let this happen again."

❧ ❧ ❧

In the operating room at St. Luke's Hospital, Dr. Henderson, Dr. Robey, and the rest of Hendu's foxhole team perform emergency brain surgery on a pedestrian hit by a *Daily News* delivery truck that ran a red light. Duck soup compared to what happened to me. No one pries into Robey's romance with Sergeant Ben Greenbaum or teases her about wedding bells. No one requests Beach Boys or Stones or Beatles or Dylan, either electric or acoustic. They operate in silence except for the communication necessary for the surgery and listen to the radio to keep current with the news from California.

"Senator Kennedy," Frank Mankiewicz, Senator Kennedy's press secretary, announces from Good Samaritan Hospital, "will be taken into surgery in five or ten minutes for an operation of forty-five minutes to an hour."

"Those California doctors must be supermen," Henderson says.

"Or superwomen," Robey says.

Mankiewicz continues. "One bullet entered the Senator's brain past the mastoid bone back of the right ear. Some fragments lodged near the brain stem."

The surgery pauses as if by reflex and Archibald Henderson and Karen Robey and Guy Stevens and Raz

Fernandez and Bobbye Briscoe and Lizzie Wrick and Ella Valery look to each other for strength and comfort. Their eyes, the only parts of their bodies visible through the surgical garb, are flat and lifeless, the eyes of corpses newly dead, the eyes of their patient on the table, my eyes when Dr. Robey removed my bandages and I first opened them. Only the discipline of the operating room keeps them from crying.

Mankiewicz continues, "Another bullet will be removed from the back of the Senator's neck. A third bullet grazed the Senator's forehead."

Henderson blinks. "Let's go people. We can save our patient."

❧ ❧ ❧

Early morning at the police stables Ben Greenbaum and Gil DeNisco ready Blue Note and Thompson for another day's duty. As they curry their horses, DeNisco presses Greenbaum for details of his most recent date with Karen Robey, asking if they'll marry. Before Greenbaum replies, a stable hand shouts from the office that there's another bulletin on the Senator's medical condition.

"The surgical team," Mankiewicz tells the nation, "has now completed three hours of surgery. Senator Kennedy lost a considerable amount of blood," Mankiewicz pauses to compose himself, "as a result of the bullet that entered and passed through the mastoid bone on the right side of his head."

When DeNisco asks where the mastoid is, Greenbaum places his finger at the base of DeNisco's skull to the left of his right ear.

Mankiewicz looks up from his notes. "There may have been an impairment of the blood supply to the mid-brain, which the doctors explain as controlling, or at least governing, certain of the vital signs – pulse, heart, eye tracking, level of consciousness, although not directly the thinking processes." An aide hands Mankiewicz another sheet of paper. "The doctors say that the next twelve to thirty-six hours will be a very critical period. They list the Senator's condition as extremely critical."

※ ※ ※

Dr. Robey visits me during her rounds. She scolds me when I tell her Kennedy won't make it, then lapses into medical jargon. "Surprising recoveries of function are not uncommon," she says. "The central nervous system and the brain have great adaptive powers for overcoming trauma." Robey looks up from the notes she is entering on my chart. "Feel up to going home?"

"I don't remember where Al's from? A friend of ours from the building. We spent an evening talking about whether he should go home after he graduates and, now, I don't remember where he's from."

"Do you remember his last name?"

"He has a dog. A French dog."

My memory is like a blank canvas and I stand before it, afraid to make the first brush stroke.

※ ※ ※

The next morning, the morning of my last full day in the hospital, first light creeps across the campus of Columbia University, deserted except for the pigeons who rest in the eaves of the buildings and the squirrels who search in vain for trees and the rats and the roaches who share habitats in the bowels of the buildings and the occasional student returning to his dorm from a night of drinking at the West End or the Gold Rail. With first light, the scars of April's rioting are still visible on the skin of these same buildings. The University has begun to scrub and scrape and sandblast these scars and someday, unlike the scars on the University's soul, they will weather into oblivion like the grave markers in Colonial cemeteries. At first light, Alma Mater still presides over Columbia University but it is a University now existing only in memory, one that ceased to exist in reality one bloody week in April. Perhaps if past, present, and future alumni become amnesiacs, maybe they will open their checkbooks and contribute to the myth of Columbia; but not me. I will never forget. No matter how much I try.

On this very same morning, as I sleep in my hospital bed Frank Mankiewicz steps to the podium at Good Samaritan Hospital in Los Angeles: "I have a short announcement to read which I will read at this time. Senator Robert Francis Kennedy died at 1:44 A.M. today, June 6, 1968. He was 42 years old."

PART II

June 25, 1967–April 24, 1968

On the fourth Sunday in June, 1967, in the afternoon of a day when the blue of the sky is the same color as the blue of the ocean rendering invisible the horizon line, the Episcopal Bishop of New York assisted by the Episcopal Bishop of Rhode Island with musical interludes provide by the children's choir of St. John's the Divine marries Dinitia Marbury Madison (who to her parent's chagrin and my delight elects to retain her maiden name) and me on an expanse of green lawn extending for several hundred yards from the elevated patio behind the Pratt family mansion on Newport's Ocean Avenue (built originally for Baldwin Pratt at the turn of the century) to a marble half wall (Italian marble from the same quarry that supplied marble to the Vanderbilt and Astor estates) in the Roman style that separates the Pratt estate from Newport's Ocean Walk, a paved foot path along the Atlantic Ocean, unfortunately accessible to the public who walk their dogs and their children and gawk at those who only wish to live their lives with a modicum of privacy. Two off duty Newport police officers garbed in tuxedos guard the steps (the same Italian marble as the half wall) lest an untoward trespass be committed.

The night before the wedding, Dinitia gives me a combined wedding and college graduation gift. "From one artist to another," she says as I unwrap it.

"I don't have anything for you."

"You are the only gift I want."

"Dali?" I ask.

"One of his *Divine Comedy* illustrations. To commemorate the 700th anniversary of Dante's birth, the Italian government commissioned Dali to create 100 illustrations of the *Divine Comedy*. This is *Inferno: Canto 25* also known as *The Punishment of Vanni Fucci*."

"We read Dante freshman year. I don't remember Vanni Fucci."

"He stole from the Church, then blasphemed God by making the sign of the fig."

Memories flood my mind. The only way for her to know is if Minnie broke his vow of silence. Maybe on his deathbed, but for all his madbrain daredeviltry that's one bed he's yet to curl up on.

"Are you all right?" Dinitia asks. "You look like you've seen a ghost."

I have, I think to myself.

Now, on the patio, waiters fill and refill crystal champagne flutes and circulate with silver trays of canapés and hors d'oeuvres, nibbles as alien to me as the exotic foods Dinitia introduced me to during our courtship, black or red caviar, cucumber sliced thin with a pâté on water crackers, escargot boiled in sea water, other things I cannot identify. I yearn for real food: a shitburger from Joe's, medium rare, with a glass of cold milk; a pizza with the works from The Depot Café; a bowl of Indian pudding from The Grist Mill; roast leg of lamb on an orange Melmac dinner plate. Over the clink of crystal and sterling and the hum of polite conversation, some guests dance to music played by a twelve-piece society orchestra that winters in Palm Beach and summers in Newport and plays only standards, Gershwin and Porter being too avant-garde. Besides, one was Jewish, the other gay, both verboten at this level of society.

A photographer interrupts my dance with my bride to pose us against a backdrop of dancing couples, stiff and formal as if we are mounted on pieces of lumber. "I wish," Dinitia whispers, "we could have someone like Vermeer paint us."

"Wrong painter."

I visualize Toulouse-Lautrec. He starts with what he sees, accepting uncritically the facts of the scene before him. Because the flat planes of his colors fail to penetrate the surface of the painting, they would accentuate the shallowness of these wedding dancers. Those who preen would be immortalized preening and their delusions of self-importance would be vivified by flaming red-orange hair or frozen acid green faces or designer clothing as costume. Somewhere in the painting Toulouse-Lautrec would place himself, stunted and deformed, perhaps in the shadow of the aristocratic bearing of his cousin, Dr. Tapie de Celeyran, perhaps as a gentleman, perhaps as a waiter, perhaps as a musician, the way I hide in my paintings a crucifix soaking in a pool of blood. The faux and the real side by side within the same frame. Ma, a flash of silver to denote her gray hair. Dinitia, a patch of white. Me? He would punish me for rejecting what is for him salvation. Too subtle to impose his deformity on me, he would use color, blacks and sooty grays, and line, thick and jagged and he would call his painting *The Martyrdom of Saint Dinitia*.

Minnie's pony tail bounces against the back of his morning coat as he dances with one of the bridesmaids.

"Are you running at Saratoga in August," she teases, then laughs when he says "I prefer contact sports to track." Club rugby at Amherst College played as if his bones, his spine, his skull, were titanium rather than bone and cartilage. Suffering enough concussions to classify him 4-F for the draft. Minnie would never hide behind a concussion. Now, he abandons the bridesmaid on the dance floor and wanders among the tables like a young child on his first visit to the zoo, both frightened and fascinated by the animals. He eavesdrops on conversations.

"What a tiny diamond," one matron says. A stray spot of caviar stains the thumb of one of her white gloves. "I don't think they insure them that small, do they Chas?"

"Lloyd's will insure anything, Petunia." Chas's morning suit barely contains him. Stretch marks disfigure the button holes of the vest. His jowls droop over the collar of his shirt and when he speaks his skin ripples like a one of Monet's quiet ponds disturbed by a pebble.

"They met at college," another matron says, obscuring her mouth with a paper fan as if doing this confers anonymity on her.

"Where he was a scholarship boy," a third hisses. She grins with the moral superiority of a tattletale, exposing a snippet of snail caught in the gap separating her front teeth.

"Honoria, please," Chas says. "Some of my hardest workers are scholarship boys. I keep their salaries low to motivate them."

"She tutored him in Oriental art," Petunia says. Her caviar stain expands as the conversation proceeds. "That's how they fell in love."

Minnie commandeers an empty seat, turning it around and mounting it as if it is one of Saratoga's thoroughbreds. "Au contraire! They fell in love when she read *Madame Bovary* to him in French." Blank faces stare at him. "*Madame Bovary*," he repeats, then continues with a low, husky voice. "And they stayed in love because she prefers Nobuzane to Monet and makes love like Aphrodite possessed." Everyone titters except Chas who harumphs and Honoria who raises her fan to eye level. Minnie dismounts the chair and moves on.

"Young man!" Petunia calls after him. "Where did you get such a horrific scar?"

Minnie removes the leather carrier housing his sacred scalpel and slaps it on the table. It catches the sun. "Self-inflicted, Madam."

"I never... "

"Yes you have, Madam."

As the party winds down, I corner Minnie. "Did you tell Dinitia?"

"Tell her what?"

"You know what."

Minnie shakes his head.

"She gave me one of Dali's *Inferno* illustrations. *The Punishment of Vanni Fucci.* She even mentioned the sign of the fig. How did she know unless you told her?"

Another head shake.

"If not you, who? Did you tell anyone? Ever?"

Minnie puts his finger in front of his closed lips.

"When you were stoned? Drunk? Too wasted to remember?"

"No."

I eye Minnie. He cringes as he reads the skepticism in my face.

The party over, the musicians packing their instruments, the wait staff cleaning up, Reginald Madison and I stand at the marble half-wall. "What's her name," I ask a young girl pushing a doll in a baby carriage along Ocean Walk. She waves and giggles and mumbles something I do not understand. Her parents step up on either side of her as if I am an ogre who kidnaps young children for profit. In her mother's lips and her father's eyes I see her destiny. Someday she will make some man miserably unhappy. On the patio, Elizabeth Madison, Dinitia, the Pratts, and Ma rest at one of the tables. Delaney Pratt snatches open bottles of champagne and finishes them.

"Don't act like a common boor," Marcie Pratt chides.

"Quite," Delaney says. "A gentleman shares his good fortune with his brother-in-law and the groom." He balances himself on the patio like a landlubber searching for his sea legs on the deck of a yacht caught in rough chop, then stumbles from the patio to the lawn, tottering toward Reginald and me. I stare into the ocean searching for some mythical sea creature, a mermaid perhaps, or Poseidon or the Loch Ness monster or the lost city of Atlantis or an explanation for why the water is different shades of blue or the horizon line is invisible. If I could swim to Ireland, I would.

"We live for Dinitia's happiness," Reginald says, "especially Mrs. Madison."

"We live for the same thing, sir." The marble retains the heat from the afternoon sun and warms my forearms.

"As a wedding gift, a dowry as our forbearers would have it, I will finance your studio for a year or three until you're established."

"That's very generous, Mr. Madison. Didn't Dinitia tell you? I've been accepted at law school. Columbia in New York."

"I can line up some commissions for you. Portraits. Corporate assignments. Things to build your name. When you're ready, one of Mrs. Madison's Vassar classmates married the owner of Boscoreale on Madison Avenue. He owes me a courtesy."

"I couldn't... "

"Of course. Of course. But you're a college graduate

with a wife to support, a wife who belongs at the Museum School. She won't let me send her; ergo, you must."

"I promised Da I'd go to law school."

"Da?"

"My father."

"What did you promise my daughter?"

"To love, honor, and cherish."

"By forcing her to become a common laborer?"

"We want to build our own life, Mr. Madison."

Delaney Pratt lumbers up to the wall and smashes his champagne flute against the marble. Shards of crystal shower Ocean Walk. "What he's doing," Pratt says to me, "is what Lorenzo de Medici did for Michelangelo. It's a vision thing, Reggie. The best man has the vision, but not the talent. The groom has the talent, but not the vision. I hope my niece chose the right one."

"He's enrolling in law school, Delaney. Columbia." Reginald puts his arm across my shoulders. "I have college chums at all the best firms, Cravath, Milbank Tweed, Coudert Brothers, White and Case. You'll have your pick." He walks me toward the mansion, leaving Pratt to hold up the wall.

"Reggie... "

"Do not despair, Delaney. I will send someone to assist you straightaway."

As we stroll across the lawn, Reginald squeezes my shoulder. I stare down at my shoes, shiny and black against the green of the lawn. The line of the mansion's shadow now bisects the lawn and as I step out of the sunlight into the darkness I feel chilled,

❧ ❧ ❧

Dinitia and I celebrate our wedding night at the Biltmore in Providence, a gift from my ushers. I work the rest of the summer to pay for our honeymoon, a week in late August in Bermuda in a honeymoon cottage with a leak in the roof right above the bed. The first time the rain awakens us Dinitia says she did not expect to share her honeymoon bed with pots and pans and I reply that the memory will grow fonder each anniversary. Our cottage is on the ocean with a living room whose roof does not leak and a balcony facing the water where we breakfast every morning on fresh fruit, eggs, sausage or bacon, croissants and jam, coffee or tea, prepared by the maid assigned to our cottage. We rent Mopeds and tour the island from east to west and west to east and visit the coves where pirates plundered, the aquarium, the lighthouse, the shops, the old city. I develop a taste for bitter, a sacrilege for someone whose Da is a Guinness weanling, and Dinitia becomes enamored of shandies. At night, we go to the Steele drum band shows at the hotels, enter the limbo contests, make love in the surf, alert for the jellyfish that sometimes wash in with the tide, and argue about my post-college plans.

At the end of the week, our disagreement unresolved, Dinitia and I, red from our honeymoon, sun burned, too painful to touch each other, fly from Bermuda to New York and move into an apartment on Morningside Heights four downtown blocks, one cross town, from Columbia University School of Law. Minnie relocates to New York immediately after graduation, a loft south of Houston (SoHo to the natives, Minnie explains) with high ceilings, natural light, and security bars on the windows. The lease, he teases, forbids dogs, cats, and law students. The Broadway line, the 1, 2, and 3 trains, Local and Express, connect us.

September, 1967 – December, 1967

On the Sunday before the first day of class, Dinitia and I walk up Amsterdam Ave. past St. John the Divine and St. Luke's Hospital where I will be designated 'Patient of the Year' for 1968 to the Viennese Pastry Shop for an espresso and a pastry. We settle into a table with a view of the law school. A faint crescent moon, pale and wan in the morning sky, hangs over the building. "A bloody pop up toaster," Dinitia laughs. An enclosed balcony (I later learn it is a reading area in the law library) protrudes from the downtown facade of the building like the lever that lowers the bread between the toasting racks. Minnie, of course, concurs, adding that the Moore sculpture on the plaza opposite the main entrance does not justify the building's existence.

"In three years," I boast, "I'll graduate golden brown, ready to be buttered by Wall Street."

"Leonardo da Vinci's father was a lawyer," Dinitia says.

"Wasn't he a bastard?" Minnie asks.

"Two days back from Bermuda and it starts," I say.

"You should have married that mill dolly," Minnie says, "the one who fucks for cigarettes."

"Soda by the case," I correct him.

"A lawyer would be a hell of a catch for her."

"Clap is all she'll ever catch," I reply.

A lawyer would have been a hell of a catch for Julia, too. In her own way, she was also a mill dolly, except her daddy owned the mill and the closest she ever came to working in it was the summer the stitchers went on strike and she bungled her away around the sewing machines, breaking two before making a stitch worth saving.

Julia would never harangue me about dropping out of law school to be a painter. Her harangue would be about my wasting time painting when I could be golfing at her daddy's country club. I doubt I would have broken par. Julia would have given me lessons for my birthday or Christmas or Valentine's Day and cheered my every putt. Every husband needs a wife who cheers for him, but no husband needs a wife who cheers for him for the wrong reason.

That evening, I ride the train downtown to meet Minnie for supper at a Cuban restaurant after which we return to his loft where he inveigles me into mixing several tubes of paint, cerulean blue. Dinitia remains at the apartment, exhausted from a day spent unpacking moving boxes, setting up the kitchen, arranging her closet and chest of drawers. Standing at a work bench, I knead a glob of pigment, adding drops of oil, kneading it, adding oil, kneading it, until it is the consistency of paste. I spread it across a thick slab of glass with a plasterer's trowel. Minnie fills two meerschaums with grass and lights his, inhaling the flame from the match head and exhaling a tapered stream of smoke. Mine awaits me, a reward for a job well done. Viridian pigment streaks his face. "Rare talent, mixing paint," Minnie says. "Especially reds."

Reds. I never could mix reds. Still can't. For the crucifix in the pool of blood I hide in my paintings I use real blood. Not mine. Not Dinitia's. Swine blood purchased from a butcher. The irony of using swine blood appeals to my sense of payback, of just deserts. Demented, I am. Perverted. Not something about which reasonable people may differ, though the unreasonable might. New York has a neighborhood known as the Meatpacking District. Perhaps I will find swine blood there.

I continue to drip oil on to the paste, then grind the mixture into paint with a glass muller, twisting the knob of the muller until my arms and wrists ache. When the mixture becomes too watery, I thicken it with a pinch of pigment, then add linseed oil and aluminum stearate. I continue mulling and mixing, mixing and mulling.

Minnie raises his pipe in a toast. "To life in the pop-up toaster."

Grabbing the other meerschaum, I collapse on an easy chair salvaged from curb side. Flakes of white fly up from a tear in the fabric and settle down like a fine ash from a dying volcano. "To secrets carried to the grave."

Minnie picks pigment out from beneath his fingernails with the point of his sacred scalpel. "The two of you are worse than a couple of cab drivers fighting over a fucking fare."

I light the meerschaum; the grass calms me. A groan echoes in my head. I hear the aches and pains in my shoulders and arms and wrists. My vision penetrates my skin and I see my muscles and the blood in my veins, bursts of color, red like the fake blood in war movies. Hollywood should use swine blood. A throb of pain accompanies each burst of color. Leonardo da Vinci's father was a lawyer; there is hope for my children.

⚜ ⚜ ⚜

With classes scheduled to start on Wednesday, I spend Monday night, Tuesday, Tuesday night, reading and rereading my assignments for the first day, three classes, all before lunch, Torts from 8 to 9, Legal Method from 9 to 10, Contracts from 11 to 12, Civil Procedure from 2 to 3. I owe Ma nothing less than Law Review, a ticket to Wall Street where I can make enough money to support her. I will live the life of an artist vicariously through Minnie and, maybe, if I have a free Sunday afternoon, dabble at the easel. "Come to bed," Dinitia calls from the bedroom. We have not made love since two Sunday mornings ago and when Dinitia asks why I tell her I'm saving myself for a mill dolly.

"You've got talent and you have to honor that."

"Fuck honor. What do you know about being poor? When was the last time the electric shut off the lights? How many winters did you freeze nursing an empty oil tank? You knew my priorities before you said 'I do'. Did you think you could change them? If I had the genius of Michelangelo, Rembrandt, and Picasso cubed, Vermeer to the fourth, my priorities wouldn't change."

"I'd rather live poor with an artist than rich with a lawyer."

"Easy to say if daddy's paying the bills."

"He would."

"I'm the son of a mill dolly and a factory man. My children will be the grandchildren of a mill dolly and a factory man. That's the gene pool you married into and daddy's check book can't change the DNA."

Dinitia closes the bedroom door. I think of the young me reading the 'Can this marriage be saved?' column in the *Ladies Home Journal* Ma borrowed every month from one of the stitchers at work. A young child afraid the next column will be about his Ma, his Da. This marriage can be saved, yes, if the couples work at it. The clockwork conclusion. Month after month. Issue after issue. Column after column. If my marriage, our marriage, were the subject of a column, the clock would stop and the conclusion would be a question: What is there for these two people to work at? I will not quit law school. I will not sell my paintings. Collectors are obsessively possessive like jealous husbands who rage if someone says 'good morning' to their wives. I will not suffer the indignity of Matisse. If I want to change blue to red or red to blue, no collector, no gallery owner, will deny me. I will not suffer the indignity of Picasso who must purchase a poster of his *Guernica* from a museum gift shop if he wishes to hang it in his home. If I owned the *Book of Kells*, to sell it would be worse than selling my birthright. My paintings are my children, the only children I will ever have who are not the grandchildren of a mill dolly and a factory man and I will never sell them. I swear on the souls of Saint Catherine of Bologna and Saint Luke. I will never stop believing my lies.

The next morning, too apprehensive to eat breakfast yet hungry because I haven't, I sink into seat number 147 in the last row of Amphitheater C on the ground floor of the law school and slip my name sign into its holder. The law school book store sells a sign to each student with name and seat number at the modest cost of $4.95 plus New York State and New York City sales tax that we carry from class to class, always sitting in our assigned seats, the same in each amphitheater, always inserting the sign in its holder. I have never been in such large classes, more than 147 since there are several students with higher numbers in my row. At Amherst College where classes were much smaller, the professors learned everyone's name by the end of the first week. Law school obviously works on different principles.

"At least we're in the back row," I say by way of introduction to Serena Adams, number 148, one of several women in the class. She dresses as if class is a job interview at a Wall Street law firm, charcoal gray skirt, double breasted suit coat, starched white shirt, tie. I dress cowboy cool as if I am still at Amherst, blue jeans and a pullover, penny loafers, no socks. I feel self-conscious as more students pour into the room, most in suits, male or female versions, a few, country hicks who graduated state universities in the Midwest or south no doubt, in ties and sports jackets.

"They have seating charts," Adams whispers. "They put marks next to our names to track how often they call on us." Her voice quavers.

"Like notches in a gunfighter's belt," one of the students in front of us says. He also wears the lawyer's uniform, male version, a navy-blue suit, white shirt, regimental striped tie, pale blue and white, Columbia colors. "Scott Steffensen." He extends his hand over his shoulder.

Before I can introduce myself to Steffensen and Adams, a tall thin man wearing a judicial robe and carrying a riding crop swaggers across the front of the room to the podium. He cracks the riding crop against the side of the podium, then lays it across the podium in view of the entire class. "I am Graham Bradley III, John J. McCloy Professor of Torts," he announces in a full-throated voice, "but you shall address me as Sir. I am the Grand Inquisitor and you are my heretics to be punished or rewarded depending on the answers you give to my questions. Most of you will be punished. Some by the death known as expulsion or, in your childish gibberish, flunking out; others by disfigurement that will banish you from Law Review and the career paths that Law Review opens. A few, a very, very few, the select few, will achieve sainthood for it is my passion to correct the errors of Admissions and eliminate the unworthy."

My heart rate accelerates and I sneak a glance at Adams who is as pale as her white shirt. I wonder which of us will faint when called upon to recite. I am no longer willing to bet against myself. I want to open my casebook, one final read through, but the room is silent, everyone still. Any noise, any motion, will call attention to me and my wardrobe, the last thing I want on the first day of class. If God loves me, Sir will go alphabetically and I'll have time to see how it's done, learn from people's mistakes, figure out what torts is all about.

Sir scans the class, his fingertips never losing contact with the riding crop. "Which heretic shall I interrogate first?" I relax as Sir fixes his gaze on the left flank of the amphitheater. "Mr. Davidow! Mr. Joel Davidow." Davidow rises, quickly, steadily, and I marvel at his composure. He is thin, a pencil line inside a black suit. Thick curly hair obscures his ears. He wears a small circular hat as white as his complexion fastened to his hair with a bobby pin. "Sir." His voice is steady, evenly modulated, as if he's Sir's nephew. Or maybe he doesn't understand what's about to happen.

"My pencil, Mr. Davidow." Sir snaps his fingers and a pencil suddenly materializes in his hand the way a bird appears in the hand of a magician. "Is my pencil a dangerous instrumentality?"

Davidow clears his throat and the echo rattles around the amphitheater. "If used improperly. Sir."

"Is it inherently dangerous as that concept is articulated in *MacPherson v. Buick Motor Company*?"

"If you mean is it by its nature dangerous," Davidow says, "perhaps when it is sharpened."

"Perhaps when it is sharpened? From which book of the *Talmud* did you get that gem of wisdom?" Sir raps his riding crop against the side of the podium. "Mr.

Malone! Is the answer in the *Book of Kells*?"

"No, Sir." I lean against the desktop to steady myself and clasp my hands behind my back where Sir cannot see them shake.

"Do you march to a different drummer, Mr. Malone?"

"Sir?"

"Your choice of clothing. Did your mother lay out your clothes for you?"

"I live with my wife, Sir."

"What you wear in your wife's presence is of no concern to me, Mr. Malone. What you wear in mine, is. Now, what say you? Is a pencil an inherently dangerous instrumentality?"

"A pencil is not inherently dangerous in the *MacPherson* sense because it would be dangerous only if misused."

"Would it matter to you whether it is sharpened?"

"No."

"Even though it is said the pen is mightier than the sword?"

I want to evaporate, crouch behind my section of desk, hide like a young boy cowering behind a tree to avoid the neighborhood bully.

"A motor vehicle, Mr. Malone. If it is not misused, would it be dangerous?"

"No, Sir."

"Nor a gun."

I hesitate. "It could go off accidentally."

"But that would be misuse."

"The function of a gun is to kill, Sir. If used properly, it fulfills its function and that makes it inherently dangerous. To kill is not the function of a pencil or automobile."

Sir snaps his fingers again and a hand gun materializes; he points it at me. Most students gasp, perhaps at the legerdemain, perhaps at the gun, perhaps at both, but Sir ignores them. "If I were to pull the trigger and kill you, would I be using this gun properly or misusing it? What say you, Mr. Malone?"

"Please point that in another direction."

Sir places the gun it on the podium, still aimed at me. "Is it inherently dangerous now?"

"I guess not."

"I guess not what?"

"I guess not, Sir."

"Why not?"

I hesitate. "It is an inanimate object. It requires human intervention to be dangerous."

"Now consider the atomic bomb, Mr. Malone. If I understand your logic, such as it is, the atomic bomb while in the womb of the Engola Gay was not inherently dangerous because it was an inanimate object."

The class titters and Steffensen whispers 'Gotcha' under his breath.

Sir continues before I can speak, "What a sturdy foundation of quicksand you would build the law of torts upon, Mr. Malone. Go back to your *Book of Kells.* What say you, Mr. Davidow?"

"I would think an atomic bomb is inherently dangerous, Sir."

"A most provocative insight. Praise be God you were not sitting under the tree when the apple fell." Sir picks up the gun and with a snap of his fingers makes it evaporate into thin air. Somewhere in the middle of the amphitheater a student starts to applaud, but stops when no one joins in. "I must say Admissions failed with the Class of 1970. You are all too dumb to teach. I shall turn the class over to Mr. Davidow and Mr. Malone who will instruct you in the *Talmud* and the *Book of Kells.* On Friday there shall be a quiz on those texts. On Monday I shall resume my attempts to teach torts but only to those who pass the quiz." Sir sticks his riding crop under his arm as imperiously as a British soldier in the colonial era and strides from the room, barely flexing his knees.

The class sits motionless, silent, paralyzed by the unknown, uncertain whether Sir will return, uncertain whether they should remain in the amphitheater until the bell rings, uncertain whether any of them will pass Torts, graduate law school, become lawyers. After several moments, one or two, then more, then everyone, turns to look first at Davidow, then me, to ask the people on either side of them whether they think Sir meant it, whether Davidow and I will teach the *Talmud* and the *Book of Kells*, whether there will be a quiz Friday, whether it will count toward their course grade, whether those who fail the quiz will flunk out.

"I'm out of here," I announce to the class. I am not the first to reach the door.

Legal Method is less abusive, as are Contracts and Civil Procedure whose professor justifies this teaching methodology as both necessary and essential to prepare us for the hurly-burly of practicing law. "The philosophy of the Marine Corps," he tells us, "is that basic training should be tougher than war. That also is the philosophy of those of us who teach first year law students. In your dotage, you will speak of us with warm nostalgia," he assures us, "and consider us milquetoasts compared to the judges and other attorneys you encounter."

"If you survive Sir," Dinitia says over supper, "you'll survive the slings and arrows of the most outrageous art critics."

"I do not plan to expose myself to those slings and arrows," I reply. She sulks and I study and she gets her period. Making love or not making love temporarily ceases to be a political statement.

Sir, as promised, gives his Torts class what he characterizes as a quiz but what I characterize as an hour exam. It fills the entire class hour and the answers to the half dozen questions, three each on the *Talmud* and the *Book of Kells*, fill two blue books. About the *Talmud*, I know nothing. About the *Book of Kells*, I know less than someone with my name should. Sir never passes back the 'quiz' and resumes teaching Torts the following Monday without banishing Davidow or me or anyone else from the class although he threatens banishment of one student or another at least once a week. No one inquires of Sir about the results of the quiz, nor whether it counts toward the grade and Sir seems disinclined to disclose this information. I wear a suit to school on Mondays, Wednesdays, and Fridays, the days I have Torts, and dress cowboy cool on Tuesdays, Thursdays, and Saturdays. I am not the only person in the Class of 1970 who adheres to one dress code for Sir, another for their other teachers.

As law school drags on through the fall and into the winter, Torts remains in a universe of its own as unlike the other first year courses as law school is unlike college. Sir wears the same judicial robe to each class and continues to perform magic tricks, at least two every class; but no more guns. Nor does he levitate any of the students. Nor saw them in half, at least not as a magical illusion. Most students, Davidow and I included, would have preferred being sawed in half to being skewered in front of the class, to dying the death of a thousand cuts, each inflicted in accordance with the Socratic method of recitation. If an enterprising law student set up a hemlock stand beside the Sabrett hot dog vendor on the corner of Amsterdam and W. 116th St., he would make such a large fortune that graduating law school and passing the bar exam would impoverish him. Or her. And best of all, from a marketing point of view, every September several hundred new customers.

When Dinitia's period ends we apologize to each

other and make love with the intensity peculiar to lovers having an affair. If our marriage is nothing more than an affair, it can't sustain itself on makeup sex.

Two weeks after Pearl Harbor Day. The winter solstice. The end of classes. The beginning of Christmas vacation, in reality a pre-exam reading period as finals start on Wednesday, January 3, 1968. Dinitia and I celebrate by visiting Minnie's loft for eggnog, roasted chestnuts, and Guatemalan Red. Her idea. My excuse, needing to study for finals, unable to persuade her to leave me home. We contribute a fifth of Bacardi Dark and a tin of cinnamon to flavor the nog. Minnie doesn't cook and doesn't know from spices. He and I share a water pipe – share meaning we alternate sucking on the pipe stem – while Dinitia indulges with a meerschaum. As we talk, the loft fills with smoke that descends on us like a lowering fog, like sewer gas Dinitia observes. As if you know from sewer gas Minnie challenges and Dinitia asks him if he ever toured the sewers of Paris. Minnie changes the subject to his Christmas trip to Italy where he will meet his parents at the Vatican for Christmas Eve Mass at St. Peter's, then travel to Firenze to visit the art he missed the previous summer, revisit the art he didn't. The joys of not having final exams, he teases.

"Absolution by the pope," I say. "What could be better?"

Minnie masks his cringe by blowing bubbles in the water pipe like a toddler playing with a straw. "Either of you do any painting this fall?"

Dinitia wanders over to the window that looks out on the air shaft separating Minnie's building from the adjacent buildings. Walls and windows are the predominant view in the loft district. Smoke from her meerschaum trails behind her like a swarm of honey bees trailing a woman wearing a flowery perfume. At the window, she sketches designs in the film of soot glazing the glass. With each sketch, the temptation to talk to her father over Christmas vacation grows, the same way her euphoria, as natural as a plastic Christmas tree, grows with each drag on the meerschaum. Her father will, if she asks, pay her tuition to the Museum School and deposit money in her bank account each week equal to what she earns in her office job. And if she doesn't paint at home, I may never find out; but if I do, I will feel she is cheating on me worse than if she sleeps with Minnie or the panhandler who cashes in several hundred dollars a week of small change in the liquor store on the street floor of our apartment building.

I suffer my hang-up without understanding it. We cobble together my law school tuition out of Dinitia's wages, savings from my summer jobs. I don't want her father paying my way in law school any more than his setting me up in a studio, arranging portrait commissions even though it would make her happy. Pride goeth before a fall, is the cliché. I am fated to read things into the way she looks at Minnie, laughs at his bad jokes, softens her criticism when comparing his paintings to mine. I wish I remembered what my Da of blessed memory said about not being mulish, a gene I must have inherited from my Da's Da.

Dinitia concentrates on the soot. On bad days, you can see the particulates in the air. On short walks such as the two blocks to the Daitch Shopwell supermarket or the four blocks to the pop-up toaster or the one block to the Gold Rail for a pitcher of beer and a cheap steak, the particulates settle in the hair and coat the skin. On long walks to the neighborhood revival movie houses for a Marx Brothers or Bogie double features or a Bergman or Truffaut or Godard or Welles retrospective, fifteen blocks to the Thalia on W. 97th St. or twenty-four blocks to the New Yorker on Broadway near W. 88th St., the particulates lodge in the nasal passages, on the tongue, on the lining of the cheeks, under the eye lids, on the surface of the eyes. In the summer, the more aggressive particulates enter the body through the pores in the skin. We no longer wear white outdoors because light colored clothing must be washed or dry-cleaned every third or fourth wearing to prevent the dingy pallor of the particulates becoming permanent. Indoors offers no refuge as the particulates seep into our apartment or the apartments of our friends or Minnie's loft through the cracks in the window frames and the openings between the window and the sash where the wood shrank or warped. Like roaches or rats, the particulates cannot be kept at bay except perhaps in luxury apartments and modern office towers where the windows, sealed against the elements, do not open. Somehow, we learn to cope.

Dinitia cranes her neck upward and peers through the bars of the security grate in search of the patch of sky hanging above the air shaft. It snows like crazy, but she can't see a fucking flake. Rarely will a snow flake survive the slow descent into an air shaft. Minnie turns on the television for the 6:00 news in time to catch the network feed from Vietnam. "Twenty-three Americans lost their lives during the last twenty-four hours," the announcer informs the United States, or at least those citizens watching NBC. Other announcers similarly inform the citizens tuned into the ABC or CBS. The NBC announcer steps to the side and the corpses of dead Americans, the bodies of wounded Americans awaiting Medivac, are guests in living rooms and dens and kitchens and bars throughout the country. "One hundred eighty-six Americans have been wounded and another fifteen are missing in action."

I stare at the dead bodies and feel my consciousness leave my body and pass through the television to Vietnam. One-third of my law school class will not return for their second year in September. Odds are several, or more, will end up in a future newscast, dead bodies anonymous to all but family and friends. I stand before the dead soldiers and I can see their skin through their uniforms and I can see inside their skin as if it is both there and not there, transparent and opaque, their muscles, their nerves, their veins and arteries, the blood no longer flowing but settling instead to the low point where gravity pulls it, their organs, and their bones, some whole, some broken, many shattered by land mines and grenades and ordnance. I am in the middle of an anatomy lesson, a life drawing lesson, a lesson worthy of Rembrandt or Da Vinci who at least learned anatomy from corpses dead from illness or other natural causes, dissected for the benefit of medical students.

"According to unconfirmed reports," the announcer who now stands beside me continues, "General Westmoreland has requested an additional 25,000 troops. He reportedly has assured President Johnson that the war will soon be over."

"Westmoreland promised the war would be over by Christmas," Dinitia says.

"Four more days," I say.

"Three," Minnie says. "Never count today."

"Four. Count today. Don't count Christmas."

"Five," Dinitia says.

"Christmas, 2001," Minnie says.

I wave the mouthpiece of the hookah over my head in a lazy figure 8, the infinity symbol. Glassy eyed and loopy from the grass I don't notice the news reporter by my side metamorphose into a pretty young thing selling tooth paste or shaving cream or mouthwash or after-shave lotion or cologne or some other toiletry no man can live without except the soldiers in Vietnam happy to be alive who would trade all the money earned by Proctor & Gambol and Colgate-Palmolive from the beginning of time to the present for passage home sitting on a seat, sipping a beer, rather than stuffed inside a body bag, a dead filling baked into a puff pastry.

She smells sweet, this pretty young thing, sweet and ripe, and I wish I could see through her clothing, but I can't because she is not dead or wounded or maimed or mauled. I reach for her, but grab only air where her breasts should be. A groan echoes in my ears, the sound of a hospital ward that has run out of morphine, and I wonder if it is the pain of the wounded soldiers awaiting triage or my own pain. I ask the pretty young thing and she tells me I will smell and taste the pain of the soldiers as if I were one with them. I have no idea what pain tastes like. Or smells like. I catalog the possibilities. The smell of an antiseptic. The taste of medicinal alcohol. Formaldehyde. The chemicals Vincenzo Minifie pumps into the veins of dead bodies to preserve them for all eternity. Or, something burning. An electrical fire, perhaps, thick with the black smoke of burning wire. A barbecue of spoiled meat. Flesh charred by a jolt of electricity, a bolt of lightning. My mind seizes up.

I wait for the smell, the taste, and when it comes it's like I haven't brushed my teeth or rinsed my mouth for weeks, grit and dust melding with the inside of my cheeks, my tongue, my lips, desiccating them, parching them, until fissures open like the fissures in a farmer's field in the middle of a summer drought, the mouth of an infantry grunt half way through a month on patrol in country with no toothpaste, no mouthwash, who won't hazard the rain water because he fears malaria or dysentery more than he fears the Viet Cong or the North Vietnamese or the incompetence of his own first looie.

I treat myself to another draw from the hookah. The grass intensifies my senses and I look up the skirt of the pretty young thing. She doesn't wear undies and her cunt, dripping sweet honey, blows me a kiss. A medic leans over me, checking my vital signs, searching my uniform for blood, asking me where I was hit, where it hurts. "*Guernica* lives," I whimper.

Minnie cracks open another chestnut and I jump at the sound of gunfire. He sucks out its sweet yellow meat. Shards of black chestnut shell cling to his sweater like bullet fragments. Others collect in his lap. A few float on his eggnog, swimming with the cinnamon. "I got us a project, O Great Musketeer of the mystic East," Minnie says.

The medic disappears. As do the pretty young thing and the news reporter. As do the bodies. In their places, today's closing Dow Jones average, Wall Street's popularity poll on Vietnam's folly. Up, down, unchanged, the war grinds on. Tomorrow's weather. The early sports. Knicks this, Rangers that; not that anyone gives a fuck. I forsake the hookah for a glass of eggnog and pour a jigger, two jiggers, of dark rum into it, stirring it with my finger.

"He's got finals around the corner and only four days between semesters," Dinitia says. Her breath fogs the designs in the soot and she erases them with the flat of her palm, staining her beautiful Carrere marble skin. A chunk of time disappears. Seconds. Minutes. Hours.

Days. I don't know. Time could not have existed before God created the universe. The Big Bang must have been the fuck of all fucks. If everyone forgets I scored Durfee's winning basket, it never happened. I down the eggnog like I'm gulping orange juice, then refill my glass, eggnog and rum, equal portions, dumping on cinnamon. It floats like brown pond scum.

Minnie perseveres. "A series of oils illustrating Eliot's *The Love Song of J. Alfred Prufrock*." He spits out a piece of shell and takes another suck on the water pipe. "I'm starting with 'I measured out my life with coffee spoons.' Except I'm going to use shells instead of coffee spoons. Ammo shells. Live or blanks? Who the fuck knows. Ol' Thomas Stearns didn't say."

"Coffee spoons," I say. "It has to be coffee spoons." I drink my eggnog, make another. Third time never fails. Minnie would not be going off to war if Kennedy had not been assassinated. Future historians will debate that, some saying yes, others no. Speculation invites partisan politics to color if not control future history. Irrelevant to Minnie. If not Vietnam, he'd find another war. I curse myself for being blasé. Shameless, I've given up on saving Minnie from himself. "Coffee spoons," I repeat.

"Nothing easy for my husband." Dinitia leans against the window. Particulates smudge her face, a parishioner anointed by a drunken priest on Ash Wednesday. "No night lying etherized on the table. No crabs scuttling back and forth. No eternal footmen."

"Something lawyerly," I mumble.

"Art offers no choice," she says.

"Fuck you."

"Love birds fighting. None of them in *Prufrock*." Minnie staggers to his feet. Chestnut shells landslide to the floor from his lap. "Your assignment." He glares at me, clears his throat three times, wags his jaw from side to side. "'In the room the women come and go/Talking of Michelangelo.'"

I raise my glass. "Wet dreaming the *David* off its pedestal for a hard marble fuck."

"The type who won't buy a painting unless their decorator approves," Dinitia says.

"Lawyers' wives no doubt." Minnie shakes his head and chestnut shells fly out of his hair like birds scared from Harpo Marx's wig in a Marx Brothers movie. "My studio is yours, O Musketeer of the mystic East."

"How big is the *David*'s cock?" I ask. "A foot? Eighteen inches? Two feet?"

Dinitia wipes her sooty hand on her dungarees. "You can't tell him from the rest of the first-year law students."

"I know his type." Minnie swigs several swallows of rum. "The artist who believes significant form is never created *ex nihilo*, but must always be found in nature and copied."

"So whose cock did he copy for the *David*?" I ask.

"Not yours, honey," Dinitia laughs.

"Whose fault is that?" I ask.

"Clay feet. Clay cock," Minnie says. I flail at him, a punch-drunk prize fighter wobbly from too many right-left-right combinations to the head. Giggling, Minnie skips out of range. "Better than the paper mâché dong you law students got."

"Not my man of steel." Dinitia dances across the loft, a high school student doing the Stroll, then bumping and grinding like a stripper weighed down by dollar bills from leering drunks. She crunches through the chestnut shells and comes to rest with her arms draped around my neck, her thigh against my groin, holding me like I'm the pole in the middle of the dance floor that the strippers partner. She wraps one leg around my waist, forcing her heel into the opening beneath my ass. "No steel tonight," she whispers, then spins away, pirouetting back to the window where she crashes into the window sill. "Enough of this bullshit," she sings, arms stretched over her head, back arched, flaunting her tits. "Din Din wants din din."

Arm in arm in arm, Minnie, Dinitia in the middle, and I, stagger through the snow up and down one after another of New York's mean streets arguing about whether to go to Little Italy or Chinatown. The snow, white in the light of the street lamps, collects particulates as it floats downward and turns to ash at eye level. It falls to the pavement and fills the gutters with a drab dingy slush that looks like water drained from a washing machine. On the avenues, the exhaust from the cabs and busses and trucks blackens the slush until it resembles charcoal dust congealed in the bottom of a barbecue left out in the rain.

"Winter," Dinitia says as she pivots us in the direction of Mulberry Street, "is not a city season."

February–April, 1968

In my introductory political science class at Amherst, there is a unit on proxy wars, added to the syllabus because of the Vietnam War. The black letter definition is simple: a war instigated by a major power that itself does not become directly involved. Future historians will argue whether the Vietnam War fits the definition. Those who contend the United States instigated the war will argue it doesn't as the U.S. was the only major power combatant in the jungles and rice paddies, the rivers and deltas, the cities and hamlets. The Soviet Union wasn't. China wasn't. If either of them was the instigator, it was a proxy war and, arguably, it was from the American perspective a just war. We argue both sides in class, but there is insufficient data to support either, dividing along lines of pro-war, anti-war. If it were a popularity contest, the antis would landslide the pros; but it's an academic exercise, intellectual, hypothetical. Unproven hypotheses are the consensus. That was spring semester, 1964. Not much help for spring semester, my first year at Columbia Law when the hypothetical became real.

There is a second definition for a proxy war, not as common but equally valid: when a fight over one thing is really a fight over something else. The war between Minnie and me fits this definition. We dare not fight over Dinitia. We dare not fight over my destroying his sculptures. We dare not fight over the secret we vowed to take to our graves. We fight a proxy war, color v. line, a prelude to a real war in a real war zone.

Minnie and I argue about color v. line. Incessantly. I accuse him of being a chromophobe and he accuses me of an underdeveloped aesthetic sense. His evidence: my preference for El Greco to the Rembrandt of the etchings. My evidence: His preference for the Rembrandt of the etchings to the Rembrandt of the oils. Children like El Greco, Minnie says. The bright colors. The distortions. The way shapes hang in the scene. The emotional surface. Adults appreciate the etchings of Rembrandt. Character, ideas, meaning, communicated through line. Color is like makeup on a woman, Minnie argues, superficial beauty to hide profound ugliness, whores and common streetwalkers being the most colorful. Color is the swan into which the ugly duckling molts, I reply. Line, Escher's line, dominates *Life with Coffee Spoons*, and, Minnie claims, portrays the infinitude of time, the finitude of life which, like the spoons of his collage, turns back on itself in ever repetitive cycles. Why aren't the spoons playing in traffic, I want to ask; or drag racing or charging a pillbox in the face of enemy fire. If God doesn't play dice with the universe as Albert Einstein once said, Minnie does. Ever since his sacred scalpel sliced and diced. Fucking Minnie.

Dinitia has a different take. Ingres v. Delacroix, she says. One a defender to the death of line, the other as passionate about color as two lovers fucking. Ideal beauty and the classical tradition counterpoise to the emotion of Romanticism. The more she prattles on the more she convinces me I'm a stranger to her, her to me. Michelangelo said he chips away at the block of marble until the sculpture appears. I'm not Dinitia's block of marble. Nothing will appear when she finishes but shards of marble.

❧ ❧ ❧

Wearing a hair net to keep his hair out of his eyes and off the canvas, Minnie gently applies a coat of damar varnish to *Life with Coffee Spoons*. Valentine's Day greetings from Uncle Sam are splayed on the refrigerator door underneath a souvenir Johnson Chapel magnet, orders to report to an induction center, then basic training, and, more likely than not, free air fare via Oakland to Vietnam. All that's missing is a red heart pierced by Cupid's arrow. Minnie spreads the damar varnish on the canvas evenly, lightly, to protect the paints without obscuring the lines. He uses a small brush to avoid getting any varnish on the coffee spoons that give his collage its third dimension. Over the centuries, much art has been lost to dirt and grime and heavy coats of heavy varnish as well as to efforts to cleanse and restore; but not *Life with Coffee Spoons*, not *Talking of Michelangelo* awaiting me on an adjacent easel. The rational side of Minnie's mind accepts that his oil on canvas in the style of a collage pales when compared to my polychromatic abstraction in mixed media and multi-dimensions. Color v. Line. Ingres v. Delacroix. Dinitia, I propose, chose color over line when she married me. In our silence, Minnie and I debate the truth of that proposition. Neither of us can convince the other.

Minnie steps away from the easel and treats himself to Mozart and a meerschaum. He reads somewhere, maybe in the *East Village Other*, that grass is standard issue with field rations in Nam. Share a joint with the enemy and make a friend for life. Free trade with Victor Charlie. Grass for opium. Opium for grass. LBJ for Ho Chi Minh. Ho Chi Minh for LBJ. Peace in our time. Peace for all time. The grass and music coat Minnie's mind, protecting his consciousness the way damar varnish protects *Life*, suppressing the involuntary memories of all that has gone before. Color becomes line and line becomes color as Minnie marvels at the way I evoke Michelangelo in a work of art in which appear no traces, no hints, no shapes or forms, nothing of the master, no reflections of his *David* or his *Pieta*, no homage to his *Moses*, nor to his two *Slaves*, one *Dying*, the other *Rebellious*, nothing from the Medici Chapel in Florence, nothing from the Sistine Chapel in the Vatican; yet a work of art that clearly evokes Michelangelo, enabling anyone who recognizes the *Creation of Adam*, anyone who sees God's finger stretch across the ceiling of the Sistine Chapel to transmit life to the human race, will understand *Talking of Michelangelo* the way an infant understands from the voice of his mother that he will be loved and fed and cared for and nurtured. If he is lucky. Art about the creation of art. Art about the metaphysics of art. Meta-art. All of this from a fucking law student with an underdeveloped aesthetic who curses himself for being inspired by T. S. Eliot rather than William Butler Yeats. A God damn motherfucking law student whose life is as empty as a coffee spoon after it has stirred sugar into the coffee.

Nothing I would ever see in a war zone would rival this.

Minnie scratches the scar that runs along his jawbone beneath his right ear. Smooth and glossy, its texture invokes the memory of M'Boto swaying from the branch of a longleaf pine, its dark green shiny needles, three in a cluster, illuminated by the glow of Gertie's fire, remnants of flayed skin flapping in the summer breeze like a threadbare curtain, and the memory of a daredevil cowering in night's blackness, real memories. When Minnie closes his eyes he is back in that field on that night hearing again those sounds, the screams and cries, the thuds and thwacks, the incessant hum of cicadas. He smells his sweat and the hay wagon and the field grass and the stink of the gas in Gertie's tank. His open wounds, his raw skin, sting and burn from the salt in his tears and the slightest motion of his mouth or jaw. The voices of that Alabama night even now invade his loft and gust around his head like a whirlwind. Yet, those memories are not real enough for him to evoke them memories on canvas in a way that will make the viewer feel that he, too, huddled in the tall grass of that Alabama field, afraid for his life, afraid for the life of M'Boto and Reverend Billington, afraid for the future of his country. A painter of nominal skill can depict a hero, but only a genius can portray a coward. Color v. line; line v. color. Ingres and Delacroix are both dead.

But, I who is no closer to that field than listening to Minnie talk about it, no closer to that field than reading police reports that profess the innocence of the natives and the guilt of the outside agitators, no closer to that field than the *New York Times* and *Life Magazine*, fucking first year law student me who sticks his paintings in a closet, refusing to exhibit them, refusing to sell them, this undeserving ass-fuck named Malone traps the animal of emotion, the fear of annihilation, the righteousness of M'Boto's sacrifice, the cowardice of the figure huddling in the tall grass, in *Death in a Combat Zone*. A work of genius, proclaims Dinitia. Twice the genius of *Talking*. Color and line. Line and color. And it sits in the closet in my bedroom in Fall River keeping company with the shirts and shoes and pants I outgrew and will never wear again. He, Minnie, lives the moment, earns his scars, pays his dues, manipulates his memories, suffers his guilt, but I paint his reality and my painting wins the hand in marriage of the fair princess. Wins more than her hand. Wins her sacrifice. No happily ever after for Minnie in this fairy tale. Nor will there be for the fair princess.

Minnie circles my easel the way he circles a Monet or Seurat or Pissaro in a museum, looking at *Talking of Michelangelo* from multiple angles, multiple distances, seeing something different from each vantage point. How easy for there to be an accident. A trip. A fall. A crash against the easel. Drunk. Stoned. Or, better yet, someone breaks in and trashes the place. Mau-mau from Harlem needing to feed their drug habit. I tried to protect your painting, but there were too many of them. Two. Three. Four. Five. Nothing I could do. Paint it again, man. You can paint it again. A true genius like you. No sweat. Michelangelo could. After all, it was Michelangelo who said of his *David*, his *Pieta*, his *Moses*, that the statue is all that is left after he chips away the extraneous marble. I repeat myself. If you chipped it away once, O Musketeer, you can chip it away a second time, a third time, as many times as there are spoons in *Life with Coffee Spoons* or lines in a Rembrandt etching. Minnie's elmwood sculptures in the style of Henry Moore, if wood chips the way marble does.

Because of me, Minnie is afraid. Not for his life. He plays with that the way we played at being artists with our John Gnagy learn-to-draw kits. Working in his dad's funeral home from an early age, he saw too much death to fear his own. No. For every great novel Vietnam produces, for every great movie, Minnie vows it will also produce one great painting or one great sculpture and it will be his name, Merisi Minifie, not mine, that will be scratched or etched or scrawled on each of these works of genius. He comforts himself that I will waste my genius painting pop-up toasters in the style of Utrillo that spew forth browned and buttered Wall Street lawyers to keep the world safe for capitalism, subordinated debentures relegated to the low rung of the financial ladder where they belong, leaving him to be the great American artist of the last half of the twentieth century. Kilroy will be there and Minnie believes to the core of his being that he is Kilroy. But standing now in the shadow of *Talking of Michelangelo*, seeing it through the haze of his meerschaum and the music of Mozart, knowing *Death in a Combat Zone* awaits its debut, Minnie realizes that I am Kilroy. Not him. He is about to go on a pilgrimage into the unknown that I will paint and this scares the shit out of him. If he could only banish color and line. Minnie sucks on his meerschaum and tries to block out the incessant buzz filling his ears. The front door of the building. Propping himself against the wall, he wambles his way to the kitchen and punches at the button to release the lock to the building's front door, bull's-eye on the fourth try, then flings open the door to his loft without waiting for the sound of the elevator, the sound of the knock. Maybe it's the Mau-mau. Or, Victor Charlie.

"We could smell the grass in the entry," I tell Minnie. For Dinitia's sake, I try my best always to be civil.

"Uncle Sam wants me to be his Valentine, me and my sacred scalpel, and I'm not even a fag." Minnie falls back against the door jamb.

"I'll set you up with someone from the National Lawyers Guild," I say. "They provide free legal services to draft resisters."

"Wops make shitty draft dodgers."

"Go to Canada," Dinitia says. "Montreal. There's a thriving art community. Paint in French."

"Not the French I don't remember from high school."

I pinch Minnie's hair net. "Wait 'til they start shaving your head."

"I'll carry some into battle for luck."

"Two superstitions are better than one," I say.

"You've got to fight it," Dinitia says. "The Guild will figure out a way."

"Your mother's health," I suggest. "Use that to appeal your classification. Tie up the draft board in litigation. By the time the court hears your case the war will be over."

"Appeals could take years," Dinitia says.

"She's got my old man." Minnie draws another lungful of smoke from the meerschaum. "Baby sit *Life* for me." Minnie hugs Dinitia, then turns to me. "Take good care of my fairy princess." Before Dinitia or I can say anything, Minnie pushes us out the door. "Gotta start my next *Prufrock*: 'I have seen it all already/I have seen it all.'"

I sulk on the walk to the subway, sulk on the platform waiting for the train, sulk as we ride the Broadway Local uptown.

"What's wrong?" Dinitia asks.

I insist on riding in the first car where I lean against the front door staring through the window at the empty track as the train hurtles forward. Dinitia sits on the bench opposite the door to the motorman's stall. She tries to stand beside me, tries to put her arm around me, but I shrug my shoulders and grunt and she hides inside Flaubert's *Trois Contes* in the original French.

Graffiti covers the outside of the subway car. Graffiti covers the inside, the walls and windows, the subway maps, the advertisements, the seats and floor, everything but the straps and poles. A tiny percentage of the graffiti is artistic, the kind of art beginning to appear in the more avant-garde galleries to the outrage of the Metropolitan Transit Authority which believes it will encourage more vandalism; but most of it is childish, punks marking their territory with scribbles the way wild animals do with urine. I stare in silence at the track bed and the signal lights and the girders that keep Broadway Local from crashing down on the tracks until, as the train enters the W. 110th Street station, I remove a black marker from my pocket and scrawl in the only open space remaining on the front window of the subway car 'Kilroy was here JSM 2/14/68'.

✳ ✳ ✳

Snow is in the forecast for the last Thursday of February, February 29, 1968, the day of Minnie's induction into the United States Army, the day he will stand naked in a line of draftees, most nervous, scared, a few looking forward to the pleasure of killing gooks. Leave it to Minnie to be inducted on a day that comes once every four years. Like a presidential election. 'Come clean for Gene.' Maybe that will save Minnie. He, Minnie, anticipates he alone will combine the sense of wonder of someone about to embark on a big adventure and the sense of regret for what might have been and the sense of fulfillment from finally having the right stage to act out on. The meteorologists predict snow, a lot of snow, beginning the day before, a nor'easter, two or three days' worth if the storm stalls over Long Island as most think it will, the kind of snow that paralyzes most places but not a city like New York. Not as long as the subways are running some sergeant at the induction center tells Minnie when he calls to ask whether there will be a snow day. Minnie doesn't want his induction postponed by the weather. To be ordered to step forward into the United States Army on Leap Day will be the invisible shield that will protect him when he's in the shit. Minnie will make it to the induction center on February 29th if he has to snowshoe.

He prepares a checklist to be completed before his induction the most important of which is to enter *Talking of Michelangelo* and *Life with Coffee Spoons* in Les Medailles de Badin, the biennial juried competition sponsored in even numbered years by the Museum of Modern Art and Francois Badin, owner of Les Artistes de Badin, one of Madison Avenue's leading art galleries. Because the entry is by invitation, Minnie forwards color slides of *Coffee Spoons* and *Talking* together with entry forms and sworn Affidavits of Originality to the Badin jury consisting of museum curators and previous Badin medalists – Badin banned himself and all other art gallery owners from the jury to eliminate commercial considerations from influencing the selection of the competitors or the winners – and both paintings are accepted. The Badin jury awards medals Olympic style, gold, silver, or bronze, and winning a Badin medal marks an artist as someone to watch, someone with a future. The roster of Badin medalists reads like a Who's Who of Art in the post-Depression twentieth century. Minnie does not ask my permission since he knows what the answer will be. Because the Affidavit of Originality must be notarized, Minnie enlists the assistance of the modern dance student who lives in the loft on the top floor of his building to forge my signature and to swear he is me in front of a Notary Public who is happy to have his vision clouded by an Alexander Hamilton and a pouch of Minnie's finest weed.

This brings Minnie to the second item on his checklist. New York's economy has its own legal tender, its own medium of exchange, and its own bankers whose vaults hold greater value than the vaults of Manny Hanny or Fat City or Toxic Chemical or Who's Chasing Rockefeller. As Leap Day approaches, Minnie liquidates his stash and deposits the cash, his seed capital for Vietnam, into a Fat City account because Fat City has branches in all major foreign capitals including Saigon and the Assistant Vice President who opens his account assures him he can access his money from any branch in the world. According to the *East Village Other*, capitalism in its truest form runs rampant in Vietnam and grunts who survive twelve months in country can return home rich if they have seed capital and know how to take care of business. Minnie figures on making a killing.

The third item on Minnie's checklist is to visit his parents which he does when he goes home to Fall River for Julia Reardon's wedding, as Jewish a wedding as an Irish lass can have. Julia marries a business major from Boston University whom her father installs in the pants factory as an Executive Vice President at a salary of $1,000.00 per week even though his only previous business experience was running the prom tuxedo rental concession his senior year at college and losing his shirt when most of the tuxes came back ruined and he had to replace them. Accountants are a dime a dozen, but entrepreneurs are the rarest coin of the realm, Mick Reardon remarks when Julia becomes engaged. Although Julia's wedding will be an unofficial fifth reunion for the class of 1963 of B.M.C. Durfee High School, Dinitia and I are not invited. Neither is Laurie Williams who cries when Minnie kisses her good-by.

Therese Minifie is not well enough to accompany Vincenzo and Minnie to the train station in Providence on Sunday, February 18th, when Minnie returns to New York. With a full house of corpses stacked up at the funeral home, four wakes and four burials squeezed into the first three days of the week, Vincenzo festinates more than he did the day he delivered Minnie to Amherst College. Take care, he manages to mumble as Minnie mounts the lower step of the coach car. Make sure Mom's alive when I come home, Minnie replies. Vincenzo mutters something in Italian and Minnie senses it is not a papal blessing. By the time Minnie settles into his seat, choosing one on the station side, only strangers remain on the platform. He waves goodby to these strangers in Providence and he waves goodby to strangers at every stop between Providence and Grand Central Station. Enough strangers wave back for Minnie to convince himself there are people in addition to his mother and Dinitia and Laurie Williams who care he is on his way to Vietnam. I care and I don't care. Yes, if he dies, part of my past will die with him. But not the secret we share.

The fourth item on Minnie's check list is to buy a camera, an SLR, one simple to use, that will enhance rather than impede his creativity, one sturdy enough to survive in the shit. A salesman in a discount camera store on 47th street with a long beard who wears a black fedora and matching suit touts the Canon FT-QL, better than Nikon or Pentax he claims, and Minnie invests $350.00 in a camera with a f1.4 lens, shutter speed from infinity to 1/1000th of a second, and a set of filters, red, green, yellow, and ultraviolet. He considers a motor drive, but doesn't know if it is wise to carry the extra weight and he passes. Minnie also buys one thousand feet of ASA 200 color film, film cartridges, and a cartridge loader that comes with instructions explaining how to roll film. Minnie rolls 36 exposures to the cartridge since this is one of the standard sizes and he doesn't want to be bothered remembering some unique number. He'll have enough on his mind when he is in country.

The fifth item on Minnie's checklist is to make up a convincing lie to explain why *Life* and *Talking* are not in his loft after he asks Dinitia to babysit *Life* for him. Dinitia makes it easy by reminding him that the paintings will not be safe on the subway, will not fit into a cab, and by calculating that the cost of renting a van is not much less than hiring experienced movers who specialize in handling works of art. Minnie offers to pay for the movers in exchange for the free storage, but relents when Dinitia insists she will deposit one-half the moving cost in Minnie's Fat City account. Minnie concedes to rescue his lie from failure. Besides, he may need the additional seed capital in Nam.

Sixth and last because it is the most important, to clean and polish his sacred scalpel with his mom's silverware polish and to repair the stitching of its leather carrier unless it fall out and be lost. It saved his life once and Minnie knows it will save his life again and again.

The snow is not yet falling early Wednesday morning, February 28, when Francois Badin accompanied by two laborers arrives at Minnie's loft to pack *Life with Coffee Spoons* and *Talking of Michelangelo* into wooden crates. Carpenters from Museum of Modern Art's maintenance department build custom crates for the paintings. Although Badin's laborers wear work shirts embroidered with the MOMA logo, they look more like stevedores than museum employees. And they have stevedore's names, Minnie thinks, when Badin introduces them, Freddie G. and Monk. Freddie G. has short black hair that clings to his skull like roof shingles that are glued rather than tacked and whose edges have begun to curl up. His neck is thick, obliterating his jaw and chin. As for Monk, well Monk just looks like the fish bearing his name.

Badin wears a velvet suit, eggplant purple, and a white shirt with a ruffled front and French cuffs adorned with gold dipped parsley cuff links. His rattlesnake boots are died to match his velvet suit. Minnie can't decide whether Badin belongs in the 16th century or the 20th, Versailles or the East Village, and he doesn't care. He prefers tee shirts and blue jeans and will never own a gallery no matter how unsuccessful an artist he is. Badin mother-hens Freddie G. and Monk as they pack *Life* and *Talking* into museum moving crates. "How will I notify you if you win?" he asks Minnie.

"When I win," Minnie replies. "Call Dinitia Marbury Madison, Malone's wife. I doubt I'll have a phone where Uncle's sending me."

"And the paintings?"

"Return to her."

"I didn't think you hippie artist types had it in you," Freddie G. says. He balances one of the crates on a hand truck. Monk balances the other.

"You'd be surprised what I got in me," Minnie says.

Monk gestures for Minnie to approach. "Go to Soo Phat's." Monk winks as he whispers. "The fuckingest whores in Saigon. I once did a dozen between beers. I did Soo Phat three times. I just love Buddhist cunt."

"She's listed under noodle houses in *The Grunt's Guide to Saigon*," Freddie G. says.

Flurries start as Freddie G. and Monk load the crates into a MOMA van, becomes a steady snow by the time the van arrives at E. 53rd Street, and a heavy snow while they unload the crates and wheel them into the conservancy to be unpacked and prepared for the competition. The snow continues falling heavily through the afternoon, through the evening, through the night, through the next morning, falling fast. It does not have time to turn ashen gray before hitting the pavement, a rare storm that transforms New York City into a winter wonderland. Wind creates drifts to bury the stoops on the uptown side of the streets, to clog the store entrances on both sides of the avenues. Taxis cannot breach these drifts. Even the busses have difficulties. But the subways run, at least the portion of the system underground and it is by subway that Minnie and Dinitia and I rendezvous at the induction center for another hug, another farewell. Minnie says good-by with another joke about the pop-up toaster and promises to write and Dinitia and I stand arm in arm as we watch him bound up the steps of the induction center to start upon his great adventure. Snowflakes land on our cheeks and dissolve in her tears. Arm in arm we slowly walk down the block through the heavy snow to the subway station and by the time Minnie reaches the top step and turns to wave, we have disappeared into a whiteout, incorporeal shadows invisible in the wind-cursed blizzard. New York City glows white like a blank canvas, now and for another twelve hours. The snow stops around midnight and the sun rises in the east on Friday morning. By Saturday morning, the streets are clear enough for the law school to hold classes and both of my classes, Legal Method and Trusts and Estates, record perfect attendance. The Rule Against Perpetuities is always a big draw. By Monday afternoon, Daitch Shopwell restocks beer, milk, and other staples. By Wednesday, mail delivery resumes. By Friday, the city finishes plowing the residential streets in Queens. In Florida, the Boston Red Sox report to Spring Training, confident they can repeat the Impossible Dream of 1967.

The first letter from Minnie arrives before the snow from the Leap Day nor'easter melts and includes a lock of his hair and a picture of him shaven and shorn taken in an amusement park photo booth. In his army haircut, he looks like a refugee from a Pat Boone movie. The second letter arrives on April Fool's Day and has large sections of text blacked out by military censors. The third letter, Minnie's first from Vietnam, arrives on tax day, April 15th.

"Edna Mae Mangel's grandson is in my platoon," he writes. "Calls himself Hobo."

The rest of the letter is about color.

"The light glows," Minnie writes, "with humidity, making the colors intense enough to taste. Ever taste green? Try to imagine what green tastes like. Mint? Spinach? Creme de menthe? None of the above. Green tastes like Beethoven's *Eroica*, like Stravinsky's *Rite of Spring*, like the opening verses of Genesis."

Color wins. Color always wins.

April 23, 1968–April 24, 1968

Columbia University School of Law does not offer courses in the law of art. Nor in the art of law. There are classes in convertible subordinated debentures, tax free exchanges, and the felony murder rule. There are professors who will teach me how to syndicate a race horse, draft a trust that does not violate the rule against perpetuities, or negotiate a ground lease. Important skills, these, as important as knowing how to crack eggs if you're a short order cook.

*　*　*

Row after row and column after column of metallic silver-colored boxes with squiggly key holes and small horizontal rectangles whose corners gently curve like the lips of a Hollywood harlot. Identical except for the apartment numbers penciled in by Frank, the building super. A perfect subject if I painted in the style of Andy Warhol. How little my photographic silk-screen of these mailboxes would differ from Warhol's Marilyns or Elvises or Campbell soup cans. They would lack Warhol's celebrity for one thing and would not be considered cultural icons even though they are iconic to apartment dwellers from New York to Chicago to Los Angeles because the United States Post Office mandates their size and shape and material and color. I don't understand Warhol's aesthetic. His art seems too personality driven. As is Picasso's, but genius always trumps mere talent. Minnie would succeed in Warhol's world.

I juggle two shopping bags of groceries, a student menu, prepared foods from the freezer case only needing to be reheated, stuffed green peppers, stuffed cabbage, Salisbury steak in brown sauce, turkey with stuffing and gravy; or foods that can be broiled, shoulder steak, shoulder lamb chops, once Cornish game hens, but only once because the amount of meat is disproportionate to the effort. Neither Dinitia nor I have time to cook and, on her salary alone, we cannot afford take-out even though the neighborhood restaurants cater to students. If Minnie wants to live off her trust funds to make art, it's his prerogative. My greed points in other directions. I have an urge to rub out the 5F on our mailbox with my thumb, but that won't stop the bills from being delivered.

Today's mail brings an invitation to the Law Review. Your mother released you from your promise, Dinitia reminds me as the elevator ascends to the fifth floor. In the apartment, Dinitia asks what's bugging me as she puts the groceries away. Maybe you married the wrong Musketeer, I say. Maybe I did. Dinitia sticks out her tongue. When the phone rings, she warns me it's seven years bad luck not to answer it and I capitulate, another capitulation in a life replete with them. Maybe that is why Dinitia tacks a cheap print of a Utrillo oil to the wall above the telephone. Utrillo's wife, Dinitia teases, didn't have to beg him to drop out of law school to become an artist. Mediocrity has its place and function, I remind her. People buy mediocrity. Pay dear for it because it has a high comfort level like a hot dog and a beer at a ball game. If it isn't offensive, it isn't challenging. It doesn't intimidate. You look at it. You don't think about it. You don't talk about it, at least not in the jargon laden art critic language ordinary folk don't understand. People hang Utrillo for one reason. Because he is French. If he were from the Bronx, they would price his paintings by the square inch and match them to the upholstery of the couch they hang above. Unless he also played for the New York Yankees.

"Monsieur Malone?"

I cover the receiver with my hand and mimic barfing.

"Je suis Monsieur Francois Badin, owner of Les Artistes de Badin on Madison Avenue and co-sponsor of Les Medailles de Badin with the Museum of Modern Art. *Art in America* did a piece on my 1966 biennial competition."

I make-believe barf again, separating my fingers slightly to allow some of the sound to seep through.

"The jury has awarded the silver medal in this year's competition to *Talking of Michelangelo*."

"How can I win a competition I didn't enter?"

"Monsieur Merisi Minifie entered your painting and one of his own. He did not win a medal, but I will give him an Honorable Mention for his service. There will be an award ceremony, Sunday night at the Pierre. Black tie. A courier will deliver your formal invitation. I would be honored to add your painting to my collection. May I propose $1,000.00?"

"It's not for sale."

"For me to acquire a young artist only aggrandizes his reputation."

"It's still not for sale."

"Think on this with care and we'll discuss it at the banquet. Au revoir."

Dinitia slides her hands into my front pockets. "What was that all about?"

"Fucking Minnie entered *Talking* and *Coffee Spoons* in Badin's biennial competition. *Talking* took the silver. He offered me a thousand bucks."

Dinitia's fingers probe my pockets. "He can make your career."

"Law Review will make my career."

"So you can spend your life sucking up to people like my father?"

I yank Dinitia's hands from my pockets. "Is Minnie doing this for you or me?"

"Doing what?"

"First he files my Amherst application without telling me. Now this. I'm a lawyer, Dinitia, not a painter. You want to marry a painter, marry Minnie. I won't stand in your way. No money grab either. Neat and clean." I shuffle some papers and a case book into my brief case. "I'm late for my Civ Pro study group. Don't wait up."

Dinitia pretends to be asleep when I crawl into bed. She maintains the pretense while I prop my Civil Procedure case book on my chest and reread *Erie v. Tompkins*. In diversity actions commenced in Federal court, it tries to answer the question of which state's law should the Federal court apply, tries to distinguish between substantive law and procedural law. Fucking Tompkins getting hit by a train walking along the tracks. I would have found for the railroad on the ground of his stupidity, but my professor will not give me credit for that answer. It's too real world. After thirty minutes, I turn off the light and settle into my sleeping position, listening for a moment to the late-night traffic on Broadway, busses, cabs, delivery trucks, the voices of drunks, usually Columbia students, but not always, sirens, city sounds, New York City's lullaby. New York City's night lights sneak between the slats of the blinds and settle on the ceiling, a fresco in monochrome. A chromophobe like Minnie would appreciate it. I roll over and face Dinitia, my eyes crunched shut. She slips her hand into the opening in my boxer shorts and whispers, Moooo.

I jump and crack my head against the headboard and Dinitia cannot stop herself from laughing. I begin tickling her. Her laughter accelerates. She tickles me and I laugh and we roll around the bed, tangling in the sheets, until I slip over the edge and she tumbles after me like Jill after Jack and lands on me, her mouth on mine, kissing, not tickling, no longer laughing, and we fuck and fuck and fuck until the bitterness of our argument is a stain on the floor after which we crawl into bed and cuddle and listen to New York's night song and fall asleep in each other's arms under the fresco of New York's night light. In my dreams, I am trapped in a Utrillo oil, a blurry stick figure on a street corner in Montmartre. In her dreams, she tells me in the morning, the Metropolitan Museum of Art acquires *Talking of Michelangelo*. Makeup sex does not always result in making up.

❧ ❧ ❧

About 1:30 that afternoon, there is a demonstration at the construction site of the new Columbia University gym being built in Morningside Park. Although the gym is sited in an unusable section of the park and the University intends to permit the neighborhood to use it, the professional whiners feel obliged to protest because it is Columbia. After the demonstration, the Students for a Democratic Society occupy Hamilton Hall, the location of the office of the Dean of Columbia College. Throughout the afternoon and evening, outsiders join the occupation including a large number of Negroes, some from the Congress of Racial Equality and Student Non-Violent Coordinating Committee, others from Harlem like the Mau-mau. Tom Hayden, one of the founders of SDS, makes several visits. By dawn on Wednesday, April 24, the Negroes take over the takeover and evict the whites. Mark Rudd, witless to the end, advocates compliance. There are enough buildings for everyone, he says. It is the beginning of what some will characterize as a crisis but in reality is a war, a culture war, a war between alternative realities, a war proving beyond a reasonable doubt, to steal a nice neat legal phrase, that LBJ and Rusk and McNamara and Westmoreland do not have a monopoly on stupidity and venality, a war with one casualty that will not succumb from its wounds for several years, if not several decades, but will succumb, for history does repeat itself. Only the names and places and dates change. Vietnam has come to Morningside Heights and the campus of Columbia University. Paint it. Litigate it. Fuck it.

PART III

June, 1962–November, 1964

June, 1962

The climb up High Street from President Avenue in the summer's heat exhausts Da and he steadies himself against the telephone pole opposite the front porch of the triple decker where we live on the second floor. The landlord promised us the first floor when it became vacant, an empty promise since he owned the tenement, lived on the first floor with his wife and children, and was unlikely to move, a promise he did not remember much longer than it took him to make it. It is a hot summer, the hottest since the war to end all wars, and the heat lingers inside the stairwell the way it lingers inside the mills. Da misses the heat in the mills, the windows that don't open, the fans that don't work, the machinery that generates heat, the furnaces being used only for hot water. It has been two summers since the Gilt Edge laid Da off, five summers since the first Mass of Father Crizal, the replacement for Father Ozoni, five summers since Minnie and I retired as altar boys. Sunday Mass is far less painful under Father Crizal.

Da grips the iron pipe railing that extends down the steps from the front porch to the sidewalk. Dry rot and termites powder the wood that anchors the railing and it sways against his weight as he uses the railing as a pulley to drag himself up the eight steps from the street to the porch. Halfway, he pauses to catch his breath. The sweat of his hands sucks flecks of rust off the iron pipe and ferries it under his skin. One of these days the railing will give way, pitching Da into the garden, into a dead and desiccated hedge leftover from the time when the garden had flowers, and the heat and hot water in the winter reached above the first floor. The hedge will offer no cushion against his fall and Da won't be able to free himself without Ma's help.

Da continues his climb one legged because his left knee aches from a work injury whenever he puts weight on it. Three bolts of cloth tumbled off a forklift and pinned his legs to the floor, laying him up for eighteen months, twelve of them in an ankle to hip cast, six months of exercises to rebuild the leg muscles. His knee is no longer right and never will be. Nor his back. Da thumps as he limps across the front porch, each thump echoing because of the hollow beneath the porch. Once upon a time, still a young father who walks like a man, we camp out in this hollow on hot summer nights. I love the diamonds of light shining through the lattice work, but the sounds people make when they walk up the front stairs and across the porch frighten me.

"It's old Billy Goat Gruff," Da says, "and we're the Trolls living under the bridge trying to capture Billy Goat Gruff for dinner."

If the hollow beneath the front porch is a poor substitute for the backyard we don't have or the tent we can't afford, I don't know any better. To me, we camp out in a wonderland created by diamonds of lights and inhabited by magical creatures. Eventually, I outgrow camping out in the hollow beneath the porch. Eventually, I outgrow everything except locking myself in my bedroom with my paintings and drawings many of which have a diamond motif and feature creatures unknown to any mythology. To Da, these diamond studded creatures are Da as clown, Da as jester, Da as monster. Only I know these figures aren't harlequins or monsters, but Da refuses to accept my explanation they are the memories of a young child camping out in the hollow under the front porch with the Da he idolizes. In truth, the diamonds remind me of the piece of cut glass in Father Ozoni's pinky finger ring. A real diamond worth tons and tons of money, he bragged to Minnie and me. Later, we learn the truth, cheap glass worth nothing.

"There's no future in the past," Da says.

"The future is only in the past," I reply. I speak only for myself. And Minnie.

But, in the early days of this long, hot summer, Da wishes for winter even though he knows that come February when the oven warms the kitchen and only I can tolerate the cold enough to sleep in my own bedroom he'll wish for summer. A never-ending cycle of going to and from nowhere.

In my bedroom, I touch up a diamond in the background of a pastel portrait of Julia, a birthday present I create from her yearbook photo. Beside my easel, I pin a reproduction of Picasso's *Head of a Sleeping Woman* I razored out of an art book in the public library. Influences and the way they converge fascinate me. Borrowing from Picasso's *Head* to create my *Julia*, means I also borrow from the archaic Greek vases and paintings by Matisse and the African sculptures in the Museum of Ethnography at the Palais de Trocadero in Paris that influenced Picasso when he painted his *Head* in 1907. Da's off balance thumping buzzes in my open window like a mosquito looking for a refill and snaps me out of my reverie and tells me all I need to know about his day, his efforts to find a job. Da never limps on the rare occasions he finds day work. I pivot the easel, my back to the window. Julia glows in the summer light. As she does in real life.

Julia won't like my *Head of a Sleeping Julia*. She won't like the way I reduce her face to a combination of curves and angles. She won't like the way the colors meld into each other, brown into black into red into green. She won't like the way I elongate her freckles into slash marks. She won't like the crucifix soaking in a pool of blood hidden in the point of one of the diamonds, if she sees it. Is that what you think I look like, she'll complain and I'll try to explain how Picasso's women lust for the opportunity to pose for him; but she'll run off in a snit and I'll have to buy her another Johnny Mathis album (which I can't afford) to make up which we'll do by making out through all twelve songs, stopping when the album stops because Julia doesn't believe in kissing without a musical backdrop. Someday, Johnny Mathis will stop making albums. That will be the day the kissing stops.

Sketches, paintings, drawings, all mounted with masking tape on the four walls of my bedroom, surround me. Rejections and start-overs litter the floor like shredded paper at the bottom of a rabbit's cage. I store finished – if that word even applies to someone like me – canvases in the closet or under the bed where they will be safe from kicks or other accidents. My output will outgrow my room before I graduate high school. If I lack the genius of the young Picasso, at least I'm as prolific. Minnie, still my friend, not yet my rival, will store the overflow. Minnie's Basement Museum featuring the lifetime oeuvre of James Stephen Malone. Everyone has to start – or end – somewhere.

"Brigid!" Gabriel's shout rumbles up the stairwell.

"Brigid!"

Once when I attempt to help Da up the stairs, his anger teaches me that Da is less ashamed accepting help from Ma than me. When you have children, you'll understand, Ma tells me. Now, whenever Ma asks why I spend time painting, I tell her when she's an artist she'll understand. I do my best to tune out the noise of Ma helping Da up the stairs by submerging myself into the pastels until I am one with the colors. There are sounds parents make a child should never hear. Making love is one. Ma helping Da up the stairs is another.

"Bring me to the chair, Briggie."

Ma walks Da to the Naugahyde easy chair and settles him into it. The chair like everything else in the living room, including Da, is well worn. Ma returns with a glass of beer. "Any luck today, love?"

"Bad luck count?" Da flashes his teeth and clenches his jaw as he struggles to take off his work boots. Ma swallows her reaction. After a lifetime of marriage, she knows when Da wants her sympathy and when he doesn't. Da's foot, still shod, falls back to the floor. "Oh, Briggie. Most tell me I'm an insurance risk. The nice ones tell me I don't know anything about this new-fangled electronics assembly."

"You could learn."

"Paterson Textiles has something in the shipping room. First box down the conveyer, I couldn't lift off. Boss gives me half a day for my troubles." Da removes a $5.00 bill from his shirt pocket. Islands of sweat darken it. "At least I can pay for this week's milk."

"Drink your beer, love."

"The boy home?"

"In his room. Painting."

"What's pickling his brain, Briggie. He says to me, Da, he says, if I go into the mills after graduation, I can work nights, paint days."

"Painting's his life."

"Art for art's sake's he says when I ask him why. Besides, it's not a man's work." Da sips the beer like a man on the edge of a desert rationing his last canteen of water. "A man's work, Briggie. If something happens to me, how's he going to care for you?"

"You know something I don't?"

"What'd I ever do for my ma of blessed memory after my da died?"

"You loved her."

"That didn't stop the electric from shutting down her power. And the bastard at the oil company wouldn't stand me a half tank." Da permits himself another sip. "Why do you think I double-shifted all these years? To have the boy go into the mills? No. College. The boy goes to college. I want him to take proper care of you after I'm gone. That's why, Briggie."

I crush a stick of black pastel against the frame of the door, pulverizing it into little pieces, then into dust, and grind the dust into the palm of my hand. I rub my palm against the drawing, obliterating Julia, transforming her into large black smudges similar to the oil smudges on the street where Da parks the car. Only the crucifix in the pool of blood remains. The smudges engulf me, sucking the breath out of my lungs and I gasp for air. Soon nothing will remain of life except large black smudges. I wipe my hands on a rag and enter the living room. "You know, Da, if I went into the mills you and Ma could use my college fund for retirement. I'd pay room and board. Da would have time for his back to heal up. And his knee."

"I had no choice," Da says. "You do. Between the money I saved up, a basketball scholarship... "

The blast of an antique car horn sounds through the windows. "I'm going out with Minnie for a while."

"No choice," Da shouts after me. "None."

"He has none either," Ma says.

Da twists around in the chair, searching for a position that doesn't pain his back. "Get me today's classifieds, Briggie. Maybe there's something new."

<h1 style="text-align: center;">July, 1962</h1>

The amusement park. Grocery wheels and mill dollies and Raphael Madonnas.

Raphael is twenty-two when he arrives in Florence, twenty-two when he paints his *Madonna of the Meadows*. Immediate success. Instantaneous even if time moves more slowly in Renaissance Florence. If Raphael does it, why not me, Malone wonders. Five years if I start now. Tonight. I hesitate. Raphael does not have a sick da who wants him to be an accountant or a ma whom he will have to support. And because if Raphael's Madonna resembles the daughter of a Florentine nobleman, gold florin will guild his purse.

❧ ❧ ❧

Lincoln Park, half way between Fall River and New Bedford on Route 6, the amusement park where I toil when I'm not summering in a local factory, assigns me to the grocery wheel. Picture a free-standing wall of shelves. Canned goods: peaches, pears, or fruit salad; wax beans, green beans, or baked beans; tomato soup. Packaged goods: crackers, cookies, macaroni elbows, chocolate covered peanuts that melt gooey in the summer heat, sugar coated breakfast cereals. A spinning wheel of fortune on the wall to my left that clicks with the constant beat of a metronome driven by a spring that slows down as the wheel loses momentum. Ten pie shaped wedges, each a unique number, zero through nine; each a unique color; each with three white light bulbs and one red. A flip board built into the counter at the front of the booth with two strips of numbers, 0 to 9, each the same color as its wedge on the wheel.

The rules of the game. The suckers place their dimes on a number and pray for one of the three white bulbs or the single red bulb to light up. If it's white, the reward is a single can or package, my choice; if it's red, a case of soda, twenty-four cans, grape or orange or root beer or cola or ginger ale, also my choice. No Coke. No Pepsi. No brand sold anywhere in the known world but at the Lincoln Park grocery wheel.

The losers, nine out of ten on every spin. Before they can steal back their money, I flip the board depositing the dimes on a moving belt that drops it into a counter except for the dimes I scoop. It's only fair. I'm worth more than $1.20 per hour the amusement park pays. I produce. Hundreds of dollars per hour gross profit. I'm a salesman and I should be paid like a salesman. By commission. 5%. 10%. 20%. Two wrongs do make a right. Do not equate artistic integrity with honesty.

Friday night. A crowd jostles for position, their pockets heavy from payday at the mills. Most in their twenties and thirties, husbands and wives with young children, but older men and women as well. Mill workers all. I know how little these people earn, these people whose only job skills are nimble fingers or a strong back, these stitchers or shipping clerks or punch press operators, these mill dollies my grandmother warns me about when I take my first factory job the summer I turn sixteen. Did you warn Da, too, I ask at the time, forgetting Ma still works in the same mill at the same machine as she has since returning from her honeymoon. Ma doesn't earn any more than the suckers shouting numbers at the grocery wheel, but at least she buys her groceries at the Brockton Public Market, not the amusement park.

Shilling the crowd. I know how to shill the crowd. I do it no matter how deep the crowd because people expect it. Management expects it. Entertain them and they forget their losses. Cigarettes and groceries aren't stuffed animals where the only players are the fathers of four-year old girls or pimply teenage boys hoping to snow their dates and get laid. Everyone's a winner every night. Suckers fill the numbers with their dimes, seven the most popular, then three. People rarely play zero unless it's in combination with some other number. I take her for a spin. The marker clicks. The pegs spin by.

Winners and losers. Six white. I tip the counter before the losers react. Two winners. Two very lucky winners. I grab a can of baked beans, a can of peas, hand the beans to a five-year old who clings to his father's neck as if he's hanging over the edge of a cliff and the peas to an old man who tells me he wants them beans. The anchor tattooed on the old man's forearm bends and turns with the folds of his skin. Its angles and folds remind me of the clocks in Dali's *The Persistence of Memory*. I imagine a painting of the old man's arm and its convoluted tattoo. *The Way of All Flesh*. I hate titles from books. *Anchors Aweigh!*

"I want them beans."

"New game. New winners. Put your money down. Can't win if you don't play."

A mill dolly pushes her way to the front of the crowd. She wears a tight white top with a plunging V neck and I admire the way her bra yanks her tits apart and exaggerates her cleavage. She leans on the counter giving me a clear view to her navel. She has a birthmark, a freckle, on the inside of her right tit and the tattoo of a rose on the inside of her left.

"Give the old man his farts, kid," she says and I do.

Break time. I lounge on the cases of soda in the storage area behind the grocery wheel smoking a cigarette and listening to Johnny Guerin beg people to play. If there's a crowd, they must be deaf mutes. Guerin usually runs the teacup ride in the children's section and isn't half the shill I am; but management switches people around at least once a shift. Everyone gets the one-hour break state law mandates. I hate working the rides. People pay with tickets and there are no overflowing conveyor belts to fund my bonuses. I French inhale my cigarette and watch the mill dolly wriggle into her shorts, wondering if she's double jointed. She sure fucked like she was.

"Award yourself a case of beans, kid," she says. I balance a case of grape soda on her shoulder and open the back door. "Better zip up before you face your public." She squeezes my ass and steps through the cloud of flies buzzing around the naked light bulb above the door.

"It's dead tonight," Johnny says.

"You gotta sell. Sell. Sell." I begin my patter, crackers for a Roosevelt, or wax beans or fruit cocktail or a case of soda. "You haven't seen such prices in fifty years," I tell the older people. "You'll never see prices this cheap," I tell the younger ones. The crowd builds, first at the center of the numbers, then spreading to the sides. At the edge of the crowd hovers Julia wearing yacht club casual. The daughter of a mill owner. The son of two mill workers. A story line out of an illustrated romance novel. Literature of the highest order. Narrative art. The diptych becomes the triptych becomes the polytych becomes the comic book. "Wheel's hot tonight, folks!" When I work the cigarette booth, I slip Julia a few packs, Luckies for me, Kents for her, and, later, perhaps on a blanket in the field where Minnie and I will merge our fortunes before summer's end, or in the back seat of my father's car, a 1952 Chevrolet convertible bought on its tenth birthday, we smoke our amusement park cigs. Sometimes, Julia lets me touch her, feel her, look at the white skin inside her tan lines, but no more, not for a case of soda, not for a carton of cigarettes, not for a birthday portrait. She holds out for a diamond from a guy who can't afford cut glass. I'd rather scrape barnacles off your dad's yacht than sail on it, I tell her and she tells me there are pills to cure seasickness.

"Can't win if you don't play."

Julia slips a dime on the ten.

"A red ten winner."

"Root beer," Julia says. I slide a case of root beer across the counter. "Anyone want this?" she asks.

A tall man, tall enough to play college basketball and not much older than me or Julia, steps out of the crowd. As pale as his undershirt, he carries a newborn infant, handing it to a woman pushing a stroller and carrying a toddler. He has a pack of Camels rolled up in one sleeve like an epaulet. James Dean lives. The tall man slaps a dime in Julia's hand, hoists the case of soda on his shoulder, and pushes his way through the crowd. I see death in the tall man's eyes, death in the eyes of his children, maybe electronic assembly instead of textiles, but the mills nonetheless. I know the tall man's children will never see my paintings no matter how many I paint, no matter how famous I become. I curse the mills, not because they imprison the tall man as they have the tall man's father, as they will the tall man's children; but because my only escape from the mill life of Ma and Da is to go into those mills.

The tall man's wife tries to quiet the baby by rocking the stroller back and forth. The infant wears a sailor's cap, tiny, infant size, maybe a gift from a proud uncle who joined the Navy to escape the mills, and a summer outfit, blue with a white anchor over the heart. The infant is too young to show its gender, but I will paint it as a boy. *Madonna with Child in Stroller*. I will model it after something out of the Italian Renaissance, perhaps Raphael's *Madonna of the Meadows*. I will set it in an amusement park instead of a field, an artificial swimming hole in the background instead of a natural lake, a bath house by its edge rather than a church or castle. Little can the tall man afford to pay for his child portrayed in *Madonna with Child in Stroller*. A can of warm root beer at most. No matter. It won't be for sale.

"Hey, kid!" someone in the crowd shouts. "Spin the fucking wheel already."

"Pick you up after work," Julia tells me. "Wait 'til you see what Daddy got me for my birthday."

"Last call for the next winner." I pull on the lever spinning the wheel of fortune. The light jumps from number to number through the bulbs, the whites and the reds. The speed creates the optical illusion of first a line, then a circle. A halo like the halos Raphael paints over his Florentine Madonnas. Unlike traditional halos, Raphael's halos are slender circles of gold that fit into the composition of circles and ovoids, an element adding a delicate depth to the face of his Madonnas. *Madonna with Child in Stroller* will have a gold halo. As will the baby. They deserve no less.

After work. When Julia kisses me, I taste the ash from the burned pepperoni pizza we shared at The Depot, a pizza joint named after its location across from the freight depot that makes up for its lousy pizza by serving beer to anyone who orders food. Three beers do not wash away the taste, nor do the amusement park cigarettes we smoke relaxing in Julia's birthday present, a 1955 Thunderbird, a gift from her dad that comes with her driver's license. On the dirt road bordering the field where Minnie and I will blend our blood we park, top down. We kiss under the stars. Julia overflows with passion, soul kissing me. I like the way her tongue moves around the inside of my mouth. I like the way her fingers caress the edges of my ears and brush the hair at the base of my neck. I like the way she arouses me. Still, I cannot move beyond the taste of ashes. I push Julia away and light two cigarettes, a Lucky for me, a Kent for her, and together we blow smoke at the stars, creating our own Milky Way. Julia aims her smoke rings at the moon, transforming it into another Saturn. The frosting of her hair, the blessing of summer's sun and salt water, flickers in the moonlight. Summer is Julia's season. I tap down another Lucky on the steering wheel. I wonder if Julia sees any difference between an accountant who carries Luckies in his shirt pocket and a mill worker who rolls Camels in his sleeve.

"He had death in his eyes," I tell her. "His wife too. His kids." I light the Lucky and launch my own smoke ring toward the moon. "Like the old men in the mills. Like my Da." My cigarette brightens with every third syllable like an accent mark over a line of poetry. Julia snuggles against me, her ear over my heart. "I've decided something," I say. "I'm not playing ball this year. I'm going to work part time and paint. When I graduate, I'm going to work nights, paint days."

"Go to business school. Daddy will take you into the business."

I suck on my cigarette. The idea appeals to me. If I have no paintings to sell, what me worry about the sign of the fig. I do not see my future as Mick Reardon's son-in-law. "His factory turns out a thousand dozen pairs of pants each shift. Four colors. Black. Blue. Olive. Khaki. Identical except for the size. Next shift another thousand dozen. From here to eternity, a thousand dozen per shift."

"Daddy will give you time to paint."

"I'm not a T Bird."

"If you don't love me, just say so."

"Who falls in love at seventeen?"

"My folks did."

I turn the key in the ignition and Arnie 'Woo Woo' Ginsburg broadcasting live from the Adventure Car Hop on Route 1 in Saugus blasts from the radio. Ginsburg cues up *Peppermint Twist* by Joey Dee and the Starlighters. "Don't," I say when Julia reaches to lower the volume. "It's what the world expects from high school kids."

August, 1962

But, my memory is not a blank canvas. I made the first brush stroke. Many years ago. 1962. Summer. August, late August, the 20th if I remember correctly. Memory, the re-creation of a past that never existed. Such a promising beginning, Minnie and I, Minnie and me. My cognitive functions have deteriorated. I don't remember the grammar drummed into me by my eighth grade English teacher. Either way, that memory I am sure of, though not how or why it ended as badly as it did. One of the memories I wish the Mau-mau would erase. It wouldn't work. Dinitia knows this story. One of the many reasons she loves Minnie, not me. She would be my archive. An incomplete archive. In the index under the letter 'O', no entry for Father Giuseppe Ozoni.

❧ ❧ ❧

Tall field grass, brown and sere from the summer's heat,

engulfs me and Minnie. Seagulls fly overhead, a shortcut from bay to inlet. Minnie wears his hair long, shoulder length, when school is out. During the school year when the principal forces him to get a haircut and Minnie complies because he knows he has to graduate high school to go to college, he wears it over his ears in a modified duck cut that makes him look like Elvis without the pomade.

Minnie unsheathes a scalpel from a leather carrier he made during Arts & Crafts at summer camp. "Is that *the* scalpel?" I ask.

"The very one. My sacred scalpel."

I sterilize its blade with a match.

Minnie laughs. "Worried about being contaminated?"

"No more than I already am. Than we already are."

I slice into my finger, deeper and deeper until, blocked by bone, the scalpel clicks to a stop. I concentrate on the ritual of the moment to numb the pain. Blood, my blood, pools around the scalpel, then spreads over my skin, sluicing into the crevices of my knuckles, around the side of my hand into the palm where it follows the lines, the life line, the love line, the money line, the memory line, moving like rainwater in a shallow gully. Blood overflows the memory line and drips on to the field grass, adding color to the drab ocher of a hot, dry summer. I pull the scalpel straight out, careful not to slice the wound open any further, then hand the knife to Minnie who wipes the scalpel on the grass and nicks his own finger. Minnie squeezes out a drop of blood and presses it into mine, smearing our fingers with the mixture. Blood, my blood, absorbs Minnie's the way the ocean absorbs rain from a passing squall, fresh water dissolving into salt water and losing its own unique properties the instant it hits the surface.

"One for all and all for one!" Minnie says.

"The two Musketeers."

"Of the art world. Minnie and Malone. The two Musketeers of the art world."

I raise my hand above my head to stem the bleeding, pointing a red stained finger toward the heavens in a sacred obscenity while Minnie fashions a tourniquet out of a handkerchief and wraps my finger. Blood, my blood, leaches through the white cloth, spreading fiber by fiber, its shade changing with the dryness, or the thickness, or the freshness of the cloth, the number of layers through which the blood passes, the distance between the cloth and the wound. The handkerchief drinks my blood, draining my life line, my love line, my money line, my memory line, with a thirst that cannot be slaked.

"Looks like the rags in crucifixion paintings," Minnie says.

The handkerchief replicates those rags, red from sopping up the blood of Christ, blood from the wounds in His side, the wounds in His hands, the wounds in His feet, but not His finger, never His finger. I hate those paintings because I know how difficult it is to recreate human blood on canvas with oils. Red on my palette, always over-mixed, is too brown, too purple, too pink, or, once, too orange. Minnie, of course, never over-mixes his reds. My discovery of swine blood hovers in the distant future.

"You can always paint off my palette," Minnie says.

"I'd rather paint with real blood," I reply.

I wipe my hands on the field grass. The stain looks as if a wounded rabbit paused to rest before continuing its flight from a pack of feral dogs.

"I'm not playing basketball this season," I tell Minnie. "I'm getting a job. Part time. In one of the mills."

"You'll blow your chance for a scholarship."

"I'm third string All County. Who's going to give me a scholarship?"

"You're starting guard for the Class A state champs and you play for a coach who always finds a way to place his boys."

"I'll work and I'll paint and if I have any money left after paying room and board, I'll save for art school."

"What for? The stuff just collects dust."

I flash an obscene gesture with my bandaged finger, but the truth knifes into me, deeper and deeper, until, blocked by bone, it comes to rest. Minnie's curse, a recklessness that makes James Dean in *Rebel Without a Cause* act like he's afraid of his shadow; my curse, art I will never sell, never display or exhibit.

"Fuck you too." Minnie plows through the tall grass toward the stone wall edging the field and I follow in his furrow, holding my hand above my head to control the bleeding. Driving home, Minnie takes the long way back. The fields bordering Johnnycake Hill Road are devoid of life except for cows clumped together in the shade of occasional trees. On the radio, Ding Dong Dave, the Afternoon Rave, alternates between the Vitalis twins, Frankie Avalon and Fabian, the Rave's daily Philadelphia hour.

"Would you go into the funeral business?" I ask. "I mean if you had to."

"Your Da still pushing accounting school?"

I flash another obscenity with my bandaged finger and the sudden motion sprays blood around the interior of Minnie's car, random drops with as much coherence as a Jackson Pollock drip painting. I don't like the new abstract art because I don't know how to talk about it. Art that cannot be verbalized doesn't qualify as art for me. Calling it abstract begs the question. As does calling it chaotic. Or using any of the other words the critics use. Maybe the language fails the art instead of the art failing the language. It makes me feel like a cave man grunting at a wall painting.

At home, Ma runs warm water over the bloody handkerchief as she unwraps my finger. Motherhood prepares her for such emergencies and this one is benign compared to most. Once I gouged my thigh on an outside water faucet, exposing a thick layer of subcutaneous fat. She propped my leg on the back seat of the car to keep the wound from opening any further and drove to the emergency room as calmly as if she were going to the store for a quart of milk. I collect scars the way some boys collect rocks. Ma thinks I will outgrow this, but there are some things you never outgrow, the reason my art now and forever will collect dust.

"I slashed it on a hubcap helping Minnie change a tire."

"The doctor should look at this." Ma pries the wound open and bathes it in hydrogen peroxide. "It may need stitches."

"Da have any luck today?"

"Or a tetanus shot."

"How'd Da make out?"

"How clean can a hubcap be?"

Red drains from the handkerchief and flows across the white porcelain until it whirlpools into the drain, a patina of light pink like mud eddies shaped by river currents. I like natural shapes because they occur randomly; or, if not randomly, uniquely. The mud eddies in one river never duplicate the eddies in any other. Of course, I can't prove this without photographing mud eddies, something I won't waste my time doing, but I believe in nature's creativity and it comforts me when I stand before a blank canvas not sure where to put the first line. Or the second. Or the third.

"Infection. If it goes untreated you could lose your finger."

"I asked about Da."

"Something will turn up. Maybe tomorrow."

"Think I'll have a scar?"

"Nothing like your thigh." She blows gently on the wound. "What about these?" She gestures toward the stack of college catalogues, unopened, on the kitchen counter, catalogues from Babson and Bentley and Bryant and other business colleges throughout the northeast and mid-Atlantic states.

"Did you ever see the Book of Kells, Ma?"

"On my honeymoon. It's a rare beauty, I tell you. I've never seen anything like it. This may hurt."

"If you could create something that beautiful..." She swabs Iodine on my wound and the pain squeezes my voice out of my throat and tears out of both eyes. "Oh, God, Ma. This stuff'll raise the dead... If you could... create something... as beautiful as the Book of Kells... would you keep it for yourself... or sell it for as much money as you could get?"

"I suppose I'd keep it." Ma lays a square of gauze on the wound. "For myself and my family. An heirloom."

"If you needed money you'd work, two jobs, three even, before selling it?"

"Isn't that how painters earn their keep? Selling paintings?" She wraps adhesive tape around the gauze, layer after layer, until my finger looks like an Egyptian mummy.

"Hemingway can go into any bookstore in the world," I say, "and buy one of his books, but Picasso's *Guernica* is lost to him forever." Lying to Ma is not a sin I intend to confess. The pulse in my finger beats against the adhesive tape, rhythmically like it's chanting an incantation. I try to decipher the beats as if they are Morse code, but they are uniform, no longs, no shorts, just a rhythmic beat against the tight white adhesive tape wrapping my finger like a mummy preserved for all eternity.

October, 1962

Devils and demons and death, a common subject of medieval art and the art of the modern world. Garsia's *Plague of Locusts* from the *Apocalypse*. Traini's *Triumph of Death*. Goya's *Los Caprichos* and *Los Disparates*. Halloween art. Garsia's Illumination illustrates the *Bible*, *Revelations* and *Apocalypse*. Traini's fresco illustrates the Plague, the Black Death. Goya illustrates monsters and beasts from the nocturnal tradition of Spanish folklore. Halloween is too tame a subject to produce great art which is why Halloween art does not progress beyond gap-toothed jack o'lanterns and witches on broomsticks. Still, I love Halloween and I rejoice over Halloween, 1962, whose devils and demons are malevolent enough to inspire great art if there were a Garsia or Traini or Goya to create it.

❧ ❧ ❧

Julia Reardon cranks up the stereo. She and Minnie can listen to music while they decorate the rumpus room in her basement for the Halloween party that Julia hosts every year the Saturday before Halloween. Now that we are seniors – the Class of '63 Rules is our motto – this year's party will be the best. Minnie gags at the opening guitar chords and harmonies of *Surfer Girl*. Julia loves the Beach Boys and their California surfer music and *Surfer Girl* is her favorite. She wears out three records listening to it. "'Do you love me? Do you, Surfer Girl?'" Julia sings, the sixth Beach Boy. "I can't help it," she says when Minnie gives her the finger, "if I'm a West Coast girl trapped in an East Coast body."

"West Coast girls wouldn't suffer knotty pine paneling."

"I think it's elegant."

"If you're a squirrel."

"Malone likes it."

"Says who?"

"Says me."

"No, he doesn't."

"Yes, he does."

"Does not."

Julia weaves streamers of orange and black crepe paper and holds them while Minnie tapes them to the ceiling. "Make him go to college, Minnie. He won't listen to me."

"He belongs in art school. Whether or not he knows it. Art offers no choice."

"Where's James?" Kate Reardon baby-steps across the floor cradling a bowl of fruit punch in her arms. Scoops of sherbet float belly up in the pink liquid like dead fish and bounce against the rim of the bowl. Waves lap against her blouse. She does not wear a bra and Minnie tries to avoid staring, but she is more compelling than the models in the nudie magazines he uses for life drawing. He turns to the side to hide his erection. He wants to ask her to model for him and she smiles as if she reads his mind and is flattered by his thoughts. "I thought James was going to help decorate."

"He's working at Schneider Tanning. They put on a weekend shift." Minnie's voice squawks as if his belt is several notches too tight.

"Just keep this infernal music down. You know how much trouble Dad has sleeping with all those goings on in Cuba."

"The Russkies will blink first," Minnie says.

"That's what the Brits said about us." Mrs. Reardon no longer smiles.

Minnie watches Mrs. Reardon ascend the stairs. If daughters grow up to look like their mothers, Julia will get more beautiful with age, something of little consolation to Malone. Julia needs to marry someone like her dad, someone with whom she will argue over nothing more serious than whether he plays golf or goes to Mass on Sunday mornings, a disagreement easily compromised by Julia taking the children to Mass while her husband plays golf or their going to Mass as a family on Saturday or, Minnie's preference, their skipping Mass. If Julia marries an artist, there will be a winner and there will be a loser and the artist will always lose. When the door to the first-floor clicks shut, Minnie dumps a bottle of vodka into the punch, then uses the empty bottle to propel the scoops of sherbet across the bowl like a hockey player shooting pucks at an empty net.

Plastic pumpkins overflowing with candy, the bounty of Halloween, surround the punch bowl as the Class of '63, or at least those seniors worthy of an invitation to Julia Reardon's Halloween party, crowd into her basement rumpus room. The streamers Minnie and Julia hung with care now dangle, unraveled, torn, damp from brushing against bodies sweaty from dancing. Twisting replaces jitterbugging, the stroll the cha-cha, and group dancing replaces couple dancing except when the music is slow and dreamy. Couples pair off and compete to see who can move the least. Statue dancing, they call it, forbidden at school dances where the chaperones make sure the dancing bodies are separated by the length of the chaperone's arm, as physically impossible as that might be. On this night, the chaperones are upstairs making better use of their arms.

The boys, except for Minnie, wear chinos and sports shirts, Minnie preferring dungarees and a loose sweater. Minnie's classmates accept him because they grow up together and because every high school clique needs its own Maynard G. Krebs. The girls wear poodle skirts. Several style their hair like Jackie Kennedy. The others, fewer than Julia's 1961 Halloween party, affect bouffants, relying on hair spray to conquer gravity. By the time she becomes a widow, Jackie Kennedy's style will conquer the Class of '63; but on this October Saturday night in 1962, thirteen months before Dallas, mere days after the Armageddon of the Cuban Missile Crisis that does not happen, most of the girls still believe in hair spray.

Fats Domino's *Blueberry Hill* blares from the record player – the Class of '63 does not share Julia Reardon's obsession with *Surfer Girl* – not yet a golden oldie or a blast from the past. Throughout the rumpus room the fruit punch works its magic. On the floor behind the bar Minnie necks with Laurie Williams, still in her cheerleader's uniform. If Maynard G. Krebs doesn't date cheerleaders, it's because television never shows high school kids kissing, at least not the way high school kids really kiss at drive-in movies, at parties, on living room couches while Mom and Dad, lost in space, pretend to sleep. In real life, a cheerleader does date Maynard G. Krebs and while both accept the fact that it is a romance that will not last beyond graduation, if it lasts that long, both also operate on the premise that as long as they respect each other, they should enjoy what, at least on this October Saturday night, is the beginning of the last carefree year of their lives. Entwined in each other behind the bar in Julia Reardon's basement, kissing with a passion derived as much from novelty as love, Laurie the cheerleader and Minnie the Maynard G. Krebs, each fueled by several cups of punch, inhabit their own worlds, at once a part of, yet separate from, each other and from the party that surrounds them. If the party intrudes into these worlds it is the smell of the football game that still lingers in Laurie's hair, a smell that at first distracts Minnie from fantasizing about Mrs. R, but which, ultimately, cannot dislodge from his mind the image of a damp translucent blouse clinging to the breast of a mature woman. Minnie knows he will have to preserve this image with oils on canvas. Yes, Laurie tells him she will model for him, hinting that she will let him decide how much or how little to wear. But Minnie's studio is at home and Minnie's mother, he knows, will insist on being in the studio while Laurie poses and, even worse, insist on Laurie's mother joining them. Minnie doesn't care if Laurie poses fully clothed. He can't paint in front of his mother or Laurie's or anyone's except for Mrs. R and Mrs. R's modeling for him, whether clothed or nude, is as realistic as Jackie K or Marilyn M or Sophia L. Minnie breaks off the kiss and buries his face in Laurie's hair. With Laurie he is rooted, yet he knows this is only transitory, that perhaps it will be the only time in his life he is. Minnie wishes he could make this moment the acorn from which sprouts the giant oak of his life, but he knows his life is trapped in a lightening- storm that the most deeply rooted oak will be unable to survive.

I arrive at the party to the opening chords of *Tears on My Pillow* by Little Anthony and the Imperials and Julia and I statue dance, sharing the floor with several other couples. In the middle of the first chorus, Stevie Flint, starting quarterback on the football team, wobbles toward us. "I didn't give you permission to quit basketball."

"He doesn't need your permission." Julia blows a pink bubble gum bubble and pops it.

"Lighten up, Stevie." Paul 'Rabbit' Costa, one of the starting halfbacks, slides between Flint and Julia as if he is slipping a tackle.

"He needs some fresh air, Rabbit," Julia says.

"Let's go howl at the moon, Stevie," Rabbit says.

"No one quits the Durfee High School basketball team." Stevie reaches over Rabbit's shoulder, but Rabbit locks Flint's arm in his and with the help of one of the other players pushes him toward the stairs.

Julia and I resume our statue dance. Julia holds me tight against her and nuzzles her mouth against the side of my neck, nibbling my skin, then making the boo-boo all better with her tongue. She presses against me and I feel her breasts, full and firm and beyond my imagination. She pulls my shirttail from my pants and works her hand inside my shirt, tracing my spine with her fingertips. We statue dance, breast to breast and groin to groin, my hands on her ass, hers on mine, pushing against each other, lost inside Elvis Presley's *Love Me Tender*, when I grab my back and double over. "I lifted a bail of cowhide the wrong way," I confess.

"Do you want Dad to take you to the Emergency Room?"

"It's just a spasm."

I bite my knuckles. The pain reminds me of the time Minnie spiked me in the hand with a hunting knife while we played stretch. A superficial flesh wound according to the doctor. A few stitches. Good as new. Better than new because I had another scar, thin and white, another combat medal. Like the scar on my finger. Julia kisses me full on the lips. Her tongue darts in and out of my mouth, sucking my tongue like a lollipop.

I gag on her bubble gum and push her tongue back into her mouth, breaking off her kiss. "I had a bitch of a day." Roy Orbison's *Only the Lonely* trails me as I hobble to the stairs. From the floor behind the bar, Laurie Williams winks at me. Roy Orbison does not sing for her.

December, 1962

In December, 1962, I find myself chewing on my pencil, savoring the lead, imagining its dark dense atoms attaching themselves to my red corpuscles, attacking my brain, turning me into a retard. That what I am. A retard. Worse than a retard. Only Bulldog Bennett schedules an hour exam the Monday before school lets out for Christmas vacation, something she does every year. I struggle to write essays on any four of Homer, Herodotus, Sophocles, Plato, Aristotle, Demosthenes, Cicero, or Virgil, identifying the person and analyzing his contribution to the development of Western Civilization, men of letters all, artists and sculptors need not apply. Nor women. Only a retard plans to read the semester's assignments over Christmas vacation. Only a retard sucks on his pencil while the Bulldog patrols the classroom looking for cheaters the way Medusa patrols her cave.

Minnie persuaded me to take the Bulldog's class in Ancient History, Greece and Rome in the time of togas. Something about the education of an artist. The way the

Bulldog teaches, it's more like the portrait of an artist as a dead youth. I tolerate the Egyptians because of the tomb art, but not the Greeks. The only paintings that survive are vase paintings, Red Period or Black Period. The flat two-dimensional figures do not speak to me across the centuries. I have comic books with better art work. I give the Bulldog my blank exam book and exit right.

Snow clouds hang low over Fall River on this cold December Monday, snow clouds reachable from the Heights where Minnie and Julia live, beyond the reach of the valley of tenements where I live. Christmas in a few days, maybe a white Christmas if it snows and the temperatures stay cold, then New Year's, then 1963 and graduation from high school, the start of real life.

Poor Da. I pity the life he lives. Working barely a month of days in 1962, never more than three or four in succession, just long enough for the bosses to figure out that someone with a trick back and gimpy knee is an insurance risk no matter how hard he works. At least Da doesn't drink, doesn't rant, doesn't rave, doesn't become the beast like most men in his circumstances. One beer at the end of the day, whatever beer is on sale, a six pack for $.79, Carling or 'Gansett or Schaeffer or Rhinegold or Piels, one beer, never more, never less, always at home, always in the same chair, always in the same living room, always in a glass with a Boston Celtics logo, an Xmas gift from a son too young to take offense at a loopy leprechaun. If it offends Da, he doesn't say. Pride, willpower, poverty, keep him sober. Maybe it's fear. Someone has to believe the priests. Maybe that's Da's curse. It was mine, mine and Minnie's. Or maybe Da has no regrets, no forgets, no feelings to be numbed, no consciousness to be fragmented into spots and dots like the points in a Pointillist painting, no guilt over the life he plans for me, his only son, his only child, a life of numbers, a life of addition and subtraction, a life of making certain the balance sheet always balances. I have guilt enough for both of us. Da does not drink. I cannot indulge in the illusion he does out of guilt. It is not fair to deny a child his illusions.

Throughout the fall as the weather cools, as the leaves fall, as the frosts becomes more frequent, I struggle to capture the essence of Da on canvas, a Christmas gift to make Da forget for a few moments that it will be another Woolworth's Christmas, a Christmas gift to challenge Da's conviction that everyone who can add or subtract should be an accountant. I can't work on Da's portrait at home. At my request, Minnie sets up an extra easel in his attic studio. He also makes excuses for me to Julia who assumes I am making up for the fiasco I gave her for her birthday. I struggle to create dignity out of line, out of color, out of shape or shading, out of light or shadow. The skills that enable me to mimic the styles and movements of twentieth century art are too undeveloped for the realism of classic portraiture, the realism of a Rembrandt, a Vermeer, a Hals. By the time of Julia's Halloween party, I have consulted every book on Rembrandt the Fall River Public Library owns, every book mentioning Rembrandt, borrowing them, renewing them week after week until the library imposes a limit on how many times a borrower can renew the same book. When the libraries at Brown University and Rhode Island School of Design refuse to accommodate me because I am not enrolled as a student, private tutoring by a R.I.S.D. professor in the past doesn't qualify me, I order two Rembrandt prints from the Museum of Fine Arts in Boston, using Minnie's name, Minnie's address, Minnie's money. By Veteran's Day, *Lady with a Pink* and *Old Man with a Gold Chain*, hang on the wall of Minnie's studio, one on each side of my easel. I study the way Rembrandt uses light and shadow to illuminate the triumphs and failures of life in the skin of his subject and to infuse the eyes with dignity. I study and I study, but little do I learn. I feel as much a retard as I do when I confront the Bulldog's Christmas hour exam.

Week after week I struggle, producing what I consider to be the crayon scrawls of a nursery school child. Where Rembrandt's wrinkles and creases, warts and boils and carbuncles, speak of nobility, mine speak of coarseness. Where Rembrandt tilts a head to portray conviction, my head, tilted at the same angle, shouts resignation, capitulation, giving up, giving in. With each wasted effort, I wonder how long it takes Rembrandt to figure it out. Throughout November into December I continue my attempts to create a portrait of Da in the manner of Rembrandt. In a few days, school will close for the Christmas holiday and I will vacation at Schneider Tanning to repay Minnie the money I borrow for the Rembrandt prints, the paints, the canvases I ruin by my many false starts. On Christmas and New Year's there will be double shifts to tend boilers that cannot be shut down, double time because of the holiday pay, almost a week's work, almost what Da earns in all of 1962. In a few days, there won't be enough time to paint a portrait of Da to put under the Christmas tree.

These thoughts haunt me as I climb the stairs to Minnie's studio where Minnie hunches over his sketch pad drawing pencil sketches of Henry Moore sculptures. A hair net, one of his mother's, keeps the hair out of his eyes. The filaments of the hair net appear electrified in the intense beam of the draftsman's light hanging over the work table. Minnie adjusts the surgical magnifying glass mounted on his head to sharpen its focus. A brick props open Erich Neumann's study of Moore to Moore's 1939 *Reclining Figure* – photographs of three views and psycho-analytical analysis of the sculpture's mysterious holes leading to unknown places. Neumann writes of early man's fascination with caves in hillsides or cliffs and modern man's need to render symbolically the womb of the Great Earth Mother. Maybe if Neumann drew or sculpted, maybe if he understood form and spatial relationships and texture, maybe if he lived in the Paleolithic era carving Venuses out of ivory tusks, maybe he would then understand that words, especially the wrong words, obscure rather than illuminate great art. Minnie doesn't care about Neumann's words. He cares only about the grain of the elmwood, the way the grain leads him by the hand in and out of the sculpture. "Marble," he says, "doesn't do that."

"What would Michelangelo say?" I reply. I mount a sketch pad on the easel and sketch Da in profile, each line as lifeless as the lines in Moore's elmwood. When I step back to view the sketch, the late afternoon sun parts the snow clouds and, for a moment, the scar on my finger glows red, as red as Christ's blood in an Italian crucifixion painting. Until it starts to snow. The snow continues throughout the night into the next day and I sleep over at Minnie's. Through the window of Minnie's studio, the Taunton River slowly disappears in the heavy snow. Some of Monet's best oils are cityscapes observed through windows or from balconies through fog or rain or snow or dirty air. I can paint this, I think, as the river fades from view. By mid-afternoon, the snow ends and the sun lights up the world. The blue of the sky is deep, too deep to be depicted in any naturalist landscape. The Taunton River reappears, a black ribbon around white gift wrap. Good-by, long Monet. It's been good to know you. Light, even and bright, reflects off the snow and floods Minnie's studio. The colors of my palette absorb the light and hurl it back at the sketch of Da. An avalanche of snow rumbles off the roof. Circles appear in the glass of water on Minnie's work bench as the vibrations invade the attic. Another difference between Michelangelo's marble and Moore's elmwood. I steady the frame of the canvas with my fingertips.

Footsteps on the stairs, a knock on the door. Therese Minifie hands an envelope to Minnie. She has always been thin, but now she wastes away like a limestone figurine exposed to heavy weather. I worry about her health as much as I do Da's. Whenever I try to discuss it with Minnie, he freezes up the way I do whenever Minnie rags me about not exhibiting my paintings. I can't equate the two. The world will easily survive without my paintings, but Minnie won't survive without his mom. Any more than I would without mine.

Minnie leaps into the air, clicks his heels, then begins twirling his mom around the studio. I squeeze myself and my easel into the corner. Minnie and his mom continue their mad twirl until Therese collapses against the door. Her chest heaves as she labors to breathe. "Your father and I once danced like that," she gasps. "If only you knew him then." Shadows of sweat dampen her blouse and I volunteer to get some water, but she shakes her head. Her cheeks puff out as she exhales, collapse as she inhales. Slowly, her breathing normalizes and the flush fades from her cheeks. "Well done, my Amherst man." Therese kisses Minnie on the cheek.

"Come to Amherst with me," Minnie says. "It's got a great studio art department."

"Do they have an accounting major?"

January 1, 1963

I spend New Year's Day, 1963, tending the boilers at Schneider Tanning while Minnie carves models out of bars of soap for an elmwood sculpture of a pregnant woman in the style of Henry Moore. He cannot control the proportions of the various elements of the sculpture. He wants the belly to be oversized, but neither pregnant nor grotesque and the breasts to be petite, the breasts of an adolescent. Soap figures recline or kneel or stand or squat like a primitive woman about to give birth. On some the facial features are recognizable, on others abstracted. Some have linear hair; others grids. I doubt the cavemen who carved the *"Venus" of Willendorf* or the *Venus of Lespugue* agonized as much. I would go to the source for inspiration, not to a derivative interpretation by a modern abstract sculptor; but I am not Minnie.

All the permutations. All the bars of soap. One is too limiting. As is two. Three. Four. If there were an infinite number of Minnies with an infinite number of blocks of elmwood, one would sculpt Michelangelo's *Pieta*. But elmwood is expensive and Vincenzo won't stand Minnie the cost. A car, yes. Clothes, yes. Records, yes. Money for dates, yes. Bribes to entice Minnie into the business of death. Da, I know, would outfit me if he could afford to. Therese, more understanding, advances Minnie the money for two blocks of elmwood to be repaid, she says with a laugh, when I am in my dotage. Minnie thanks her with a silent prayer she will one day have the corpulence of a Moore sculpture.

Minnie transports the two blocks of elmwood from his front porch to his attic studio by a series of ramps and pulleys that would make Leonardo da Vinci proud, Rube Goldberg prouder. As he gently sands one of the pieces of elmwood (sanding with the grain) with fine grained sandpaper, Julia asks him to file an application at Amherst College for me.

"He's afraid," she tells Minnie. "Afraid of me. Afraid of you. Afraid of the world outside Fall River."

"That's not what he's afraid of."

Minnie resumes sanding. After each stroke, he blows away the dust. He doesn't want to sand the grains back into the wood and pit its surface, mar its smoothness, dull its sheen. He understands Moore's infatuation with wood. It has the intimacy of a fine woman and, soon, it will have the shape. The wood absorbs Minnie's attention as does the barely audible whooshing of the sandpaper against the wood, and all he can hear is the voice of the elmwood whispering to him as he attempts to transform it into a work of art, a sculpture in the style of

Moore.

"If you believe he has that much talent," Julia says, "do this for him."

And Minnie does. He sorts through my portfolio and sets aside six pieces, three water colors, two oils, and a pastel. He submits slides, slides he photographs himself, and the originals never leave his studio. Minnie swells with cleverness, convincing himself I will never know. But, I know everything and I explode into his studio like a hydrogen bomb shrieking that he had no fucking right! I slap the elmwood out of his hands, splitting it in two against the radiator. When I lunge for another sculpture, he intercepts me and slaps me across the face and wrestles me to the floor where we roll around like children who don't know how to fight. I immobilize him with a half-Nelson and charge his work bench, kicking it over. Two sculptures crash to the floor and splinter into toothpicks.

"If you want to play God," I taunt, "put Humpty Dumpty back together again."

The scar on my fingertip pulsates, it's whiteness like a line of headlights in the distance. The click of a scalpel against bone echoes in my mind. Blood overflows my memory line and stains my palm. A bloody handkerchief wets my pants. I kick Minnie in the gut and, ignoring his groans, slam the door behind me.

It is a debilitating winter, the winter of 1963, each storm further weakening Da, each edging him closer to death. A chronic cough. Recurring fevers. Treated with hot tea laced with honey. Medicated with aspirin. No money in the budget for doctors or prescription drugs. Someday the snow will melt, flowers bloom, sun warm the air, dry out the lungs, calm the fevers. Someday.

In 1811, Caspar David Friedrich painted *Winter Landscape*. In the center foreground, a cripple without crutches leans against a rock, raising his hands in prayer to a crucifix set before tall evergreens, vigorous in their youth. Grass pokes through the snow. The sky glows with the dawn. Salvation. Resurrection. Hope. Spring is in the air. Friedrich, mediocre in comparison to German romantic poets like Goethe or Schiller, nevertheless fancies himself a leader of the German Romantic movement. He does not paint air or rocks or snow or trees; he pontificates about the way these natural objects reflect the soul and emotions of the artist. (Not even love-struck high school seniors talk like this.)

Where you see a mountain or a waterfall, Friedrich sees an allegory of religious symbolism. (A caution: do not view Friedrich's *Abbey Graveyard under Snow* on a full stomach.) Bullshit to the nth power I say. Friedrich's glow of dawn is the fading embers of dusk. The cripple raises not his hands in prayer. He tosses his crutches aside in anger and curses the crucifix. Not every cripple is another Isaiah. Or another Da. Not every crucifix soaks in blood.

❧ ❧ ❧

Friedrich painted a romantic winter, a winter existing only in bad poetry and German Romantic painting, not a real winter, not the hard winter of my senior year in high school with snow on the ground from early December to late March, rare for southern New England, a winter of colds and coughs and flu and cripples who understand the efficacy of a good curse. Da catches his cold Christmas week and it soon evolves into the flu, lingering through January and February into March, no match for the aspirin and hot tea with honey, the only medical care Da can afford. Around St. Patrick's Day, the weather patterns begin to shift, the snow storms begin to edge across the continent to the north, hints of spring tentatively arrive.

Despite a voice rattling with phlegm when he says good morning, despite mucous clogging his nasal passages and perpetually sours his stomach, Da travels to Boston by bus day after day after day where he sometimes finds casual labor through one of the temporary employment agencies. Before Boston he tried Providence where the bus ride cost half as much and took a quarter of the time, but Providence doesn't depend on temporary workers like Boston and the owner of Providence's one temporary agency always runs out of assignments before he runs out of buddies who buy him drinks or kickback half their earnings. And Providence pays less than Boston. Much less.

During hockey and basketball seasons, Da picks up trash at Boston Garden. He can tell by the amount of trash whether the Bruins or Celtics win. Happy fans buy more hot dogs, more popcorn, more beer or soda. Professional wrestling fans eat and drink the most. Maybe they are the happiest. In April, the Red Sox will return to Fenway Park and there will be more work. Red Sox fans are rarely happy, but Fenway Park is much bigger than Boston Garden and there is work after every game, win or, as is usually the case, lose. Da likes working Boston Garden and Fenway Park. It's day work and Ma cooks dinner and we eat together. The food tastes better. His one beer is colder.

Once in a while when one of the regulars is sick there is custodial work in one of Boston's office buildings, vacuuming the corridors, cleaning the rest rooms. This pays better, much better, and is easier on Da's back, but it is night work and he arrives home in the morning to an empty apartment, Ma at work, me at school, empty like the months he goes from factory to factory looking for regular work. Empty, the apartment doesn't feel like home and he feels like Goldilocks who broke in while the people who live there are away. He walks around taking care not to touch anything, not to wrinkle the couch. If he uses a glass or a dish, he washes it and dries it and returns it to the cabinet. He will only eat a piece of bread if there are enough slices in the loaf for a missing one to go unnoticed. The night's wages in his pocket don't make up for returning home to an empty apartment. Maybe if Da had a permanent job on the night shift, he would conquer these feelings. Maybe not. All he knows is that on those mornings when he returns home from a night of cleaning Boston's office towers, he never has an appetite and goes to bed without breakfast.

When there are more men than assignments, something occurring about a third of the time, he takes an early bus. On these occasions, he skips dinner, eating instead the sandwich Brigid packs for his lunch, and goes to bed before she returns from work, before I come home from school. On these nights, eating dinner with Ma and me seems a sacrilege. He isn't working full time and the round-trip daily bus fare to Boston is expensive and the agency takes a commission off the top, but he is working and brings home a little money each week and can at least look himself in the eye each morning when he shaves. By the end of March, the winter passes. The snow melts. Da's flu eases up. His cough slows. His voice no longer rattles. He can taste food again. Maybe as the weather warms, he will find something full time in one of the local mills. Maybe life will return to normal.

"You haven't made love to me all winter," Brigid says one night as she snuggles against her husband's back, her nightgown still under her pillow.

"I wasn't much of a husband this winter."

"I want to make love because I love you, not to reward you for working."

Gabriel rolls over to face his wife and kisses her eyebrows. Their familiarity comforts him. She slowly guides his hand along the side of her neck, across her breast, over her stomach, to the inside of her thigh where she presses it against herself.

"Oh, Briggie. I don't deserve you."

"You deserve all of me." She shifts her hips and pushes his finger into her, then unsnaps his pajama bottoms and reaches for him. His penis lies in her hand, partially aroused but too soft to enter her. With one hand she strokes him while she nibbles his ear lobe, then kisses him on the neck, then on the mouth, open, the way he likes. His penis hardens slightly, still not hard enough for intercourse, and she continues to massage him and kiss him. And she makes little noises because she knows how much better he responds when he thinks she is becoming aroused. His penis hardens a little more and she lubricates it with her saliva, wetting it from the tip to the base and sliding her hand up and down. "Now," she says as she rolls on to her back and places him inside her.

"I'm no better here than on the factory floor," he says after he slips out with his first thrust.

"Shhh!" She raises herself to help him enter her, but again he slips out.

"Oh, Briggie! Such a failure am I." He rolls off her and pulls the sheet up to his chin. "You'd think I'd drunk a keg of Guinness."

"You should be that Irish." Brigid reaches for him again, but he intercepts her hand and brings her fingers to his lips and kisses them.

"I love you," he says.

"And I love you." Brigid cuddles against him, draping her leg over his thighs. Her breast rests on his forearm and she rocks gently. The hair on his arm caresses her nipple.

"This college Minnie's going to... "

"Much better than those business schools you're pushing on James."

"What's the good studying art?"

"It's like going to Trinity College, Dublin." She kisses Gabriel's shoulder and shifts her weight to center his thigh between her legs. The friction of his skin against her keeps her aroused. "Give him your blessing. He won't go if you don't."

"If he goes to one of those business schools, Mick

Reardon'll have a job waiting for him. Not on the floor. In the office. Good money. Enough to take care of Julia. Enough to take care of you."

"James has his own life to lead."

"He's got obligations, Briggie."

"Give him your blessing."

"I won't have you end up like my ma of blessed memory." Gabriel's voice breaks.

"If you don't, I'll release him from those obligations."

Gabriel tries to turn away, but Brigid locks her arm against his cheek and massages his penis again until it is hard enough to enter her and she positions herself astride him and lowers herself on to him and moves up and down and bends forward and brushes her breasts against his face. The scratch of his whiskers against her nipples arouses her even more all the while cradling his head in her hands. His mouth finds her nipple. And as she rises and as she falls and as she rises and as she falls she repeats her request that Gabriel give James his blessing, not begging, not demanding, but somehow making it sound right. She cannot be refused and he cannot refuse her and when he says yes he will her nerves vibrate like the budding branches of a sapling in an April breeze and the vibrations quicken, deepen, shaking the sapling standing tall against the hurricane, bending but not breaking, always snapping back, rooted deep in the earth by her love for her husband and his love for her; and she enjoys the sweetest orgasm in many, many years.

With Gabriel still deep within her, she rolls on to her back and positions her legs, her knees almost opposite her ears and cries 'faster' as Gabriel starts moving and 'faster' as she lowers her legs to move with him, and 'faster' as she raises herself off the bed to accept his thrusts, and 'faster' as she slaps her thighs against his ribs, and 'faster' as she bounces her heels off his buttocks. She is young again. They both are. Young and strong. Their future still ahead of them. No aches. No pains. No trick backs. No sore knees. A man and his bride. A bride and her husband. "Because I love you," she says.

"Because I love you," he replies.

And together they lie, conjoined and united, and together they sleep, conjoined and united, and, in the morning, when the sun awakens them, they are still one.

※ ※ ※

At 14, Picasso gains entrance to advanced classes at the School of Fine Arts in Barcelona. At 16, he enrolls in the Royal Academy at Madrid. At 18, he joins the avant-garde at Els Quatre Gats. In his early twenties, Picasso conquers Paris. Running away from home leads to no good, unless you run away to join the circus.

※ ※ ※

Rain blows against my bedroom window as I lie on my bed and study the chalk propped against the bedpost. The rain makes a clawing sound like a prisoner with long fingernails scratching the stone walls of his cell. It is not a rain for singing in. I cannot decide whether the chalk is worth the investment of canvas and oils. I ration my supplies and false starts are beyond my budget. Minnie can afford to fail, to experiment, to learn his craft. I can only afford to be perfect the first time, unless I switch from oils to watercolors; but the reputation of an artist who works in watercolors is as permanent as a watercolor exposed to heavy rain. The language tells it all. If it were otherwise, watercolorist rather than painter would be the common synonym for artist. Minnie disagrees. In the days when we were on speaking terms, he insisted poverty would force me to learn discipline, to learn to discriminate between good and bad, to learn to make judgments. Like he's an expert. He wastes more canvases in a month than I use in a year. At one time, Minnie gave me those canvases. I reversed them on the frame, paint on the back. It was worse than wearing thrift shop clothes, hand-me-downs from someone else's older brother. I hear Da's footsteps outside my door and open it before he knocks.

Da holds his back rigid to contain the pain and limps across the room. "Big crowd at Fenway last night, Yankees and all," he says. "With the rain made for a long day." He eases himself on to the desk chair, sitting forward to transfer his weight from the base of his spine to his feet and legs.

"I went from school to the tannery." I rotate the chalk 180 degrees and face it toward Da. "What do you think?"

"This college Minnie's going to... "

"I'm not going to college with Minnie."

"You got my Da's temper. Don't be the mule he was."

"They don't teach accounting at this college Minnie's going to."

Da clenches his teeth and raises himself with his arms to relieve the pressure on his back. "Your Ma says a President of the United States went there. Says he was a lawyer before he was President. Says painters have lawyers. Museums. And the... the... " Pain traps the words in his mouth.

"I'd rather go into the mills."

"You won't be able to take care of Ma when my time comes. She deserves better than what I did for my ma."

"What do I deserve?"

"That's the mule talking. I'm not asking you to promise law school. Just think about it. Promise me you'll think about it and you have my blessing."

"How come all of a sudden?"

Da loops his hands together under his right thigh behind the knee and lifts his leg off the floor. "Because... " He bares his teeth as he tries to straighten his leg. "Because your Ma was right and I was wrong. Just like you're wrong about Minnie. Make peace with him."

"He won't..."

"Let him say no for himself."

"Cover your eyes." I slide all of my clothes to one side of my closet and ease out a sketch pad that I open and set on the easel. "Open sesame. It's a study for an oil painting I'm working on."

"Me? I'm not dead yet."

"Most portraits are of the living."

Da grabs the bedpost and pulls himself out of the chair. "You made me look too good."

"It's called Realism, Da." I hug him across the shoulders. I don't want to aggravate his back.

❧ ❧ ❧

On a chilly Tuesday evening during April school vacation I bring Minnie a peace offering, a painting, synthetic polymer on finished plywood, of Minnie and Laurie holding hands in an abstract version of the sculpture garden at the Museum of Modern Art in New York. The crucifix soaking in blood blends in with the sculptures. When I knock on the door of Minnie's studio, a light, bouncy knock, a request to enter, not a demand he shouts, Not now, through the door. I knock again and when Minnie opens the door, I hand him the painting. "I came to apologize."

"Will you let me destroy one of your pieces?"

"I'm sorry."

"You make toothpicks out of my sculpture and you want to skate by with 'I'm sorry'? Me and Laurie, huh? Where are we? A cemetery?"

"The sculpture garden at MoMA."

"These black splotches are sculptures? I'll bring this to our fiftieth reunion. Painted by the class genius, I'll say. The Michelangelo of his time."

"I won't be there?"

"In Paris. The Louvre will beg for your discards. Fall River won't exist. Me, Julia, Laurie, we'll all drink a toast and talk about the good old days when art offered no choice and Michelangelo Malone played backcourt for the state champs. Maybe someone will have an old *Fall River Herald*, the one with your picture on the front page, hanging in midair, the ball in flight, the clock at zero, Durfee down by one on the scoreboard."

"Not the one with the editorial crucifying me for quitting the team?"

"You never could mix your reds." Minnie grabs me and hugs me, then kisses me on both cheeks European style. "The Two Musketeers of the art world." Minnie nudges me toward the door. "I'm in the middle of something and you know how temperamental us Artistes are."

The next day I receive a letter of acceptance from Amherst College. At Julia's insistence, we celebrate under the stars in the field where Minnie and I became blood brothers. The night air is clear and crisp and the stars shine like they do on a winter night, the type of starry sky that inspired Van Gogh. I doubt he shared it with anyone. Julia and I share body warmth on a blanket beside Julia's car. A stone wall shields us from the road and the Westport police who routinely arrest teenagers with alcoholic beverages. I doubt the judge will be lenient because we drink champagne rather than beer. Julia traces the outline of my ear with her fingertips. "A lot of Amherst grads go to business school." She blows the words into my ear. "Harvard. Sloan. Stanford. All the top schools. You'll take us public. Turn a little ol' pants factory into an international conglomerate. We'll be zillionaires."

"What if I went to law school? Went into art law? Represented Minnie? Other artists? Art galleries? Museums?"

Julia interrupts me with a kiss, tangling her fingers in my hair while she pulls my shirt out of my pants and struggles to undo my belt buckle. I roll on to my back and face the starry sky. The stars draw my mind out of my body the way a magnet attracts iron filings and I feel my mind drift upward until I am looking down from above, watching Julia, then myself pushing her hands away and rolling to the side and zipping up my pants and telling her no. I love you, she says, her voice wee and small because light years separate us. Above me the stars wink out and I plummet down like a skydiver whose parachute fails to open.

Paintings are different sizes. There are miniatures that require magnifying glasses. There are gargantuan works whose dimensions are measured in tens of feet that overwhelm the largest galleries. Tintoretto's *Crucifixion*, for example, is 17 feet 7 inches by 40 feet, 2 inches. Picasso's *Guernica* is more than 11 feet tall, more than 25 feet wide. Gros's *Napoleon on the Battlefield at Eylau* is more than 17 feet tall, more than 26 feet wide. Ingre's *Apotheosis of Homer*, Delacroix's *Massacre at Chios*, both exceed 10 feet in height, 10 feet in width. And, of course, there is Jackson Pollock. Lives, too, come in different sizes. Like all oversized works of art, Minnie's life is best viewed from a great distance.

❧ ❧ ❧

August. 1963. Summer. Rock and roll's favorite subject after unrequited love. Rock and roll sings not of my summer. The grocery wheel at Lincoln Park. Subbing on the cigarette wheel. Soda for mill dollies who fuck by the case. A rerun of the summer of '62 except this summer I also work a shift in the mills, third shift, midnight to seven, sneaking the money to Ma while telling Da it's walking around money at college. A real world summer, a summer of staring blankly at the spinning lights on the grocery wheel or cigarette wheel or making cardboard boxes from flats in the shipping room or stacking full boxes on the loading dock or hauling raw cowhide into the tanning room, finished cowhide out of the curing room, or smoking Luckies on the loading dock during the ten minute break I receive every four hours. Not the summer of a high school student, this summer of nights in the mills with dinner at 2:30 AM, breakfast at shift's end, standing at the easel for an hour before going to bed, sleeping, then working afternoons and evenings at the amusement park to begin the cycle again with another night in the mills. Quit the mills, I'll have a life. Painting mornings when the light is strong, working the amusement park afternoons and evenings, but the amusement park doesn't operate year 'round. In September and October, it opens only weekends. By Halloween it closes for the winter. With Labor Day a week away, the amusement park prepares for the switch to weekend hours and I am pink slipped effective Labor Day with the rest of the summer help. If I pass on Amherst and move to Florida or California where amusement parks operate year-round... , but college, liberal arts, not business, means a lot to Ma. Da means well, but he doesn't have it in his genes to be the father of an artist. Few fathers do.

"I'm going to Washington for the civil rights march," Minnie tells me one day in late August as he drives me to work. "It'll be worth a dozen paintings." Minnie parks in the shadow of the roller coaster.

"You sure that's why?"

"Come with me."

"I'll paint from your photos."

"Picasso didn't paint *Guernica* from a still life."

"And Michelangelo was present at the creation?"

"I'll babysit your sacred scalpel."

"It goes where I go."

"Think it through, Minnie. Security will be tight. They'll see it as a weapon and confiscate it. It'll be lost to you forever."

"Not where I'll hide it." Minnie slaps the inside of his thigh, then flashes me the finger. "Shit, man! Today. Tomorrow. Two lousy shifts. You'll be back for the weekend."

I jump out of the car, then lean inside the window. "We come from different worlds, Minnie. You and me. In yours, moms stay home and bake cookies. In mine, they sit at sewing machines stitching pants. In yours, daddy's credit cards gas up the car. In mine, kids skip lunch to have bus fare. I don't belong in your world any more than you belong in mine. Go. Have a wonderful time. March for civil rights. Come back and paint the greatest paintings ever painted and maybe you'll be the better artist because no one gives a rusty fuck about paintings of punch presses or grocery wheels, but if that's what I have to paint that's what I'll paint because that's my world."

Minnie guns the engine; the lake pipes roar like a wounded animal. Peeling rubber, he almost takes my head with him. On Wednesday, I switch shifts with the shill who works the stuffed animal wheel. Julia and I watch Walter Cronkite report live from the March on Washington. Thousands and thousands of people cram the Mall in the heart of D. C.

"A vast army of America's middle class," Walter Cronkite informs the nation, "marches today on the streets of our nation's capital."

Julia sets a tray with a pitcher of lemonade, two glasses, and a box of sugar cookies on the coffee table.

"Everywhere," Cronkite continues, "well behaved groups of young children clap their hands and sing freedom songs. Despite the crowd, everyone is friendly. There's the atmosphere of a summer outing, part political convention, part fish fry, part fair ground. Freedom has never been celebrated with such dignity."

Julia settles on the couch beside me and drapes one leg across my lap. Her tan is rich and dark against the pale pastiness of my factory skin. Dark enough to pass for colored. She wets her fingertips on the moisture condensing on the sides of the pitcher and traces designs on my face.

❧ ❧ ❧

On the Mall in Washington, Minnie, sporting an "I was there" button, snakes his way through the crowd, stopping every few seconds to take another photograph. Close-ups. Mainly people. Their faces. Their expressions. The look in their eyes. The set of their mouths. And their hands because hands are as important as faces. Not to record the event. His five senses do that, but to recall the event, what he sees, what he hears, what he feels, what he smells, what he tastes. When he sits in his studio on some cold winter night, his mind and his heart and his hands will be in Washington.

Words hang everywhere. Words hang on the signs carried by many of the marchers, "Pass the Bill", "We march for integration", "We'll be free by '63". Words hang from loudspeakers, some conciliatory and reassuring, "We are not a mob. We are the advance guard of a massive moral revolution for jobs and freedom." Other words challenging, threatening, "We shall splinter the segregated South into a thousand pieces, and put them back together in the images of God and Democracy." Still others, pleading, exhorting, "You've got religion here today. Don't backslide tomorrow." Words hang in the very air itself, a steady chant from the distant Lincoln Memorial, "Pass the bill! Pass the bill!" Words hang in song, Josh White, Odetta, Mahalia Jackson. And words hang between the clapping hands of the people Minnie photographs:

> "I'm gonna tell My Lord
> When I get home,
> Just how long you've
> Been treating me wrong."

Minnie walks backward along a gravel footpath photographing long lines of marchers. He composes, then recomposes, the scene through the viewfinder of his camera, adjusting its focus as the distance from his subject changes. Minnie pans the crowd with his camera searching for the next perfect face, the next perfect expression, the next perfect painting, when a blonde fills his viewfinder, more beautiful, he thinks, than Ingrid Bergman in *Casablanca* or Lauren Bacall in *To Have and Have Not*. Minnie maneuvers toward her through a group of elderly Negroes carrying miniature American flags. He picks up his pace and trips over an elderly Negro woman, falling at her feet. A small American flag flutters down beside him as he brushes bits of gravel from his cheeks. The Negroes form a semi-circle around him, most of them old enough to be the son or daughter of a parent freed by the Emancipation Proclamation. "Excuse me, ma'am." Minnie picks up the flag and returned it to her. Out of the corner of his eye he notices the coed watching him. "My fault. Sorry."

"First time a white man's ever sorried me." The

woman wears a black dress, long sleeve with cuffs at the wrists, gloves, and a hat with a mesh veil. Her hair, as white as the stars on the flag, extends below her hat like the fringe on a surrey. A 'We'll be free by '63' sash loops from one shoulder to the opposite hip crossing over her heart.

"Can I walk along a spell?" Minnie asks.

"Edna Mae Mangel. Alabama."

"Merisi Minifie. Massachusetts." He extends his hand. "The world calls me Minnie."

Edna Mae hesitates before shaking Minnie's hand. "President Kennedy's Massachusetts, Mr. Minnie?"

"There's only one Massachusetts, Miss Mangel."

"Call me Miss Edna."

The group moves along the gravel, no longer talking or singing or chanting. Riding north on the freedom bus, there were warnings: The F.B.I. might infiltrate to spy on the marchers; segregationists might infiltrate to provoke breaches of the peace. That is the greatest fear. An incident. Something that will distract white America from the justice of the Negro cause. Something that will justify a Congressman's decision to vote against the bill. Something that will persuade President Kennedy to delay again until another tomorrow. This march is about today. Not tomorrow.

"Drive up, Miss Edna?"

"My Lord! Think a body can afford a car? Boarded a freedom bus yesterday in Birmingham. Eight dollars. You know how long it takes my Joseph to earn eight dollars?"

"A day?"

"I heard wages up north were high," another Negro says. "I'm Miss Nellie, Miss Edna's sister. Her older sister."

"$1.15 an hour in the mills," Minnie says. "Minimum wage."

"Not in Alabama," Miss Nellie replies.

Somewhere, in the distance, Bob Dylan sings *Blowin' in the Wind.*

꙳ ꙳ ꙳

I nibble on a sugar cookie, holding the pieces on my tongue, enjoying the way they dissolve.

"See anything worth painting?" Julia asks.

"Amazingly enough," Walter Cronkite tells the nation, "the rest of downtown Washington is as quiet as a Sunday morning when everyone's still in church," Cronkite's voice is calm and reverent as if he's reporting a miracle. "This may be one of America's proudest moments."

꙳ ꙳ ꙳

"First march, Mr. Minnie?" Miss Nellie asks.

"First march."

"Miss Edna she's a real veteran. Twice jailed. Stitches. Broken leg once. A keepsake from Bull Connor."

"Miss Nellie likes to talk things up," Miss Edna says.

"Can I take your picture?" Minnie asks. "Both of you? Together?"

"No!" An elderly Negro in a black wool suit worn shiny with age at the knees and elbows and seat of the pants, plants himself between Minnie and Miss Edna. "He may be Hoover or Klan."

"I'm an artist. I just want to paint them when I get home."

The coed materializes out of the air and thrusts a pencil and a sheet of paper with the day's schedule mimeographed on one side at Minnie who does a quick sketch of Miss Edna and Miss Nellie. "I'm Dinitia Marbury Madison, Mr. Minnie." She offers her hand. "I'm a trained observer keeping my eye out for troublemakers." She withdraws a walkie-talkie from her knapsack. "Shall I call a parade marshal?"

"He looks harmless enough," says the Negro who stands between Minnie and Miss Edna and Miss Nellie.

"Is that really why you're here?" Miss Nellie asks Minnie. "To paint people?"

"I'm here for the same reason you are," Minnie says.

"No white man can be here for the same reason we are," Miss Nellie says.

From the direction of the Lincoln Memorial, a soft chorus of *We Shall Overcome* rises up and pours over the marchers, row by row, file by file, rank by rank, like a flood passing over the land depositing bottom soil, making fertile what once was barren.

"Miss Nellie," Miss Edna says, "me, all the rest of us who rode that freedom bus, we can't afford to eat at fancy restaurants like they got in Birmingham or Mobile. But if I want to save my money, if my Joseph wants to save his, if we want to go to one, maybe for a birthday or anniversary... it's only right isn't it?"

Minnie bows his head, the better to hear Ms. Edna's voice.

"It seems silly, doesn't it? All these people. All this trouble for my Joseph and I to be able to eat at the fanciest restaurant in Alabama. But it's not, Mr. Minnie, 'cause every white here today can and we can't. And only your Mr. Kennedy can make it right. That's why I paid eight dollars and rode the bus night and day. And that's why no white can be here for the same reason we are."

"It's what your Mr. Kennedy said this last June," Miss Nellie adds, quoting the President's statement: "'If an American because his skin is dark cannot eat lunch in a restaurant open to the public, then who among us would be content to have the color of his skin changed and stand in his place?' Them be fine soundin' words, Mr. Minnie, but we can't eat words. That's why we're here. We're tired of dining on fine words and not fine linen."

Minnie walks along without saying anything while Miss Edna and Miss Nellie join in singing *We Shall Overcome*. There are not a lot of Negroes in Fall River. Not a lot at Durfee High School. Portuguese, yes. And Cape Verdeans. They live where they want, though most clump together in certain neighborhoods. They eat at the lunch counters in the five and dime. They go to the same schools as the other kids, play on the same teams, belong to the same clubs. They vote, electing one or two to the City Council, the School Committee. Hell, some get invites to Julia's Halloween parties.

But Miss Edna isn't Cape Verdean. Miss Nellie neither. Nor are the Negroes who surround him. He reads about civil rights, watches television news, talks about it in Civics. He knows, everyone knows, the Negroes only want what the Portuguese and the Cape Verdeans have, and the Irish and Italians and Jews. Reading the paper, watching television, isn't the same as seeing their faces, hearing their voices. Such faces. Such wonderful faces. He will paint these faces and if he's good enough maybe hundreds of years from now portraits of Miss Edna and Miss Nellie and the others will hang in a museum and a mother and a father and their children will stand before the paintings and the parents will tell the children that this is what it was really like at the civil rights march in Washington, D.C. in the United States of America in August of 1963. If he is good enough. Some he will pose like the Heads of the Apostles in Masaccio's *Tribute Money* Others like Francis Bacon except that he will hang bodies, Negro bodies, not sides of beef, in the background. More artists come to mind. Orozco. Giotto. Caravaggio. Jacob Lawrence, but not the flat, linear style of the early Lawrence. Let

Malone mount Rembrandt posters beside his easel and paint from pictures. Minnie will paint from life. If he is good enough.

"You're right, Miss Edna," Minnie says. "I'm not here for the same reason you are. But maybe I can make sure no one ever forgets why you're here. I'm sure going to try."

"You want to see things worth painting?" Miss Edna asks. "Come to Alabama."

"There's plenty of seats on the bus," Miss Nellie adds. "Enough for both of you."

"You're serious, aren't you?" Minnie says.

"Life's too hard to be frivolous," Miss Nellie says.

"Amen," say the other Negroes in the group.

"You have to earn the right to paint me, Mr. Minnie," Miss Edna says. "Marchin' in Washington, well it leaves you four pecks short of a bushel."

"Ain't that God's truth," Miss Nellie says.

"Amen," the group choruses again.

In the distance, distorted by the static and feedback of microphones and loudspeakers, a man, his voice not recognizable where Mr. Minnie and Miss Edna and Miss Nellie and Miss Dinitia stand, speaks of his dream.

❦ ❦ ❦

"It's Minnie," Julia says. "Calling from Washington. He's going to Alabama."

I hold the phone away from my ear. Julia eavesdrops. "Why Alabama?"

"Miss Edna says I have to earn the right to paint what I see."

"Who's Miss Edna?" I ask.

"Be careful," Julia shouts. "You can't paint from the grave."

"It beats watching life on television," Minnie shouts back.

❧ ❧ ❧

"Negro lives worth nothing in Alabama," Reverend Martin Carmichael explains to Minnie and Dinitia. They sit in the back of a freedom bus deep inside North Carolina on the return journey to Alabama. The night, cloudy with neither moon nor stars, obscures the rural landscape in dark shadows, perfect for nightriders. The freedom riders, exhausted from a long day, a long night, sleep. The excitement of Dr. King's speech fades before the bus reaches Richmond. Miss Edna, Miss Nellie, the others, know that Dr. King's words mean one thing on the Mall in Washington D.C. In Alabama, the words mean something else if they mean anything at all. Negroes in Alabama have nightmares, not dreams, and words, no matter how powerful, are never strong enough to chase away nightmares. "White lives," Reverend Carmichael continues, "worth less than nothing if they befriending Negroes."

Minnie tries not to think about Reverend Carmichael's warning as he tosses and turns in an effort to find a comfortable sleeping position on the derelict of a bus. Its frame rattles whenever the driver accelerates, shudders when he brakes. Cracks in the macadam might as well be potholes half a wheel deep. The seats, vinyl with duct tape accents, have the give of poured concrete and the smell of an unventilated locker room.

"Where'd you learn to paint?" Dinitia asks Minnie when he stirs.

"Self-taught."

Dinitia retrieves a sketch pad from her knapsack. "Flick your Bic." She holds the flame while Minnie flips through her sketch book. He stops at a pencil drawing, *Dr. King and the Devil*, depicting Dr. Martin Luther King riding a stallion through a dark valley toward a horizon where the first glimpse of the morning sun can be seen. The sun illuminates Dr. King's suit of armor in the medieval style and decorated with the lilies of Christ. "From St. Paul's Epistle to the Ephesians," Dinitia says. "'Put on the whole armor of God that you may be able to stand against the wiles of the devil.'"

Devils, carrying Klan hoods, peer around trees and from behind boulders and crowd the path behind Dr. King's stallion. They raise dark clouds of dust like a horde of scavengers tracking a wounded animal. Dr. King rides eastward, ignoring the devils, ignoring their dogs nipping at the hooves of his stallion, ignoring all that is behind him. His eyes focus forward to the horizon and the first glimmer of the rising sun. "I modeled it on Durer's *Knight, Death and the Devil*."

Minnie feels as inadequate as an eighth grader flunking art. "I got a friend back home who could do something like this." He places his hand on top of hers, but she withdraws her hand and stuffs it under her thigh, then curls toward the window, her back to him.

❧ ❧ ❧

Dinitia rides shot gun in a station wagon. Like the freedom bus, it rattles and heaves and vibrates with every bump in the road. Too much grit and grime clog its air filter. Too many fumes constipate its tail pipe. Reverend Ashley Billington, a Unitarian minister from Montgomery whose mother named him after her favorite character in *Gone with the Wind*, drives. Minnie and M'Boto Kenyatta, an exchange student from Ghana who plans to enroll in Yale, sit in the back seat. Kenyatta wears a dark suit, white shirt, narrow black tie knotted tightly at the neck. Minnie wears dungarees and an Amherst tee shirt. His camera rests in his lap, its lens cap in his pocket.

Billington nicknames his station wagon Gertie after an old dray horse that lived out its life on his grandfather's plantation. On hills, Billington coaxes Gertie with gentle words and a promise of high-test gasoline at the next fill-up. Sometimes Gertie responds; sometimes she doesn't, the same as his grandfather's Gertie who left the dray in the field if she wasn't in the mood to haul it. Neither Gertie responds well to kicks or slaps or angry words. Gertie sways with the curves as the road corkscrews through the Alabama countryside. Billington drives slowly, in part because he doesn't want Gertie to collapse from over-exertion, in part because farmers in this part of the county aren't too particular about where they park their tractors or hay wagons for the night. The air hasn't cooled much since sunset and Gertie's open windows provide a breeze but no relief from the heat. There is no moon, no stars, no source of light.

"You named after Ashley Wilkes?" Dinitia asks.

Billington nods. "I doubt northerners will ever comprehend what Mitchell's book means to southerners of my parents' generation. My generation, too." Despite his pedigree, the University of Alabama denies Billington tenure in the Department of Religion and fires him as an Associate Chaplain because of his involvement in the civil rights movement. Bear Bryant doesn't recruit Negroes for the Crimson Tide and the University trustees don't tolerate Negro sympathizers ministering to the religious needs of the student body. In a few weeks, Billington will join the University of Michigan faculty to teach Christian Ethics.

"What's it like in Ghana, M'Boto?" Dinitia drapes

her arm along the top of the seat and rests her chin on it.

"We are a free country." His accent reminds Minnie of Rex Harrison in *My Fair Lady*. "The first black nation south of the Sahara to proclaim its independence."

"Why Yale?" Dinitia asks.

"My generation will modernize Ghana and soon it will be a great nation like yours."

"What are you doing here if you're going to Yale?" Minnie asks.

"If I intend to fight for freedom at home, I must first learn how."

Gertie's engine light flashes red like the bloodshot eye of a wild animal. "She's overheating," Billington says. "I hope the gas station at Five Corners is open."

The shrill whine of cicada competes with Gertie's wheeze and rattle. She shudders and bucks as she crosses from smooth macadam to the unpaved gravel fronting Norris' Gas. Two gas pumps, one for regular and one for high test, rise out of the gravel, the pump for regular listing to the right like the leaning tower of Pisa. A single bulb hangs over both, but a lampshade of flies and moths and other winged insects obscures the light and the service station itself is more shadow than anything else. The neon sign on the roof hums like an air raid siren warning of an imminent attack. The two r's in Norris and the G in Gas flicker like they are in their death throes. Minnie flashes a photograph. One day he'll find out what the place looks like.

"Don't stray," Billington warns.

A door opens and a stiletto of light splits the gravel lot and punctures Gertie's hood. Minnie now sees that Norris Gas is a wooden building with a step-up covered porch littered with two couches, an ice cooler, and used automobile parts. Strips of flypaper hang from the porch's ceiling like streamers from a 'grand opening' celebration that happened several generations ago. Minnie flashes another photograph.

A hulk steps into the door, his gut touching the frame on each side. "Whad'y'all want?" His voice is too small for his body and it squeaks as if his balls are caught in a vise.

"Where's the loo?" M'Boto asks.

"Don't work here." The hulk steps into the dim light cast by the bulb hanging above the gas pumps. He has a rounded skull, similar to a bowling ball, except for the bridge of his nose and his recessed eyes. He has a small mouth, barely large enough to wrap around the neck of a bottle of sour mash. He wears a dark blue work shirt with a white name emblem above his right breast, Norris in red script, ornate and flowing, like the calligraphy some other Norris might wear to a society ball sponsored by the Daughters of the Confederacy. A large white carbuncle grows out of the right side of his nose. Minnie wants to pop it, to liberate the geyser to spew forth and flood the gravel lot. It would be white as milk, but thick like milk curdling in the heat of an Alabama summer.

"Massys would love this guy," Dinitia whispers. "Marinus too." Minnie nods as if he knows their work, but his memory doesn't function properly in Dinitia's presence and he cannot think of any artists who make ugliness their primary subject.

"He means the john," Dinitia says to the hulk.

"Him neither."

"The rest rooms, Billington says.

"For his kind, outhouse round back."

"What about my kind?" Minnie asks.

"Your kind. His kind. Same kind to me." Norris snorts the words. Minnie moves toward the side of the gas station, but Norris, as nimble as an interior lineman on one of Bear Bryant's national champion football teams, beats Minnie to the corner of the porch. "Customers only."

"Fill it up," Billington says. "And add some water to the radiator, please."

"Cash only." Norris backs Minnie toward the pumps.

Billington holds up a ten-dollar bill.

"Can't make change."

"No matter."

A moth flutters down, then returns to the light as Norris cranks the gas pump. The sound reminds Minnie of his mother's eggbeater and her warnings to keep his hands out of the mixing bowl or else the eggbeater will snap off his fingers. He curls his fingers into fists and shoves them to the bottom of his pockets. While Dinitia and Billington wait with Gertie, M'Boto sneaks around the side of the station and Minnie follows him. Halfway back are a pair of doors, one labeled Johnny Reb, the other Scarlet O'Hara. Johnny Reb hangs on its upper hinge, tilting like a drunk soldier clinging to a wall. Scarlet O'Hara has a hole where the door knob should be. Between the two, there is a square of plywood on which 'Whites Only' is painted in block letters. Not knowing how to read will not excuse this trespass. Behind the station an outhouse perches on cinder blocks beside a mound of tires. Shit piles up beneath it like mounds of cow patties in a pasture. On the door, 'Niggers' in black paint. Minnie photographs it and the sudden light of his flash bounces off the glass face of the gas pump like a moth crashing into a closed window.

"I'll stand guard." Minnie opens the door labeled Johnny Reb.

"I can't go in there," M'Boto says.

"Bullshit!" Minnie photographs M'Boto entering Johnny Reb, then helps him swing the door closed. Again, the flash illuminates the glass face of the gas pump. Norris hangs the nozzle on the side of the pump and retreats into the station where he dials up the sheriff, using a pencil because none of his fingers fit into the holes of the dial. "Some nigra's using Johnny Reb, Cyrus," Norris says.

"Delay 'em, now. I'm on my way."

Norris fills a water bucket and hauls it to the station wagon. "Radiator's too hot to open. I'll check the oil." While he fiddles with the dip stick, he disconnects the wires linking the distributor cap and the spark plugs. Glancing sideways, he watches M'Boto exit Johnny Reb. "Still too hot." Norris splashes some water on his face.

"I've got to pee," Dinitia whispers to Billington.

"Can you hold on? We're almost there."

In the distance, sirens wail, the groans of an out of tune pipe organ. At the first sign of lights sweeping across the trees and fields and gravel lot of the gas station, Dinitia locks herself in Gertie. Fear aggravates her need to pee and she squeezes her legs together until her muscles ache.

Two sheriff's cars peel into Norris' Gas, kicking up loose gravel that bounces off Gertie like hail stones off a tin roof. They pin Gertie at the pump, one in front, one in back, their sirens creating a stereo concert. Red lights sweep through Gertie, bathing Dinitia in their glow. She feels she is in a horror movie, trapped in a car by flying saucers, dreading the inevitable moment when the aliens appear, yet wishing they would hurry up, curious, anxious, to see what they look like. Three heads, maybe, or eyeballs on stems, or scaly bipeds evolved from dinosaurs, or gelatinous blobs. Starving because of their interstellar flight. Carnivores coveting flesh, human flesh. And dehydrated. Desperate for blood, human blood, to slake their thirst. Or human pee. She would piss in their mouths. If they have mouths.

Instead, Sheriff Cyrus exits the front car. Lean and lanky and without an ounce of body fat, he is about her father's age, steel gray hair, a comforting face except for a scar starting under his left eye and curls beneath his ear. Cyrus sweeps the parking area with the spotlight on his cruiser and gestures for M'Boto and Minnie to step out of the shadows. Then he taps on Gertie's window with the butt of his gun and motions for Dinitia to roll it down.

"It's not too smart being out at night with a nigra," Cyrus says. "Deputy Clem will take you to the Reverend Lovejoy's."

Deputy Clem materializes at the sheriff's left. Dinitia knows him from somewhere. She's positive. Clem smiles and the shock of recognition makes her forget the need to pee. On Huntley/Brinkley. In *The New York Times*. A voter's registration march. After water cannons dispersed the marchers, the police descended on them like locusts on a wheat field, clubbing them into submission, men, women, children. Deputy Clem was the whistler, whistling *Dixie*. Over the screams and shouts, over the crack of the clubs against the skulls of marchers, Deputy Clem could be heard as clearly as if he was on stage spiked and miked. "Alabama calls itself the Heart of Dixie," David Brinkley told the nation. Chet Huntley nodded in agreement.
"I'll stay here, thanks," Dinitia says.

"You'll be safer at the Reverend's overnight. My missus will take you to the Greyhound in the morning."

"I'm fine. Really I am."

"Clem you take the lady to the Reverend's. You go straight there. No stoppin' nowhere 'long the way." Cyrus offers Dinitia his hand the way a gentleman would a lady and escorts her to Clem's cruiser as if he is walking her to a horse drawn carriage after a plantation ball in the antebellum south.

"We'll be going," Billington says.

"Whoa, now!" Cyrus says. "I've got a report a serious

crime's been committed here and I got to investigate. How can I investigate if the suspects go on their merry way?" He turns to M'Boto. "You the nigra don't know how to read?"

"He's from Ghana, Sheriff," Billington says. "He doesn't know our customs."

"Customs? Shit!" Minnie says.

"You from Ghana, too?" Cyrus asks Minnie.

"Massachusetts."

"Yankee, are ya?"

"Red Sox fan."

"You making fun of me, boy?"

"No, sir."

"Being that you're a Yankee and all," Cyrus says, "you may think funny of what Southern hospitality's really like. Why don't y'all be my guest for the night. Free room. Breakfast in the morning. Wherever you're going, you'll have an easier time findin' it in the light."

"We wouldn't want to impose, Sheriff," Billington says.

"Why a true southerner don't know the meaning of the word impose."

❧ ❧ ❧

Thirty minutes later, M'Boto balances himself on a wooden stool in a basement cell, raising himself off the dirt floor too high for the rats to gnaw his toes or ankles. He shivers at the noise of rats chewing on the legs of the stool. He knows these sounds from a jail cell half a world away when President Kwame Nkrumah held his uncle in a similar cell under the Preventive Detention Act of 1958 for publishing an editorial warning about the folly of depleting Ghana's foreign reserves. Nkrumah charged his uncle with sedition and detained him without trial, first for five years, then extended it to ten to frighten Ghana's other newspaper editors into self-censorship. His uncle's cell, built when the Gold Coast was a British colony, could be the model for this cell in Alabama, or vice versa, the same dirt floor, the same cinder block walls, the same steel door with a flap at the bottom for sliding in a plate of food, the same rats. Who is more the victim—himself or his uncle? Who is more the villain—Sheriff Cyrus or President Nkrumah? Which is more democratic—Alabama or Ghana? A useless debate. The rats are the only certainty. In the world of ugly, the rats of Alabama twin the rats of Ghana. Or vice versa.

Meanwhile, upstairs, Minnie and Reverend Billington pace the cement floor of a clean jail cell, no rats, no vermin of any kind except, according to Deputy Clem, the prisoners themselves. "It makes no sense the way he let Dinitia go," Billington says. "Most of these sheriffs rape female civil rights workers. Rape one, scare off a hundred."

"What's going to happen to M'Boto?" Minnie asks.

"An accidental fall."

"But we're witnesses."

"The only difference between Alabama and Siberia is we rarely get snow."

In his office, Sheriff Cyrus finishes his phone conversation. "The missus will drive her to the 9 o'clock Greyhound. No one better interfere with that bus, ya hear?"

"The boys ain't gonna like it," Clem says.

"You let'em go at midnight. All three. I want 'em leaving here in perfect health, ya hear? Perfect health."

"I'll take pictures," Clem says.

"Movies. Take movies. In the cell but move the nigra upstairs first. Getting into the car. Driving off. With movies no fuckin' Kennedy can say we harmed one hair on their pointy heads."

"Jesus, Sheriff. You're brilliant."

"That's why I'm the sheriff and you're the deputy."

Shortly after midnight, Gertie chugs along, backfiring and bucking because Norris does not reconnect all of the wires from the distributor cap to the spark plugs. The night is as black as a piece of Alabama anthracite and as hot as the inside of a coal furnace. Minnie drives because he has too much nervous energy to be a passenger. Reverend Billington searches the radio dial for something other than Reverend Deacon's Salvation Power Hour. M'Boto dozes in the back seat. Around a bend in the road, a hay wagon.

"Lock the doors and back up," Billington says.

High beams blind Minnie and he does not see six men in Ku Klux Klan regalia step out from behind the hay wagon.

"Cut through the field," Billington says.

Minnie steers hard to the left and guns the engine, but Gertie dies, her weakened systems, disconnected distributor cap, unable to digest the sudden influx of fuel. The Klan surrounds Gertie, some carrying rope, others bats or shovels, whips and chains, one a pick ax that knocks off Gertie's door handles, her outside mirrors, smashes her windshield and side windows, punctures her gas tank, destroys her headlights. Minnie reaches for his sacred scalpel, ready to slice and dice and kill some Klan, but fear freezes his hand. He chickens out of the ultimate game of chicken. Outside Gertie, the sounds of people being beaten fills the air. Grunts. Cheers. The thud of shovel against skull. The crack of whip against flesh. And screams. Three voices. Then two. Then one. Then none. Minnie crawls into the underbrush, hunkers down when he hears them searching for him. Flames. In the light of Gertie's funeral pyre, Minnie sees M'Boto swinging from a tree, naked and flayed as if they harvested his skin to make a lamp shade. Minnie listens to Gertie burn, to the explosion of her gas tank, to the roar of her fireball, to the sounds of trucks receding into the dark, to the creaking of a rope swaying on a branch over his head, to his own heart. A body's shadow swings back and forth on the ground beside his head and Minnie feels trapped in a pit beneath a descending pendulum, the pendulum of his sacred scalpel.

❧ ❧ ❧

Sometime later, Minnie awakens in a private room in Massachusetts General Hospital in Boston. Bandages swaddle his head and face. He is groggy from a morphine drip, but he recognizes his mother by her hair style, classic Italian monumental. *The Price is Right* plays softly on the television mounted on the wall above the foot of his bed. The contestants bid on a Mardi Gras trip to New Orleans and their guesses range from $559.00 to $1,864.00. Dinitia Marbury Madison stands at the window staring out at the triangles of white dotting the Charles River. It is perfect sailing weather.

"Where... Where..." Minnie's voice sounds like he is underwater.

"Mass. General. Boston," his mother says.

"They lynched M'Boto." Dinitia buries her face in her hair the way a song bird buries its head under its wing. "The Reverend's in a hospital in Mobile." Dinitia's hair billows as she speaks.

Minnie tries to process this information through the haze created by his pain killers. "Dinitia?"

"I talked my way on to the med-plane."

"I'm here," Laurie Williams says.

"They skinned him alive."

"It wasn't your fault," Laurie says.

"I made him use the men's room. I backtalked the sheriff. When it counted, I pissed my pants."

"They killed him because he was a Negro," Dinitia says.

"It's not your fault," Laurie whispers.

Dinitia says, "They were drunk. They didn't know you were still alive."

"I froze. Did nothing. Played dead hoping they wouldn't find me."

"You were beaten unconscious," Dinitia says.

"I saw him hanging there. I could have stopped it."

Laurie squeezes Minnie's hand. "You couldn't have taken candy from a baby."

Minnie shakes his hand free. "Get out. All of you. Go." He gasps and lapses into unconsciousness.

On *The Price is Right*, a Negro couple from Chicago wins the Mardi Gras vacation with a guess of $1,334.00 and elect to take the cash.

Most (but not all) paintings are rectangular. The geometry of the rectangle dictates the decisions the artist makes in laying out the compositional elements of the work. In some paintings, the artist clearly marks the boundaries between these elements like the boundaries between the states on a map of the United States. In others, the elements blend into each other in a seamless transition. Compare Hopper's *Nighthawks* or Magritte's *Time Transfixed*, for example, with any painting from Monet's Rouen Cathedral series. Amherst College marks a boundary and a transition. I leave it to you to decide whether my painting is a Hopper or Magritte or Monet. As if it matters. Ask Hopper or Magritte or Monet. They'll laugh you away.

✦ ✦ ✦

Amherst College. Freshmen year. September, 1963. If we knew then what we know now... As Einstein said,

God does not play dice with the universe. God did, first semester freshmen year.

The weather blesses the Pioneer Valley and freshmen move-in day for the Amherst College Class of 1967 is sunny, warm, a slight breeze not fierce enough to dislodge leaves from the oak and maple trees shading the grassy quadrangle where James and Stearns cluster with North and South, Appleton and Williston, and Johnson Chapel. Freshmen wearing purple beanies with a white 67 drag trunks, boxes, crates, and suitcases into James and Stearns. The college assigns Minnie and me to 406 Stearns, a two-room corner suite on the top floor. One room looks out on the quadrangle and the War Memorial honoring the men of Amherst who died in World War I, World War II, Korea; the other on the Pratt Museum, the geology building. An abundance of many Pratts: a museum, a dormitory, the football field. I thumb through the freshman mug book, happy there are no Pratts. Nor are there other Malones. Or O'Malleys. Or Finnegans. Or Finnigans. But one Ryan there is, and one Kelly. Too few to demand the dining hall serve corned beef and cabbage on St. Patrick's Day.

Not all peace offerings, not all hugs with man kisses in the European style, lead to peace. Some lead to a cessation of hostilities, but not every such cessation equals peace. Without telling the other, each of us asks the college to assign us elsewhere, but there are no available rooms in the freshmen dorms and as freshmen we are barred from empty rooms in the upper-class dorms. Rooming together, peace or war, will it result in the death of one, perhaps two. At least we're not in love with the same woman. Not yet.

Minnie feels at home but I sense from the awkward way Vincenzo and Therese wait by the car, Vincenzo tightening the knot of his tie every few seconds, Therese shifting her weight from foot to foot as if she is standing on hot coals, that they feel like immigrants dining at society's table. Vincenzo wears a black suit, white shirt, dark tie, a man who came from the funeral home and will return to the funeral home. Therese wears the dress she wore when the Cardinal celebrated Mass at their parish to honor Father Giuseppe Ozoni's years of service to God and Church. The dress fit her then, accentuating her figure in a tasteful way. Now the dress's bodice droops and the waist hangs and the hem, once fashionably below the knee, skirts her ankles. At the rate she is losing weight, she will atomize before we graduate.

Minnie leans against the fender of his dad's car, a misaligned hood ornament. The sun's warmth soothes Minnie's face. Bandages cover his forehead above the bridge of his nose and his cheeks below each eye. The scars from the shallow wounds are healing, some enough to expose to the air without risk of infection. Those glow pink in the bright sunlight. Minnie hates his scars because of the way people stare, but they give him a way to break the ice with his new classmates, a way to impress the coeds at Smith and Mt. Holyoke mixers. I marched on Washington, he boasts. I survived a lynching in Alabama. He doesn't confess how he blames himself for M'Boto's lynching. One scar will be permanent to remind him, the scar along his jaw bone below his right ear. Minnie will see it and feel it every time he washes his face, every time he shaves, every time he combs his hair, every time he sees his reflection. And, when his hands and fingers heal enough to allow him to hold his paint brushes, to control his paints, he vows to memorialize M'Boto in oils. A penance painting.

For the hundredth time Minnie's mother reminds him to apply the ointment every day to prevent infection. My scar, a tiny white squiggle on my fingertip, the legacy of our once and former brotherhood, Minnie's and mine, doesn't require any ointment. Two scars.

Symbol without meaning; metaphors for nothing.

Minnie doesn't expect many visits to campus by his parents. No football Saturdays. No concerts or plays. He doubts they'll come for Parents' Weekend. He hopes they attend graduation. Almost fifty years in this country and his parents still float above it like an oil slick on water. After they die, they make him promise to ship their bodies to Italy for burial.

I hug Ma while Da swings his leg to he can climb into the passenger's seat. I try to hold back my tears, afraid I'll embarrass myself in front of my new classmates who are shaking their fathers' hands and kissing their mothers on the cheeks as if they are already Amherst graduates, captains of industry, bankers or doctors or lawyers, men of wealth and means and social position.

"I envy your tears," Minnie says when I join him.

October, 1963–November, 1963

His name was Giorgio Vasari. He lived from 1511 to 1574. His basic work was *Lives of the Most Eminent Painters, Sculptors, and Architects*, a mere ten volumes in English translation. Many credit him with codifying the development of the idea art history now labels the Italian Renaissance. Read Vasari with caution, today's critics warn. Check him against current scholarship. The arrogance of these so-called art historians who write today, some 400 years after the fact, that they are better qualified to explicate Michelangelo than Vasari who knew him. I envy Vasari for talking of Michelangelo by talking with Michelangelo. I laugh at the prospect of Vasari's descendants deigning to write my biography. Or Minnie's. What you are now reading will be the definitive text, until the next definitive text.

꧁ ꧁ ꧁

September becomes October. We adjust. To college. To being in some of the same classes. To rooming with each other. We divide our space with a Berlin Wall, invisible but not imaginary. We cultivate different friends. Still, we're lumped together as if we constitute a school of painters. American art had the Hudson River School. Amherst has the Fall River School.

※ ※ ※

Minnie and I wait nervously beside our easels as Professor Delaney Pratt prowls his studio with a black Magic Marker. Pratt's Life Drawing class is a prerequisite for all studio art courses and he runs it like a Marine drill sergeant runs basic training at Paris Island. Only the survivors receive departmental permission to major in Studio Art. Pratt's portrait, a life size oil, hangs above the platform where a life model will soon sit. In costume and artistic style, the portrait steals from Gainsborough. In it, Pratt positions his right hand over his heart, his fingers under the lapel. His left-hand rests on the hilt of a sword in a scabbard. His eyes are black, without ambiguity. His hair is slicked down and combed back, cemented in place, more a helmet than a head of hair. The portrait has no signature, no attribution, no provenance, but for a campus myth that it is a self-portrait. There is an alternative myth whose believers argue Pratt signs what he paints. According to this myth, the portrait was the thesis project of a former student, a *Phi Beta Kappa* who gained representation by a New York gallery as a result of the A+ Pratt bestowed on him. What is not myth is Pratt's power within the art department, the power of a dictator for life and the ego to exercise it. Neither students nor untenured faculty dare question him, not even behind his back.

"No!" Pratt slashes one student's drawing with his black Magic Marker. "No!" Another. "No!" A third. "A thousand time's no." Pratt rips my drawing from the easel and lights it with a cigarette lighter, a World War II vintage Zippo emblazoned with the white battle ax against a field of blue, the symbol of the 65th Division, Combat Engineers. "Have you considered majoring in Fire Science, Mr. Malone?" Professor Pratt hands the flaming paper to me and smiles as the ashes drift to the floor, then claps his hands. A model, draped in modesty, arranges herself on the platform beneath Pratt's portrait. Dinitia Marbury Madison.

"If the sight of the female body excites you, Mr. Minifie," Pratt says, "perhaps you should switch to Autopsy. I'm sure you will do very well." Pratt re-arranges the draping to expose her knee. "The last student who attempted to date my niece flunked out of school. Gentlemen. Please do not embarrass yourselves with your usual puerile drawings. Mr. Malone. Sit out this exercise."

"Out of lighter fluid?" I ask.

"The only difference between a wit and a twit, Mr. Malone, is the extra 't'."

Before I can respond, a helicopter emblazoned with the seal of the President of the United States lands on the lawn outside the studio, then a second, a third. President Kennedy will visit the campus to dedicate the cornerstone of the Robert Frost Library and the Air Force tests alternate landing sites for the helicopters that will transport him from Westover Air Force Base.

"Saved by the President, Mr. Malone, but I trust you will drop my class by Monday when Mr. Kennedy will be back in Washington."

❧ ❧ ❧

Indian Summer flies north with President Kennedy. Red, white, and blue bunting garnishes the campus and accents the deep reds, oranges, and yellows of the foliage that peaks later than normal because of unseasonable warmth. Temporary fencing similar to the slat fencing erected at Pratt Field to control the crowd at football games encircles the quad. The Massachusetts Turnpike Authority loans surplus toll booths for use as security check points. Minnie and I pass through three to access the seating reserved for undergraduates. The faculty and their families who sit much closer to the podium pass through a fourth. Only the campus squirrels move about freely and unrestrained. The crowd is as festive as the weather is beautiful and, under the watchful eyes of the Secret Service and the Massachusetts State Police, is orderly and respectful.

I balance a sketch pad on my lap and lay two sets of pencils on the grass at my feet. At each checkpoint the Secret Service examines the sketch pad and pencils, flipping the pages, tapping the pencils, even drawing lines, before letting me pass. My first sketch, President Kennedy and Calvin Plimpton, President of the College, Kennedy laughing at something Plimpton whispers in his ear, a souvenir for Da, not the caricature with exaggerated hair and teeth favored by editorial cartoonists, but a drawing of the man who guided the nation safely through the Cuban missile crisis. I want to capture the strength, the dignity, the courage. Someday I'll do an oil on canvas of Kennedy at Amherst, a gift to be hung inside the Robert Frost Library, or perhaps a gift for the President and the First Lady when they retire to Hyannisport. Today's sketches will be my memory of this day, better than photographs because the pencil is a much sharper instrument for recording a scene than the shutter of a camera. Nothing mediates between the subject and object in a photograph. The light hits the film and freezes the image for all time. Yes, it can be doctored in the darkroom, but the negative is what the negative is. Unlike the photographer, the artist mediates his subject as part of the act of creation. Light does not mechanically create an image on canvas by the opening and closing of a shutter. Cameras create souvenirs and I have left my Brownie in my dorm room. By the time Kennedy receives his honorary degree, I will be on my twelfth drawing, enough raw material for a third, a fourth, perhaps a fifth, oil painting. I continue sketching as Kennedy begins to speak.

"Robert Frost," Kennedy says, "was one of the granite figures of our time in America. He was supremely two things: an artist and an American. It is hardly an accident that Robert Frost coupled poetry and power, for he saw poetry as the means of saving power from itself. When power leads man towards arrogance, poetry reminds him of the richness and diversity of his existence. When power corrupts, poetry cleanses. For art establishes the basic human truth which must serve as the touchstone of our judgment."

I stop sketching.

"I see little of more importance to the future of our country and our civilization," Kennedy continues, "than full recognition of the place of the artist. If art is to nourish the roots of our culture, society must set the artist free to follow his vision wherever it takes him. We must never forget that art is not a form of propaganda; it is a form of truth."

Kennedy pauses and flashes his famous grin as one of the campus squirrels scampers across the stage. "They're better behaved at Harvard."

He continues after the laughter dies down, "But in a democratic society, the highest duty of the writer, the composer, the artist is to remain true to himself and to let the chips fall where they may. In serving his vision of the truth, the artist best serves the nation." Kennedy slowly scans the crowd as if he is speaking directly to each individual. "I look forward to an America which will not be afraid of grace and beauty."

The President waves to the crowd. With every wave the cheers became louder, more insistent. As the Secret Service escorts Kennedy to his helicopter, he gives the crowd a thumbs-up and the cheering renews itself, continuing as he boards his helicopter, continuing as it becomes airborne, continuing until it is barely visible in the sky above the Pioneer Valley. When the helicopter disappears, the Secret Service opens the gates and most of the students head to Pratt Field and the homecoming football game against Wesleyan. I sit and resume drawing. For the moment, Delaney Pratt doesn't exist.

❧ ❧ ❧

Indian Summer departs with President Kennedy and November turns slate gray, the leaves weightless and brittle and crunchy, a lifeless brown. The football team defeats Wesleyan, Trinity, and Williams in Williamstown. Minnie goes to the Williams game in the hope he will bump into Dinitia, but I listen to the game on the campus radio station and work on my first Kennedy oil. I still attend Pratt's Life Drawing class even though he ignores me, refuses to grade my work, refuses to comment on my assignments. At least he does not burn me at the stake in the center of the studio. At the last class before Thanksgiving, Dinitia Marbury Madison returns, her draping less modest, but still far from nude. The leaves on the trees outside the studio are brown, withered, too dead to appreciate her beauty. A few leaves always stick to the trees throughout the winter, surviving the blizzard's gale winds, the January thaws, the snowball fights between the freshman and sophomore classes, falling only when pushed aside by the buds of springtime. Perhaps these are those leaves.

As we work, Pratt patrols the studio, weaving in and out between the easels, flicking his Zippo like a pyromaniac looking for a building to torch. Minnie is the day's third victim, the first time Pratt burns one of Minnie's drawings. "I don't see you saluting now, soldier," I whisper to Minnie as flames consume his work.

"Perhaps you should show him how, Mr. Malone," Pratt says.

I take a deep breath. "I don't salute what I don't respect. Sir." As one, the class looks up from their easels.

"Since you will fail this course anyway, Mr. Malone, perhaps you will spare us the embarrassment of your attending class." Dinitia wraps herself in the draping.

"I've paid my tuition. If I'm going to fail, I will at least get my money's worth doing it." Pratt flicks his Zippo and approaches my easel, but I knock the lighter from his hand and it skitters along the floor. He retrieves the lighter and flicks it twice like an old-fashioned teacher whipping the air with a hickory switch preparing to inflict corporal punishment. Before Pratt can burn my drawing, a student rushes into the studio.

"Kennedy's been shot in Dallas. He's dead."

The class freezes. Pratt pockets his lighter. Dinitia slouches from the room. My life drawings are now still lifes and that sunny Saturday, not even four weeks past, is now part of another age, another epoch, like the Roman Empire or the Pharaonic dynasties of ancient Egypt or the lives of the artists Vasari wrote about. I tiptoe from the studio, abandoning my drawing.

※ ※ ※

At home in Fall River, I watch President Kennedy's funeral on television. I fiddle with the rabbit ears, but cannot eliminate the ghosts that distort the black and white images, the riderless horse, the funeral caisson, the mourners who are as lifeless as their murdered President, their heart beats slowed to the rhythm of the muffled drums. When John John salutes his fallen father, the President's voice rings in my head, "I look forward to an America which will not be afraid of grace and beauty." Only then do I cry.

A boundary and a transition. Einstein was too gentile when he said God does not play dice with the universe. Craps is the name of the game and God does play craps with the universe. As well as with the lives of those who inhabit it.

December, 1963–February, 1964

For a painter, Christmas should be a season of Adorations and Nativity Scenes, but I have no energy, physical or emotional or mental, for painting. Broke as usual, I spend Christmas vacation of my freshman year of college the same way I spent Christmas vacation of my senior year in high school, working at Schneider Tanning, double shifting both Christmas Day and New Year's Day, double overtime pay, the equivalent of eight days pay in two. I work days, not nights and I don't know whether it is Professor Delaney Pratt or the Kennedy assassination or the rut I find myself in with Julia, or rooming with Minnie, or a combination of the four that keeps me from the easel; but I sense that Pratt and the assassination are excuses while Julia is what my physics professor describes as the equal and opposite reaction that necessarily follows every action. I hate physics and would not suffer through it but for the two-semester freshman science requirement. I earn a 72, if earn is the right word, and maneuver my one second semester elective to create a schedule conflict that lands me in the class of the easiest grader in the physics department. The 92 he gives me, and gives is the operative word, is as accurate a reflection of my abilities as the 72.

⁂ ⁂ ⁂

I continue dating Julia while Minnie haunts the mixers at Smith and Mt. Holyoke, competing with guys from Dartmouth and Yale, Harvard and Brown, Williams and Wesleyan, for a name, a phone number, a date. By the third weekend of the semester, my Saturday nights have become as predictable as the motion of the planets around the sun, damn that physics course, something to eat, maybe in Valentine Hall or the Leaning Tower of Pizza or Barselotti's, a movie or concert or hall party, then a speed walk across town to the University of Massachusetts to return Julia to her dormitory before curfew. I can't visualize myself marrying Julia and see no future in our relationship; but, as the song lyric goes, breaking up is very hard to do.

I decide to do it on the Friday night before Christmas. We would go to the Durfee High/New Bedford High basketball game, then a late supper at the Venus de Milo in Swansea, and back to Julia's house. There, in her living room, with Johnny Carson cracking jokes while Ed McMahon tries to induce the dog of the night to eat its Alpo, I will explain our future is in the past. My plan crashes and burns as soon as we walk into the Durfee gym. New Bedford dethroned Durfee in the 1963 Class A Tech Tourney championship game and Coach told the *Fall River Herald* that Durfee lost because its most experienced guard, the only guard capable of containing Wendy Miranda, New Bedford High's sophomore sensation, quit the team. "He could have postponed fingerpainting a few months," Coach said. The reporter printed the quote and every other negative statement Coach made about me. I sent a letter to the newspaper explaining I work nights in the shipping room at Schneider Tanning. The newspaper prints it under the headline 'A Quitter's Reply'.

On the Friday before Christmas, as the two Bristol County rivals warm up for their first game since the championship final, the first game in their annual home and home series, the boos begin when Julia and I enter the gym. People drape coats and jackets across open seats wherever we go. "Sit on the New Bedford side," someone shouts and the crowd takes up the chant. One of the cheerleaders rips a page from the game program, wads it into a ball, and hits me behind the shoulder. Within seconds, wave after wave of paper cannon balls pelt me from the Durfee stands. "Qui-t-t-t-er!" the crowd chants. "Qui-t-t-t-er! Qui-t-t-t-er! Qui-t-t-t-er!"

Sirens wail and a dozen cops flood the floor. Some escort the New Bedford players to their locker room. Others surround Julia and me. "The gym will be cleared," the police announce, "or this game will be forfeited." Like air escaping from a tire with a pinhole leak, the crowd quiets and begins filing out until the gym is empty except for the referees and other game officials, the Durfee team and coaches, the police, me, Julia.

"Arrest them," Coach demands.

Julia holds out her arms, her wrists close together, inviting the police to handcuff her. "Coach," Julia says, her voice calm and even. "I can take my punishment like a man. Can you?"

"I spoke to your father, Miss Reardon," a police captain says. "He's on his way." "Arrest them, God damn it," Coach shouts.

"We'll let you play," the police captain says. "but we won't let the crowd back in."

"Play or forfeit," the head referee says.

"Once a quitter, always a quitter," Coach says as he signals his team to form two lay-up lines under the home basket.

That night, I try to visualize an allegory of bravery in the style of Vermeer's *Allegory of the Faith*. Julia will personify bravery. A white flowing gown. A sword. A shield. A banner. A resolute visage. A lion at rest beside her who makes eye contact with viewers who stand before the painting. A horse behind her. White. Rearing up. Enemies dead at her feet. Others fleeing toward a horizon of mountains. An angel with a trumpet peeking from behind a cloud. Either the iconography of bravery or Joan of Arc transformed into a cliché. I lack Vermeer's connection to his subject. Perhaps I should paint *Allegory of the Quitter*. The next day I look up 'quit' in the dictionary. Seven definitions, the first being 'to free oneself', the seventh being 'to give up or abandon'. I will paint the first. Julia will see the seventh.

❧ ❧ ❧

Reading period, final exams, semester break, and unusually heavy snow combine to prevent Julia and me from seeing each other in January and the chaos of the beginning of the new semester keeps us apart in early February. We speak on the telephone, stilted conversations about exams and the weather and our new classes. We punctuate our conversations with silences that encapsulate our words the way a background wall encapsulates the figures in a painting. We inhabit a common space, but we do not share it. Still, on Valentine's Day, 1964, a Friday, Julia's sorority at the University of Massachusetts celebrates with a Winter Wonderland Party and she invites me. The weather cooperates, covering the Pioneer Valley with a foot of fresh snow, soft and fluffy, what skiers call powder, not the wet, heavy slush that falls when the temperature is near freezing.

Paper Cupids alternating with red hearts and hand cut paper snowflakes decorate the sorority house. Left-over mistletoe hangs from the center of every lintel. The menu caters to the college palate: kegs of beer, bowls of pretzels and chips, tubs of onion dip. $2.00 buys a 16-ounce cup and unlimited refills. Lose a cup and it costs another $2.00 to replace it. Two fisted drinkers can buy two. The Rolling Stones boom out of the stereo, *Satisfaction*, *The Singer Not the Song*, *I'm Free*, *Gotta Get Away*, the great cuts from their first two albums. UMass fraternity guys pack the sorority house. Some dance in the living room. Others hang close to the kegs, guarding their cups with their lives and searching for courage in the beer's foam. The lucky ones descend to the make-out pit in the basement where blankets draped over clotheslines separate the mattresses. I hate the pit. Everyone smokes and the air is thick with it and I have to send my clothes to the cleaners to make them wearable again, an expense my budget can't afford.

Julia pulls me on to the dance floor. We slow dance to *As Tears Go By*. "Why do you treat me like shit?" Julia locks her hands behind my head. "I love you." She presses her hips against me and sways to the rhythm of the song.

I stop dancing and push Julia away. Outside, I shove my hands into my pockets and hunch over to shelter myself from the wind and cold. The sidewalks are not plowed and I share the streets with cars, people on skis, people on snowshoes, people on foot, drunk college students pushing other drunk college students on sleds made of dining hall trays. My eyes tear from the wind and the tears diffuse the headlights of the oncoming cars. They twinkle like exploding stars. The chains on the wheels chatter against the snow like the teeth of a child suffering frostbite. My nose drips and I let it accumulate on my upper lip and sluice into my mouth. Soon it will freeze, an icicle hanging from a twig. The storm swirls around me, blowing snow in my face. My cheeks grow numb and my toes tingle and I walk faster, worried I'll lose feeling in my toes before I get back to my room. My bladder feels like it is about to explode. Behind me, a car horn blares and I see my shadow on a snow bank. My shadow foreshortens as the horn grows louder and I leap into the snow bank to avoid being hit by a skidding car. My hands and arms plunge up to my elbows to break my fall. Snow fills both ears, both nostrils. The car bounces off the snow bank like a pinball off a bumper, missing me by inches, and careens across the road into another snow bank. The driver tries to free his car from the snow and the stench of hot rubber from spinning tires stings my eyes. I shake the snow from my sleeves and brush it from my hair and resume my trek toward campus. I laugh at the absurdity. Every artist needs a great creation story. This near-death experience is not mine.

I stop phoning Julia and refuse to take her calls. *Allegory of a Quitter* will not be an allegory.

Winter is, however, a Pioneer Valley season.

The beauty of late winter asserts itself and inspires me to return to the studio where I try to paint the Octagon, the home of the Amherst music department, as it dissolves into winter's twilight. Weathered and gray and barely visible in dim, overcast light, the Octagon has the perfect 'now you see it, now you don't' quality for Monet if he painted with John Singer Sargent's palette. I conceptualize the painting as a black and white photograph in oils and decide to use only the four or five tones from the middle of Ansel Adams gray scale that I will expand into eight tones since the Octagon is an eight-sided building. The Octagon will be a shape without lines or boundaries melding into the snow-covered ground that surrounds it, the snow laden sky that huddles over it. There will be hints of doors and windows, hints of a front stoop, hints of shrubbery, shapes that will change depending on the distance of the viewer from the work, the angle of vision, the quality of lighting in the room where the picture is hung. The more ambitious I conceive the project, the more at home I feel and, by the end of my first session in the studio, I feel I haven't been away at all.

On the second Saturday of March, a day when diamonds of ice stud the trees and the sun burnishes the whiteness of the snow with a blinding intensity, a day on which the Octagon thrusts itself into its space with sharp, crisp boundaries, its windows reflecting the sun, its shrubbery gleaming and glistening, its gray stucco glowing against the sky's blue, Minnie drags me away from my easel to an exhibit of 'Feudal Art from Japan' at the Smith College Museum of Art. I suspect his ulterior motive and only go because I sense he needs someone to ride shotgun and no one else is foolish enough to do it. He fears someone may rob his stagecoach. Certainly not me, he is confident.

At the museum, Minnie and I argue from gallery to gallery about the art, what it can teach us about vision, about technique, about a way of seeing that neither of us have encountered before.

"Saying Cezanne paints apples," Minnie tells me, "isn't experiencing what Cezanne paints."

We hurl the names of European artists, the names of European paintings, at each other like infantrymen lobbing hand grenades, but most of the grenades fail to detonate and the explosions from the few that do explode harm neither of us. "Fuck you and the horse you rode in on," Minnie says in exasperation as we enter the final gallery of the exhibit, nine hanging scrolls on paper depicting the life and death of Michizane by Fujiwara Nobuzane, a Japanese artist from the Kamakura Period who lived in the late 12th and early 13th centuries. Dinitia Marbury Madison stands before one of the scrolls. She wears a flannel work shirt, blue jeans, and work boots, and carries a copy of Flaubert's *Madame Bovary* in the original French. Minnie circles the gallery to approach her from her other side, struggling to contain his excitement, to exude the ultimate Cowboy Cool, until he trips on his own shoelace and stumbles toward her like a rodeo rider punch drunk from being thrown from too many bulls.

"If you read Flaubert in French," Minnie says in an effort to display his sophistication, "you must love Monet."

"Well, if it isn't the Hardy Boys," Dinitia replies. "What great art world mystery are you trying to solve today?"

"How many painters does it take to change a light bulb?" Minnie asks. "None because painters prefer natural light."

Dinitia smiles at him as if he were a young child spouting his first 'Knock, knock' joke, cute rather than funny. "Still in love with Monet?" she asks. "I prefer Nobuzane. His *Hell Panorama* walks you into Hell the way Dante did, deeper and deeper as you go from scroll to scroll. See the devils carrying Tokihira's spirit toward the gates of Hell. And the flames. Did you ever see such scarlet?" Dinitia moves down the wall to another scroll. "Or such jolly devils? You can hear them whistle while they work."

I study the scroll. Cat-faced devils with rusty blades saw slabs of flesh from the bodies of men while others pour hot lead down their throats or nail their tongues to the floor. Viperous insects can march across them. Cooks stir cauldrons of human broth to ladle out to the assembled masses who hunger for it like orphans in a Dickens novel. I glance at Minnie. I wonder if he imagines himself as one of the victims of the cat-faced devils. The way he crosses his arms to hug himself answers my question.

"Those figures look like rejects from Botticelli's etchings of Dante's *Divina Commedia*," Minnie says. "Especially the horny green one tearing the body apart."

She shakes her head. "Legend says Nobuzane died at his easel brush in hand trying to conceptualize a passageway through Hell in a color no human eye had seen before. Will either of you die at your easels?"

"Where do you come up with this shit?" Minnie asks.

"I major in art, not Western art," Dinitia replies without looking away from the scroll. "Still planning on law school, Malone? Call me if you change your mind. Fourth floor Martha Wilson."

Over the next two weeks Minnie returns to the gallery with his sketch pad to do studies of *Hell Panorama*, but Dinitia does not reappear. When he telephones Martha Wilson or stops by unannounced, she is always out and never returns his calls. Once he decides to wait, but after two hours campus security suggests he leave. On his sixth visit to the gallery, he finds a piece of folded paper wedged between a picture frame and the wall with a message written in English with Japanese style letters: 'Sometimes lightning strike only once.'

That night, Dinitia calls me, feigning anger because I haven't called her. "I haven't changed my mind," I explain.

"How about supper Saturday night at Mei Ling's? Downtown Hamp across from the Calvin. Meet you there at 7."

"I don't have a car."

"Hitchhike like every other Amherst freshman."

Mei Ling's is too far from Boston's Chinatown, or New York's, to attract decent chefs yet many of its patrons, especially the faculty and students at the Four Colleges, Amherst, Smith, Mt. Holyoke, and UMass, demand the exotica of Chinatown menus. To satisfy them, the Ling family simplifies the recipes to the level of cooks rather than chefs and exaggerates the description of each dish to sound more foreign than it really is.

For its other patrons, the locals who work for one of the neighboring municipalities or for building and grounds at one of the colleges or at the gas stations lining the Hamp Road or till the fields of the onion and potato farms, the people for whom Chinese food consists of rice, sprouts, or noodles with side orders of egg rolls, pork strips, or spare ribs, Mei Ling's offers drinks in hollowed pineapples or coconuts with colorful paper parasols and names like Scorpion's Revenge and Three Delights, and a variety of chow meins and chop sueys, beef, chicken, pork, scallops, shrimp, whose menu descriptions are as nondescript as the food itself. Although the seating is egalitarian, first come, first served, reservations not accepted, more often than not, the economic class to which a person belongs can be discerned by what he or she eats or drinks at Mei Ling's. I avoid the class war by allowing Dinitia to order which she does in Chinese.

"They have a secret menu," Dinitia confides as she pours a cup of heated rice wine. She laughs when I screw up my face like a child swallowing castor oil.

"Must be my western palate." I drink my water and half of Dinitia's.

"It's an acquired taste. It took me two cups and I've been loving it ever since."

I try another sip. "Could be worse."

"I really like your work," Dinitia says as one waiter replaces the flatware with chopsticks and another serves the first dish, baby squid in lobster sauce. She divides the food between us. "You belong at a museum school."

"I don't like spies."

"I didn't spy. Your professor showed it to me."

"He doesn't have the right." I fumble with the chopsticks and pieces of squid rain down on the table, my lap, my sleeve, in my water, everywhere but my mouth.

"Like this." Dinitia positions the lower of the chopsticks in the crook of her thumb and the upper between the tips of her first and second fingers. "Use your thumb to hold it in place. The bottom one stays fixed and your finger moves the upper one. You tweezer the food off the plate into your mouth." She maneuvers my fingers to demonstrate. "This should be easy for a painter. Both chopsticks and paint brushes require highly developed fine motor skills." Dinitia uses the chopsticks as if she were born to them.

"I'm not hungry."

"Uncle Delaney's a failed artist. Jealous of genius. That's why he's hard on you. The more he dumps on you, the more talent he thinks you have." The waiter brings the second dish, Orange Spicy Beef. "Eat around the red peppers unless your mouth's lined with asbestos." She pops one in her mouth and smiles. "My mother's a Pratt, Delaney's older sister."

"My ma's a Johnson. Her grandfather had a motor car. Liam Clancy wrote a song about it."

Dinitia frames my eyes between her chopsticks. "You're serious, aren't you? Did your mom's grandfather ever meet Yeats?"

"He was at my mom's baptism. Parnell, too."

"And you're a painter, not a poet?"

"I never said I was a painter."

"You must be one of these people who's always the last to know." She refills her wine cup. "Don't you like the food?"

"Hamburger and fries. Hot dogs for a change of pace."

"Uncle Delaney is a hot dog. He worships at the altar of mediocrity. His self-esteem depends on creating failures."

"Did he create you?"

"I intimidate the hell out of him. My work, I mean. And I'm not half as good as you." Dinitia signals the waiter to bring me a fork. "Only on first dates." She clicks the tips of her chopsticks together, then resumes eating. I use the fork to play with my food.

May, 1964

Spring never returns to the Pioneer Valley on the same day or during the same week or, sometimes, in the same month each year; but, sooner or later, like an unreliable lover, it does return. In 1964, spring weather returns well ahead of the season. The construction of the Frost Library picks up as the weather improves. What should be a celebration of Robert Frost instead is a memorial of Dallas. A piece of black bunting tacked to a 2 x 4 marks the spot where President Kennedy stood when he delivered his Poetry and Power speech. Every Monday a representative of the Hampshire County Building Trades Council places a single white flower at its base. Some students call for the redesign of the library's entrance to make room for a permanent plaque to commemorate that spot. Others want the library to be renamed. The memory of an October Saturday is a permanent shroud for the Frost Library. Spring weather persists, sunny, warm, enough rain to green the grass; but winter refuses to yield and probably will not for several cycles of the seasons. To take advantage of the weather,

Professor Delaney Pratt moves his studio class outside because, in his words, "painting in the sunlight has a long and noble tradition in the history of art."

There is no sunlight on my canvas, nor on Minnie's, as each of us labors to portray the August night in Alabama when M'Boto Kenyatta died because of the color of his skin and Merisi Minifie, cowering in the tall grass, survived because Clem and the other Klansmen were too drunk to realize he still lived. My painting is dark, a series of shadows, lumps, seemingly abstract and formless, barely visible in a light, dim because its only source is the stars flickering in the background of the night sky like distant candles; but on close inspection, intimate details escape the darkness, Minnie's cheek being split open by a chain, the skin of M'Boto's chest hanging over his pelvic region like a loin cloth, the charred remains of a car, the childlike joy on the faces of Clem and the others, a crucifix in a pool of blood. Starlight reflects off the white of their teeth, the whites of their eyes, conjuring up distant suns in the dark night sky and illuminating the faces of the Klansmen the way dying embers illuminate the Christ child in a Renaissance Adoration. The darkest of painters, El Greco, Goya, Caravaggio, mix the paints on my palette and guide my brush; but there is a flatness about the painting, not the flatness caused by a lack of depth of field, but the flatness that comes when the artist is a member of the audience watching from afar rather than an actor on the stage.

Minnie struggles with his version of the same scene, but his command of light and form and color pale beside mine and his painting resembles a panel out of one of the Marvel comics we buy each month at Hastings, the panel depicting the moment of desperation that always occurs immediately before the superhero, Spider-man or Daredevil or Captain America, vanquishes the villain and saves the day. The Fantastic Four never lose the battle of the Baxter Building. Thor never loses to Loki. But there were no superheroes in Alabama. No Spiderman. No Daredevil. No Captain America. No Iron Man. Only villains, super villains, and an aura of emotion and outrage emanates from Minnie's painting, elements mine lack. Not bad for second hand, Minnie cracks and I now understand that Picasso could not paint his *Guernica*, that Hemingway could not write *The Sun Also Rises*, without first going to war. Professor Pratt orders me to prop my canvas against the legs of Minnie's easel and gestures for the class to gather around. "Vision is all, gentlemen. Not technique. Vision. Mr. Minifie has it. Mr. Malone doesn't. Mr. Minifie sees. Mr. Malone doesn't. The blind do not artists make."

⁂ ⁂ ⁂

That night, I meet Dinitia at The Satire Room, one of Northampton's many college bars that serve underage drinkers as long as they don't act like high school kids. A scruffy folk singer does covers of *Blowin' in the Wind*, *If I Had a Hammer*, other tunes out of the Peter, Paul and Mary songbook. I am deep into my second pitcher of 'Gansett. Dinitia sips coffee because she has to write a term paper for her course in Epochs of Chinese and Japanese Art.

"This summer," I say. "You want to know what I'm doing this summer?" I chug directly from the pitcher. "Excitement City. Days I'll be hauling cowhide at Schneider Tanning. Nights I'll be running the grocery wheel at Lincoln Park." I wave at the waiter. "Another, my good man. Pratt," I spit out the name as if Dinitia is responsible for her uncle's conduct, "slammed me again today. I don't have vision, he says. I paint like a blind man, he says. Get a Seeing Eye dog, he says."

"The more he dumps on you the more talent he thinks you have. How many times have I told you that?"

"He wouldn't know talent if it stuck its head up his ass and yanked his cock." I burp and the odor of over-ripe beer hangs in the air. "I gotta take a picked wiss." I lean on the back of my chair for balance and push it along the floor. "I gotta wiss," I announce to each table, whether occupied or vacant. Inside the Men's Room, I plant my elbows on top of the urinal, leaning into it until my forehead rests against the wall above the flush lever. "Wissing picked good," I say as gallon after gallon of 'Gansett flows from me. "Oh, shit," I say when I reach down to zip my pants and realize I forgot to unzip them. The waiter arrives at the table with the third pitcher of beer at the same time I stagger back from the Men's Room.

"He's reached his limit," Dinitia says.

The waiter laughs. "House rule. Can't serve anyone drunk enough to piss his pants." People at neighboring tables snicker.

"I have not yet begun to drink."

"Buy you another round, buddy," a guy sitting at the bar says. He dresses like a biker in a Hollywood movie, long hair, black leather jacket, skull head tattoos, but Dinitia sees him bagging groceries at the local super-market and doing odd jobs around Hamp. A chorus of 'me too' spreads throughout the room and six pints of draft beer materialize on my table.

"Chug a lug! Chug a lug!" Hollywood stands over me clapping and leading the chant. "Chug a lug! Chug a lug!" Everyone but Dinitia joins in.

I slowly raise the first pint, close my eyes, and throw my head back. Half the beer makes it into my mouth, the other half pours down the front of my shirt, a few drops dribble down Hollywood's leather jacket. Everyone claps and hoots and shouts for more as if I'm a stripper showing tit. I down the second and third pints the same way. "I gotta picked wiss." Hollywood leans on my shoulders; I can't stand.

"Let him up!"

"Make me, bitch."

Dinitia picks up a full pint and throws it in Hollywood's face. He reaches for her, but she grabs his wrist, yanks him forward, and slams his face into the table, smashing his forehead against the salt shaker. It breaks, scattering shards of glass and grains of salt. As he struggles to rise, Dinitia clasps her hands together and brings them down on the back of his head like a pile driver. The metal cap of the salt shaker cracks his cheekbone and blood pools on the table, combining with the beer and salt and glass, flowing toward me until it dribbles over the edge of the table like a waterfall weakened by drought, slopping on my piss drenched pants. Dinitia glances at the bartenders who react as if they've seen it all already, then steps over Hollywood and slips into an empty booth to catch her breath. I hug the beer pitcher to my chest and stagger over to join her.

"You'll be summering with Uncle Motherfuck, I s'pose."

"Newport for the tennis."

"Ah, Newport." I try to slide into the booth, but can't find the opening between the table and the bench seat. I flop down on the floor beside her, resting my chin on the pitcher's spout. "If you're in my neighborhood stop by and I'll fix it you win a case of soda. Grape. Orange. Root beer. Any fuckin' flavor you want."

"There's a difference between suffering for your art and being insufferable."

"I must've missed Uncle Motherfuck's lecture on that."

Dinitia rips the pitcher from my arms and empties its dregs on my head. As she steps over Hollywood, he raises his head, but she flashes him the finger and he sinks back into the puddle of blood and beer. When she reaches the exit, she bows, then backs out like a gunslinger retreating from a saloon, fuck yous flashing from both hands, her thumbs cocked like the hammers of Colt 45s, her middle fingers the gun barrels. The Satire Room responds with an ovation.

I am not well read enough to know if there is a tradition of great literary bar fights. Perhaps in the pulps, but I know little of them. I do not know of any paintings of bar fights. Probably a failure of my education. Gangster movies and westerns do not count. Bars and cafés or people in bars and cafés, on the other hand, are a traditional subject for art. Van Gogh's *The Night Café* is but a single example. Van Gogh is the perfect artist to paint the fight Dinitia and I had in The Satire Room. The perfect marriage of technique and subject, line and color. Check out *The Night Café* if you doubt me.

*   *   *

Because of this bar fight, the second semester of my freshman year at Amherst College ends without my seeing or talking to Dinitia and I return home to Fall River before I can apologize. I want to write, send her a watercolor as a peace offering, Paradise Pond at sunset in the style of late Monet or the Connecticut River at sunrise with the Amherst and Smith crews practicing in the style of early Monet, but I don't have her home address. There is no see you in September date after the last term paper, the last final. There is no celebration of surviving our freshmen years. There is no exchange of addresses and phone numbers. We do not say good-by for the summer or make whatever promises or pledges or plans our hearts urge on us. As usual, my best laid plans go astray.

By Memorial Day, I have already worked two weeks in the tannery, one week in the amusement park. By the summer solstice, the dog days arrive and by the 4th of July the summer heat bakes the odor of the chemicals used to tan cowhide into my skin. Brown and dry, it looks like it suffers from too many days at the beach rather than inside a factory. Long showers don't wash away the odor. Deodorant doesn't neutralize it. After shave lotion doesn't disguise it. I become used to it, as do Da and Ma, as do the people who patronize the grocery wheel who don't complain because they, too, live or work where factory smells are as commonplace as the smells of beer and a chaser after work, the smells of sausage at dinner time, the smells of a car engine that burns oil, the smells of a skin bracer slapped on the cheeks on a Saturday night. If anything, the familiarity of my odor attracts people and the grocery wheel is busier than the previous summer. I'm rewarded with a raise of $.10 an hour to $1.35, $54.00 per week, the only college student working at the amusement park who earns more than the minimum wage because the park management believes my ability to shill the crowd and not my body odor produces the customers. Dimes diverted before they reach the coin counter add another couple of dollars to my hourly rate. There is a little bit of a Marxist in every college student.

"A string of winners tonight, Ma. They just about accused me of giving the food away." I flop down at the kitchen table opposite Ma who sits in front of a portable fan sipping iced tea. Midnight and the temperature is still well above 80 degrees, the tenth consecutive day of daytime highs in the upper nineties, overnight lows in the mid-eighties. Ma slides the ice tray across the table and I refill it. Moths and other insects of the night collide with the screen in the kitchen window, bouncing off with soft pops that sound like the pebbles Romeo threw when he tried to get Juliet's attention, the Drama Club's play my senior year in high school. The bugs that bypass the screen at the corner where it is torn away from the frame flit around the ceiling fixture. The audio from the television in the living room sneaks between the blades of the fan. Ed McMahon is massacring another Alpo dog food commercial while Johnny Carson taunts him, teases the poor dog that refuses to eat, makes fun of the product. Ma always plays the television or the radio when her men are not home, its voices the guard dog we cannot afford. She rattles the ice cubes in her glass and rubs it against her forehead, but the condensation evaporates in the fan's breeze before it cools her. She closes her eyes and presses the glass into her forehead.

"What's wrong Ma?"

"Your Da's got too much pride." She tilts the glass. The ice slides to a stop against her lips. "Old country pride," she says into the glass. The ice cubes flutter as she speaks. "Third shift's no good for him. He doesn't eat right. Doesn't sleep right. His back's no better."

I stand in the shower, letting the cold-water seep into my soul. A telephone call, one fucking phone call, and Da would be a foreman at Reardon Manufacturing, working days, easy work, bossing people, checking the raw material in, the finished goods out, lugging nothing heavier than a clipboard with a few sheets of paper. And

Ma, too. Training the stitchers. Filling in once in a while if the orders fall behind or someone is out sick. One fucking phone call. Maybe if I can teach Julia to appreciate the act of creation. She never will the way Dinitia does. But if she can be made to understand what it means to create, to be creative, maybe marrying her won't be that bad. The next morning, I awake earlier than usual and call, suggesting she come over while I'm painting.

"You inviting me up to see your etchings?"

"To see me etch. Just a crazy idea. I thought if you watched me, maybe you'll understand better."

"Which one of us is the mill dolly?"

I spend the rest of the morning tidying up my room, picking up the false starts, discarding drawings from the floor and bagging them for the trash. I replace the works in progress leaning against my bookcase and dresser and desk with paintings I did at Amherst, paintings like *The Octagon at Dusk* that earned me an A- in Professor Delaney Pratt's studio art course, the highest grade in the class.

I catalogue my works in progress, trying to decide which one to work on for Julia. For Dinitia, I would work on a drawing in the style of Toba Sojo, a Japanese artist of the feudal era Dinitia introduced me to whose drawings are pure line, but line with a sweep of motion that makes the horses, dogs, bulls, frogs, and goats that populate his drawings come alive. No color. Just line. Dinitia understands, appreciates, how one line lives and breathes and dances on the page while another line, drawn with the same pencil, as thick and dark as the first, is as inanimate and immovable as a tie rod extending out of a slab of concrete. Dinitia appreciates the act of creation that produces a line that lives and understands that a dead hand only produces a line that doesn't.

Not Julia. For all her promises about giving me time to paint, I can't help but feel that in Julia's mind giving her husband time to paint is no different than giving him time to play golf or go fishing or play poker with his buddies. Very few wives share golf or fishing or poker with their husbands. My wife will have to share the act of creation or I'll be another factory worker with a pack of Luckies rolled in the sleeve of my tee shirt and she'll be another fuck on the cases of soda in the storage area behind the grocery wheel. I tack a study of Toba Sojo's *Battle of the Bulls* beside my easel, an exercise he drew in an effort to understand how to make pure line come alive. Toba Sojo will be my master. Julia Reardon will be my subject. *Mill Dolly* will be my title.

The following morning, I wait by the front door, ready to open it before Julia rings the bell. Da had another difficult night. The second line at the cannery, the orange soda line, jammed, backed up, and spewed unsealed cans of orange soda throughout the cannery, contaminating the cola and ginger ale lines, closing them down as well. Da and the night shift were hosing down the conveyer belts when the morning shift arrived and the foreman clocked them out and made them finish the cleanup before allowing them to leave. He also fired two at random and canceled the night shift differential, $.15 per hour. "It'll put a hole in our budget, Briggie," he told Ma over the cup of tea they share each morning during the few moments of overlap after he returns home and before she leaves. "Get your rest, love," she replied, "before the heat ruins the day."

I open the front door as soon as I see Julia's Thunderbird turn the corner. She wears short shorts and a halter top and looks as beautiful as a Raphael Madonna, but not as virginal. I feel more nostalgic than I want, but I don't know what I'm nostalgic for. We tiptoe in silence to my bedroom. "You look like you're having a good summer."

"You smell like you're having a bad one."

"The tannery."

"Doesn't smell like that in a pants factory." Julia taps two cigarettes out of her pack.

"Not while I'm working."

"That supposed to be me?"

"The idea of you. The emotion of you. The memory of you. The meaning of you. It all emerges out of form and line and color. When it works, I capture the vibrations of your soul. When it doesn't, it's like a paint-by-numbers portrait that looks nothing like its subject."

"I have one of those. My dad sent my high school yearbook picture to some company in New York and got back an oil painting. It's a perfect portrait of what I'd look like if Minnie's dad did me up for my wake."

I help myself to one of Julia's cigarettes and smoke in silence, exhaling through the screen. Giving away a painting is the same as selling it. Receiving Julia's love in return is the same as being paid money. A gift is a sale. But she already loves me; I'd be getting anything new. I would not be profiting. My life after death rides on the answer to these questions. From the bathroom the sounds of Da coughing up phlegm and the toilet flushing intrude like an unwanted chaperone. "It's an act of mimesis. Not an act of creation."

Julia glances at her watch. "I'm running late. I'm meeting mom for lunch in Padanaram. The Packet has its fall line in."

The following week, Julia visits again. "Remember the time you tried to teach me how to shoot foul shots," she says. "You explained spin and aim and arc and follow through and I understood everything you said, but I still couldn't make a shot. I bet Bob Cousy's wife can't make foul shots either, but that doesn't stop him from loving her. Or the guy who invented polio vaccine.

I bet his wife doesn't know the difference between a Bunsen burner and a pipette." Julia lights two cigarettes and gives me one. "I signed up for a course in the history of art. I don't want to embarrass you in front of your painter friends."

"It's not the same."

"If my name was Julia Child instead of Julia Reardon, I'd love you even if you didn't know the first thing about French cooking."

"It isn't the same."

"It's exactly the same. You're just too stubborn to admit it."

July's heat burns into August and my summer persists as unremitting as the temperature: late night conversations with Ma, morning visits from Julia in my bedroom studio while Da sleeps that evolve into morning visits to Julia's, her mother out, shopping or sailing or playing golf or tennis, wistful thinking about Dinitia while we argue about Bob Cousy and Julia Child, foreplay without intercourse. Julia has little tolerance for the way I stink like a piece of partially cured cowhide. Whenever my odor overwhelms her, she douses me with cologne and massages it into my skin. She learns things about my body that I myself have yet to learn and I frequently come before her hands reach inside my pants. With the arrival of the dog days of August, I feel I am slipping into an addiction I will never escape.

To celebrate her birthday, Julia insists we spend the night in the dunes at Horseneck Beach, skinny dipping, English Leather massages, swigging cheap Scotch mixed with warm ginger ale, making love, cuddling under a canopy of stars wrapped in a Milky Way ribbon. "Somewhere out there," I whisper in Julia's ear, "there's a planet with intelligent life and telescopes. Millions of years from now, billions of years, when the light from Earth reaches them, they'll see what we do tonight."

Julia nibbles my ear. "Let's put on a show they'll never forget."

At daybreak, the sun peers over the horizon, unrolling a red carpet on the calm surface of the ocean. When the first rays reach the dunes, we awaken, bathe in the ocean, and make love to the cries of seagulls searching for breakfast. "This is the best birthday present ever," Julia says as we snuggle.

"Better than the T Bird?"

"Much better, but not as good as next summer's." She wiggles the ring finger of her left hand in my face. Julia drives along the back roads of Westport at half the posted speed limit. "What's your rush?" she demands when I ask her to drive faster.

"Breakfast is the only time Da and I have together."

Julia floors it and the Thunderbird races down the country roads, a hot rod on a drag strip. City traffic slows us as we pass from Westport into Fall River. Turning into my street, she downshifts and begins the long descent down the hill. When she sees Minnie on my front steps, she toots the horn and waves, braking hard when Minnie rushes into the street like a young child chasing a ball. "Your Da took a stroke." Minnie vaults over the hood and wedges himself into the car. "I've been waiting all night for you."

The T Bird roars up the hill and I wrap my arms tightly around Minnie's waist, an anchor to keep me from being thrown from the car when Julia hits the flats of the cross streets. "When?"

"The shift supervisor found him. On the floor. Under the conveyor."

In the Intensive Care Unit, Ma sits on the floor at the foot of Da's bed clutching her rosary and being comforted by Father Octavio Crizal while an orderly takes apart the oxygen tent still enveloping Da's head and shoulders. Two others wait in the shadows to remove the body and transport it to the hospital morgue where the coroner in consultation with the attending physician will determine the cause of death, decide whether to require an autopsy, when to release the body to the Minifie Funeral Home whose hearse is already en route.

"He is with God, my son." Father O'Malley walks me around to the side of the bed opposite the orderly. "He passed in his sleep. Without pain. God's blessing."

Fucking language. Doesn't respect the truth. Da died. He didn't pass. He'll be buried. Not laid to rest. A corpse. Not earthly remains. Father O'Malley administers the last rites, reciting the sacrament in Latin because he knows Da wanted it that way. Latin makes death real in a way English cannot. Latin ferries the soul to God in a way English cannot. Latin, not English, is the language of saints. Latin, not English, is the language spoken in Heaven. Latin, not English, is the language that will bury Gabriel Stephen Malone. I kneel beside Ma and bury my face in her lap and she comforts me and I am a young child again suffering the terrible hurt Minnie and I will take to our graves and she cries but I do not and above us the Latin words hang in the air like a hovering archangel while Father O'Malley positions himself to block our view of the orderlies who wheel Da from the room as he makes the sign of the Cross over Da once, twice, a third time, a fourth, to make certain that God instructs St. Peter that this knock on His pearly gates is not to be ignored on penalty of being expelled from Heaven for all eternity. And we pray.

The heat abates slightly on the night of Da's wake and the high 70's seems a cold wave. Fall River's factory society lines up to pay their respects, mill workers and their spouses, the shipping room clerks, cutters and stitchers, loom operators, machine mechanics, hey-boys who lug in the raw material, haul out the finished goods, even the foremen and shift supervisors. Some are ill at ease wearing their church clothes because it isn't Sunday; others wear freshly laundered work clothes, the spare set everyone has for emergencies or for wakes. The Reardons, Kate and Mick and Julia, wait in line with the other mourners. Mr. Reardon wears his Padanaram outfit, a blue seersucker suit with a paisley tie, as does his wife, a sleeveless summer dress with a floral print. Julia wears tropical weight slacks and a dark blouse.

In the main parlor of the Minifie Funeral Home, Ma and I accept condolences beside an open coffin. Da appears to be alive. I'm convinced he will sit up, greet everyone by name, propose a toast. Instead, as each mourner kneels before the coffin, a memory flits from Da to the mourner and, then, when the mourner hugs me or kisses my cheek or shakes my hand the memory enters me and opens up inside my mind's eye like a home movie. Once again, Da and I camp under the front porch. Once again, we fish for yellow perch on a lake in Brewster on the Cape. Once again, I go long in the school yard at the top of the street and Da wobbles a football into my outstretched arms. Once again, Da confiscates my comic books because I dip Patsy's braids into the inkwell at school. Once again, Da is healthy with no hurts in his back or his legs or his knees, going to work before I get up for school, having supper at home at the end of the day. Each mourner brings a new memory and there are enough mourners for me to relive almost my entire childhood. I see no memories in Ma's eyes.

When the Reardons reach us, Julia wraps her arms around me and cries into my shoulders. She brings me no memories, only a void as if the bulb in the movie projector inside my head burned out, and I can't help but think that Da is angry with me for not being at home when he took his stroke, punishing me by placing me inside the same void where his soul now awaits Judgment. I stand stiffly, my arms hanging straight down, my elbows locked, my entire body suffering from its own rigor mortis. Julia leans her head back and stares into my eyes which are dry and blank. Julia's arms slowly slide down my side, catching momentarily on my belt, and she steps back until we no longer touch. The void dissolves as Julia follows her parents to the rear of the parlor but the next mourner in line brings no new memories from Da. Nor do any of the others. And when I glance at Da I do not see someone who looks ready to jump up and dance a jig. I see a corpse and I know that the memory of Da as a corpse will accompany me throughout life and, if I do not earn my own passage into Heaven, will be my punishment in Hell.

In the back of the parlor, the Minifies, Vincenzo and Therese, sit quietly, with the Reardons. Julia joins Minnie in a corner, talking softly with some high school classmates who have come to pay their respects.

Later, after the crowd thins and the line of mourners no longer extends through the foyer into the parking lot, Dinitia Marbury Madison quietly enters and approaches the coffin. If I see her, my eyes do not send the information to my brain. If I recognize her, my brain does not process this information. If I intend to react, my muscles do not respond to the orders from my brain. But Minnie recognizes her and reacts and responds and smiles and coughs and gives a little wave that a stranger might interpret as his running his fingers through his hair, but which he hopes Dinitia will interpret as a greeting, an invitation to join him after she pays her respects. Dinitia lowers her head without looking toward Minnie, but Minnie's brain, in its own way as dysfunctional as mine, interprets her motion as a nod of acknowledgment, an acceptance of his invitation, and he leans over to whisper in Julia's ear to remind her who Dinitia is.

In the front of the parlor, Dinitia crosses herself, kneels before the coffin, then, after several minutes, crosses herself again, rises and touches me lightly on the shoulder. When she whispers how sorry she is, home movies again flood my mind's eye, the Christmas visit to the model train store above the bus station when all we can afford to do is look at the trains and make up stories about the little plastic crew who operate them and passengers who ride them, the St. Patrick's Day when I am finally old enough to go with Da to Gallagher's for corn beef and cabbage and a sip of green beer that makes me sick, my seventh birthday party when Da puts a sign on the front porch of the house announcing 'Party in Rear' and my friends tease me for weeks about where the birthday party takes place, our first television, a used black and white, cheap because color has been in the stores for a few years, and the first television program I watch at home, *The Lone Ranger* who rescues a widow from claim jumpers who murder her husband to jump his claim to a silver mine before he files it, memories and more memories, the film running through the projector at two, three, ten times, normal speed, more memories than all the previous mourners together bring me. I hug Dinitia and she hugs me and we hold our embrace for as long as our feelings are deep and, at long last, I cry for Da.

"How'd you find out?" I ask.

"One of the yard boys left a *Fall River Herald* by the pool. I saw the death notice."

Dinitia comes to Fall River for Da's funeral, then returns to Newport with a promise that she'll see me in the fall. "I may take some time off," I tell her. "Build a nest egg for Ma. When the amusement park closes, I'll work graveyard and paint days. You know what the great

God Pratt says about morning light." I expect an argument from Dinitia but all she says is that we'll talk later and I sense that she'll forget me long before I forget her, but Ma comes first.

Minnie doesn't call after the funeral, not once, and I don't have time to call him. Julia explains that Minnie is in Firenze studying Florentine art at the time of the Medicis. As good a place as any to run away from life, I say. I expect a post card, several, but Minnie doesn't send any. I write and ask why, but he does not answer my letters.

I divide what little is left of the summer of Da's death into three parts like the ancient Gaul I read about in high school Latin class, one part work, one part painting, one part mourning; but the parts are not equal. Measured in hours, work takes the most time, two jobs, graveyard shift in a factory, afternoons and evenings at the amusement park, eighty hours a week, sometimes ninety if I take someone else's Sunday hours at the amusement park, something I do about half the time I'm asked. I confine painting to the few Sunday afternoons I take off, first morning Mass, then Sunday dinner with Ma who always insists on cooking regardless of how hot it is, then painting while listening to the Red Sox on the radio. Mourning overlays everything. I mourn with each spin of the grocery wheel, with each load of cowhide I carry into the tanning room, with each box of finished leather that rolls down the conveyor belt into the shipping room. I mourn with every pitch of every inning of every Red Sox game. I mourn with each stroke of paint I apply to the canvas. I mourn each time I hug Ma or help her with chores around the house or think of Da's ma sitting in the dark without heat, without light.

If I survive it is because chronic fatigue leaves my emotions anesthetized. It also anesthetizes my creativity. My paintings are dull and flat, uninspired, subjects like the tree outside my bedroom window, the three decker across the street, the bridge across the Taunton River. Fatigue mires me in realism, the shape of the branch, its colors and shades, its texture, all have to be reproduced with an exactitude available only in photographs or in the imagination. The more I try, the more I fail. I paint as if my eyes are disconnected from my brain and my brain from my hands. I paint as if I am painting portraits from year book photographs. Acts of mimesis, not acts of creation.

An intellectual exercise to busy a washed-out mind: If Marcel Proust were a painter rather than a writer, how would he paint *Remembrances of Things Past*? Impressionist or Post-Impressionist? Fauve or the Expressionist? The Cubist? Abstract Expressionist? Unlikely Dada or Surrealism as he died too soon. He could he paint different parts of his epic in different styles, experimenting like the young Picasso. On a blank canvas, he could organize his memories differently. Someone as verbal as him probably could not communicate visually as effectively as he did verbally. His convoluted and complex sentences cannot be translated into line and color; or just line, nor just color. The medium is not be the message.

Yes, there is an honorable tradition of narrative painting in art, both Western and Eastern; but the spectator oft times knows the narrative before viewing the painting. I believe the appreciation of the narrative (as distinguished from the appreciation of the work of art) comes from that foreknowledge, not from the painting. For critics and art historians, narrative is an afterthought discussed in service of artistic technique when they compare and contrast paintings on identical subjects. See e.g., the thousands of paintings of the life and death of Jesus Christ. Imagine a Sistine Chapel ceiling painted by Proust. Rinsing the washed-out mind.

If the narrative was not part of our cultural heritage, no one would understand the story the Sistine Chapel ceiling tells. This is not a trivial question problem. There is no individual to interpret the life of my art and the art of my life when I am dead. There is no collective consciousness intimate with the story of my life. If I do not take over the art world, biographers will not compete to publish the story of my life. Da's memories depart with his soul as did the memories of Father Ozoni. As will Minnie's. Dinitia's memories encompass barely 20% of my history. Julia keeps her own counsel for which I am grateful. Ma's memories – few, if any, serious biographers of men rely on the memories of their subject's mother. I alone can explicate and interpret my life. I regret that I lack the skill with line and color, shape and form, that Proust had with words.

On the Monday after Labor Day, 1964, I return from my shift at the tannery to find my underwear ironed, folded, and neatly stacked on the living room floor beside my

trunk. And my jerseys and shirts. And my chinos and dungarees. And my socks and ties and belts. And all the other clothes I need to return to college for my sophomore year.

"I want to take some time off," I tell Ma. "Build up a nest egg for you. Paint."

Ma vacuums the inside of my trunk. "You'll be drafted."

"I'll apply for a hardship."

"Maybe if you didn't quit basketball the draft board would be sympathetic."

"I'm the primary support of my family. It's in the law."

"Mr. Reardon offered me a job." Ma places my pants in the bottom of the trunk, hanging the legs over the side to be folded after she packs the underwear, a trick to keep the pants from creasing. "Hand me your undershirts, dear. I won't be working the machines. He needs someone to supervise the stitching room, train the stitchers. A forelady he calls it. Same as a foreman. Good money."

"He offer you this after Da died?

"When Da got laid off."

"Why didn't you take it?"

"Da wouldn't let me." Ma smoothes a wrinkle out of one of the undershirts. "He didn't want any of us beholden to Mick Reardon."

So cruel a reminder that the accuracy of a memory is independent of its veracity. Children understand this better than adults. For the balance of the summer after Da's funeral, Julia was a cup of coffee and a donut on the way from the amusement park to the factory, an occasional beer and pizza on a Sunday night, breakfast once or twice a week at the Green Diner. She never bitched about Dinitia or whined about the future. She didn't cry when my exhaustion prevented me from responding to her efforts to arouse me. She substituted cuddling for sex. A new Julia. Instead of draining me, she renewed me. If I appreciated her in a new way, I felt the same about her as before, still unable to love her. Like a cartoon hidden under a painting, beneath her new tenderness, as sincere as it might be, lurked her desire to gift wrap me for her twenty-first birthday.

"Two, three years," I say to Ma. "Maybe four. I'll finish school later."

I argue my case for dropping out as Ma continues to pack. I argue my case the next morning as we drive down Route 6 from Fall River to Providence, then Route 146 from Providence to the Massachusetts Turnpike, then west on the turnpike to Palmer, through South Hadley on Route 116, the Notch Road, to Amherst. I argue my case as I unload the car and carry my trunk and suitcases into Davis, one of the Social Dorms. I argue my case as we eat shitburgers at Joe's. I argue my case as we walk across the Town Common toward campus. When she asks what peace will Da have if I quit school, I lose the argument. Freshmen wearing Class of '68 Beanies and burdened with bags of books scurry past us. The Betas and the DU's play Frisbee football on the grass between the two fraternity houses. The Psi U's lounge on their front lawn drinking beer. Three or four students line up on the Hamp Road, thumbs out, begging a ride to Smith. "I have to rest," Ma says when we reach Converse Memorial Library.

We sit on the library's shallow granite steps. To the side. Beside a black wrought iron lamp post. As still as architectural elements. In the shade, the chill of the stone seeps through my shorts, my underwear, frosts my ass.

"Let's find someplace warmer," I say

"I release you," Ma says. "I will not be the sow who eats her own young."

The shadows deepen. Freshmen troop in and out of the library. Some congregate on the steps, complaining that the reading assignments for the first class in History I, the first class in Humanities I, are checked out of the reserve room. Their college careers are in ruins before their first class. I put my arm on Ma's shoulder and give her a hug. I help her to her feet and she puts her arm in mine and we walk across the Freshmen Quad and down the hill past Barrett and Chapin and Fayerweather to the parking lot beside the Social Dorms. A pair of squirrels chases each other round and round the trunk of a maple tree. Someday, James Stephen Malone, Attorney at Law, will buy his ma a house in Fall River's Highlands.

The next morning, I wait in Mead for the art department offices to open to arrange studio space for the coming semester. Amherst College has a modest art collection, a few bequests from alumni including one of Degas' dancers, a few acquisitions, nothing as elaborate as Harvard's Fogg and the Busch-Reisinger and its many other museums or even Williams College whose students have access to the Clark as well as the college museum. Still, Amherst has an extensive collection of color slides that reproduce the best of the Louvre, the Ufizzi, the Hermitage, the Metropolitan Museum of Art, the Tate, the V & A, the Museum of Fine Arts, the Art Institute of Chicago, the best of the world's great art. If gaps exist in the collection, thousands of art books in Converse fill them. I have the entire history of art from the earliest cave paintings to the latest multi-media constructions available to me and this enables me to learn from the masters. I linger before the Degas in Mead trying to decide whether dressing the bronze in muslin and silk heightens the realism or transforms it into an oversized doll a rich girl might find under her tree on Christmas morning. Minnie arrives and when he sees me a blush tinges his cheeks and whitens the scars, now healed, that fleck his face. I head for the door.

"Wait up, man?" Minnie follows me into the court-yard between James and Stearns.

"What the fuck you want?" I demand.

"You could've told me."

"Don't go fucking jealous on me."

A stray bit of sunlight navigates its way through the branches and reflects off one of the dormitory windows. The reflection bathes Minnie's cheeks in a pale, washed out yellow and the scars on his face begin to glow. The glow intensifies and the pupils of Minnie's eyes narrow to points, his eyes darkening until they are black like an Alabama night in mid-summer.

"Dinitia knows it wasn't your fault," I tell him.

"I didn't even try."

"You were beaten within an inch of your life."

"I could have distracted them. Make them come looking for me."

"He would have bled to death anyway. The F.B.I. explained that to you."

The sunlight slips from the dormitory window and its reflection slips from Minnie's face. The glow dims and recedes into his scars. The pupils of his eyes expand and their natural color returns. From above, a hooting sound. A crow. The bells in the Johnson Chapel clock tower ring, ten minutes before the hour. "I'm late for class," Minnie shouts, bounding down the stairs behind James toward Chapin. "Bullshit," I call after him. The crow swoops down and picks up something shiny, a piece of tin foil, perhaps from a stick of gum or a cigarette pack or a candy bar.

In my mail, a dinner invitation from Professor and Mrs. Delaney Pratt. Saturday night. Eight o'clock. "My idea," Dinitia tells me. "You and Minnie."

"No, I say."

"And risk alienating Uncle Delaney?" she asks.

That evening Julia calls and also invites me to dinner Saturday night, the French King, a restaurant on the Mohawk Trail. "Next to a motel overlooking the river," she says. When I explain the situation, Julia tells me her period's a month overdue. I remind her I pulled out, but she dismisses my explanation: "It's not the Immaculate Conception."

October, 1964–November, 1964

I kick at the early autumn leaves, premature casualties in winter's annual war, as Minnie and I walk down South Pleasant Street in Amherst to Professor Delaney Pratt's house. Each kick makes my stomach queasier. Julia finds a doctor in Belchertown who performs abortions. At night. In an apartment over an auto repair shop. Cash in advance. Pocket change to Julia. Two year's tuition to me. Assuming she really is pregnant. She must be bluffing. She knows what I did last summer. Hauling cowhide. Shilling groceries. One night in the dunes when I pulled out, spilling my sperm on the sand. Above, a crescent moon balances atop the Holyoke Range, standing on one toe, and I think of the m∫an in the moon stories Da read to me at bedtime from a storybook Da's Ma gave me one Christmas. On its cover, a boy holding a fishing pole reclines in the moon's crook. I delay bedtime by asking Da how do boys fly to the moon and when can I fly to the moon, and Da says the boy's really from Mars and boys on Mars have space ships the way boys on earth have bicycles, and I beg Da to move to Mars, but Da says earth boys will die from breathing the Martian air, and eventually Da kisses me on the cheek and turns off the light and I have a bad dream about the baby Julia will have if I'm a Martian. The crescent moon absorbs the queasiness from my stomach. Julia has to be lying. Or someone else is the father. A man in a tuxedo answers Pratt's door and escorts us into the living room.

"A curator I know at the Metropolitan helped me select the pieces," Professor Delaney Pratt says by way of a greeting. Pratt sports a blue blazer, yellow silk slacks, powder blue dress shirt with an ascot. I feel like a hobo in my sports jacket, sport shirt and tie, white Levi's, penny loafers, no socks. Minnie doesn't dress any better, black Levi's instead of white, tennis sneakers instead of penny loafers, also without socks. "It was my idea, of course, to accent the Federal period pieces of Joseph B. Barry with some Philadelphia Chippendale." Now, I feel like a hobo in a foreign country who doesn't speak the language.

"May I offer the gentlemen drinks, sir?" The man in the tuxedo appears at the door, balancing a silver serving tray on the fingertips of his right hand.

"Wine for the gentlemen." Pratt rolls his tongue around the word gentlemen as if he cannot decide whether we fit the definition. "The usual for me. A Beaujolais," Pratt tells us. "Last season's Nouveau. I think you'll find it acceptable. Now for the tour." Pratt moves around his living room like a docent in an art museum. "That high chest of drawers is Philadelphia Chippendale. This pier table is by Barry. Mahogany, of course. A William Whitehead breakfast table. Also, mahogany. A tea canister from Joseph Smith's workshop. Earthenware. A tad older than the chest. It all works marvelously well together. If you promise not to spill, you may sit on the Queen Anne's."

"Which are neither Philadelphia Chippendale nor Federal period," Mrs. Pratt says as she enters the living room. She wears a white blouse open at the neck to display pearls that dip below the top of her cleavage, a long black skirt, and a smile.

"Must you Marcie?" Pratt asks.

"I can't have you misrepresenting the furniture, dear." She offers her hand first to me, then to Minnie. "Don't let my husband cower you. He would have failed Matisse if he had the chance."

"Marcie!"

"Well it's true, Delaney. You said it yourself."

"A throwaway line at a lecture."

"Dinitia has told me about both of you. She will be down momentarily. Gentlemen, please. The chairs do not have ropes across them."

"Am I sitting on a million dollars?" I ask after I lower myself into one of the Queen Anne chairs.

"Of Baldwin Pratt's money," Mrs. Pratt says.

Pratt reddens slightly. "Times were different in Baldwin's day. Taxes were non-existent. You kept what you made. Shipbuilding. Railroads. Oil. Baldwin dabbled in all of them. Now your generation," Pratt extends his glass in our direction, "thinks making money is sinful."

"And he gave much of it to the college." By the tone of her voice, Mrs. Pratt chides her husband for not being as generous. "One makes different choices if one inherits the money."

"Sometimes not having money frees you to make the choices you really want." Minnie smiles at me.

"Delaney the Dilettante." Dinitia bounces into the room. She wears a calico print floor length dress with a scoop neck accented by a gimp necklace with some scrimshaw dangling from it. She reminds me of one of the Mamas, the thin one. "That's what my mom calls Uncle Delaney."

"My niece sounds more and more like her great grandfather Baldwin every day," Pratt says.

"Baldwin made the family fortune," Dinitia says. "He was a spendthrift, but he always made money much, much faster than he spent it."

"Let's not spoil dinner with talk of Baldwin," Delaney says.

The butler appears at the door, ringing a silver bell.

Delaney assigns seats, Minnie and myself below the salt, Dinitia, himself, his wife, above. "Now this dining room set... ," Delaney begins when everyone is seated.

Mrs. Pratt interrupts, "Don't bore them, dear, with provenance."

What about the toothpicks, I wonder. Or the candles. Or the light bulbs. I smile at Dinitia through the centerpiece of fresh roses and she smiles back. Dinitia's mother and Delaney Pratt must be as different as a brother and sister can be. To appease Pratt, I feign interest in the table settings. Crystal. Bone china. Sterling. A different world, a different universe, from the orange Melmac, tin flatware, and glasses, originally grape jelly containers decorated with cartoon figures, that graced the table where I ate roast leg of lamb, Ma's special meal for special occasions, the night before she drove me back to campus, the same orange Melmac, tin flatware, and glasses for the roast leg of lamb Ma served the night before my first day of kindergarten, the evening after my first communion, to celebrate my graduations, first from elementary school, then junior high, then high school, the night of my confirmation, Da's fiftieth birthday, their twenty-fifth wedding anniversary, the night of Da's funeral. We measured our lives in roast legs of lamb on orange Melmac plates.

The meal progresses with a fruit course, a soup

course, a salad course. We engage in the chit chat of people who do not understand why they are together at the same table. Or, the same universe. Minnie, to my relief, ignores me and indulges Pratt's gossip about the art world, feigning awe as Pratt drops as many names as there are grains of salt in the silver salter. Having nothing to say to either of them, I divide my attention between the food and the Ladies Pratt who swap family anecdotes. I recognize some of the food, the orange and grapefruit sections in the fruit course, for example, but not the green fruit, sliced thin and circular, the tomatoes and cucumbers in the salad, but not the lettuce, deep green, almost a spinach green, with tinges of purple around the edges of the leaves. Most of the food is as alien to me as a foreign cuisine. I want to ask about it, what it is, where it comes from, but I don't want to endure another Pratt lecture on provenance nor the gibes Pratt will hurl at me in class. All hail Malone, the would-be artist who cannot identify the food he eats. Maybe Dinitia will tell me later like the time she taught me to eat with chopsticks or introduced me to sushi, not a better educating a lesser, but one person sharing her likes with another. As the butler places a boned breast of quail in the center of my plate as small against the white of the plate as an eagle soaring against a puffy cloud, I wish Dinitia and I were eating roast leg of lamb off orange Melmac.

After dessert, another course I do not recognize, there is cognac, cigars, and more chit chat to fill the awkward silences rather than communicates real thought. When the Pratts excuse themselves, Dinitia offers to walk us back to campus. The crescent moon no longer balances atop the Holyoke Range and the absence of street lights makes South Pleasant Street dark and foreboding. We angle away from the street and begin the long climb up the hill from Alumni Gymnasium toward Johnson Chapel and the Octagon. About a third of the way up, Minnie breaks ranks and doubles his pace. Dinitia sprints ahead and wraps her arms around him. "You couldn't have saved him." Minnie struggles to free himself, but Dinitia squeezes tighter. "I love Malone because I love Malone. Not because M'Boto died in Alabama."

"I will always believe if I saved him, I would be your Prince Charming."

"My hero, but not my Prince Charming."

The semester proceeds. Whenever I ask Julia about Belchertown, she tells me not to worry. The Art department faculty approves Minnie and me as Studio Art majors. Professor Pratt's vote is not made public. Minnie un-pledges his fraternity and moves into a vacant bedroom in my suite in the Social Dorms. If he is not free of his demons, he conceals them. I do not feel as out of place as I did freshman year, but I miss Da and Da's face haunts me at the oddest times, at breakfast one morning when the scrambled eggs have white streaks, falling asleep in Evolution while the professor drones on about Darwin's finches or Mendel's peas, learning the butterfly stroke during gym, working at the Reserve Desk in the library. There are other times as well, explainable occasions, such as the Saturday night Dinitia wore the same skirt she wore to Da's wake which she changed when she saw my face bleach white. On the phone Ma hints the same is happening to her. Maybe there is life after death. Maybe the soul lives in some other world and penetrates this world now and again. The truth behind the myth of the Guardian Angel. I do not believe in Guardian Angels. I believe in boys from Mars who cast their lines into space's vast oceans from crescent moons.

❧ ❧ ❧

Outside the ivory tower, candidates campaign for president, pluck petals from daisies, countdown to a nuclear holocaust, remind us that in our hearts we know who's right. Inside the ivory tower I am too young to vote; I ignore the election. I would not have if I knew the future as you do. Not if I knew Minnie's name would one day be carved into the Amherst College War Memorial with the names of the other men of Amherst who die in this century's great wars. In the fall of 1964, those wars of generations past and their great battles are more a part of the campus than that nasty little skirmish in Southeast Asia. Vietnam will intrude before I graduate, protests, sit-ins, teach-ins, editorials in the *Amherst Student*. The Class of 1966 at its graduation will stand and turn its back when President Calvin Plimpton awards an honorary degree to Secretary of Defense Robert McNamara whose moral certitude about the rightness of Vietnam condemns Minnie and a multitude of other young Americans to premature death. It is our curse.

Election night and Democrats everywhere except Massachusetts celebrate.

The light of the homecoming pep rally bonfire the Friday night before the Williams game obliterates the crescent moon hanging over the parking lot of Converse Memorial Library. Sparks dance in the night air like drunken fireflies while drunken students, part of America's academic elite when sober, do a circle dance around the bonfire, shimmying and shaking and wailing like a prehistoric tribe invoking the spirit gods to bless their hunt and grant them the kill of their quarry, Williams, in Saturday's football game. As the flames of the bonfire die down, the embers glowing red in the night breeze heat the air beyond the tolerance of the celebrants who drift off in small groups, in couples, some solos, many heading to one of the fraternity houses to continue their revels, others to their dorm rooms with the same intent. Minnie wangles invitations to Chi Psi whose party feature kegs of imported beer, pouches of Acapulco Gold, and the Valley Rats, a local rock group that does covers of top forty hits. On this night its play list sticks at *Louie, Louie,* its rendition of the lyrics no more decipherable than the original by the Kingsmen.

Since the beginning of the semester when Dinitia told Minnie that Alabama is not the reason she loves me not him, Minnie has dated only sorority girls from the University of Massachusetts who are 4-F's, (find 'em, feel 'em, fuck 'em, forget 'em), never the same one twice. Double dating is awkward. If Dinitia and I want to see the latest Bergman or Godard or Fellini movie at Kirby Theater, Minnie's date votes for the latest Elvis Presley flick at the Amherst Cinema. One saw every Presley movie four or five times and insisted that *Love Me Tender* was better than *The Seventh Seal* or *Breathless* or *8 1/2.* At least you can understand it, she pouted. When the three of us debate whether D. H. Lawrence is a novelist of erotica, Minnie's date ends the discussion by announcing that *Peyton Place* has the best sex scenes she's ever read and she can't imagine any man writing them better. It's like a training manual she says. By the book, Minnie tells me later that night. Three times Dinitia offers to introduce Minnie to some of her Smith classmates (art majors, she promises.) and three times he declines.

"Not Chi Psi," Dinitia says.

"You have a better idea?" I ask.

"I signed out to Uncle Delaney's."

"He who's worse than Smith's worst housemother."

"No. He who's in New York with Aunt Marcie visiting my cousin Nathaniel. Homecoming's one of the many traditions Delaney doesn't believe in."

On the lawn in front of the fraternity house the Chi Psi's play rugby against the Psi U's, everyone moving in slow motion because the booze and the pot disconnect their brains from their nervous systems. The scrum staggers across the lawn like a piece of tumbleweed caught in cross winds.

"I'm going whether you come or not," Dinitia says. Thirty minutes later, we let ourselves in through the Pratt's back door. "No lights. We'll use Nathaniel's room. There's a streetlight outside his window." His room has the artificial neatness of a place that is no longer lived in. Felt banners from Phillips Exeter Academy and Amherst College hang on the wall over the bed, the diplomas on the opposite wall above the desk.

"Uncle Delaney counts his bottles," Dinitia says as I uncork a bottle of his Nouveau Beaujolais. She extends two wine glasses into the light from the streetlight. "He'll go crazy not knowing what happened to this one."

"You'll get in trouble."

"Aunt Marcie will convince him he drank it and doesn't remember." Dinitia gives me the glasses and rummages through some records lining the floor next to the desk. "Coltrane's *Ballads*?"

We sit on the bed, side by side, sipping wine, barely touching, yet nestled within a cocoon of intimacy that Coltrane's saxophone, lush and lyrical like a young mother humming her infant to sleep, spins. I maneuver my arm until it casts a shadow puppet on the opposite wall and though my real hand is several inches from Dinitia's head, my shadow caresses her shadow and she turns toward me as if she can feel my touch through her shadow. Our shadows hug, then separate, then sip more wine as the web of Coltrane's saxophone encircles us.

"The promise you made your Da. You never promised you'd give up painting. Only that you'd go to law school."

I raise my wine glass over my head and a blister of light swims across the wall. Dinitia does the same, creating a second blister, and the two merge and separate, bounce off each other, circle each other, charge and retreat, until they stop, facing each other across the diplomas. "It's either/or, Din-Din."

"It doesn't have to be."

"Please don't." I refill the wine glasses and we exchange sips from each other's glass.

"Nathaniel's Assistant Curator of 20th century art at the Modern in New York. Uncle Delaney took color slides of your portfolio to show him. Delaney fancies himself being a footnote to your fame."

"Why didn't he ask me first?"

"You'd say no." Dinitia moves toward me but I turn away. Only our shadows kiss. "Minnie told me the *Guernica* story. It's bullshit. A crutch."

"If you only knew, Madam Freud. If I'm afraid of the empty canvas, how come I have a portfolio for Uncle Delaney to photograph?"

"Because that's not what you're afraid of. Whatever it is, it isn't that." She abandons her wine glass on the headboard. "I wish you had Minnie's bravado."

"He's yours for the taking."

"I want you. The real you."

"You saw the real me in the Satire Room last spring."

"That's not the real you." Dinitia puts her finger to my lips. Coltrane's saxophone repairs its cocoon and when we emerge, we wear only his music.

PART IV

September, 1949–1957

September, 1949

It is September, 1949, and I sit at a table in the church basement (Parish of Saint Monica) in front of a piece of paper wider than my arms can spread. Across the table is another four-year old whose name I cannot say because it has too many funny sounds that make me giggle. This upsets the nuns who punish giggling because Jesus was not a giggler and He is our Savior. Giggling is a sin, the nuns tell me, and I promise never to giggle again because I want to go to heaven if I die in my sleep. The nuns bless me.

"Call me Minnie," the boy says.

"Minnie Mouse," I say.

His face puffs up like he's going to cry until one of the nuns reminds him that our Savior was not a crybaby even when they nailed Him to the Cross. Minnie sucks his tears back inside his eyes. He wants to go to heaven too. We all want to go to heaven. We will do anything to go to heaven.

"Just Minnie," he says. "No mouse."

"Malone," I say.

Between us like a fence is a row of jars. Paints. Finger-paints. Red and yellow and green and blue. And a pile of those wooden things the doctor puts in your mouth when he looks down your throat. Ugh! Share, the nuns say, and we do.

"The sky," I say, as I streak blue across the top of my paper. "The sun," as I drop a blotch of yellow.

"My yard." Minnie spreads green from side to side.

"That big?"

"Bigger." He pushes the green over the edge on to the table. A nun slaps the palm of his hand with a rule and makes him clean up the mess. "No crying," she reminds him.

I put a dot of green at the bottom of my paper. "My yard."

"Come play in mine."

Minnie draws a black line across the green and adds a stick figure on it, another below it. "Me sitting on a wall. Me falling off."

"Humpty-Dumpty," I say.

"Sat on a wall," Minnie replies.

"Humpty-Dumpty," I repeat.

"Had a great fall."

"All the king's horses," I say, "all the king's men."

"Couldn't put Humpty-Dumpty back together again."

We both laugh. Again, a nun cracks the back of Minnie's hand with a ruler. As she reaches for mine, Minnie sticks out his tongue, then knocks the ruler out of her hand before she can swat me. "Did Jesus hit children?" he says.

"Jesus did not backtalk," she says as she rushes off to find Father Giuseppe Ozoni.

"We'll never go to heaven," I say.

"Neither will that stupid nun," Minnie replies.

"Aren't you scared?" I ask.

Minnie laughs. "My dad runs a funeral home. Dead

bodies don't scare me."

Father Ozoni is fat and his face is always red and he sweats a lot, his white collar always wet like my shirt if I'm caught outside in the rain. He has a giant freckle on his cheek under the corner of his left eye with a single hair growing out of the middle of it. And he smells funny. Minnie says he smells like garlic. "Ma doesn't cook with garlic," I say.

Father Ozoni looms over us like a water balloon in the hands of a bully. "Come," he says, "so I may instruct you in God's ways. Private instruction about which you will zip your lips and tell no one."

Later that week, I do play in Minnie's yard. After nursery school. In a sandbox full of sand like the beach and a bulldozer and a steam shovel and a dump truck and pails and shovels just like the ones grownups use except they are the right size for us. We are happy because Father Ozoni has told us we are good boys will go to heaven.

"Let's dig a hole to China," Minnie says.

"Where's China?"

"The other side of the world." Minnie tosses sand over his shoulder. "If we dig deep enough, we'll come out on the other side."

"We'll fall off."

Minnie laughs.

"I don't want to dig a hole. I want to finger-paint."

"Did Jesus finger-paint?" Minnie asks. "If Jesus didn't, it's a sin and we won't go to heaven if we die in our sleep."

"We finger-paint in church," I say.

"I want to be just like Jesus."

"Me too." Later, Ma picks me up and I have five finger-paintings for her and Da that she promises to tape to the walls of their bedroom. And she does.

It's 1954 and Father Ozoni is fatter, much fatter, fatter than a cow, and still sweats a lot and still smells like garlic and Minnie and I have to suffer him because we are altar boys and we have Sunday school and he will be our fate unless we move to another parish, something we will never do. Ma and Da can't afford to move out of the tenement where we live and Minnie's parents won't go to church in a parish where the priest is not Italian.

Minnie's folks have a television. Black and white. A small screen in a very big cabinet with an Adoration and a plant on the top, the wood protected by a doily. It has one knob to change the channels and another to adjust the volume and an antenna that sits between the plant and the Adoration called rabbit ears because it looks ears of a rabbit, except they're not floppy like real rabbit ears. We nickname the antenna Crusader Rabbit after a television cartoon character. At home, Ma and Da only have radios, two, one in the living room and one in Ma's and Da's bedroom, both in plastic cases that get dirty whenever they are touched. I don't like radios because there is nothing to see. I ask why we don't have a television and Ma says because TVs cost a lot of money. I offer my penny collection. She smiles and kisses me on the forehead.

Minnie's television only receives two stations, Channels 10 and 12 from Providence. The Boston stations are fuzzy with ghosts and no matter where we put the rabbit ears the fuzziness and ghosts do not go away. Sometimes we play with the rabbit ears, pointing them this way and that, and try to make three ghosts instead of two. Once we made four. Minnie's mom doesn't like us to play with the rabbit ears.

"Is she afraid of ghosts?" I ask.

"She's afraid of everything," Minnie says.

One day on Channel 10 we see a program where a man teaches people how to draw pictures. He says if we can draw a ball, a cone, a cube and a cylinder, we can draw a real picture the first time we try.

"Like an ice cream cone without the ice cream," Minnie says when the man draws a cone.

This man has a beard that ends in a sharp point and a moustache and wavy hair and when Minnie's mom sees him, she shrieks and says she won't have the devil in her house. She confesses to Father Ozoni that the devil appeared on her television screen and he assures her this man is not the devil, but a well-regarded teacher who teaches children to draw, and that it is far better for young children to watch his drawing lessons than cartoons like Crusader Rabbit that make a mockery of the crusades that took back the Holy Land from the infidels. With Father Ozoni's blessing, Minnie's mom lets us watch the drawing man. Later, we learn the man's name is John Gnagy and the name of the program is *Learn to Draw*. Minnie and I watch it every week and soon we are drawing pictures, real pictures, trees and people and buildings, drawings that Gnagy calls landscapes and seascapes and still lifes.

We are excited, but we get bored because we draw the same pictures Gnagy draws on TV and we want to draw our own pictures, pictures of things we don't see on television but see in real life. We want to draw our teacher who we call Triceratops behind her back because of the way her nose sticks out from her face. We want to draw Mr. Joosse who lives across the street from Minnie because he has hair growing out of his nose and ears. We really want to draw Father Ozoni because he is the funniest looking person we know. "We can sneak into the church and put the drawings on the bulletin board," Minnie says. "He'll crucify us," I reply. Minnie shakes his head. "That's a cardinal sin."

We try drawing Father Ozoni from memory, but we can't get it right. In mine, he's too fat; in Minnie's he's not fat enough. In mine, his head is shaped like an apple; in Minnie's, a pear. His lips look like the candy lips filled with sugar water sold in the penny candy store. His nose grows out of his face like those funny things that grow out of potatoes when they sit on the shelf too long and have to be thrown away because they are too rotten to eat except Ma cuts those funny things out because food is too precious to waste. His eyebrows are like the brush Da uses when he lathers his face to shave. His ears look like pieces of fruit that were run over by a car. His giant freckle looks like an ink blotch someone tried to clean up by wetting their finger. The single hair stands erect like a flag pole.

"We need one of Gnagy's kits," Minnie says.

Gnagy sells a Learn to Draw kit on his show. It has pencils and chalks and a lesson book and everything you need to become a real artist. Minnie and I want to become real artists. We want to draw pictures people will hang in their living rooms. I ask Ma and Da to buy me a kit, but they say it is too expensive. Everything is too expensive. Minnie's folks say no because they think drawing pictures is frivolous and a waste of time even though they have books with pictures of paintings and sculptures by great Italian artists. "They never open those books," Minnie tells me. We do, all the time, careful not to wrinkle or tear the pages. God. Mary. Madonnas. The Christ Child. Jesus on the Cross. Jesus off the Cross. Apostles. Angels. Saints. We marvel at the pictures. Once we ask Father Ozoni why there are no pictures like that at Saint Monica and he scolds us and says boys who ask questions like that do not go to heaven. We still want to go to heaven and he promises to help us get there.

But we want to go to heaven as artists, not as a funeral director like Minnie's dad or as factory workers which is what Ma and Da are. We want to draw God and Mary and Madonnas and the Christ Child and Jesus on the Cross and Jesus off the Cross and Apostles and Angels and Saints like the great Italian artists whose pictures are in the books Minnie's folks never open. And we want to go to heaven to meet them. Without Gnagy's kit, we will never get there.

"An idea," Minnie says one day. We are in his room surrounded by bad drawings of Father Ozoni, too bad to be funny as cartoons. "We borrow money from the collection plates. A little each week until we have enough for two kits. Small amounts he won't know are missing. If you can hide yours here, your parents don't find out." As altar boys, we know where Father Ozoni hides the money before he takes it to the bank, an old cupboard with a lock easily opened with a little silver knife Minnie always carries with him, something we once did just to see if we could do it.

"What's that?" I asked when he first showed it to me.

"A scalpel. Dad has a drawer full."

"What's it for?"

"Cutting bodies. Dad calls it making an incision."

"Won't he miss it?"

"He don't count them and if he does, he'll figure it got thrown out by mistake."

Now, I say, "That's stealing. We can't steal from the church."

"Borrow," Minnie says. "We'll pay it back. No one will miss it."

"God will."

"God will forgive us because of the beautiful pictures we'll draw."

I am not convinced, but I want the Learn to Draw kit more than I've wanted anything in my whole life, more even than a television, and I swear to myself I'll pay back twice, no three times, what Minnie and I borrow and confess my sin after I do and receive absolution and be forgiven and go to heaven and meet all the famous Italian painters.

❧ ❧ ❧

When we watch Gnagy's television show we draw in front of the TV. We watch it every Saturday morning except when Minnie's dad is home, something that does not happen very often. On those Saturdays we watch *The Lone Ranger* on the other station, Channel 12. I like the idea of wearing a mask, the idea no one will know who I am. Maybe I will someday. I'll call myself The Lone Artist and when people look at my paintings they'll ask, 'who is that masked artist?' I'll tie up Silver outside my painting room in case I have to chase after a bank robber or claim jumper or a kid who steals from church collection plates and shoot them with silver bullets.

It takes six months for the money to add up. We have our Learn to Draw kits for several months now and work our way through the lesson book twice. We want to graduate from pencil drawings to watercolors, but we don't have the money to pay for watercolors, not even toy store watercolors. Again, we borrow from the church. It has been a long time since the last time and Father Ozoni has not said a word. We figure we're home free. A dollar a week, we agree.

One Saturday I tell Minnie he draws bodies really great.

"Dad makes me help out in the funeral home. I see dead bodies all the time."

"Yuck!"

"You get used to it. At least to some of it. The ones who died peacefully look like they're sleeping. I have trouble with bodies of people who died in accidents. All beat up. Open wounds. Smashed up heads. Bloody blood blood."

"I've never seen a dead body. When Da's ma died they wouldn't let me go to the wake."

"We can take our pads and sketch them."

"Your dad won't mind?"

"Who's going to tell him? Not me."

❋ ❋ ❋

Watercolors, real watercolors, are much more expensive than the Learn to Draw Kits and it takes us a long time before the money adds up. Four or five Sundays from having enough money to buy two sets of watercolors, two sets of brushes, and two pads of the special paper needed for watercolors, Minnie and I talk excitedly about the number of home runs Ted Williams of the Boston Red Sox hit during the past week, especially three against the hated New York Yankees, as we count out the nickels and dimes for that week's loan. Usually one of us stands watch in the sanctuary while the other borrows from the collection plate money. If someone comes, we say we're tidying up the sanctuary, neatening up the prayer books and hymnals, cleaning Father Ozoni's office, to explain our presence in an empty church. Father Ozoni appreciates our efforts and makes jokes about what great janitors we'll make someday. If he happens by, loud talk about the day's readings, how much we liked sermon or the pretty music of the hymns, warns the other who closes the cupboard where the collection money is hidden and busies himself straightening out Father Ozoni's office.

"If we borrow a little extra," Minnie says, "we can afford to go to Fenway with the CYO and see him live." I know better than to ask Ma and Da for money to go see the Red Sox. Minnie's folks can afford the cost of the trip, but they don't believe in baseball even when it is an official outing of their parish church. About some things his folks are as dead as the bodies his dad buries.

Before I can reply, a bright light flashes, then another. Father Ozoni leers at us from behind a camera. "Well, well, well," he says. "Stealing from God." It's not a question the way he says it.

"Borrowing," Minnie says. "We'll sign IOU's."

"For twice the amount," I add. I'll bargain up to three times if I have to.

"What would your parents say?" Father Ozoni snaps another photo. I blink at the brightness of the flash. "Or the police? Or God who has a special place in Hell for those who steal from Him. Reform school in this life, Hell in the next. Your futures are well set."

"We steal for Him, not from Him," I say.

Father Ozoni chuckles and gestures for me to continue.

"Minnie has a book of paintings of famous Italian painters who glorify God. We want to paint like them, but we can't unless we borrow from Him."

"How much do you owe Him?"

Minnie and I glance at each other. A lie to Father Ozoni is a lie to God and that is a sin God will not forgive; we confess. Everything. About the Learn to Draw Kits. The watercolors. Everything.

"What about art lessons?" Father Ozoni asks. "Oil paints and canvases?"

"We haven't thought that far ahead," Minnie says.

"Of course not," Father Ozoni replies. "Thieves who steal from God never do."

"Borrow," I say. Father Ozoni's garlicky smell makes me nauseous. I want to heave my breakfast, but I swallow it down. My mouth tastes like rotten meat. I am too afraid to ask for a glass of water. Minnie looks like he did the time our teacher caught him cheating on the spelling test. His dad spanked him with a belt. He had to stand in class for three days, shamed because his skin was to raw, his butt too sore, to sit.

Father Ozoni clears his throat. He bares his teeth like he does when he lectures us on sin and the need to live a sinless life. We are doomed. Worse, we are damned. He clears his desk, then walks over to the bookcase and removes a book, one of three identical books, big books, heavy books. He carries it with two hands. He lays it on the desk, opens it, turns the pages, stopping at a page with Canto XXIV on the top with ornate letters. The capital 'C' is like a small painting. Serpents snake around the letter, baring their fangs the way Father Ozoni bares his teeth. The other letters I recognize as Roman Numerals, but I cannot translate them into numbers.

"God's roadmap of Hell," Father Ozoni says. "A guidebook for sinners to what awaits them after death. Into the Seventh Bolgia of the Eighth Circle of Hell, God hurls thieves, eternally jailing them in pits of vipers. These are not ordinary snakes, harmless like the ones you find in your backyard. No. These snakes feed on the thieves." Spittle accumulates in the corners of Father Ozoni's mouth and dribbles toward the point of his chin. "Close your eyes and imagine this. Malone. A viper approaches you, lunges at you, bites you in the belly, the soft part of your belly where your belly button is. You and the viper stare at each other." He licks his lips, then wipes them lips with the back of his hand, cleaning the spittle from the corners of his mouth. "Slowly, you become the viper and the viper becomes you. To become yourself, you must now bite Minnie who will become a viper and then bite you ibn order to become Minnie again. For all eternity you will bite each other, changing from boy to snake to boy to snake to boy to snake because you are thieves.

"But that is not your fate. That fate would be too lenient, too merciful, for thieves like the two of you. No. God ordains a far more severe punishment for those who steal from His Church." Father Ozoni turns the page. Canto XXV headlines the new page. Again, the capital 'C' is like a small painting. I look away. "Those who steal from the Church," Father Ozoni continues, "upon being bitten by a viper are incinerated by God's flame into a lowly pile of ashes only to return to human form to be bitten and incinerated and returned to human form, again and again and again, a cycle that endures for all eternity." Father Ozoni leans across his desk until his face is inches from ours. The fat of his belly covers the book. He rests his tongue on his lower lip like a dog suffering the heat of a summer day. The stench of garlic makes me gag. "Think of the worst pain you have felt in your young lives, then multiply it. Not by ten. Not by one hundred. Not by one million. Multiply it by infinity and you still will not have the pain inflicted by God's flame, the pain suffered by those who steal from His Church. There is no such thing as borrowing from Him." Father Ozoni leans back in his chair and taps his fingers on the fat of his belly. "I shall pray to Him for guidance on the best way to address this. For the time being, run along and beg God for His mercy."

Two weeks later after Sunday Mass Father Ozoni tells our parents he would like us to stay to help him clean the rectory. They consider it a blessing Father Ozoni chooses us over the other altar boys. We have never been in the rectory and we are willing to scrub the floors, polish the pots and pans until they shine, do whatever Father Ozoni asks, if God will absolve us our sins.

"I have prayed to God," Father Ozoni tells us, "and in His infinite wisdom and mercy He has shown me the way to your absolution."

I look up at the living room ceiling and silently mouth 'thank you.' Minnie's eyes remain fixed on the floor as if he sees Hell through the carpeting.

"Do you remember the fate of the sinner who stole from His Church?" We both nod. "That sinner further blasphemed by cursing God with an obscene gesture." Father Ozoni makes a circle with the index finger and thumb of his left hand. With the thumb of his right hand, he penetrates the circle, rapidly sliding his thumb in and out. "The sign of the fig."

Father Ozoni lowers his hands and rests them on his desk. "God will grant you absolution if you pass two tests. First, you must prove to Him you can resist temptation. Not just today or tomorrow, but for the rest of your lives. To make it difficult for you, God ordains you will both become artists, painters, but He will consider it the sign of the fig if you ever sell your paintings. You will be tempted by riches, fame, adulation, but selling your paintings will be the sign of the fig in His eyes and will condemn you to the Seventh Bolgia of the Eighth Circle of Hell no matter how pious and sinless a life you lead from now to the day of your death."

Father Ozoni stands and steps out from behind his desk. "God's second test. Fetch my shirt and pants," he orders Minnie. "Remove my cassock," he orders me. "Hang it in the bedroom closet."

When I return, Father Ozoni is standing in the middle of the living room in his underwear. There is a bulge in his underpants that looks like a sock puppet trying to escape. "Kneel," he orders Minnie. "Watch," he orders me. He lowers his underpants and his prick springs to life. I have never seen such a large one. "In your mouth," he orders Minnie. Minnie hesitates. "God ordains this," Father Ozoni says. "It's your only path to heaven. If you don't want to spend eternity in Hell, you will bow to God's will, obey His command." Minnie places Father Ozoni's prick in his mouth. "In and out," Father Ozoni says. "Slowly. Slowly." Tears run down Minnie's cheeks. I puke my breakfast. "Suck. Suck harder." Father Ozoni moans, a moan I have never heard before. His eyes, closed, bulge from their sockets. His mouth twists open and his lips peel back exposing his teeth. His breathing speeds up, fast, short pants like he has finished running hard and needs to catch his breath. He screams and Minnie gags. "Swallow," he orders. He withdraws his prick from Minnie's mouth and pulls up his underpants. The sock puppet has disappeared. "Next week your turn," he tells me, "or maybe later today. Now clean the rectory. You'll find everything you need in the closet in the kitchen."

This continues and continues and continues, week after week, month after month. After a while, Father Ozoni asks our help on Wednesdays, then Tuesdays and

Thursdays. Three times a week. Tuesdays, Thursdays, Sundays. As a reward, because God wants it, he explains, Father Ozoni buys us watercolors and brushes and special watercolor paper. He pays for art lessons at the Rhode Island School of Design in Providence. He drives us and treats us to supper after each lesson. When we are ready, he buys us oil paints and canvases and a different set of brunches. He admires our work and urges us to continue. He especially praises our portrayal of Christ on the Cross although they are childish and crude compared to the paintings in the books Minnie's parents never open. He promises to hang our paintings in the rectory, perhaps in the church itself if they are good enough, when they are good enough. "I will sell them," he says, "and use the money for God's good works."

"To repay our loans?" I ask, but Father Ozoni makes believe he doesn't hear me.

Later, Minnie says to me, "Straight into his pocket."

We say nothing to anyone about what Father Ozoni forces us to do. We fear eternal damnation. We fear no one will believe us. We fear Father Ozoni really has God's blessing. Our fears keep us from squealing. We endure and endure and endure until one day Minnie says, "This stops now."

I say nothing. Whatever Minnie has in mind, I do not want to know.

That Sunday is my turn to suck Father Ozoni's prick. Minnie watches because Father Ozoni always insists the other watch. As Father Ozoni's face screws tight with ecstasy, I notice a flash of silver out of the corner of my eye. I stumble backward, Father Ozoni's prick still in my mouth. I spit it out. Father Ozoni screams, collapses on the floor. Blood gushes from where his prick used to be. Minnie wipes his scalpel on Father Ozoni's underpants, then plunges it deep into

Father Ozoni's left eye. Only the very tip of the handle shows. Minnie withdraws it, then swipes it across Father Ozoni's throat. Another geyser of blood erupts, an Old Faithful of blood. Again, Minnie wipes the scalpel on Father Ozoni's underpants.

Father Ozoni moans as the kinetic energy of death takes control of his muscles. His handshakes as he struggles to lift his crucifix from where it hangs around his neck to his lips to kiss it, but death seizes him before it reaches his lips and it falls, unkissed, to the floor beside his head. Blood gushes from where his prick once was. And blood gushes from his throat, from his eye, and pools around his head, around the crucifix, slowly rising, like an incoming tide, until it blankets Jesus on the Cross, first to His knees, then His waist, His head, stopping before the Crown of Thorns sinks beneath the blood. A final death spasm and another wave of blood spurts from the eye, the throat, the groin, plunging the crucifix beneath the depths, drowning Jesus on the Cross.

I stand transfixed. I have never seen a person die before. I have never seen that much blood. I have never seen Jesus drowned in blood. The Italian artists in the book Minnie's folks never open never painted this. The head of John the Baptist on a plate, yes; but never this. Someday I will, a crucifix sinking into a pool of blood, and maybe my painting will end up in one of those books or on the wall of a museum or the nave of a church. If I don't die before my time and go to Hell to spend all eternity sucking the prick of Father Ozoni.

"Ozoni's curse of the sign of the fig is Satan's, not God's. It dies with him," Minnie says. "Let's amscray." Running faster than we've ever run before, we hide in the wooded area of a park near Minnie's house, invisible from the basketball court and baseball diamond, invisible from the street. "Our secret," Minnie says. "We take it to our graves." I nod.

"Promise on your soul," Minnie says.

What soul, I want to ask, but don't and join Minnie in making the promise. We hide in the woods until the skies darken, then go home and face the wrath of our parents for being late for dinner. Ma and Da send me to bed without supper. Minnie's folks make him eat his cold.

That night, I cannot sleep. I don't understand how Minnie knew it was the Devil talking, not God. I can't figure out why Father Ozoni would buy us art supplies and pay for lessons if he were not following God's command. Let Minnie tempt fate. I am too cowardly. With Father Ozoni we have toured Hell, both in this life and the next. I do not want to return. Not selling my paintings no matter how great the temptation will be a small price to pay for salvation. I doze off, my mind conjuring up the temptations God will place before me to lure me into making the sign of the fig. I pray I am strong enough to resist.

That night while his parents sleep and I lie awake, Minnie sneaks into the bathroom. Flushing to toilet to create an excuse if one of them asks why he got up in the middle of the night, Minnie immerses the scalpel in hot water. With the scouring powder his mom uses on the bath tub, sink, and toilet bowl, he cleans the blood and residue from the scalpel until the blade is as shiny as it was before. My sacred scalpel, he thinks, as he buries it in the bottom of his shoe box of baseball cards.

Two days later, the Boston Archdiocese announces Father Guiseppe Ozoni died after a long undiagnosed illness. He receives all the honors the Church bestows on a deceased priest. Decades later when the child abuse scandal rocks the Church and Boston's Cardinal who covered up the scandal and did not punish priests like Father Ozoni, but reassigned them to unsuspecting parishes where there were new victims to prey upon, when this Cardinal is granted asylum and diplomatic immunity by the Vatican, I understand the true nature of Father Ozoni's undiagnosed disease. Someday, I vow, I will make an Easter Sunday pilgrimage to the cemetery where the Church buried Father Ozoni and spit on his grave.

Part V

June 6, 1968–June 16, 1968

June 6, 1968

The day is gray, monochromatic, Zone 5 on the black and white scale. The sky is as milky as a one of the watercolor washes of my childhood. No contrast. No light and shade. No shadows. I can't paint without light and shade. Without shadows. Without my shadow, I feel incomplete, soulless. Rain would restore the color, but none is forecast. Memories shadow me and my mind operates like the landscapes I paint, the portraits, the still lifes. Representational, not conceptual. Each memory is a separate painting. All the colors of my palette. Even the reds, colors I still cannot mix properly. Minnie's last laugh. Now that he's dead, I have no one to mix reds for me. Swine from the Meatpacking District, a shitty fallback. If the world's museums have enough wall space to hang my oeuvre, I do not have the infinite number of lives to paint it. Fucking reality.

I wonder how this can be. In my law school Evidence class, we read studies proving that eye witness testimony is too unreliable to be the basis for criminal convictions. People think they remember what they see, but they don't. The professor demonstrates it for us. Someone bursts into the class, screams, squirts the professor with red dye, then escapes. Write an eye witness statement for the police, the professor orders. Describe the assailant. Physical appearance. Age and gender. Race. Clothing. Describe the weapon. What the assailant said. When we finish, the assailant reappears and reenacts the attack in slow motion. We compare our eye witness statements with what actually happened. Less than half the class has the majority of the details correct. Yet, the law says our testimony is sufficient to affirm on appeal the assailant's conviction. Of murder. Of a death sentence. We are eye witnesses. We are complicit.

I lack a photographic memory that remembers everything. My memory doesn't function that way; maybe memory itself doesn't. The mind, the intellect, organizes bits and pieces, shards of memory, into a coherent narrative, part real, part wishful thinking, part as made up as the memoir you are now reading, and this coherent narrative becomes memory, whether these events happened or not, whether they were eye witnessed or not. Which is why we are all unreliable narrators. Even the dead. Especially the dead.

❧ ❧ ❧

Several cabs, some empty, some with fares, some off duty, drive by the Amsterdam Avenue entrance of St. Luke's Hospital in New York's Morningside Heights neighborhood. The drivers ignore my wife Dinitia Marbury Madison, and her waving hand and her shouts as if they believe we want a ride to the South Bronx. With my wheelchair, I'm as undesirable a passenger as a Negro whether wearing a suit or rags.

Because of one-way streets, the cab ride to our apartment is twice the length of the walk; but hospital policy dictates that discharged patients be driven home and a taxi is cheaper than an ambulance. On an ordinary day, I would insist on walking, challenge the hospital to prevent me, and, with exaggerated winks and raised eyebrows, remind everyone that I am a first year law student, a Columbia University School of Law first year law student, in search of my first case; but on this achromatic day, humor no matter how innocent, how innocuous, how well intended, would be in bad taste. As resentful as Dinitia was when she used to pose for one of my life studies, I sit and wait and lament the absence of my shadow.

All the cabs have long strips of black crepe streaming from their radio antennas. Just black. Not red and black like the cabs and police cars and school busses and private cars that once paraded down Route 24 from Boston Garden to Fall River. Not red and black like the school bus of champions with a hero named Malone and the rest of the B.M.C. Durfee High School basketball team, the coaches, the mascots, the cheerleaders, the chaperones, the police escort. Not red and black like the school busses with the pep squad and the band, the caravan of friends and fans in private cars, Julia, Minnie, Ma and Da, still alive, still healthy, still working. The world was swathed in red and black that night. The absolutely positively best night of your lives, Coach roared in the locker room after the game. Absolutely positively.

A police car with a black stripe over the seal of the City of New York on its door, the blazon for police cars in funeral processions for fallen comrades, cruises by. Private cars have black cloth tied to their bumpers or door handles or taped to their hoods or trunks or fenders. Sheets of black paper cover the advertising panels on the sides of the city busses. Black wreathes are wired to the grills of the city sanitation trucks. Pedestrians on Amsterdam Avenue, heads bowed, walk to the slow cadence of the bells in the carillon of St. John the Divine, the bells with the lowest notes sounding every fifteen seconds, the other bells, the bells of joy and merriment, silent. Though they walk singly and are strangers to each other, the cadence of the bells binds them into a procession. Black bunting caps the garage doors of the fire station on W. 113th St. and its flag, red, white, blue, hangs at half-mast. The firefighters who often play cards on the sidewalk outside the station or entertain the neighborhood children with sleight of hand or other simple magic tricks comfort each other while they watch the news on television and pray they will not be interrupted by any alarms, real or false.

Photographs of Senator Robert F. Kennedy bordered in black grace the window of the Viennese pastry shop and the door of the candy store that sells magazines and comic books and the counter of the Post Office substation and the fire escapes of the apartment buildings and the windows of the apartments. Identical photos are taped to cash registers in the Green Tree Hungarian Restaurant and the V & T Pizzeria and the croissant shop where Dinitia and I sometime eat breakfast with the newspaper on Sunday mornings. The city, wearing widow weeds, announces to the world that it mourns Senator Kennedy's assassination.

As for Dinitia's efforts to hail a cab, they roll past the hospital, the drivers preoccupied with their own thoughts until success, at last. This cab, too, has a banner of black crepe attached to its radio antenna. More black crepe rims its rear-view mirror. I hoist myself out of the wheelchair into the cab. The driver wears a black button with a ribbon of black cloth pinned to his shirt over his heart, torn half way down like the one Joel Davidow wore after his father died.

"Where to?" the cabby asks through the plastic partition separating the front seat from the back.

"One twelve and Broadway," Dinitia says. "Tom's Restaurant."

The cabby's eyes, puffy and bloodshot, shine through the dirt and grime and scratches clouding the partition, the eyes of a person who cried himself to sleep, Ma's eyes and mine after Da's passing. I understand now that New York mourns Senator Kennedy like a member of the family and for the first time since Dinitia and I married and moved to New York the previous summer I count myself a New Yorker. The cab navigates around the cars double-parked on West 113th Street. It moves in slow motion as if someone stole the octane from its gas or injected downers into its carburetor. When the cab stops at Broadway for a red light, the headline of *The New York Times* catches my eye: 'Kennedy is Dead, Victim of Assassin; Suspect, Arab Immigrant, Arraigned; Johnson Appoints Panel on Violence.'

"Get me a paper."

"We have one at home."

Home. Once, a three decker half way up one of Fall River's hills. Camping out with Da in the crawl space under the front porch. Digging a hole to China in the backyard with Minnie. Trying again at the beach. An underground ocean. Not blue like the real ocean. Secrets to be carried with us to the grave, Minnie having journeyed there long before his time. Once upon a time we were friends. Once upon a time Minnie saved my life. I repaid him in spades. B.F., Before Dinitia. No colors. No red. Only black.

The light at West 113th Street and Broadway turns green and pedestrians walking with the same slow gait as those on Amsterdam continue to cross in front of the cab. The cabby doesn't lean on his horn, but stares down at his hands folded in his lap as if he is praying to the bobble head doll wearing a New York Mets cap mounted on his dashboard. Blue and orange beneath the black. Still no red. When a pedestrian hesitates, the cab inches across Broadway and turns left to head downtown. The old men who usually play chess or checkers on the benches in the median strip just sit, not talking, their newspapers spread across their laps like blankets. The Senator stares up at them, all teeth, all hair, the sparkle in his eyes shining through the dull gray newsprint. No one pokes or prods or pinches the produce at the Korean green grocer's in search of the freshest firmest tomatoes or peppers or grapes. No one browses the used furniture on the sidewalk in front of the hardware store. No one waits in line for lunch at Tom's Restaurant or to buy a sandwich at Mama Joy's or a square of Sicilian pizza at Antonio's. No one panhandles the street opposite the liquor store. New York is like a car with a rundown battery. Dinitia squeezes my hand. At our apartment building, the cabby sighs and waves off the fare.

"Make a donation in the Senator's memory," he says.

Our living room is all shadows in the sunless light seeping in through the windows facing the air shaft. No artificial suns illuminate the shaft this day and I shake my head when Dinitia reaches for one of the lamps. "Brew some coffee," I say as I spread the *Times* on the table where we eat our meals. The letters clump together like paint too long on the palette. My eyes still don't focus well enough. Someday they might. Someday. "Read this to me."

"He was shot dead," Dinitia says from the kitchen. "What more do you need to know?"

"Why do we have his stuff?" Since I awoke from the coma, my mind confuses past and present and I'm never sure whether I'm living in today or yesterday. Someday, maybe, I will; maybe not. The doctors don't know. It's not their fault. Medicine is an inexact science. That's why, I tell myself, I won't accept medical malpractice cases when I hang out my law shingle. If I hang out my law shingle.

"It's in his will."

"Bastard."

Minnie's studio supplies are stashed in the corner next to the desk where I wrote my appellate brief for the first-year moot court competition. A legal issue only a true-blue attorney would love: Does an international treaty limiting the amount of monetary damages that victims of air crashes on international flights may recover from a United States airline preempt the New York wrongful death statute that has no limitation? In real life, a few million dollars would be at stake; in moot court, A's and B's and C's. Minnie's easel sags against the wall between the windows. In the dead of winter, I stared out those windows as I struggled to comprehend the Rule Against Perpetuities. Twenty years after the death of the last life in being at the time of the testator's or trust settlor's death. I see nothing wrong with perpetuities, no reason to have a rule barring them. Everyone wants forever.

Minnie's last creation, *Life with Coffee Spoons*, an oil on canvas, leans against the arm of the chair where I studied Torts and Contracts and Criminal Law and Civil Procedure. There are pens and pencils in an Amherst College glass on the desk, a legal pad, an eraser, case books, a protractor and compass. Not six months since we argued about that painting, me and Minnie and Dinitia. It was our proxy war, arguing about painting to avoid arguing about what we really should have been arguing about. Minnie's concept, my opening salvo, prosaic, as unimaginative as greeting card art. Coffee spoons spiraling into infinity, disappearing into the painting's first vanishing point; a variety of spoons, big and little, plastic and sterling, engraved and plain.

"Would the spoons be full or empty?" I asked Minnie.

"Eliot doesn't say," Minnie replied, "so it's for me to decide."

My mind wanders back to the coffee spoons. Some are empty. Some full. Some have coffee beans or ground coffee or instant coffee granules or liquid coffee. There are spoons with white sugar and spoons with brown sugar, some in cubes and some in packets and some granulated, and spoons with milk and spoons with cream and spoons with cinnamon and spoons with chocolate syrup and spoons with things Minnie refused to identify.

"Heroin," Dinitia said, but Minnie used only soft drugs. We all used only soft drugs. Heroin was cutting edge, the outsider drug for serious artists. LSD, also. Neither suitable fo a Sunday painter. The source of Dinitia's resentment, that I am a Sunday painter. It's not like she didn't know. I massage my forehead. Close my eyes to rest them. I feel like I'm drugged, a side effect of my meds.

There are coffee grinders in Minnie's painting regressing into infinity at the second vanishing point. Old fashioned hand-turned grinders. Sleek modern electric powered grinders. But no percolators or drip coffee makers or espresso machines because, as Minnie boasted, he boils his coffee like a trail hand on a cattle drive in the old West.

"The concept flames," I said. "It opens no narrative space. It won't be worth the time or the canvas."

How angry Minnie became, his anger intensified by the pot we smoked, until Dinitia said she agrees with me, one of the rare times she sides with me in our arguments with Minnie. Wives are supposed to side with their husbands, right or wrong. "Möebius strips," she said, tearing a strip of paper, twisting it 180 degrees, taping the ends together. Two sided and one sided at the same time. She traces a line on both sides of the paper without lifting her pencil. "This is what it means to measure out your life in coffee spoons."

Minnie took Dinitia's advice because he still loved her and wanted to marry her and always will even after his death did them part, but never held it against her, or me, that she married me. Or, if he did, he buried it far beneath the surface paint where the most powerful X-ray machine would not uncover the chalk that lay directly on the canvas. I was not as forgiving. Minnie did not measure out his life in coffee spoons, but drew it on Möebius strips, hieroglyphics to tell his life story like the wall paintings in a Pharaoh's tomb in ancient Egypt. Minnie must have had a premonition. A glimpse into the future. His future. I wonder if he also glimpsed my future. Two would be painters who were going to take over the art world. One now dead; the other a husk one-third of the way to becoming a lawyer.

Dinitia places a tray with two mugs and a coffee pot on the table and sits beside me. "Laurie Williams called. Funeral arrangements. I told her we'd be there."

"Minnie's cheerleader. Perfect for him." My delusions survive my head injuries, my brain surgeries, my coma, my month plus in the hospital. I sip some coffee, then press the mug against my chin. Steam slides up my cheeks. Dinitia dries my tears with her fingertips.

I dump the contents of my attaché case on the floor, my law books and course outlines and legal pads and pens and pencils, then fill it with paint brushes, first Minnie's, then mine; but not Dinitia's. Hers still have a lifetime of brush strokes. Her lifetime. Maybe she'll paint my memories. She has the vision. The talent. More than Minnie and I combined. Squared. Cubed. She should be at the Museum School or studying privately, not working some shit job to support a dead broke law student. I fear the angry God she's appeasing by her sacrifice.

"Where's his sacred scalpel?" I ask.

Dinitia eyes me as if she thinks what little is left of my mind now runs free, stampeding down the streets and avenues of New York like a wild beast escaped from its cage in the zoo, fleeing the zookeepers who would drug it and haul it back to its cage if they don't kill it first.

"His sacred scalpel," I say again. "The one we used when we became blood brothers. The one he used to save my life."

A pall of skepticism about the accuracy, the authenticity, of my memories floats across Dinitia's face. She does not know about Father Ozoni, about the vow of silence Minnie and I took. Minnie has kept his. I wrestle with the question whether his death released me. I grab an umbrella from the back corner of the closet to use as a cane and hobble toward the door.

"Where are you going?"

I pause, my hand on the door knob.

"To take a ferry ride."

"You're recovering from a traumatic brain injury. You shouldn't be wandering the city alone."

"Come with me."

Dinitia tries to wrestle the brief case from my hand, but my grip is too tight. "Traumatic brain injury. No strenuous exertion. You heard the doctors."

"If you're worried, write out the directions and pin them to my shirt. If I become confused or get lost, the kindness of strangers will send me on my way." I start dictating step-by-step directions. Exit the apartment building. Walk down Broadway to the 110th station. Broadway Local downtown to South Ferry.

Dinitia interrupts. "I'm not going to aid and abet

you giving up painting."

"Nice legalism. Aid and abet. Makes you sound like a law student."

"What happened to the man I married?"

"I'm not Minnie. Never was."

She flashes me the finger.

❧ ❧ ❧

While I ride the Broadway Local downtown, my wife walks down Broadway to the Gold Rail, her cadence slow, like a person in a funeral procession, a funeral procession of one. Kennedy's assassination slows the rhythms of the city, silences the background noise. Broadway is hushed, less traffic, fewer pedestrians. Cabbies drive less aggressively, not leaning on their horns at the slightest provocation. Busses accelerate slowly, tamping down the rumble of their engines, their exhausts.

The Gold Rail is empty, one or two at the bar hunched over their glasses, their sorrow making their heads too heavy for their necks to support. The tables in the back are unoccupied. And the Gold Rail is quiet. Television off. Radio off. Juke box unplugged. Signs advertising various brands of beer dark. No small talk about the Yankees or the Mets or the stock market. Ordering one of their cheap steaks, a better value than some of the East Side steak houses, and a pitcher of draft beer, Dinitia selects a table near the window that opens on the air shaft between the buildings. Like all ground floor windows, even those that do not open on the street, metal bars prevent intruders from breaking and entering. New York, New York.

Nineteen days shy of our first anniversary, Dinitia grapples with the possibility that the marriage, her marriage, may be a failure; that the man she tries to mold into the husband of her dreams lacks the courage to allow her to do so. I am a contradiction she does not understand, courageous enough to defend a law school classmate against a horde of Mau-mau, yet too cowardly to give up the law to paint. She would accept my rationale, that I promised Da I would support Ma in her widowhood, a promise Ma released me from, if I sold *Talking of Michelangelo* and gave Ma the money. $25,000.00 would make her life much easier; but I refuse. It's not as if I'm holding out for the painting to become more valuable. I wouldn't sell it, I swear, for a million dollars. She wishes she believed me when I prattle on about how selling a painting is like selling a child. In a letter she asked Minnie for the truth about my refusal to sell, but that letter will now forever be unanswered.

Dinitia refills her glass. Half a pitcher down, half a pitcher to go. The beer warms her head. Her mind floats, observing her as if it occupies the chair across the table. The steak arrives and she cuts away the gristle, not the fat. It is red in the middle, the way she likes it. She lets the French fries soak in the meat's juices, then tops them off with ketchup. She moves the vegetable, steamed broccoli, to the side. It's not that kind of day. She wonders from which side of the family, Pratt or Madison, she inherits her peasant tastes; or, is her bloodline not as pure, not as patrician, as she's been led to believe.

Divorce. The word surfs the beer's foam. It would devastate me even though I'm convinced she loves Minnie, not me. Many times, I offered her her freedom. Minnie would be alive if she had accepted. Othello's jealousy pales beside mine for Minnie. Not emotionally but financially. Scholarships and student loans cover my tuition, fees and books, but her job pays the rent, buys the food, the day to day expenses of everyday life. Without her, how cannot pay for them. Still, I would not sell my precious paintings. I'd drop out of law school, get a job, maybe return to Fall River and go into the mills like Ma and Da before me. Third shift, I once said. Work nights, paint days.

Physically, I don't know whether I've recovered enough to work hard labor. Or, to return to school in September. Memory will be a problem, Dr. Henderson explained. Short term and long term; but, Dr. Robey added, the brain is malleable. Connections reestablish. The condition may ease, self-correct.

Maybe a divorce in two years. Three years if he has to take a year off. He graduates, passes the bar, becomes self-supporting. With law review on his résumé, he has a choice of Wall Street firms to work for. Kiss each other good-by; move on with separate lives. She would have to be very cautious about sex. Children would ruin the equation. Minimize the fucking, double up on birth control, pills and a diaphragm or pills and an IUD, or pills, a diaphragm, and a rubber, chart her cycle to track when she ovulates. If she could afford two rents, she would move out. Daddy would pay, but she doesn't need his unending 'I told you so'. Separating the twin beds would be a start. An air mattress in the living room.

She finishes the steak and French fries, refills her glass and cleanses her palate by draining it. If she shares her thinking with me now, divorce becomes inevitable, irrevocable. Wait and maybe things will work out in an unexpected way. She wishes she could convince me she married me because she loves me and never loved Minnie in that way, that she nags me about painting because she loves me and not because she wants to transform me into another Minnie, that the marriage would work if I weren't pigheaded, mulish, Othello-ish.

She pours the last half inch of beer from the pitcher

into her glass; stares into it. The beer absorbs its bubbles. The liquid's surface calms, flattens. The darkness of the Gold Rail comforts her. Outside's bright sky frightens her. She chides herself. She wishes it were as simple as it was in *Casablanca* when Bogie said to Bergman, Our problems don't amount to a hill of beans in this crazy world. Mine, she thinks, aren't worth one bean out of that hill.

❧ ❧ ❧

I stay on the downtown Broadway Local rather than change to the Express at 96th Street, the same subway car where I scrawled 'Kilroy was here' the day of Minnie's Army induction. My initials, JSM, superimposed on each other, the way I sign my paintings because I am either too arrogant or too ashamed or too timid to use my full name. Or all three. Graffiti now cover everything, the doors and windows, the floor and ceiling, the seats, the inside walls, the outside walls, my 'Kilroy was here', my initials. For every graffito that shows talent, there are dozens that would fail nursery school finger-painting. Beneath the streets in the subway tunnels where night and day are as interchangeable as Jackson Pollock drip paintings, the graffiti are full of color, bold and fluorescent, color that bombards my eyes like the Mau-mau who attacked me on the Columbia campus, wave after wave until my skull was breached, my brain overrun, color that coats the skin and lodges in the membranes of the mouth and nose like the particulates that dirty New York's atmosphere, color that oozes like gangrene from dead tissue. Color. Acra red, cadmium, ochre, ultramarine, sap green, lampblack, Payne's gray. There is no escape. Change cars, change trains, change cities, no matter. Underground, color is everywhere.

The other passengers ignore the graffiti, reading their newspapers, the *Times*, the *Daily News*, the *Post*, page after page of stories about Senator Kennedy's assassination, photos of Ethel, the children, the cousins, Rose from Hyannisport being comforted by Ted. Like everyone else on the subway, I feel like the member of a family on its way to a funeral.

At 103rd street, a priest enters and sits down opposite me. He is fat, as fat as a cow, fatter than a cow. I can smell the garlic from across the subway car. He wears an eye patch like the man in the Hathaway shirt ads. I think I have seen this priest before, but I do not recall where or when thanks to the scrambled eggs of my memory. The priest smiles at me and makes the Sign of the Cross. I do not feel blessed. He exits with a flock of other passengers at 96th to await the Broadway Express.

At the far end of the subway car, a young Negro, high school age, tall and thin, his knees half way up his chest, sits and dribbles a basketball, its grain worn smooth from playground asphalt. He wears a red tee shirt and red Converse sneakers and red gym shorts. He dribbles the basketball with his fingertips, his fingers slightly arched, the flat of his hand never touching the ball, the way Coach taught. He has long fingers, this Negro, long and slender, good fingers for palming the basketball, good fingers for dunking, good fingers for taking the pass in the pivot and shooting a hook shot. Something else Coach taught. Few players shoot it now. Except for Lew Alcindor. Few players know how to defend it. Except for Lew Alcindor. Maybe I should have stayed with basketball.

I tap my umbrella against the floor to the beat of the basketball. That's where I would be if I didn't quit the team. A second state championship. A wife named Julia. Business school. Studying to turn a factory that makes pants into an international conglomerate. Minnie would be alive. He would have to be. His sacred scalpel would have willed it. We would still be friends. We'd have to be. No one else would taunt me and tease me for the road not taken. Art offers no choice was his mantra. How fucking portentous. I would have played senior year if it meant Minnie's life. I would have married Julia and let him marry Dinitia. I would have let him take over the art world without me, the one Musketeer. My head throbs, synchronized to the bounce of the basketball, and I want to ask the black kid to stop; but I don't want trouble. I close my eyes as the train rumbles into and out of the stations at 68th Street, 59th Street, 50th Street, Times Square, 34th Street, 28th Street, 23rd Street, 18th Street, 14th Street where the kid with the basketball exits as if he's leading a fast break, 8th Street, 4th Street, the rest of the stops until South Ferry, the last stop on the Broadway Local.

At South Ferry, I pay my nickel and hobble aboard the Staten Island Ferry. The click of my umbrella first on the gangplank, then the wooden deck of the ferry, becomes the sounds of footsteps across a wooden porch. Billy Goat Gruff to a young me hiding under the front porch with Da who spun out fairy tales of strange and fantastical creatures and magic beans and talking Billy goats. Diamonds of light from the lattice work. Diamonds of light from the cut glass of a fake and phony pinky finger ring. Leaves dry and crunchy. Filaments of spider web. Dust and dirt, damp if it recently rained. Clothes to be washed, hung on the line to dry; but Ma never complained. She understood the importance of illusion. Much more important than memory.

In the stern of the ferry, a young woman, a violin case at her feet open for contributions, plays Bach, one of the Orchestral Suites. Her hair, the same rich polished brown as the wood of her violin, cascades over her face. The ferry moves into Upper New York Bay and the wind tangles her hair in her bow and the strings of her violin and she pauses to untangle it, then ties her hair behind her head and resumes playing, the Second Movement from Bach's *Third Orchestral Suite, Air*. The waves are choppy and the hull of the ferry slaps against the water like a drummer who cannot keep the beat. Oil slicks streak the water beside the ferry, a rainbow of reds and greens and sickly yellows against the gray of the sky, the dirty blue of the bay. White caps accompany the ferry like seagulls hoping for handouts. Beyond the stern, seagulls congregate, circle, hover and eye me like I'm a piece of raw fish. They swarm above me now, undecided whether I'm dinner, screeching Quitter! Quitter! Quitter! Me. Minnie. Oblivious to the seagulls, the violinist closes her eyes, absorbed in her music that she obviously loves. The music hovers about her as it would wherever she played, whether in the stern of the Staten Island Ferry or on the stage of Carnegie Hall or the orchestra pit of the Metropolitan Opera House in Lincoln Center or in the privacy of her bedroom, and I wonder if it will protect me from the seagulls.

I want to step into the music, but I can't without disturbing her. I listen from afar. Musicians have an advantage over painters, sculptors. Performing does not dispossess them of their art. They can always play it again. And again. The lies I tell myself. After a few moments, I limp to the railing, hook the handle of my umbrella on it, and open my attaché case. One by one I take out the brushes, my own and Minnie's. The brushes are jumbled together. I can't tell whose are whose. First the watercolor brushes, then the bristle brushes, the oil painting brushes, the badger brushes Minnie called his 'sweeteners', the single stroke brushes, the fan brushes, the lettering brushes, all the brushes, one by one, and I break them into twos and I throw them piece by piece into the waters of Upper New York Bay where they are greeted by the whitecaps as if they are returning home after a long absence and by the seagulls who, still in search of something to eat, swoop down and circle above the brushes, cawing in disappointment because the brushes are not edible. I apologize to the waters for not offering up Minnie's sacred scalpel, but they do not believe my explanation any more than I do.

Quitter! Quitter! Quitter!

I close the attaché case and raise it to the level of my chest, to the level of my nose, just below my eyes, where I cradle the flat of its side in my palm, my fingertips bent. My palm makes an opening the size of a golf ball, the way Coach taught me, taught all his players, to shoot jump shots. I bend my knees, gritting my teeth from the pain, then square my feet and leap, an inch or two, maybe three, above the ferry's deck. At the apex of my jump, I extend my hand over my head and propel the attaché case forward over the waves with a flick of my wrist. It spins, perfect rotation, and it arcs, perfect arc, and it soars over the waters of Upper New York Bay, upward, ever upward, toward the seagulls the way a basketball once soared toward the championship banners hanging in the rafters of Boston Garden. I land with a jolt that collapses my knees and I crash to the deck, feeling more pain than Da ever felt and for a moment, a moment no longer than a heartbeat, I want to roll myself beneath the bottom rail into the choppy water and swim after the broken brushes and hold on to them as if they are pieces of drift wood big enough and sturdy enough to support me until I make landfall on some deserted island, my mind cleansed of memory by the salt water, a blank canvas, the terror of facing the blank canvas more comforting than the terror of memory. Instead, I hoist myself on to the bench opposite the railing and peer out at the water where I think I see the waves part and I think I see a hole open, a hole the size of a basketball hoop, and I think I see the attaché case, still in perfect rotation, still with a perfect arc, swish through the hole. In my mind's ear, the thumping of the ferry's hull slapping against the waves is the applause of an arena full of fans and the whistle of the wind is their cheering. In my mind's eye, the attaché case spirals deeper and deeper into the water, beyond the reach of light to where the only illumination, the only color, comes from the creatures who inhabit the deepest depths, sinking deeper and deeper into the water the way memory sinks deeper and deeper into the past, until it comes to rest in the muck at the bottom of the bay with the wreckage of ancient ships and the detritus of modern life. I'm tormented by not knowing how far back in time my memory would have to go until it came to the exact instant, the exact moment, the exact experience, when I lost my future. I doubt I will know when I am there. Like my attaché case, my journey into the past most likely will stop where it stops because I have come to rest in the muck.

❧ ❧ ❧

The muck. A tricycle wheel. Willem de Kooning. De Kooning does not paint tricycles. Nor do I. But I learn to ride my trike about the same time I learn to finger-paint and, somewhere, deep inside the mangled ganglia of what remains of my brain, a linkage reestablishes itself, between what I can and what I cannot say, and I stand once more before De Kooning, my first exposure to *The Time of the Fire* and *Detour*. The debate of modern art, whether color and form may exist alone as expressive means without imitating visual reality. For some critics, his paintings inchoate, fragmentary, senseless, (assuming these words have meaning in the context of discussing an oil painting); for others they convey meaning in their spontaneity, their lack of schematic preparations. Fuck the art critics and their pronouncements from on high, especially those who pontificate that 'No shred of visual reality can be recognized.' They speak of the obvious, the dominance of reds and greens and yellows, the strong passages of black and white that force the eye to move from vortex to vortex as if the paintings are an aggregation of miniature tornadoes sucking the viewers into the canvas. We are all Dorothy on our way to Oz. Except for those of us who are Toto. I listen to young mothers who wheel strollers through the museum exposing their toddlers to art in the hope that in sixteen or seventeen years Johnnie will get into to Harvard or Johanna to Radcliffe. 'You can fingy-wingy paint better than that,' they say in the lilting voices of young mothers cooing at their first born. Once, could I.

❦ ❦ ❦

In the stern of the ferry, the violinist begins the Third Movement of Bach's *Third Orchestral Suite*, the *Gavotte*. I welcome the music. It lifts me out of the water on to the ferry's deck. Maybe if she plays long enough, maybe if I listen hard enough, maybe I will find that instant of time, that moment, that experience, when I lost my future and time will wash over me and purify me and restore me to the moment before the decay began, the moment before oil slicks desecrated the bay and I still had a future. Father Ozoni's curse of eternal damnation haunts me.

I hobble over to the violinist as the *Gavotte* ends and when she starts the *Bourrée* I remove a ten-dollar bill from my wallet and anchor it under her resin, weighed down against the wind. I smile at her when she mouths her thanks. As she starts the *Gigue*, the final movement of the *Suite*, I hobble back to the railing. By the time I get there and unhook my umbrella, the brushes and the attaché case and the seagulls and the oil slick and the violinist have vanished and I am alone, as alone as a point in a pointillist painting.

⁂ ⁂ ⁂

On the deck of the Staten Island ferry, I emerge from a cocoon of Bach. The helmsman steers the ferry into its slip. The bow nudges the dock; the starboard side scrapes wood pilings. Vibrations rattle my bones, more brittle than I realized. I rode the subway down to South Ferry, my bones anesthetized on adrenaline. None remains. I shake at the thought of how I will suffer the lurching, the sudden starts and stops, of the uptown trip. I feel like chips of marble at the base of an unfinished Michelangelo sculpture. Not every block of marble houses a statue within it. I am destined, at best, to be a discard, a block of marble repurposed as a finial or a gargoyle. The crew secures the ferry to the pier. Using the railing, I pull myself into a standing position. The wind raises a chop and the ferry rocks back and forth. My umbrella becomes the third leg of a tripod, the only way I can maintain my balance.

A hand on my shoulder. The woman with the violin, newly encased. "Why?" she asks.

I wince and she eases her grip.

"Your brushes. Why?"

I try to think of something witty to say, something profound, but my mind blanks, unable to muster a cliché much less an original thought. The new, improved me. Tomorrow I will call Dr. Robey. If I remember.

She loops her arm in mine, grasping my upper arm to steady me. I hold the umbrella in my opposite hand, tap, tap, tapping it against the deck. I try to disguise my limp as she guides me along the rail toward the gangplank. People with no time to spare jostle us as they eddy around us, some muttering under their breath. "It must have been a horrible accident," she says.

We disembark into the sunlight and open air of Battery Park. Black bunting on the street lights whips back and forth in the sea breeze. We enter the dark, windy canyons of Wall Street. The green greed of money, the yellow jealousy those who earn less harbor for those who earn more, ebb and flow around us. Lawyers and bankers and stock brokers rush to wherever they must rush, their moment of silence for the late Senator the briefest interruption in their workaday lives. Soon I will rush with them. If my limp allows me. If my mind escapes its prison of clichés. I fear for my mind.

"Do you have a minute?" I ask. The violinist nods. We break free of the pedestrian flow and angle toward the observation platform that overlooks the World Trade Center construction site. She helps me up the stairs, her hand in the small of my back gently pushing.

"Why?" she asks again when we reach the top.

I look down into the foundation hole, deep, the bottom not visible. Men in hardhats wearing fluorescent orange vests, as small as ants, scurry about. Construction equipment wrapped in black, trucks and bulldozers and steam shovels and cement mixers, rumble back and forth, as small as the toys I once played with in a Fall River sand box in Minnie's back yard. A flag flies at half-mast. "Digging a hole to China."

She laughs. "Entrance to the underworld."

"Isn't there supposed to be a river? A ferryman? A dog?"

"The underworld entered through the dark wood."

A familiar phrase. One I have heard before, though I don't know where, don't know when. My mind fails my memory, my memory my mind. I am too proud, too embarrassed, too afraid, to ask. Not of appearing ignorant or dumb; rather afraid my mind will not find meaning in her answer. Tonight, I'll ask Dinitia. If I remember.

On the platform's railing, binoculars commonly found at tourist sites. Slip a quarter in the slot and the lens cap slides open for a minute, maybe two, maybe three. I hobble up to it, fumble in my pocket for a quarter. She covers the slot with her hand, feeds it a quarter. I bend forward, my forearms resting on the railing. The stretch of my back muscles pulls on my ribs. I clench my teeth, shielding my tongue from them. Through the binoculars, the construction workers, the construction equipment, the flag, are almost life size. The black bunting is streaked with the dust of the construction site. The lens cap closes. She offers another quarter. I shake my head. Stand. Blink the tears out of my eyes.

"Play something. Please."

"Here?"

I nod.

"If you tell me why."

"Please." I feel like a starving panhandler begging a dollar to buy something to eat.

She removes her violin from its case, tunes it. "A request?"

"Your choice."

"For the Senator."

A funereal sound, many layers weaving in and out of each other like ocean currents, like autumnal breezes on the cusp of the change of seasons, like snowflakes caught in a whirlwind, like the colors of a braided rainbow. Below us, some of the ants no longer scurry. Look up. Remove their hard hats. The layers coalesce into a single tone, not a monotone, but a single tone, a long tail that balances the body of the music.

"Your composition?" I ask.

"*In Paradisum*. A Gregorian chant for funerals. My arrangement. Recast for violin. Multiple violins, actually. Multiple voices require multiple violins. The movement I played, they all chant as one."

"It's yours forever. Whenever you want it, you take out your violin and it's yours. That's why."

"I never thought of it that way." She returns the violin to its case.

"If Picasso wants his *Guernica*, he has to buy a poster."

She clicks the case shut and looks up at me. In her eyes I see an understanding Dinitia does not have, Julia does not have, an understanding she shares with Ma who would never sell the *Book of Kells* no matter how desperate she is for money. I lean forward to kiss her. She angles her head and my lips brush her cheek.

"What's your name?"

She puts her finger across her lips, across mine.

She helps me down the stairs of the observation platform, supports me on the long walk to the subway entrance, down the stairs, through the turnstile, on to the uptown platform. I no longer hide my limp. On the Broadway Local, we find seats. She balances her violin on her lap; it extends on to mine. The train pulls into Chambers and she stands.

"Uptown Express?" I ask.

"Brooklyn."

"I want to see you again. I owe you an answer to your question."

"You answered it."

Before I can say I didn't, a swarm of people rushing to switch to the Express engulfs her, sweeps her out the door. I think I see her hand thrust above the throng, waving. Slowly it sinks into the throng, the hand of a woman drowning in a roiling ocean, of a crucifix in an ocean of blood. But, I'm the one going under, beaten down by waves gentle enough for children to play in. I try to stand, follow her, but by the time I make it to my feet the door closes and the train begins its uptown journey to its next stop, then its next and its next until it arrives at Broadway and 110th where I disembark wishing I were in Brooklyn.

In the apartment, a note from Dinitia. 'Someone called in sick. Have to go to work. Supper in the fridge to be warmed in the oven.' I eat it cold.

So begins a dark and empty night.

Riding the Broadway Local to South Ferry in the hope of running into the mystery violinist on the Staten Island ferry, I thumb through the articles Dr. Karen Robey gave me on traumatic brain injury, TBI in medical lingo. I prefer the lingo, the initials less threatening, less ominous, than the words. Control the language, control the perceptions. Most of the articles presume a level of scientific knowledge greater than mine, a familiarity with medical jargon, an understanding of scientific words and phrases, and I wonder why Robey wasted her time copying them; but one, written in ordinary English, is understandable.

"Patients suffering traumatic brain injury," according to this article, "are often unaware of their own conduct." The paper offers several examples: a teenage girl who attacks her father but has no memory of doing so; a middle age man convinced his wife is his executioner who has to be restrained in her presence; a young mother who screams at anyone who enters her hospital room and denies ever having given birth. When told of these incidents, the patients routinely claim no knowledge, deny they ever happened. One patient who learns of his behavior by reading his sister's diary she had carelessly left out becomes incensed and sues his sister for libel and defamation.

I pray Dinitia doesn't have a diary. A record of my behavior. What I said. Did. What I have no memory of. My medical records. I dread secrets in the hospital files. Minnie's secret, I hope I didn't babble it in my delirium. If I did, I hope no one believed me.

"In many cases of TBI," the paper continues, "it is often difficult if not impossible to determine whether behavior patterns are a result of the trauma or were a part of the patient's personality matrix pre-trauma."

The narrative of my life, my post-TBI memories undermine, displace, pre-TBI events. I don't remember whether Minnie and I became blood brothers or I was careless slicing a tomato. Whether I destroyed his sculptures out of anger or he smashed them against the floor out of artistic rage. Whether I'm going to law school to fulfill my pledge to Da to care for Ma or because I am afraid of the blank canvas, afraid of experiencing the world, cowed into being a mere observer. Whether Dinitia lusted after Minnie. Whether he killed Father Ozoni. Whether I did. Whether his pinky finger ring was a real diamond.

"To control the past," the paper asserts, "one must first re-experience it. Often revisiting the site of the trauma triggers the release of suppressed memories." The site of the trauma. The corner of the Columbia campus where the Mau-mau beat down occurred. I don't know if I'm brave enough to unlock the secrets of my past; or the truths. It will be like scratching a scab before the underlying skin heals, if it ever does.

Arriving at South Ferry, I toss the papers, all of them, aiming for the nearest trash barrel, missing it, moving on, another pile of trash for the janitors to clean up, throw away. Would that amnesia was as easily suffered.

※ ※ ※

Meanwhile, in Times Square.

The late afternoon light temporarily blinds Dr. Karen Robey and Sgt. Benjamin Greenbaum as they exit Loew's Capitol after spending almost three hours in a dark movie theater on their third date watching *2001: A Space Odyssey* on a movie screen several stories high, several buildings wide, curved to avoid optical distortion. They linger under the portico while their eyes adjust. Pedestrians stream up and down Broadway like schools of fish homing in on destinations by biological imperative rather than conscious choice.

"Uptown or downtown?" Greenbaum asks.

Downtown lies Times Square where movies houses show first run releases, double feature revivals, or porn, sex porn, violence porn, sex and violence porn; where electronics stores selling cameras, radios and TVs, stereos, luggage, put up their 'Going Out of Business Sale' signs the day after taking down their 'Grand Opening Sale signs; where shills stand at the entrances of peep shows with private booths, strip shows with private booths, lap dances with private booths, luring all with guarantees their show is the lewdest in New York; where marks line up trying to outhustle the masters of Three-card Monte who lure the marks in by employing come-on men, never women, who mislead the marks into thinking they can actually win and utilizing sleight of hand or misdirection to make sure they never do. Cheap steak joints, never more than $3.99, promote hand cut steaks, baked potatoes, beverages, cooked to order. Smoke rings from the Camel billboard garnish the air like errant rings in a child's ring toss game.

Uptown lies Carnegie Hall, Columbus Circle, Central Park, 57th St. whose stores neither Greenbaum nor Robey can afford to patronize.

"Uptown," Robey says.

"I didn't get the ending."

"What's to get?" Robey says. "You're born. You live. You die. Life goes on."

"Is that what the infant symbolizes? Life going on?"

Robey shrugs. "I don't know, Ben. I'm a doctor, not a philosopher."

"What hope does a cop have?"

"Did you like the movie? That's all that counts."

"Do you think Pan Am will offer moon flights in 33 years?"

"Honeymoon packages."

At 52nd, they cut over to 7th, avoiding the sidewalk salesmen trying to hustle tourists on to the tour busses.

"What I love about this city," Greenbaum says. "The selling never stops."

It's early for dinner, but tourists line up at the Carnegie, the Stage.

"Do you think computers will run our lives in 2001?" Robey asks. "Robot cops. Robot surgeons."

"Robot husbands. Robot wives."

"Robot brains for patients like Malone."

"We'd all be immortal."

"Aren't we already?" Robey says.

At Columbus Circle, they take Central Park West uptown, walking past the apartment buildings where the rich and famous live, The Dakota, The San Remo, The Beresford; further uptown, the New York Historical Society, the American Museum of Natural History.

"Isaac's favorite museum. He wants to be a dinosaur hunter."

"If you'll settle for something simple," Robey says,

"we can eat at my place. I've finally mastered scrambled eggs."

"I have a doctorate in omelets. Our Sunday morning routine. The only one that's survived Esther. Is there a bodega in your neighborhood?"

"Is there a neighborhood on the Upper West Side without one? I'll buy the ingredients."

"Cheap wages for a master chef."

"A one trick pony master chef."

"But what a trick it is."

As Greenbaum dices the peppers, onions, chorizo, fresh rather than cured, Robey brews coffee, then grates the mozzarella. By hand, he beats six eggs, adding a dollop of milk for each. "The trick," he says, "is to fry the eggs for a minute or two before adding the other ingredients, then bake rather than fry the omelet. Is the baguette fresh?"

"This morning."

He gently pushes on the crust. "I like my bread raw. Jam or jelly?"

"Blueberry preserves. Hendu picked it up at a farm stand upstate."

"Hendu?"

"Dr. Henderson." She pours two cups of coffee. "It was tough morning. Sad. A consultation with Malone. Sugar? Cream or milk?"

"Black."

"Someone made a reference to the dark wood leading to the underworld and he missed it."

Greenbaum raises his mug to his face, not to drink but to hide his ignorance.

"As soon as I mentioned Dante, it all flooded back. Freshman year at Amherst. Humanities I. Even the name of the professor. The *Divine Comedy*. The opening canto of the *Inferno*.

Greenbaum lowers his mug without drinking.

"What's wrong, Ben?"

"Criminal justice at CCNY. No match for liberal arts at Smith."

"Do you smell something?"

"The eggs." He rushes to the oven. "God, I can't even get this right."

"Hey, I once burned water boiling it for tea. Scorched the bottom of the kettle. It had to be replaced."

"Most of it can be salvaged, but I ruined your skillet."

In silence they eat except for pass the salt, pass the butter, pass the blueberry preserves, offering a refill on the coffee, dividing up the washing and drying of the dishes, him to wash, her to dry.

"I'll replace it," Greenbaum says as he dumps the skillet in the trash.

Robey rescues it from the trash. "I'll scour it back to new."

"It's only a skillet."

"It was only his brain. I can't scour that back to new." She hugs the skillet as if it were a new born. Charred eggs muddy her blouse. "They don't teach it at med school, how to cope with the failures."

"Not at the police academy either." Gently, he pries open her arms, pries her fingers from the skillet's handle, places it on the counter; then wraps his arms around her, pushes her head against his chest, kisses the top of her head.

"It's been a long time," she says, "since I've listened to a heartbeat without a stethoscope."

"How does it sound?"

"Strong and healthy."

"I wish."

She lifts her head and brushes her lips against his, back and forth, back and forth, until he steadies her head between his hands and they kiss, long and deep, losing their balance and knocking the skillet from the counter, crashing it to the floor, the noise causing them to break out in laughter, and they laugh all the way into her bedroom where the laughing stops as they undress each other. After, she rests her head against his chest.

"Still strong and healthy?"

"Stronger. Healthier."

"Muscle over mind."

She raises her head. "Sad? Why?"

"Like you said. You're born. You live. You die. Life goes on. But it doesn't. Not for those left behind." He strokes her arm. "I've hidden from life since she died. I don't want to anymore."

Silently, she curls his chest hairs around her little finger, releases them, curls them again. "Ouch," he says in a mocking tone when she gently tugs.

"Don't you dare," she says when he curls her hair around his forefinger.

"I can't decide whether it's time for you to meet Isaac."

"Five, six, weeks. Three dates."

"This is more than a date."

"He'll resent me. Hate me. Take it out on you."

"Now. A month from now. A year from now. What's the difference? He's at the age where he blames me for the accident. What am I supposed to do? Put my life on hold 'til he's an adult?"

"'Til he's old enough to understand."

"Please, Karen. No excuses. If you don't want to, just say no."

"I'll never replace Esther. You'll never replace Rennie."

"That doesn't mean we can't love each other."

She pulls the sheet up to her chin. "Love takes more than listening to jazz."

"Too embarrassed to bring a cop to your next Smith reunion?"

"Let's see how the summer goes. Maybe come September."

"Think?"

"I don't know, Ben. It's bad for me right now. I have nightmares about Malone. Rennie rises from the grave and scolds me for botching the surgery. Last night Bobby Kennedy joined him. Maybe in a few months. I'm not ready to say yes. If you insist on an answer here, an answer now, it will be no."

"What does that make me? A gigolo? You need to get laid and figure I'm a safe bet. I haven't been with another woman since Esther died and you turn this into shit."

"I'm sorry, Ben. I'm just being honest."

Rolling off the bed, he grabs his clothes and quickly dresses. "Me, too. This," he says, encompassing the room with his arms, "is the dark wood leading to the underworld."

"Ben... "

Several days later, Ben Greenbaum takes his son Isaac to see *2001: A Space Odyssey*. Although the memories and associations are fresh and painful, they go to Loew's Capital theater in Times Square because *2001* is a movie that demands being seen on as big a screen as possible. Ben guides Isaac to the left-hand section of the theater, two-thirds of the way back, as far away as possible from the area of the theater where he and Karen Robey sat. Seeing the movie a second time, Greenbaum notices small details he initially missed; yet, these details flee his mind before reaching the part of the brain housing memory, forgotten before they can be remembered. He feels like the hominid in the opening sequence when it realizes that a femur bone can be used as a weapon to destroy other hominids. Or, like Karen's patient, Malone, whose mind darts around like a minnow in a bucket. Greenbaum shuts his eyes as the femur rises into the sky and morphs into a space station.

Details he missed on first viewing continue to slip in and out of his mind. He now appreciates Malone's suffering. He can't imagine living without remembering Esther. One blow to the head, a fall from Blue Note, a bat wielding rioter, and she would be lost to him forever. On the screen, the Discovery is deep into the Jupiter mission. Dr. Frank Poole exits the spaceship to reinstall the AE-35 unit in the dish assembly. Maneuvering in open space outside his space pod, Poole approaches the assembly. Suspended against the cold, desolate backdrop of the universe, there is a balletic feel to Poole's movements. Greenbaum wonders where that word comes from. Balletic. Not a City College word. A Smith College word. A memory of something Karen once said. He has never been to the ballet.

Poole's EVA pod looms behind him. Without warning, Poole tumbles into that backdrop, spinning over and over, fumbling for his air hose that has been disconnected. The further Poole spins away from the Discovery, the slower his struggles until he is a statue spinning, a spinning he would have continued for all eternity except that Commander Dave Bowman retrieves his body. The HAL 9000 computer, omnipotent and omniscient, disclaims all knowledge of the how or why of this tragic accident.

Greenbaum fidgets in his seat, shifting his weight from one side to the other, then back again. Poole, he realizes, is destined to spin eternally through an unforgiving universe because Bowman is too late to save the life of his shipmate. The parallels, the intersections, are uncomfortable. Like Poole exiting the Discovery, he raced from Robey's apartment. Karen does not attempt to rescue him, or, at least, retrieve his lifeless body. HAL has imprisoned her in her apartment, preventing her from opening the front door to escape the way HAL refused to open the pod bay doors to allow Bowman reentry to the Discovery. He, Greenbaum, Bowman, the helmet of his space suit with its oxygen and life support systems behind on the Discovery, alone and forgotten in his hurry to retrieve Poole.

Bowman, Poole. They are interchangeable to HAL, to each other. One lives, one dies; it could be either. Little does it matter. Within the four corners of the movie, it would make no difference. Robey, Greenbaum, also interchangeable. One lives, one dies; whichever it will it be, no difference will it make. Karen explains the movie. You're born. You live. You die. Life goes on. Greenbaum crosses, then uncrosses, his legs.

"You okay, dad?" Isaac whispers.

"Having trouble getting comfortable."

"Move over a seat."

"Always the pragmatist."

"What's a pragmatist?"

"Shhh," says someone behind them."

Greenbaum leans over and whispers in Isaac's ear. "Bathroom break. Another popcorn?"

"Butter and extra salt."

In the lobby, Greenbaum hunts for a payphone. Poole died. He doesn't have to. Nor does Karen. Unless HAL wills it. He wishes it were as simple as pulling crystals from HAL's memory center. Karen, Karen, give me your answer do, I'm half-crazy all for the love of you

❧ ❧ ❧

Meanwhile, in Morningside Heights.

In the lobby of my apartment building, I chitchat with Frank, the building super, while the mailman sorts the mail. Frank knows my situation and tolerates my gibberish. Some obscure postal regulation not taught at Columbia Law School makes it a Federal crime for the mailman to hand our mail directly to us. Other residents, on their way to or from errands, also wait. Some nod, one or two murmur a hello, but most avoid me, afraid I'm contagious, afraid they'll catch a beating the same way they catch a cold. I wish I were contagious. I would breathe all over them. Turn them black and blue with my breath. Exhale abrasions and bruises. Zephyr a few scars. Frank tells me every Sunday him and the wife light candles for me. His words, him and the wife. You're both saints, I reply. The mailman finishes and locks the mailboxes and grants us leave to retrieve our mail. I would salute his devotion to the letter of the law, but it would be petty in light of his black armband and the black crepe dangling from the strap of his mailbag. It takes a tragedy like the Senator's assassination to connect strangers in a city like New York.

"A letter from Minnie," I tell Dinitia. She packs for our trip to Fall River for his wake and funeral. "Read it to me."

She says, "He wrote it in San Francisco and mailed it from Saigon."

'Dear Lawyer Lobotomy and Saint Dinitia: SanFran-FuckingFrisco. 48 hours to go, then into the great unknown. Most of the guys are out drinking and looking to get laid. Me, too. Found a gallery that rents studio space, easels, brushes. You supply canvas, paints, which they sell and inspiration which they don't. Buy that on any street corner in the Haight. Bishop Hippo's. 397-398 Augustine Way if you're in the neighborhood. Several potentials, a Mary two easels over. Before I could say the magic words, she told me she was betrothed to another. Her exact words. Like she could read my fucking mind. She did pose for me. Head shot only but she has a face Mona Lisa would cry for, die for. If she won't fuck a nobody maybe she'll fuck Minnie da Vinci but I doubt it because she's betrothed to another and told me in no uncertain terms she's as faithful as a chastity belt. Her words again. Exactly. Not a total loss.

She let me in on the secret, the secret secret, the secret we're not supposed to find out 'til after... no I'm not going to tell you, not now anyways, and it's got me painting my first masterpiece. Mon. Badin here I come. Or is it M. Badin? I should have paid better attention in high school French since they say French is spoken in Saigon. Fucking digressions. Mary will not countenance, her word again, me calling it *The Secret*. Says it's malum prohibitorum. More her words. You took 4 years of high school Latin with The Fog; translate for me. *Book XI*. Her title. I ask her what it means and she says surprise surprise it's a secret. Serious as a nun. No more NYC for me. Too many lawyers. It's SanFranFuckingFrisco all the way. Bishop Hippo will babysit *Book XI*. One less thing to distract you from the pop-up toaster. Happy buttering! Ciao! Minnie the Magnificat' PS. Sacred scalpel safe and secure.

❦ ❦ ❦

"It's real," Dinitia says.

"Call Hippo's," I say. "Maybe we can get it air freighted in time for the wake."

I ignore her questions and lock myself in the bathroom. I turn off the light. The darkness soothes my eyes. The pain of being able to see has decreased day by day, the physical pain. The emotional pain has flatlined at a level high above my comfort zone. The bathroom door muffles Dinitia's sobs.

The phone rings and rings and rings until it finally stops ringing.

I would comfort her if I could. She's mourning two deaths, Minnie's and our marriage's. She belongs in the Museum School. I belong in law school. Fifty years from now, if I live that long, I'll be taking watercolor classes in some Florida retirement community and following Dinitia's career from afar. Maybe if Lawyer Lobotomy wins enough cases, he'll be able to afford to buy one of her paintings. A small one. An early one. Before she establishes her career. Before the prices skyrocket. Saint Dinitia the Magnificat. There will be no Malone the Magnificat.

Dinitia pounds on the bathroom door. I twist the knob, unlocking it. She collapses beside me.

"Laurie Williams called. Funeral's postponed indefinitely. Minnie's lost. The army can't find him."

In Fall River, Therese Minifie dies from the news. If and when the army finds Minnie, there'll be a double wake, double funeral. Not before. Vincenzo won't bury an empty coffin.

June 8, 1968–June 16, 1968

Day after day I ride the Broadway Local to South Ferry. Day after day, hour after hour, I board one ferry in South Ferry, a different ferry in the Staten Island terminal for the return trip. Day after day, hour after hour, I quiz the ferry crew. Do any of you remember, I ask, the woman who played the violin in the back of the boat. Most say no. A few tease me for not knowing the back of the ferry is the stern. None say yes. I treat it as a job, first ride to Staten Island no later than 9, last return to South Ferry no earlier than 6. Day after day, hour after hour, the mystery violinist never reappears.

On days that it storms, I ride the Broadway Express into Brooklyn, exiting in each station hoping to find her, a busker in the dry of the underground. I never do. I ask the clerks in the token booths, the janitors who sweep the platforms, random people waiting for the subway, whether they have ever seen a young woman carrying a violin case, playing in the station. None have.

I revisit the observation platform over the World Trade Center construction site. I ask the pipefitters, the heavy equipment operators, the electricians, the journeymen, the laborers, whether they remember the woman who played the violin the day after the Senator's assassination. I remind them many removed their hard hats when she played. A few say no. Some shake their heads. Most brush by, unwilling to be delayed from their end of shift beers by someone who wears bandages in place of a baseball cap. One or two curse.

I'm beginning to doubt she exists. That, in reality, she's a creation of my imagination. *Ex nihilo*? A post-TBI occurrence. A memory fresh. For all I know, TBI corrupts, erases, memories of current events, robs me of my future.

Dinitia becomes curious, then suspicious. "Where do you go all day?"

"I ride the ferry," I explain. "The water calms me."

She does not believe me. I don't blame her.

"Join me," I say.

"I work," she reminds me.

"On your off day."

"I'd call your bluff if I didn't have better use for my free time."

I consider contacting Dr. Robey, but I doubt she has, anyone has, a magic potion that will cure me. If I confide in Dinitia she will nag me about therapy, perhaps threaten involuntary commitment if I refuse. An easy way to dispose of me; I won't give her the opportunity. I'm alone, locked inside my traumatic brain injury. Words now replace initials. Words are harder to run from.

Laurie Williams calls. The army locates Minnie in Mobile, AL where he was shipped to the Minofia Funeral Home by mistake. "The wake and funeral are set," she tells us, giving us the date and time. I want to ask if the army recovered Minnie's sacred scalpel, but my vow silences me.

"We'll be there," Dinitia says.

We travel by train, Dinitia and I, and Laurie Williams meets us in Providence. Minnie's cheerleader. A hurricane cannot rip her roots from the soil. Deep enough, strong enough, to anchor two, four, six generations. Nothing disturbs them. She cries when she sees my scars and bruises and stitches and the funny way my hair is growing back and color drains from her eyes and cheeks and lips and her skin collapses in on itself, the skin of a victim of a long famine. We hug, but she is beyond comfort because she is beyond grief. She will have to assimilate the loss in her own way.

"Minnie's dad did it," Laurie says.

I do not want to know what he did. I stuff my ears with my fingertips like a four-year old who believes that if he does not hear it, it is not said; if it is not said, it did not happen. I retreat to a baggage cart and sit behind shipping boxes waiting for the next freight train. The train I arrived on recedes down the track until it disappears into its vanishing point.

"He sold the funeral home."

I am a captive audience.

"He's going back to Italy. Minnie and Therese will be buried there. A cemetery in the hills outside Florence. Overlooking the Duomo."

"He belongs in the Medici chapel," I say. Dinitia rests her hand on my shoulder and I know she wants me to bite my tongue. Buried in Italy. No grave in Fall River to visit. I don't know if this makes Minnie more dead or less dead. I glance at Dinitia. Whatever her reaction, her face remains impassive.

Italy. Minnie's vanishing point. Not carved of marble by Michelangelo, but a photo in our high school yearbook. A photo in our college yearbook. An obituary in the Amherst alumni quarterly magazine – I am asked to write it, but decline, – a listing with the deceased alumni in the alumni directory until the last member of the Class of 1967 dies and the magazine and directory delete the Class of '67 from the institutional memory of the college. We say Minnie lives in our memories. Mine and Dinitia's and Laurie's and who knows who else's. Mine are no good. I don't even know whether the mystery violinist exists or not. Whether Minnie killed Father Ozoni; or, whether I did.

Memories survive only as long as the brains that store them. As long as those brains don't suffer traumatic brain injury. And, we say, Minnie lives in sheets of papers in government files, official documents created by, belonging to, the Selective Service Administration, the United States Army, the Social Security Administration, the Alabama State Police, the Civil Rights Division of the Department of Justice; maybe the F.B.I.; maybe the Alabama state police; maybe in the moldy file cabinet in the office of a country sheriff. And newspaper morgues. Traces in archives until the paper turns to dust or the government decides the records serve no purpose, useful or otherwise. In *Life with Coffee Spoons*. In *Book XI*. In whatever sketches and chalks and studies and oils and water colors and pastels and drawings and sculptures Vincenzo does not destroy when he abandons the New World for the Old. For the moment, we all share Minnie's vanishing point.

In the distance, a whistle and the train from Boston

to New York emerges from its vanishing point. A handful of people disembark. A man and woman with four young children. They mill about, uncertain where to go. Two elderly men, perhaps brothers, who talk softly while they wait for the porter to bring their luggage. A man in a suit carrying an umbrella and a leather satchel who strides through the double doors into the station, a man on a mission. Three college students, male, tie-died tee shirts, cut-offs, sandals, pony tails, tottering as if they stepped out of the Death Cage at Lincoln Park. They dance toward the double doors as if life is a ballet to be danced out of step to unheard music. Another whistle and the train pulls out of the station, gathering speed, until, once again, it disappears into its vanishing point.

The next day, the wake. Open coffins. In death Therese gains weight and appears thin, not emaciated, her restoration a work of art by a true artist, Vincenzo's valedictory which, if God is good and God is great and God is merciful, will give him peace. Minnie looks alive, asleep, the same as Da at his wake. Vincenzo erases his scars including his memorial scar to M'Boto. Without his scars, he isn't the real Minnie. If they meet in the next life, M'Boto and Minnie, he won't recognize Minnie.

Minnie is bold and brave in his military haircut, peaceful and contemplative in his suit and tie. No uniform, no medals on display, no Silver Star or Purple Heart that the Army awards him posthumously, no flag, no military color guard. Vincenzo buries a son, not a soldier, a truth he grasps in his dour, funereal manner but that eludes Minnie in death as in life. At the head of Minnie's coffin, *Book XI*, a miracle of modern transportation. At the foot, *Life with Coffee Spoons*.

Book XI. The meaning of its title does not die with Minnie. He never knew. No one will ever know except Mary who will never say. The secret secret will forever be a secret. Line dominates. Color is an afterthought. Minnie's way. His last argument in our perpetual debate, now eternal. A collage of Möebius strips turning back on themselves in ever repetitive spirals. Dinitia, his inspiration. His final rebuttal to our perpetual argument. Ever smaller, each Möebius strip. Ever smaller. Spiraling back and back until they disappear into the painting's vanishing point. Each spiral itself a Möebius strip comprised of a multitude of Möebius strips. One side and two sides at the same time. A strip of paper. Twist one end 180 degrees. Tape it to the other end. One side. Two sides. Trace a line. A line on each side. A line on both sides. Without lifting the pencil from the paper. A magician's trick. A shell game. Three Card Monte in Times Square. No. A topological phenomenon essential to the comprehension of three-dimensional space. The discovery of a German mathematician who donated his name and received in exchange immortality to endure for as long as the study of topology exists, which will be for as long as physicists and mathematicians study three-dimensional space which will be forever because simple things are often the things we never understand. The definition of immortality. Time without end. The infinitude of time. The finitude of life. Beginning and ending at the same place. Like Möebius and his strip. Like *2001: A Space Odyssey*. Born. Live. Die. Life goes on. What is the ratio of immortal artists to immortal lawyers? Ten thousand to one? Ten million? How many Clarence Darrows does it take to make a Michelangelo? No number of Clarence Darrows will make a Michelangelo.

Book XI. To an untrained eye a reprise of *Life with Coffee Spoons*. Substitute Möebius strips for coffee spoons. Art is not that simple. In that substitution, Mary's secret of secrets lurks, hides, awaits discovery.

As does Minnie's. As is the sacred scalpel hidden within, among, the Möebius strips. With a magnifying glass, I will search for the secret of secrets, the sacred scalpel. They're there in *Book XI*, I hear Minnie shouting from outside time, if you are smart enough to decipher it. As if he had. Minnie bequeaths this mystery, this secret of secrets, to me in his Last Will and Testament that Uncle Sam, *in loco parentis*, forces him and every other raw recruit to execute before dispatching them to their fates. *Book XI*.

Julia, round with child both in belly and face, pecks me on the cheek. She stares with the curiosity of a young child and I follow her eyes as they travel around my head. I'm okay, I say before she asks. Julia's husband, the once and future pants king, gazes down at his shoes and mumbles hello and shakes my hand, his grip limp and lifeless. I want to feel for his pulse.

"I gave up smoking for the baby," Julia says.

No longer is she *Head of Sleeping Julia*. One after another, people line up to pay their respects to me as if I, not Vincenzo, am Minnie's father. Some I know. Some I know of. Some remain strangers even after they introduce themselves. Sister Monica who assures me Minnie resides with God because he died a just death that redeems the blackest of sinners. Hobo who shows me a sketch and tells me its story. Miss Edna and Miss Nellie who wear their March on Washington clothes. Classmates from high school. Classmates from college. Bishop Hippo who flies *Book XI* east, debunking a miracle that saddens me, not his presence but the debunking of the miracle. He declines to explain the meaning of *Book XI*. With every woman unknown to me I hold my breath, then try not to show my disappointment when she does not introduce herself as Mary from Bishop Hippo's. When I ask Hippo after her, he shrugs his shoulders and says I might as well ask him to explain the origin of the universe. SanFranFuckingFrisco. A few people drift from me to offer condolences to Laurie.

The crowd thins. Vincenzo putters about, distracting himself with busy work. The Riordans depart as do Julia and the future pants king and the unborn child for which she gave up smoking. Miss Edna and Miss Nellie sit themselves in the living room as if posing for a still life, resting their weary feet, each holding her gloves in her lap. Hobo approaches, wary as if he cannot decide if he wants to say something. Dinitia joins us.

"You with Minnie when he died?" I ask.

Hobo nods.

"Please," Dinitia says.

Hobo shifts his weight from one foot to the other. His muscles tense. His eyes moisten. He takes a deep breath and holds it in as if he's underwater

"Please," Dinitia repeats.

"It be hard," Hobo says.

I motion Laurie Williams over and I introduce her as a close friend. Hobo acknowledges her as if he recognizes her name. I want to ask if he does, but restrain myself. Even in death, Minnie is entitled to his privacy.

"We back from R & R, back from Saigon." Hobo shakes his head. "Don't know if I can do this."

I lead Hobo into a private sitting room. Dinitia and Laurie follow, Dinitia with a box of tissues. I pull up four chairs. We face each other, knee to knee to knee to knee. Dinitia balances the tissues on her knees where Hobo can reach it. In the distance the air conditioning hums and I wonder if it reminds Hobo of a helicopter approaching the landing zone. Little, if anything, do I know about the sound of approaching helicopters. I've never been there. The old debate resurfaces.

"We back from R & R," Hobo says again. "The LZ, it ringed with sand bags. A wall of sand bags."

Dinitia offers him a tissue and he dabs his eyes.

"We play games with the VC. Line up empty cans on the wall, target practice for the snipers. Crazy bets. How many hits. How many misses. Coping best we can."

The door to the room opens. A head appears, no one I recognize, quickly withdraws. The door closes.

"Mail call. He waiting on a letter from you," Hobo says to Dinitia. "About him." He glances at me. "Nothing. Only one in the platoon without mail. Worse kind of being alone in a combat zone there is."

I nod, begin to say something, but Dinitia taps my foot with hers. Laurie closes her eyes as if she anticipates what Hobo will say next and doesn't want to hear him say it.

"We all reading our mail. Paying no mind to Minnie. I finish my letters and look around for him. He be sitting on top of the sand bags. I yell for him to get down before he be killed. Run over to pull him down. Before I get there, one shot and he falls like Humpty Dumpty." Hobo swallows a sob, then buries his face in his hands. "He knew. He fucking knew. We all fucking knew."

The air conditioning cycles off. The room is silent but for the sound of our breathing, ragged, muffled, as if we're suffocating. Laurie can't hold back her tears.

"Positive?" I ask.

Hobo nods.

I rub the scar on my finger, wonder if any of Minnie's blood still flows in my veins, my arteries. There must be one or two corpuscles, maybe more. There has to be more. One reaches my brain and triggers a realization. Minnie was not an artist because he painted or sculpted. More than anyone, he knew how mediocre his work was. He knew Bader bestowed an Honorable Mention on *Coffee Spoons* not because it was worthy but as a reward for entering *Talking* in the competition. No, Minnie was an artist because of the way he lived his life. And the way he died. The art was the performance, the performance the art.

The corpuscle triggers a second thought. Minnie did not understand this. Dinitia does. Observing the work of art unfold is her attraction to Minnie. The notion of his creating a work of art unable to be hung on a museum wall, mounted on a museum pedestal, fascinates her. I look into her eyes and read her mind. She will paint Minnie's life, however many paintings it will take. Maybe she'll squeeze me into a corner or in the background peeking out from behind a burning bush. Maybe not. Love will guide her brush strokes. Love for Minnie as a work of art.

A third realization, damn corpuscle. I never outgrew nursery school finger-painting. Dinitia must realize this, She'd be a fool if she didn't.

Hobo blows his nose, clears his throat, glances at his watch. "We need be going or we miss our bus."

Hobo stands and Dinitia hugs him. "Thank you," she whispers. He hugs Laurie, then me. Pain from my partially healed ribs rakes my body. Without the pain, I wouldn't be alive.

On the sidewalk we, Laurie, Dinitia, me, wait for the cab with Hobo, Miss Edna, Miss Nellie, each of us mourning our fallen Humpty Dumpty in our own way.

One day. Two days. Three days. We observe the rites. The rites of the Church. The rites of secular society. The rites we create for ourselves. We say good-by to Minnie and Therese. The Kennedy's, the nation, say good-by to the Senator. We cry. They cry. We celebrate Minnie's life, Therese's life. They celebrate the Senator's life. We do not know how to act. They do. We do not know the rules. They do. We are too young to be burying one of us. They are not. On the fourth and fifth day we visit with Ma and on the sixth day Laurie Williams drive us to the train station in Providence. We will return to New York for the seventh day when we will rest.

The train chugs from the station, westward to New York. The rhythmic motion, slightly swaying side to side; the wheels, clicking like a metronome, lullaby me to sleep and I dream of Laurie standing on the platform, waving, watching, waiting until the train disappears into its vanishing point. I dream I am in that vanishing point. At least I think I am because in my dream I am in a place of infinite size blacker than the inside of Minnie's coffin. I call out but the ether absorbs the sound of my voice and I do not hear myself. I flap my hands with the speed of a hummingbird's wings, but feel no breeze. I stick out my tongue, but taste no taste. I inhale through my nose, but smell no smell. I sit, or at least assume the position of someone sitting, but there is nothing beneath me; yet, I have no sensation of plunging into the abyss. No sensation of being suspended. No sensation except the absence of sensation.

I awaken when the train crosses the city limits into the Bronx. I press my face against the window with the wonderment of a four-year old when the train enters the long, black tunnel, a tunnel the adult me knows leads to Pennsylvania Station. Or, Grand Central. The adult me doesn't know. The train accelerates, pushing me into the cushion of my seat. Centrifugal force pushes me against my arm rest, then the window. The acceleration continues. The torque increases. Like the death wheel at Lincoln Park. The interior lights malfunction and I am in the dark. The train rolls on. I search for lights in the tunnel, but see none. There are always lights in train tunnels. Naked bulbs hanging from wires. Red exit signs over emergency doors. Signal lights for the train's engineer. But the tunnel is as black as my dream. Like the lights are switched off. Like New York is suffering another blackout. Like I've slipped into another coma. Gone blind. I wish I knew if it were a dream; or, real.

The train races through a station, too fast for me to

recognize the platforms or read the signs. For an instant, light illuminates the inside of the car. The window by my seat is blank. Without my reflection. Dinitia screams. I do not hear her. Like the violinist, I am not there.

—END—

S. Frederic Liss

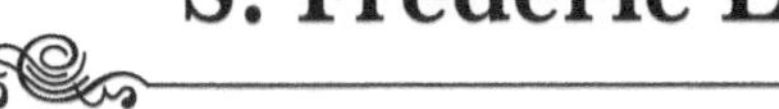

Liss is a multiple Pushcart Prize nominee, a nominee for the story South Million Writers Award. He was also a finalist for the Flannery O'Connor Short Fiction Prize sponsored by University of Georgia Press, the **St. Lawrence Book Award** sponsored by Black Lawrence Press, and the **Bakeless Prize** sponsored by Breadloaf Writers' Conference and Middlebury College.

He has published or has forthcoming 65 short stories and has received numerous awards and other forms of recognition for individual short stories including **The Florida Review Editor's Award for Fiction**; **James Still Prize for Short Fiction** sponsored by Wind; **Midnight Sun Award for Fiction** sponsored by Permafrost; Third prize in the **Arthur Edelstein Prize for Short Fiction**; Finalist for the **Raymond Carver Award for Short Fiction** sponsored by Carve Magazine; and Honorable Mention in the **New Letters Literary Award for Fiction** and the Glimmer Train June, 2014 Fiction Open. Liss has also published in *The Saturday Evening Post*, *Alfred*

Hitchcock Mystery Magazine, *The South Dakota Review*, *The South Carolina Review*, *Dogwood*, *The Worcester Review*, *Fifth Wednesday Journal*.

He earned a BA from Amherst College, Amherst, MA; a JD from Columbia University School of Law, New York, NY; and an MFA from Emerson College, Boston, MA. He was the recipient of a Grant-in-Aid in Literature from the *St. Botolph Club Foundation*, Boston, MA where he led a workshop in writing fiction for over 10 years.

Also by S. Frederic Liss

Fiction

Talking of Michelangelo
Pierian Springs Press, 2025

In Zugzwang:
Stories of Ilion Heights
Pierian Springs Press, 2025

The Charles River Pogrom
Pierian Springs Press, 2025

Sugaring Time:
Stories of Thebesford County
Pierian Springs Press, 2026